Nick Hopton was born in M
York and educated at Camb
the Foreign Office. *In Pieces* i

"Nick Hopton is a fresh new talent"
AMANDA FOREMAN

"A wry look at the world of journalism with an undertow of menace"
SEBASTIAN SHAKESPEARE, TATLER

"An enjoyable read for any football fan, particularly those who follow Manchester United"
SIR BOBBY CHARLTON

"A striking combination of football, terrorism and journalistic shenanigans. Nick Hopton has kicked off with a winner"
TOM LEONARD (media editor) DAILY TELEGRAPH

"A wry, intelligent story of London life in the nineties"
VICKY WARD, NEW YORK POST

"An absorbing saga of popular culture and personal loyalties. Football is presented as a plausible component of life, not merely a literary obsession"
GEORGE BROWN

"Hopton's prose sparkles both on and off the pitch"
WILF McGUINNESS

"A brilliant debut"
WILL CASH

"An accomplished, entertaining and thought-provoking first novel. Nick Hopton is definitely one to watch"
ROBERT BEAUMONT

IN PIECES

by

Nick Hopton

TIGER & TYGER
LONDON

In Pieces is a work of fiction. Names, characters, places and incidents are either the product of the author's imagination or are used entirely fictitiously.

PUBLISHED IN THE UK BY
TIGER & TYGER

DISTRIBUTION:
Unit 9, Ormskirk Industrial Park,
Old Boundary Way,
Burscough Road,
Ormskirk,
Lancashire L39 2YW

Tel: 01695 575112
Fax: 01695 570120

Printed and bound in the UK by Watkiss Studios

First Published 1999

ISBN 1 902914 04 X

For Alejandra

These fragments I have shored against my ruins

The Waste Land
T. S. Eliot

Behind our daily mirrors lie our dreams,
Part of every breath but hard to see:
Our guardian angels, watching us at night,
And guiding us by day towards what's right.

But often we are blind and will not see,
Let slip our dreams, relive banality.
So we must breathe betimes and, unconstrained,
Soft sense an angel's smile for dreams attained.

The Book of Dreams
P. Donoth

PROLOGUE

The summer came late that year. Thursday the fifteenth of September was one of those days for which it's worth weathering a torrential July and August. Not too hot, but sunny and with the first intoxicating scent of autumn in the air. Those unfortunates stuck in offices longed to stroll in the parks and kick the first fallen leaves into the slight breeze. But enough Londoners remained masters of their time to ensure that the pavements were bustling and the cafés full.

On the dusty Strand shoppers rushed along tumbling over themselves. A great flood of humanity washed past Charing Cross and down towards the Aldwych. Tourists, office workers and the homeless jostled along together. The traffic moved more slowly, grinding its way along the choked road in peristaltic bursts. Exhaust fumes hung in the air and mixed with the sunshine, refracting primary colours onto the tired grey flagstones.

It was the end of summer and yet an optimistic air of expectation hung on the day.

When the explosion ripped across the street at two minutes after one o'clock, it seemed to fulfil the prophecy which had permeated London all morning; here was the great event foretold by the sunshine and the excited pedestrians. But once the stiletto splinters torn from shop windows had fallen back to earth, and the twisted metal sculptures wrought from scaffolding collapsed with an apocalyptic boom, all optimism evaporated.

The bomb destroyed over one hundred metres of buildings and broke windows a mile away in the City. Many of the victims had to be identified by their dental records.

WINTER

Mini Bournemouth stared out of the window and for the first time in over a year allowed herself to behave like a woman. The tears gouged through the powder on her slightly wrinkled, porcelain cheeks, but she didn't bother to mop them up. She just kept on facing out of the window, staring blindly at the twinkling brilliance of the London Docklands. In the distance she could make out Canary Wharf, blazing away like a Roman candle in the crisp, snow-filled night. It suddenly appeared a perfect metaphor for her own career; strange how she'd never noticed it before now.

It wasn't easy being the most successful woman in British journalism. Of course, the benefits outweighed the disadvantages—Mini was the first to admit that she loved the attention and the chance to play role model to thousands of bright young women. The letters she received still gave her a buzz and in her more philosophical moments, of which there had been an increasing number recently, she persuaded herself that it really mattered that she continue to make a success of her job. She wasn't just working for herself. No, it was as much for the generations of women coming after her, benefiting from the barriers she had broken and the inroads she had carved into newspaper chauvinism.

But being a pioneer also had its disadvantages. Since breaking through the glass ceiling and being appointed the first ever female editor of a major national newspaper (some would say *the* national newspaper), Mini had hardly seen her family. And this hurt because she had always taken pride in telling her many professional admirers, especially those interviewing her for glossy magazine articles, that she had succeeded in combining her career with a happy home life. Her three kids were doing fine at school and Mark, her husband—her *only* husband, as she occasionally emphasized to her much-divorced friends—was loyal and loving.

When she accepted the job at *The Courier* she had known it wouldn't be easy. What she hadn't expected was that the man who hired her, Sir Lesley Johnson the media tycoon, would prove so impossible.

The problem became evident after only a few weeks, but Mini thought she could overcome it and even use it to her own advantage. After all, that's what she'd always succeeded in doing in the past when faced with a difficult situation or a cantankerous superior.

Sir Lesley, as he liked to be known, was to prove the exception. He objected to editorials which deviated even slightly from his own politics and seemed to forget when talking to Mini that she had a track record in the media almost as long and as impressive as his own. He patronised her dreadfully, but this she could bear.

What really got to her was the self-censorship which she began without really noticing. She started to lose respect for herself, slowly at first, but after a year she realised that it was a long time since she had even tried to challenge Sir Lesley's brittle opinions through her editorial column. The fire which had carried her so far seemed to be burning out.

The inevitable reaction when it came was predictably strong. Mini banged out several polemical leaders, which brought an incandescent Sir Lesley to the phone.

'What the hell do you think you're doing, young lady?' he bellowed. 'I've told you I don't agree with euthanasia.'

Mini had wanted to tell him not to call her a young lady—she was almost fifty after all—and to defend her argument that euthanasia was justified in certain cases; for example, in Sir Lesley's. But her career mind overrode her emotions and she bit her tongue.

'I'm sorry, Sir Lesley,' she heard herself saying demurely, 'I'd forgotten that.'

'Well, don't forget in future.'

'I won't.'

'You'd better not...' He'd left the threat hanging in mid-air and had become more explicit a few weeks later when

Mini chanced her arm again with a stinging attack on the current legal practice of allowing women to be cross-examined in court by those accused of raping them.

'For God's sake woman, *The Courier* isn't some sort of feminist rag. If you want to write that kind of tripe, go and work for *The Guardian*...'

'Sorry,' was all Mini managed through clenched teeth.

'Sorry? You'd better be. If this happens again, you'll be looking for a new job.'

Mini hadn't answered, but she knew it was only a matter of time before her self-respect got the better of her again. She started weighing up the options and made a few discreet enquiries of old friends.

Her natural home, *The Daily Telegraph*, had recently appointed a new editor and all the other top positions were filled. *The Mail*, where she had worked before coming to *The Courier*, also offered no escape route. She couldn't face the prospect of sloping back to her old editor with her tail between her legs; it would look like she couldn't handle the pressure, and she was under no illusions that many of those who had scribbled so enthusiastically about her arrival at *The Courier* would write even more vividly about her departure. Suddenly her position as a feminist icon seemed to be a millstone around her neck.

Mini tried to pull herself together and stared hard at the sparkling night lights of East London, imploring them to provide the moral strength she so desperately needed. She wiped away the damp patches on her cheeks and powdered her shiny, porcelain skin. The mirror showed that her eyes were red beyond repair, but that couldn't be helped. She dabbed a bit and then turned to the task in hand. The important thing was to act before Sir Lesley did.

A beacon on top of Canary Wharf winked at her and the idea that she had a fellow conspirator cheered her slightly. Mini watched the snowflakes fall past her for a while; even the night seemed to be crying cold tears for her, she thought. Then she walked back to her huge black desk and surveyed the papers arranged in neat piles across the glass surface. The paper had gone to bed and the worst of the mess had disappeared. Odd articles and a few abandoned drafts still remained.

She ignored these and picked up the framed photograph which occupied pride of place. She paused and planted a wistful kiss on it. Mark and the kids grinned back at her. Sasha was now frighteningly fifteen but Tarquin was still an adorable twelve-year-old cherub. She realised with a pang of guilt that she'd not always lived up to the high ideals of motherhood she had championed as a columnist. The picture had been taken three years ago, when life hadn't been quite so serious. Before she'd had to neglect her family in favour of dawn starts and midnight finishes at work. That had also been long before she'd started to harbour even the slightest doubts about her husband's fidelity. Well, that was one good thing about all this. She was going to have much more time to spend with the three of them; she might even be able to save her marriage— after all, as yet she had nothing concrete to suggest it couldn't.

Mini put the photograph in her bag and called her secretary Martha Rogers, on the intercom. Martha, single, middle aged and unassumingly charming, was an institution at *The Courier*. She'd been there longer than any of the staff journalists, long before the paper moved to Docklands, and she provided a point of stability among the musical chairs to which everyone had wearily become accustomed. Invariably neatly dressed, tweed skirts in winter and cotton floral print dresses in summer with a cardigan cast over her narrow shoulders, Martha could be relied on to be efficient and calm when everyone else was rushing around chaotically. She also provided continuity between editors— her reputation was such that no newcomer would dare to sack her immediately and within a short time they came to rely on her utterly.

'Martha, darling. Could you pop in a minute?' Like the rest of the staff, Mini thought Martha was a star; in Mini's book, her secretary was one of the best things about working at *The Courier*. She would miss her.

'Sure, no problem, Mrs Bournemouth.' Martha's head appeared round the door, illuminating the room with a gentle smile.

Mini smiled back.

'Everything all right?' Martha asked. Perhaps she'd noticed the red eyes.

'Yes, fine. Everything is...fine.'

Martha looked at her expectantly.

'Right, sorry. I just want to dictate a quick letter and then we'll both get out of here. God knows, it's late enough.'

Martha shrugged but was clearly grateful. The clock on the wall showed ten to eleven. Settling herself in the seat opposite Mini, Martha took the letter in shorthand, and, apart from a sharp intake of breath on a couple of occasions and the onset of a pained expression, she did not react to what her boss said.

'... So it is with the deepest regret that I have to tender my resignation with immediate effect. Yours sincerely, Miranda Bournemouth,' concluded Mini.

'It's always better to jump before you're pushed,' she offered by way of explanation to the shocked Martha. 'Come on, cheer up. This isn't the time for tears. I'm going to spend more time with my family after all.' Mini managed a wry smile at the cliché and Martha stifled her sobs.

'Now I need you to get that letter to Sir Lesley at about eight tomorrow morning. I know it's a bit early, but I want him to receive it just after he's read the paper and before he can get on the phone.' Mini smiled broadly and surprised herself with her levity. 'God, he'll love that editorial! Absolutely love it!'

She picked up her bag, crossed to Martha and gave her a peck on the cheek. 'Thanks for everything, eh? Don't worry, I'll stay in touch. Look after yourself. Goodness knows who he'll appoint after me... But you know you can always give me a ring if you need a move. Okay?'

Martha nodded, dumbstruck by the loss of her boss. She had enjoyed working for Mini far more than for her predecessors.

Mini turned and walked purposefully across the room. At the door she glanced back and waved briefly. Then she was gone.

⚽ ⚽ ⚽

Dougy McCormack, Political Editor for *The Scribe*, a critically-acclaimed but commercially-failing broadsheet, was having breakfast at his desk. 'Hey, are there any more croissants?' No answer. Dougy sighed. You just couldn't get the staff these days. What kind of a PA abandoned him at such a crucial moment of the day? The kind he had, that's what.

He turned to *The Courier*, a rival paper, but one which he respected and tried to keep broadly in step with. He knew as well as most that it offered the most accurate media barometer for the government's policies. While he could read the gauge and reflect it in his columns, everyone knew that *The Courier*'s owner had a symbiotic relationship with key members of the Cabinet. What was less clear was whether Sir Lesley's contribution to government policy exceeded the government's influence on his newspaper. Dougy suspected it did.

'Wow, that's odd!'

'What is?' came a nasal voice from the next room.

'Oh, you're back are you? Thought you'd already left for the day.' The sarcasm seemed to wash over Serena, his secretary.

'No, Dougy, I'm here for several more hours yet. At least until lunchtime.'

If I ever get another job, I'm going to give up being Mr Nice Guy with my staff, vowed Dougy. No more modern management for me. I'm going to be taken seriously, and I'm not going to take any crap from my subordinates.

'What is?' insisted Serena. For the moment it was obviously too late, Dougy sighed.

'What is what?' snapped Dougy.

'What is odd?'

'Oh, yeah. I was just reading this, that's all.' He shook a copy of *The Courier* above his head.

Serena immediately lost interest.

Dougy read the leader again carefully. That didn't look like Sir Lesley, not at all. Criticising the government's education policy—not the usual line at all. And not just criticism, but a damning attack.

What was going on? His brow furrowed as he puzzled this mystery and sipped his coffee. Blast, it was cold. 'Serena!'

❁ ❁ ❁

Mark rolled over and stretched a languid arm out. He knew the bed would be empty. Mini was always gone by six and it was now nine. He understood why she went and was never there when he felt like making love to her; but no amount of conscious understanding could completely eradicate the nagging irritation and growing resentment. How could she expect him to be the perfect husband when she was either too tired or absent? It was a lot to ask. Although he knew his job was low-key compared to hers, he wondered whether Mini worried about the small cares of an interior designer any more.

Mark's hand brushed against something. Something soft and silky which yielded pleasingly to the touch. He opened his eyes with a start. 'What are you doing here?'

Mini yawned and stretched. 'What do you mean? This is my bed, isn't it, and aren't you my husband? Or were you expecting someone else?'

'No, of course not. That's not what I meant. Shouldn't you be at work?'

'Yes, probably.'

'Is it a holiday?'

'You could say that,' said Mini thoughtfully. She took his hand and placed it on her silk night dress. Mark looked at her, puzzled, unaware for a moment that he was cradling her breast. He wondered what Mini was playing at. But then he felt a demanding warmth surge into his groin. There would be time for explanations later. He grinned and leaned over towards his wife.

'Hey, you... Come here...'

⚽ ⚽ ⚽

'You offering me the job?'

'What do you think?'

'Well, Sir Lesley, it's a bit of a bolt from the blue...'

'Well, don't hang around admiring the show. Do you want it or not? There are plenty of others who'd jump at the chance.'

'Yes, yes. Of course I do.'

'Good. There are certain conditions attached.'

'Of course.'

'But we can talk about that when you come in later today.'

'Today? What time?'

'Why, are you busy?'

'Uh, no... Of course not. Anytime, that's just fine by me.'

'Good. That's what I like to hear.' Sir Lesley knew he'd got the right man already. 'Let's say twelve, okay? We'll sort out a few details and then take some lunch. Quaglino's okay?'

'Yeah, sure.'

'Right. See you at twelve.'

Dougy still pressed the receiver to his ear as the line went dead. 'Wow! Wow, bloody wow!' he shouted.

'What's wrong now?' asked Serena.

'Wrong? Wrong? Nothing's wrong. Nothing is wrong at

all! In fact... Everything... Even you... Everything is perfect.'

Serena looked at her boss suspiciously. He'd clearly lost the plot completely this time.

⚽ ⚽ ⚽

Simon Simpson, tall and modestly handsome in a weak-chinned English sort of way, wrinkled his brow and scanned the first edition. It wasn't there. He pursed his lips and exhaled through his nose. His friend Jimmy, who'd got a mention in the sports pages for his goal in Millwall's Second Division victory, had contributed more to the paper than he had.

Si slumped in his chair, swivelled forty-five degrees and undid the cuffs on his electric blue shirt before carefully rolling them up. Damn. He'd spent all day researching that story and then Slimey Stevens, his loathsome boss, had pulled it. He might have guessed this would happen. Si put it down to jealousy but knew that if he didn't get out soon his career as a journalist would be over before it had really got started.

While wondering how to salvage the day, he twiddled his pen and stared absent-mindedly at the screensaver on his desk-top computer: *Success isn't the ball at the back of the net, it's getting it there. Success isn't the*—The red text scrolled endlessly across the aquamarine background. Apparently, this was a quotation from the poet-footballer Eric Cantona. Si's boyhood football-fanaticism had faded to indifference after puberty; he only took a passing interest in the game these days, and only then when it concerned Jimmy's fortunes. So he found it hard to pinpoint what had attracted him to the aphorism; but after seeing it printed large on a sports page he had adopted it for his idle moments—at least until he found something more interesting.

Slimey Stevens, *The Standard's* Diary Editor sidled over to the desk where Si had spread out the paper. 'Hi Si, how are you today?' Slimey was forty-three, thin on top, squeezed ridiculously into a yellow check waistcoat and in the last couple of years had been forced to concede that his parabolic career curve had irrevocably flattened out. As a result he had added spite to his rich collection of personality defects, which already included insecurity and bitchiness. Talented and attractive but inaccessible young men, such as Si, had become favourite targets for Slimey's queening acerbity.

Si looked up at Slimey's approach. 'Fine... Well actually, no. I'm bloody pissed off.'

'Oh, why's that?' Slimey was doing a bad job of hiding his *schadenfreude*.

'Because you pulled my story, that's why.' Si knew he had to hold back and control his temper. Otherwise he'd be out of a job.

'Oh that. Yes, I know, sorry luv. But it just wasn't up to it. That's all.' Slimey made to move off. 'It's a tough old world, journalism. You'll just have to get used to it.'

'But it was a perfectly good story. You know it was.' Si was about to accuse his boss of doing him down deliberately, but just bit his tongue in time.

'No it wasn't. It was crap. Far too political for us. If you can't understand that, then you'd better reassess your options, I'd say.'

'You would, would you?'

But Slimey didn't bother to reply. He'd had his fun. He turned his back and walked over to his own desk to start the day's work. If Simpson could be riled so easily, then he'd have no problem getting rid of him before long. But not quite yet; he wanted to enjoy the situation a bit more first.

Si watched Slimey waddle away. He ran his fingers through his mop of wavy hair and rested his head in his hands, crumpled over the desk. This was awful. Where had things gone wrong? Until only a few weeks ago he'd been doing great. 'The high-flyer' was how he'd heard someone describe him. But now it was all about to go down the pan. When the phone rang he watched it for about ten seconds, too depressed to answer.

'Why don't you answer your phone?' Slimey called across. 'It might be a story and, God knows, honey, you need one...'

'Hello, *Standard* Diary...'

'Hi, can I speak to Simon Simpson please?'

'Speaking.'

'Hi, Simon. This is Martha Rogers. I work for Douglas McCormack.'

Si sat up. Like the rest of the media world, Si was very aware that McCormack had just been appointed to succeed Mini Bournemouth at *The Courier*. 'Yes, of course...'

'Mr McCormack was wondering if you could pop into the office later today. He has a proposition for you.'

'Really? Can you tell me what exactly?'

'No, I'm afraid I can't. Only that you may find it worth your while. Mr McCormack has seen your work and he likes it. I think you'll be interested in what he has to say.'

'Oh, right. What time?'

'Say about three?'

'I'll be there.'

'Good. See you then. Bye.'

'Bye.' Si's heart was thumping. The excitement was almost painful. Could this be it? The break that would take him out and above the likes of Slimey Stevens? He didn't dare to hope, but it was impossible not to. Three o'clock seemed an eternity away.

'Another?'

'Yeah, why not?'

'It'd be rude not to, eh?'

'I guess so.' Jimmy stood up, pulled up his jeans and tucked in his tee shirt. He wandered over to the bar and returned soon after with two handsome pints.

Si and his best mate Jimmy were in their local, The Feathers. The pub provided them with a refuge and a second home. They sat on high backed chairs in the corner at their usual table, a rough wooden rectangle covered in beer mats and the circular stains of a thousand pints, many consumed by Si and Jimmy. A dozen other tables clung to the walls, but most of the pub was given over to space before the long L shaped bar. On Friday night this space would be filled by a heaving mass of drinkers celebrating the end of the working week; but during the day it was empty and the bare boards, uncluttered by drinkers, made the pub seem much larger and lighter than it really was. On the other side of the polished, oak barrier, the bar staff shuttled up and down in the deep slot as if attached to a rail. Their reflections flickered in the hanging beer glasses and stencilled mirror, which ran the length of the bar. The Feathers was nothing special really—much like several hundred other Edwardian pubs in south west London. But it was important to Si and Jimmy and associated inextricably with their friendship.

Si watched Jimmy weave his way towards him. His friend was poised, the natural athlete balancing two full glasses carefully. A girl turned her head as Jimmy passed, clearly impressed by his trim body, clean-cut good looks and smiling eyes. The extra-short haircut was neat, and baggy jeans concealed large thighs—always, reflected Si, a winning factor with girls.

'Thanks for that,' said Si, sipping carefully so as to preserve the spumey head for as long as possible.

'You look like you're seducing it, not drinking it.' Jimmy wasn't malicious, just mucking about. He knew Si well, better than anyone probably. They'd grown up together and, although they'd now gone different ways, they still saw enough of each other to know what was what. 'You take your tongue out of there, you pervert. You can get arrested for that, eh?'

'Piss off,' said Si matter-of-factly and resumed drinking.

Jimmy laughed and took up his own pint purposefully. 'So how's it going?'

'What?'

'The new job, what else?'

'All right. It's all right.'

'Is that all?'

'Yeah, it's really good now I come to think of it. Most of the time.'

'I s'pose that's true of everything.'

'Not everything, but work anyway. I catch myself thinking there must be more to life than turning up to an office and working all day. Know what I mean?'

'Yeah, suppose so.'

'Not that you've ever worked in an office, mind...'

'Hold on. Football is a job too, you know. Bloody hard work too...'

'Yeah, sure. I wasn't saying otherwise. Only you don't work in an office, do you?' They drank quietly. 'The thing that gets me, you know, is how broken up modern life is... D'you see?'

'No, can't say I do,' answered Jimmy. He was used to the reflective side of Si. He sat back expecting some obscure musing from his friend and was ready to humour him. He wouldn't respond; he never did. Not that he minded listening. It was just that he didn't understand what Si was on about half the time.

'Well,' said Si patiently, 'we all run around like headless chickens doing things, work and going to the pub and meeting people and so on, but much of it doesn't make sense. What's lacking is something to hold it all together. You know, a structure.'

For once Jimmy broke his rule and tried to get his head around Si's philosophising. 'You mean like a jigsaw puzzle in a box?'

'No, not really,' said Si gently, slightly surprised by Jimmy's observation.

He paused for thought and watched his friend drinking. He hadn't expected his friend to participate and had been using Jimmy much as a dandy uses a mirror when dressing: to glance vainly into from time to time just to confirm and take pleasure in his wondrous appearance. But Si wasn't an intellectual snob and was prepared to consider Jimmy's simile.

'That assumes it all fits together to make one picture. No, I'm not that optimistic. All I want is the sense that some of it matters... Some of the bits of my life, that is.'

'Mmm, I see what you're getting at,' lied Jimmy happily. Through the warm fug of the bar he dimly perceived that this was a special moment. One of countless instantly forgotten good times which make life bearable. Jimmy valued his evenings in the pub, almost as much as he prized his friendship with Si. Not that he'd ever articulated either idea; not even thought them through clearly. But they were the bedrock of his life.

❀ ❀ ❀

Si stood in his bathroom horrified. He should have known; of course he should. The trouble was, he half-suspected he had known. But he'd ignored the signs and not bothered to take pre-emptive action. He looked down with a mixture of dismay and fascination.

The shards of glass spread like a mosaic out from the epicentre of the explosion. Silvered slivers, sharp as needles and some as big as daggers. The late morning light slanting through the blinds played with the blunt angles revealed by the broken mirror and refracted rainbows onto the white bathroom tiles. Si noticed how a yellow blur melted quickly into a hot orange just above the taps.

'Damn,' he muttered unconvincingly. What now? He couldn't really move, standing as he was, barefoot in the middle of the broken glass. But he had to get to work. 'Damn.'

He had an idea. He spotted the carved frame of the

mirror—an Oriental design in dark, painted wood. The frame lay on the floor where it had fallen. Like a guillotine blade the mirror had slipped off the loose hook and fallen softly to the floor, exploding with a surprisingly loud bang. More of a crack really, like a whiplash at the circus or static electricity. As the smooth face of the mirror smashed and slid into itself, over itself, sending sheets of glass skidding across the floor, the wooden frame remained upright for a second, as if stunned. In shock; like a shot man realising that death is upon him. Then it had gently toppled over.

Si retrieved the frame and shook the remaining glass out of it. Then he used it as a stepping stone to reach the door. He decided not to bother sweeping up until later. There wasn't time.

'Damn,' he muttered again as he closed the bathroom door on the scene. Now the prospect of cleaning up would hang over him like a black cloud all day. But worse, and he hated to admit it, he could feel the primitive suspicions of his childhood weighing upon him. He thought he'd laughed them off years ago. But the thought of what his mother would have said made him shiver.

Si looked at his watch. Twelve ten. Time to get to the pub. Jimmy would be waiting.

The Feathers was always quiet at lunchtime, even on Sundays. Si and Jimmy's table faced the big video screen. When there were soccer matches on satellite TV, about twice a week, the screen would become the focus of the pub. At other times, like today, it would appear a strange appendage, hanging there like a drying sheet. Ugly.

Jimmy was tired. After yet again scoring the winner in yesterday's key Second Division match against York City, he'd gone for a few beers. Ignoring the manager's injunctions against getting drunk during the season, he'd got plastered. He regretted it now.

To deal with his hangover, he ordered a strong Bloody Mary. With everything. As he'd known it would, the vodka was already kicking in and making him feel better.

Si had spent the previous evening watching a film on TV. Some instantly forgettable action movie with a thrilling if implausible plot. He'd gone to bed feeling faintly dissatisfied with his life. Normally, such feelings evaporated overnight. But when he woke up, he'd been surprised to find himself suffering from a mild depression.

'D'you ever wish you were doing something else?'

Jimmy looked up and stopped playing with his swizzle stick, which he'd been spinning on the edge of the glass. 'Eh?'

'Like, d'you ever want to do something else? For a job?'

Jimmy looked thoughtful, raised his glass but didn't drink. 'Haven't we had this conversation before?' No response. Si seemed to be waiting for an answer. 'Well, now you come to ask... No,' he said.

'You're lucky... I do. Well, sometimes. Like now.'

'Why? I thought you enjoyed being a journalist.'

'I do sometimes.'

'And you were telling me how wonderful your new job is.'

'Have you ever read it?'

'Read what?'

' *The Courier*? You know, the paper I write for.'

'No,' Jimmy admitted coyly. He didn't like it when Si went off on masochistic tracks like this. Si was his friend—he wanted him to be cheerful and crack a few jokes, not get all introspective. Jimmy tried to raise his spirits. 'You know I don't read much. But I'm sure it's really good and you can influence people...'

'Can I?'

Jimmy sighed. It clearly hadn't worked.

'I wonder. Most of the time I think I'm writing rubbish and feel like I'm being manipulated by people whose real intentions I don't understand.'

'Eh?'

'Oh, nothing. It doesn't matter.' Si sighed in turn.

Jimmy didn't give up and looking at his friend said brightly, 'You always wanted to be a journalist. You're natural for it.'

'I didn't always want to be. It kind of happened, really. It seemed the best option at the time, but I never thought I'd spend the rest of my life doing it.'

'Who said you would?'

'Well, it's difficult to change careers once you've got going.'

'My arse. It's only difficult if you think it is. And you're being bloody stupid 'cos you're only twenty-seven. You could stop tomorrow and become...whatever. No problem.'

'A footballer?'

'What?'

'Could I become a footballer? Tomorrow like?'

Jimmy's brow creased. 'Well, no. It's a bit late at twenty-seven.'

'Exactly, that's my point. It's already too late to do most things. Even at twenty-seven. And the thing is, nobody tells you that when you're twenty.'

'I never knew you wanted to play soccer.' Jimmy was clearly puzzled. 'You were crap at school.'

'I know. I don't want to play soccer.'

'So why did you say you did?'

'I didn't. I just meant... Anyway, the point, is even if I wanted to, I couldn't. I don't suppose there's much I could do if I wanted to change.'

'You could become a dustman. I had a cousin who became a dustman when he was made redundant at forty.'

'Yeah, I suppose so. I could become a dustman. That's a relief, isn't it?'

Jimmy failed to notice the irony and nodded. The conversation had woken him up and, combined with the healthy measure of vodka, had buried his hangover.

'It's not that I really want to change jobs...'

'Great, I don't think you'd make a very good dustman anyway. No offence, mind.'

'None taken. I think really, I'd just like to know I could do something else if I wanted. To have the option. Often I feel like I've no real choice in how I lead my life. Know what I mean? Things just happen and we react to them. We have no control.'

'Yeah, it's a bugger, isn't it?'

They lapsed into Sunday morning silence and sipped their drinks.

'Gagging for a fag,' said Jimmy.

Si recognised the beginning of a well-practised routine. He took up the script. 'Have one.'

'Can't. The manager'd kill me. Anyway, I don't really want one. It's three years since I last smoked and mostly I don't miss it much.'

'Never saw the appeal myself.'

'Oh, there's nothing like a cigarette. Especially with a cup of coffee after breakfast.'

They fell silent. Si wondered what had happened to the rest of Jimmy's habitual eulogy of smoking. He hadn't even mentioned the post-coital bit, which he always did, with a great cheesey grin when it came to the most purple part of his speech. Instead, Jimmy slipped into a nostalgic reverie.

'Sometimes I think that whatever we do we'll end up at the same place.'

'What?'

'Well, you know, even if I'd stayed at *The Standard* and not moved to *The Courier*, I doubt it'd have made much difference in the end.'

'Yeah, I suppose we all die eventually,' said Jimmy cheerfully, the urge to smoke clearly conquered.

Si looked dismayed. 'No, I wasn't being morbid. Only that I reckon we can probably follow a thousand different paths, maybe even simultaneously, and still end up at the same point. I'd probably end up a sad old lushed-out hack, whatever...'

'Now you're losing me.'

'Oh, it doesn't really matter. But it does make a mockery of choice, I reckon.'

'This is way too serious. Remember, I've still got a hangover. Treat my brain gently.'

'Yeah, you're right. Sorry.'

'Another one? '

'Yeah. Another Bloody.'

'Right you are.' Jimmy slipped off to the bar. As he watched him go, Si chewed the lemon slice from his last drink and wondered why he spent so much time in the pub. It wasn't as if he was an alcoholic or anything. The social conditioning of his generation, he concluded. Jimmy returned smiling, gripping two long red glasses firmly in his hands. Red, the colour of Sunday mornings.

⚽ ⚽ ⚽

Si was working late. He flicked on the TV. It was tuned to the Parliamentary Channel. He'd sussed out from the start that the way to Dougy's heart lay through his politics. And on several occasions when Si had been summoned to Dougy's office, the TV had been tuned to the Parliamentary Channel.

Now, as far as Si could work out, Dougy supported the Government. But it wasn't always clear. And often Dougy would run stories as a favour to individual members of the Opposition. He obviously had a foot in both camps. This made it difficult for Si to know what he should and shouldn't put in his column. He seemed to have got it right so far. But he knew that when he didn't, he could expect a rollicking from Dougy. To minimise the risk of this, Si had taken to watching coverage of Parliament at every spare opportunity. He thought this would help him to tune into what made Dougy tick.

At the moment the Opposition party were doing well. They were ahead of the Government in the polls, and exuded a cocky assurance that they would form the next Government. But there was no date for elections to take place and Si knew that Dougy was working to position himself to gain the maximum from whatever turn the political scene took.

'Doesn't the Honourable Member for Bognor South realise that education in our schools is a disaster? Worse, it's an unmitigated disaster. Since this government took power, funding for the education sector has been cut by 26 per cent in real terms. How can he claim that the Government has improved education for our children? It hasn't improved it; it's virtually destroyed it.' The Opposition Spokesman subsided into the empty acres of green leather bench—there can't have been more than a dozen MPs present. His opposite number on the Government benches stood up.

The Secretary of State for Education dismissed as nonsense what had just been said, and fiercely defended the poor backbench Member for Bognor South, who had been so savaged by the fluent and acerbic onslaught.

The backbencher, pink-cheeked and tightly upholstered in wide pinstripe, huffed in indignation at the Opposition's attack, hear-heared his Right Honourable Friend and looked forward to a good dinner at the end of the debate. It was jolly unfair of the Opposition to single him out for attack. He was only doing what the Whips had told him to do. It was damned annoying that they'd forced him to come along to this debate at all. What did he know or care about education, anyway? Confound them. He hated having to feed questions to Ministers. The sooner he found his own rightful place on the Front Bench, the better.

The Shadow Spokesman had forced the Minister to give way again. 'In response to the Minister's challenge, let me tell him this. When *this* party is in power, we will consult widely with leading representatives of all the main religions in this country and will work closely with them to improve moral standards and to improve the education system...'

A sarcastic voice from the most distant of the benches opposite shouted, 'Is that a policy? If so, it's the first yet.' Howls of exaggerated laughter greeted the comment.

'Yes, it *is* a policy. And it's more than the government can offer us. They are bereft of new ideas and morally bankrupt and that's why they will soon be out of power. Yes, it *is* a policy and I am grateful to the Honourable member on the opposite benches for highlighting this point. This party believes that you cannot divorce religion from education and that to improve education standards in this country we need to involve religious leaders in seeking ways forward. 'The Shadow Spokesman sank back as the Minister impatiently sprang up and thrust forward to the dispatch box, gripping the metal-banded box, eager to seize back the initiative.

Si's interest was already drifting. He wondered if Dougy had been watching. It would be interesting to see how *The Courier's* editor decided to play it in tomorrow's edition. Certainly, there was considerable scope for journalistic soap boxes; religion and education were two very emotive subjects.

Si and Jimmy started out about seven at The Feathers. Quietly at first. Just a few pints and some gentle banter. The usual comfortable and sporadic conversation. Neither had any fixed plans for the evening.

It was best to get to The Feathers early on a Saturday night, if you wanted a stool at the bar; and if you didn't get a stool, there was little chance of chatting up the girls as they waited later in the evening to be served. When it got really busy about ten, they were standing three deep at the bar, sometimes for up to a quarter of an hour. That was Jimmy's favourite time to strike. Like tickling salmon, he described it. Taking them when they were most vulnerable. Belly up, half-drunk on lager, and starting to forget themselves.

The Feathers wasn't a bad pub. It attracted a mixed bunch: balding young bankers trying to stay awake and biding their time before moving up the road to Chelsea; paunchy, jobbing builders from the North East missing their families, shooting their mouths off and waving fifty pound notes around; chintzy divorcees pretending they were still young; a scattering of raucous tarts game on for a big night out; and, of course, Jimmy and Si—the only professional footballer and journalist among the regulars, but, in common with most of the clientele, non-native Londoners.

Like the bankers and the tarts, Jimmy and Si didn't hang out with their schoolfriends, most of whom had stayed in their home town and now spent their spare time playing darts and snooker. Another trait shared with many Feathers' regulars was a degree of insecurity; they might be doing okay today, but the future was uncertain, even threatening.

It always amazed Si that people made it past forty. How did they do it? So complicated, confusing. Mortgages, endowments, marriages, kids, tax returns. Even organising a holiday could appear a challenge at times. Did it all become blindingly clear at some stage? wondered Si, awe-struck. Or was everyone else simply born knowing how to deal with life?

Jimmy felt this less acutely, but occasionally he also expressed the idea. 'I mean, what happens afterwards? No, not after I'm too old to play soccer but after *everything*? I mean, shouldn't we be doing something about it now instead of faffing about like this?'

But in the face of all this terrifying doubt, Si and Jimmy had found one island which offered temporary refuge: The Feathers.

Sometimes, after last orders, they went on to a party. On this particular evening, Brenda Bassett suggested the venue. Brenda used to work behind the bar, before getting a job as a Public Relations assistant. But she still came in for a drink. 'It'll be great, free booze, beautiful people, even famous ones...'

'Famous? Like who?' Jimmy raised his eyebrows.

'Oh, I don't know. You shouldn't be so...' Brenda searched for the word. Jimmy waited, watching her, amused. 'So *pedantic*,' she concluded triumphantly. 'But there will be 'cos this guy whose house it's at is pretty flashy. He drives a sports car, and he's on the radio. I met him through work.'

Jimmy smirked, but Brenda didn't seem to notice.

Brenda was all mouth—always had been; even three years before as a sixteen-year-old wearing make-up and boasting about what she'd done with her twenty-three-year-old boyfriend the night before. 'You see that mark there... No, not there, there on my knee? Yeah, that one. That's where...' And so on, trying to impress them all as she pulled the pints.

Yet, despite her crudity, Brenda was an attractive girl in a raw, sexy kind of way. She rarely wore skirts larger than a handkerchief and had the legs to carry them off. Her tops were invariably too tight and allowed her breasts to reveal themselves impressively through the thin material. Combined with her raunchy laugh and undistinguished but acceptable face, she had something which made most men enjoy her company—Si had once described it as her 'mistress quality'. She was an archetypal Other Woman.

Si had known a girl like Brenda at school. He'd shared illicit cigarettes with her and a crowd of others during lunch breaks and used to watch her inhaling carefully, imagining what she'd be like on her own. Just him and her. She used to take a mouthful of smoke expertly and, pouting smudged lipstick, blow out the blue-grey stain into the insipid air, which shone with a billion drops of cold, lemon sunshine.

'He's posh then, is he?' cracked Jimmy, but Brenda didn't smile.

'You don't need to come if you don't want to. Nobody's forcing you. But it's you who's missing out if you don't.'

'Only joking. Course we'll come. Won't we, Si?'

'Well, I'd been thinking of starting back soon,' Si muttered dubiously.

Brenda made a face. She'd always thought Si was a bit wet. But quite sweet all the same. Not that she gave any credence to those pub regulars who suggested that Jimmy and Si were queer. She knew Jimmy wasn't for a start. And Si, always so repressed, distant, too clever by half—she half-fancied him really. He was different. At least he wasn't on the dole.

'No, come on! You don't need to stay long if you don't want to. Time to party, eh, Si?' And as usual Si couldn't be bothered to object. Jimmy won the day.

'Yeah, suppose so. Why not?'

⚽ ⚽ ⚽

Two hours later Si found himself in a party from hell pressed in on all sides by sweating bodies, drinking an unhealthy-looking cocktail through a straw and discussing television with a boring stranger. Brenda, Jimmy and everyone else he knew had disappeared. What am I doing here? I hate parties, why did I agree to come? he wondered.

He abandoned the loquacious girl who'd cornered him, even though she was still in full flow about the sad demise of the TV dinner. He went in search of Jimmy and found him near a table straining under the weight of a large metal bucket containing bottles of beer and icy water.

'I scored two today against Tranmere,' Jimmy boasted as Si came within hearing range. 'It's only a matter of time before one of the big clubs spots me and then I'm away…' He'd been celebrating those two goals all night, but the wafer-thin, pallid girl didn't seem to mind. She listened absent-mindedly.

The goals had become more spectacular during the evening with each telling. The tap in from a goal-keeping mistake had, after a few more drinks, become a volley from ten yards. Now it had become an overhead bicycle kick from the edge of the box into the top right hand corner. Amazing, thought Si. Nobody else seemed to notice or care that the truth had been lost somewhere between The Feathers and the party.

'Baby, we should go someplace else,' Jimmy intoned. He seemed unaware of Si, standing beside him.

'Do you know I'm a super-model?' Si tried not to look surprised. It was true that she did have a strange, haunting quality to her; but how could she be a model—she was all skin and bones?

'Yes, baby. Sure do. You've told me four times already.' Jimmy flashed his killer smile and Si looked away, his stomach turning. Sometimes Jimmy was too much. Even for Si, who had known him all his life. Even as a kid, when they were playing soccer in the street and the ball had gone off course, destroying someone's rosebed, even then Jimmy had charmed himself out of trouble. Often it had been Si sent to retrieve the ball and to receive the abuse, while Jimmy and the others snickered around next door's hedge.

But Si kept these thoughts to himself. He knew that at the end of the day Jimmy was the only real mate he had. The only one who would put himself out, any time, any place, to help him out. For example, dashing across the world to get him out of jail when his smuggling project went wrong—not that he'd got a smuggling project yet. But if he were to, then Si knew he could rely on Jimmy. Yes, Jimmy's smarmy sweet-talk and loyalty would come in handy as they blasted their way out of the dank cells and abseiled to freedom.

So, gratefully thinking how Jimmy had risked his all to get him out of jail, he forgot his rancour. 'D'you want a drink, you two?'

'Hey, Si, where've you been?' Jimmy grinned broadly. 'Yeah, I'd love a drink. You're a good man, Si. How about you, baby? By the way, this is my oldest mate, Si Simpson.'

'I can't drink,' moaned the girl. 'It'll make me fat and ruin my figure, and you know how difficult it is to stay at the top when you're a super-model.'

Si sighed and Jimmy guffawed. 'You look like you could put on a bit of weight.' The model looked askance at Jimmy. Maybe she'd noticed that his Texan bar drawl had faded and crossed the Atlantic—a slight twang now underlay each coarse vowel. But Jimmy seemed impervious. 'Well, I'll have a beer and Daisy here will have a carrot juice.'

'Maisy, my name's Maisy, not Daisy.'

Jimmy roared with laughter again, drowning out the waif's protests. 'Oh baby,' soothed Jimmy recovering his misplaced drawl, 'what's in a name? It's the real you underneath I'm interested in.'

Maisy poked him in the chest with a bony finger. 'If you think you've got any chance of sleeping with me, then you'd better learn my name pronto, buster.'

Si got the drinks in. He'd seen, and heard, it all so many times before.

When he returned five minutes later, Jimmy and Maisy had disappeared.

After a few moments, Si gave up waiting for them to return. With all that story-telling, the bugger's probably scored his hat-trick by now, he reflected; best leave him to it. Tired, Si pushed his way through the gyrating throng. God, he felt sober. This was no longer his idea of fun. Was it ever? he wondered.

At the door he paused to recover from the effort of walking ten paces. A hand stretched out and touched his forearm. Si turned in surprise. 'Hi, you had enough?'

'Uh huh.' Si made to leave.

'No, don't go yet. Let's have a drink. Come on, don't be shy. I don't know anyone here and somehow I think we'd get on.'

Si hesitated but, seeing the proffered can, he took a closer look at the girl. Finding himself transfixed by a pair of large, almond eyes, he accepted. 'Yeah, okay. Why not? What's your name?'

'Roberta. What's yours?'

'Si.'

'Hi, Si.' She smiled winningly.

Si hated small talk, although he could manage passably well when necessary. There seemed to be no alternative, so, summoning his scant, remaining energy, he launched in. 'Do you know who that guy over there is? The one with the bizarre bow tie? I hate bow ties. Something lacking and inadequate about them. Like wearing one's insecurities on one's sleeve.'

The girl wasn't responding. She looked at him from under hooded lids and smiled as if slightly amused by what he was saying.

Si gave up on the small talk.

'Don't you think this party's awful?'

'A party from hell,' Si agreed.

The girl laughed attractively. 'Yes... Exactly.' She had a musical, soft voice; not local. He looked at her suspiciously. Was she taking the mick?

Someone bumped into Si. 'Are you leaving or not?' slurred a voice. Si stood back to let them past.

'Come on. I know somewhere quieter.' Roberta led him to a door which slid back. Taking him by the hand, she led him into a dimly lit room. Si followed the tall, slim girl obediently and, despite promising himself that after one final drink he'd go home, his mind raced ahead. Roberta sat cross-legged on the floor and gestured for him to sit down opposite her.

Intrigued by the stranger's compelling presence, he did so, leaning back against the wall, legs stretched out in front. 'So, Roberta, what are you doing here?'

'Well, I'm a student and I've been living in London for four months.'

'Where are you from, if you don't mind me asking. I mean you've got great English, but you just don't seem totally English.'

Roberta seemed to take this as flattery. The truth was that she had a strong and seductive foreign accent and a cool beauty to match. She twiddled a strand of long black hair as she replied. 'No, you're right. I'm from Khartoum. D'you know where that is?'

'The Sudan?'

'Yes, well done. Most people just give me blank stares if I say Khartoum.'

'It sounds wonderfully exotic. I'd love to go to the desert sometime. I've never been. Only seen the films, you know.'

'Well, if you're good, then maybe I'll take you.'

Si shot her a startled look. She seemed to be playing with him. Otherwise she was terrifyingly forward. 'That's a bit rash. We've only just met. How do you know I 'm not a serial killer?'

'Well, if you are, I'll find out soon enough and I won't take you.' Roberta smiled broadly. She had a large, inviting mouth and bright teeth.

Si laughed. He found this self-confident girl rather attractive, even captivating. Odd. He hadn't started the evening with any intention of meeting anyone. But, he reflected, in London you should never be surprised by those you meet; that was part of the city's diaphanous attraction and, of course, its horror.

His mother, in one of her eastern religion phases, at about the time she claimed to have the gift of medunity, had taught him that all the time an infinite number of options, invisible to the conscious self, unfold like a card deck; and chance, not choice, selects the card determining the future.

Si had a less mystical view of London life. Roberta was certainly special; but, he thought wryly, this wasn't exactly the first time he'd found himself in such a situation. He'd seen, and heard, it all before. So, another party, another pick up. And no doubt tomorrow would yield another morning after. Or perhaps, he thought as his natural optimism shone through, it might be one of those magical moments which only reveal themselves with hindsight?

❀ ❀ ❀

'Morning, Si, do you want some coffee?'

'Yeah, okay.' Si groped his way to the desk and sat down. Mondays were always difficult but this one was proving trickier than most. 'Milk and one sugar please.' Bill grunted as he left the room.

Si had been at *The Courier* for two months. The domino effect initiated by Mini Bournemouth's resignation had gathered pace and eventually acquired the force of a tidal wave. Many journalists were caught up in it and for several weeks the whole profession talked about nothing apart from who was moving where and who'd been sacked by their paper. Some hadn't been so fortunate as Si. He'd heard of at least a dozen established journalists who'd lost their jobs.

'Often happens in the build-up to an election,' commented a hoary hack who'd survived the shake-up.

The tidal wave crashed from one editor's office to another, from newsrooms to features desks, and wobbled and dislodged hundreds of staff. The secondary ripple, which had shaken Si loose from his niche at *The Standard,* had washed him from a junior position to become Diary Editor on *The Courier*.

Following that unexpected meeting with Dougy McCormack, less than a fortnight had elapsed before he had taken up his new post. The promotion carried a degree of risk. Certainly, he was more exposed than in his previous job. For the first time people began to know who he was.

The smell of success terrified him not a little. Surely they've made a mistake in picking me, he panicked. I find it difficult to go shopping on my own, let alone help to part-edit a major national newspaper with millions of readers.

Si started unconvincingly, somewhat overawed by his new responsibilities; but realising he enjoyed the support of the newspaper's editor, he had started to feel more confident by the day. Now he realised that he could do the job.

Si worried a bit about managing the Diary staff, particularly his assistant, Bill, who seemed slow to learn the ropes, although he'd already worked for six months at *The Courier* under Si's predecessor; but Si realised that Bill and the others were still coming to terms with the new regime. It was early days yet and he was sure it would work out. Above all, he was determined to be a better manager than Slimey Stevens.

After a month, Si began to enjoy his work. He was still trying to tune into what his editor Dougy wanted, but the gentle satirical style required came easily; and, in contrast to his previous job, he was encouraged to take an interest in political stories. He'd always had certain compunctions about what he wrote, but he quickly learnt that Dougy would only accept well-substantiated stories. Surmise and rumour had no place in *The Courier*'s Diary.

Si found it best to let his victims stitch themselves up rather than put the boot in himself. Not that he was naturally malicious. But he knew that he would have to cultivate a hard edge if he was to make a success of the job. Fortunately, he found that those who had something to hide normally hoisted themselves by their own petard. He just published what they said and let the reader judge.

Justice was normally done; for instance, in the case of the backbench MP who bombarded the Diary with daily faxes about his latest exploits but seemed not to care that they were rarely used. In fact, on the few occasions Si had to resort to these offerings, the published pieces reflected badly on the MP and his inflated self-opinion.

'Bloody good journalism' was how Dougy described such stories.

Si was delighted. Praise from his boss, which he'd noticed was not frequently forthcoming, produced a heady feeling not dissimilar to the effect produced by breathing in deeply over a mouthful of single malt whisky.

'Did you hear about the bomb?'

'Hear about it? I was caught up in it. The underground

was shut for hours. What a mess.'

Bill plonked the mug down on his desk. 'Coffee, one sugar.'

'That's great, thanks. By the way, how are you getting on with the Minister of Sport and his fling with that Olympic shot-putter?'

'Not so wonderful, actually.'

Si hated the word "actually" and ground his teeth.

Bill continued unaware. 'There was nothing in it.'

'Who told you that? Mavis or the Minister?'

'Neither. I found out that he was bonking his secretary.'

'Oh.' Si sighed. 'Well, we'd better drop it then.' He knew what Dougy thought about stories involving Ministers and their secretaries. They weren't news. So many of them were at it, so why make a big deal? And, equally importantly, Dougy didn't want to incur the wrath of his political connections without being sure of his ground. The trouble with secretaries was that they hardly ever kissed and told. Far too loyal and always half-hoping that their boss would eventually divorce his wife and marry them. Anyway, Si knew perfectly well that Dougy would never accept a story unless he was sure of its pedigree. It had to be proven to run. Especially in these politically tense times. He silently cut Bill's story from that day's page and thrust a fax into his subordinate's hand. 'Check that out. It may be a runner.' Bill took the paper and, reading it, left the room.

Si picked up the phone and dialled Jimmy's number. A girl answered. Surely not the super-model from Saturday night? It hadn't looked serious enough. Jimmy would have booted her out on Sunday morning if he was behaving true to form. 'Hi, can I speak to Jimmy, please?'

'He's not here.'

'What, is he training?'

'God knows. Why don't you ring back later?'

'Yeah, okay. Will you tell him I rang?'

'All right, if you tell me who you are.'

'Oh, sorry. Just say Si called.'

'Right.' The girl hung up.

Strange. Si felt disconcerted by the conversation. The voice had been oddly familiar, but the girl had shown no indication that she knew him.

The coffee was good. If nothing else, Bill could do one thing well. The phone rang.

'Hi kid, look, have you got a moment?'

At the sound of the gravelly tones Si sat up in his chair. 'Yes, of course.'

'Well get your butt up here. I want you to do something. And it's urgent. Five minutes max, okay?'

'I'm on my way.'

⚽ ⚽ ⚽

'Go straight in,' said Martha softly. The sparkle had disappeared from her eyes in the last few weeks. Although he hadn't exchanged more than a few words with her, Si suspected something was wrong. She appeared to be on the verge of tears. But now was no time to express sympathy and, smiling, he strode through the door.

Dougy beckoned him to a chair as he walked in. Below them Si could just make out the silvery flicker of the Thames' edge. The sky which occupied the majority of the panoramic windows was Airfix grey. Winter in London. How long until spring? wondered Si. He hated this depressing weather.

Even in such a short time, the room had changed since Mini left. In particular, the meticulous tidiness had been replaced by chaos. Dougy's jacket sprawled over the back of a chair and every surface was covered with old newspapers and magazines.

'Sit down, sit down.' Dougy swivelled his chair and leaned across the cluttered desk towards Si. 'I've got a job for you. I want you to run a series of pieces in the Diary about religion and education. Okay? Treat them...well, as usual. And don't be afraid to dish a little dirt. Understand?' Not waiting for an answer, Dougy went on: 'The important thing is the theme.' Dougy smiled malevolently. 'Do you think you can do that?'

'Yeah, course I can.' It didn't take a genius to work out that Dougy's sudden enthusiasm was connected to education's rapid rise up the political agenda. In particular, the Opposition's promise the previous week that, were they to be elected, they would involve religious leaders directly in the formation of education policy. Education was rapidly emerging as the main issue upon which the next election would be won or lost.

'Good, good. Well, you get on with it. I want to see about half a dozen stories over the next few weeks. Then we'll take another look and see how it's going, right?'

Si nodded. He closed the door respectfully after him. Dougy was already on the phone.

Back in his office he pondered his task. The problem was that he didn't know which way Dougy wanted the stories to spin. He'd feared to ask as Dougy clearly assumed Si knew. Should they support or undermine the Opposition's initiative? Normally *The Courier* supported the Government, but the forthcoming election had undermined all the usual assumptions.

It didn't help that Sir Lesley Johnson had become increasingly unpredictable in his political loyalties. Of course, *The Courier*'s ambiguous position wasn't exceptional. These were strange times. Many habitually pro-Government tabloids appeared to have been working towards an Opposition victory for months, probably with the intention of placing themselves in opposition as soon as possible; after all, what journalist enjoys propping up a creaking Government more than writing critical copy?

Aware of this and knowing what he did of Dougy's personal politics—the man was anti-establishment by nature and loyal only to his own interests—Si decided to play safe and go for the critical approach. As a journalist he found it usually paid off. People took you more seriously if you were hyper-critical and cynical.

With growing interest in his task, Si decided he would paint a picture of morally bankrupt religious leaders. He would make his readers wonder how the future of the nation could be entrusted to such individuals. Defrocking a few priests shouldn't be too hard, thought Si, and he resolved to publish his first piece within the next two days. A pro-Government line was the traditional *Courier* approach; it seemed the safest course to take in the circumstances.

❀ ❀ ❀

'Scratch my back. No, not there. There.'

'There?'

'Mmm, there... '

It was a dull February day and Si was at his flat with Roberta. She was a demanding girl. 'Work hard play hard' was her motto, taught to her by her father at an early age. And, as far as Si could see, she stuck to the letter of it. During the first few weeks of their affair he had seen her rarely, as she studied hard at the college library. During the weekends she never left his side. It was novel for Si. Not far away on the river a long barge drifted past and Si heard the horn boom in the mist. An echo from a slower and more civilised age.

'Tell me about your family.' He rolled away from her and admired the curve of her breast, unveiled by a lazy sheet.

'There's not much to tell. I've told you most of it already.'

'I know, but tell me again.' Roberta's exoticism fascinated him. All his previous girlfriends had been wilting middle-Englanders with little to distinguish them from every other pasty-skinned plain Jane. Si also had a weakness for routine and repeating successful formulae. To recognise a series of phrases or actions helped him to impose some sort of structure on the amorphousness which always threatened to engulf him.

'Well, my parents lived in the Sudan. My mum's German, and they met when my dad was studying in London. He also had a scholarship. It's quite odd that he's so English in many ways and yet when he's in the Sudan he becomes extremely… pious, I suppose, for want of a better word.'

'Does you mother work?'

Roberta looked at him strangely. 'You know she doesn't. Si, I've told you all this before.'

'Yeah, I know. But I want to hear it again. Go on.'

Roberta sighed. 'Well, no, she doesn't work. Not any more. When they first met she was a teacher. But after they left for the Sudan, just before I was born, she stopped. It's difficult for her to work as a woman and now virtually impossible. Anyway, my father forbids her.'

'Forbids her?' This was uncharted territory for Si. A land where men could stop their wives doing things. With the authority of the law. Weird. Medieval even.

'Yes, since the change in power he has become much more Islamic in public. Of course, at home he knows my mother would not tolerate it, but she accepts that in public we must cover up with the *hijab* and behave respectfully.'

'But she's not a Muslim, is she? Why should she behave like one? '

'She is now. She converted when they got married. I don't think she thought much about it at the time, but now she seems quite committed to certain aspects. Of course, she's brought me up to recognise my equality as a woman and she's still very western in many ways. But my father has become more Islamic as he's got older and I don't think she wants to make him unhappy… By flouting his beliefs, you see.'

'Beliefs or customs?'

'Is there a difference?'

Si decided not to pursue this. 'So what brought you to the UK? Your mother?'

'Partly. But also my father supported the idea. He is very much in favour of educating women and thought that it would be good for me to study at the same college as him. I don't think he realised quite what was going on when he was a student here. He must have been very diligent and I don't think he socialised very much. He's quite a serious man.'

'Have you told your parents about...about us?' Si winced at his own question. It sounded so melodramatic. He wasn't even very sure what he meant by it. They'd only been together a short time after all; and he, at least, was not consciously serious about the relationship. The future would arrive in its own good time. There was no point in hurrying it. Still, he was surprised that he'd felt the need to ask the question.

Fortunately, Roberta seemed to have sense enough for them both. 'No. And I've no intention of doing so.'

'Why not?'

'Why should I? It'd only cause problems. My father would probably order me to take the next plane home if I did.'

'Really?'

'Yes.'

Silence followed and Si could just hear the barge hooting downriver.

'I want another scratch.'

'I've just given you one.'

'I know, but that was at least twenty minutes ago and I want another now.' Roberta was headstrong and sometimes, it seemed to Si, rather demanding.

'Can't we wait a little while... Just a few more minutes?' Worried about his performance, Si thought he might just have an inkling what lay behind Islamic chauvinism.

'No, I want one now. Now.' And smothering his protests, Roberta lithely rolled over on top of Si. She stifled further debate with a judiciously placed kiss.

⚽ ⚽ ⚽

'Brenda! I thought I recognised the voice when I called you... Jimmy mate, how could you? Anyway, I thought you were well away with that other girl at the party. The super-model. The one you'd been boring all night about your goals.'

Jimmy looked faintly embarrassed. He stared hard at the TV. 'Yeah, I know. I think that was the problem. She disappeared and left me and, you know, when I came to go home I just happened to bump into Brenda. We'd both had a few and...Well, you know how it happens.' Jimmy lapsed into silence and Si looked at him incredulously. Well, it was Jimmy's mistake, not his. Why make it more difficult for him? He made a conscious effort and for the first time since Jimmy had arrived at Si's place he looked closely at the programme on TV.

They slouched side by side on the faded sofa having cleared a space among the debris of Si's life. Beer cans stood on the low table before them, reflecting in the glass top. A few fraying shirts hung off the back of the chairs caught in limbo between the washing and ironing which Si had promised himself he would do yesterday; somehow there never seemed to be time for such household chores. On her bimonthly visits, his mother chided him to do better: 'Get a cleaner Simon, if you don't have time to do it yourself.' Si normally nodded in acquiescence but then failed to do anything about it. Anyway, he liked his flat: it was, as he liked to describe it, 'lived in'. And it was very much an extension of his personality, from the framed prints on the wall to the books piled up in the corners having overflowed the packed shelves, and to the CD collection spilling out all over the rush-matting on the floor; each object was associated with an event or period in Si's life.

'That's just ridiculous,' Si moaned pointing at the TV accusingly.

'What is?' Jimmy sounded apprehensive, probably fearing

that he was about to be taken to task again for sleeping with Brenda.

'Didn't you notice? Most of the Top Ten are bands we first saw fifteen years ago when we were kids.'

Jimmy brightened. Si had let him off the hook. 'Yeah, I guess so. But what's wrong with that, eh? They're good songs.'

'What's wrong? What's wrong? It's the death of western civilisation, mate, that's what's wrong. Pass us another can, will you? Cheers.' Si unlatched the ring pull and sucked hard on his lager.

Top Of The Pops was playing out with this week's number one. A Bee Gees cover sung by four lads who looked like their mothers were backstage handling their wardrobes and haircuts.

'Pathetic,' moaned Si. 'Punk might as well never have happened.' He was in a boisterous mood and enjoying his self-appointed role as arbiter of modern British culture. There was scope for some light-hearted Diary pieces somewhere in all this.

'I don't see what the big deal is. I like Gary Numan and the Beatles are the greatest thing ever. You told me that yourself once.' Jimmy wasn't about to give way in an argument about pop music.

'Did I? It must have been when I was a kid. Tastes change, you know.'

'Actually it was about ten years ago,' conceded Jimmy. They looked at each other and cracked up laughing.

'I suppose some of them are pretty good,' agreed Si grudgingly. 'I liked that neo-punk band that was just on. The one where the singer looked like that girl who sang *Happy Birthday* years ago. D'you remember her? Clare someone, that's right... Clare...' He sifted the dregs of his memory for the surname but in vain. 'She was from Scotland,' he offered lamely.

'Yeah, they were good. Didn't last long, though.'

'Never do. I think that was their only hit. I remember

someone gave me it for my sixteenth birthday. It was really big then.'

'But I see what you mean,' said Jimmy, looking unusually thoughtful. 'There's not a lot new about. Kind of depressing, really.'

'That's my point. All this rehashing of old anthems, styles and so forth. Nothing new. I mean pop music is dead really. There's only dance and then all this retro stuff. And look at the kids today...'

'Yeah,' nodded Jimmy.

Warming to his theme, Si went on: 'They all look daft wearing those baggy flares, trainers and seventies haircuts. Grunge... I mean, some of the music's okay. I like that band Nirvana. Kurt Cobain. Really cool, he is.'

'Didn't he top himself?'

'Oh yeah, he did. So that wasn't one of the coolest things to do, but the music's okay.'

'Kind of modern Jimmy Hendrix.'

Si looked doubtful. 'Maybe, kind of... Anyway, I saw my cousin the other day, he's seventeen. Nice kid, Paul, but totally brain dead like the rest of his generation. They think they're the first to ever hear of these bands... As if history began in 1992. Know what I mean? And what's more, they're so serious. Really depressing talking to Paul. He wants to be an accountant. Can you believe it? Seventeen and wants to be an accountant. We may as well top ourselves now. The world's going to be a pretty boring place in ten years time if everybody's holding down serious jobs and the height of their aspirations is being an accountant. When I was seventeen...'

'Yeah?' challenged Jimmy.

'When I was seventeen I wanted to be a rock star.'

'Really?' Jimmy sounded interested. He thought he knew most things about Si but he'd never known about this teenage ambition. Despite himself, Jimmy felt irritated. He tried not to show it. 'Like Kurt Cobain?'

'Well, sort of.'

'Fat lot of good that did him.'

'Well, or a writer. But not an accountant.'

'You're beginning to sound a right old codger, you are. Moaning about the younger generation. All you need is your pipe and slippers. You're not one to talk anyway, are you? Look at you, twenty-seven and a respectable journalist. That's pretty serious.'

'No, it isn't. Journalism's a totally different kettle of fish. Far more adventurous and individual. And in a way I'm a writer like I always wanted to be. It's creative too. Not like accountancy. And I'm far from respectable. You should have heard what someone said about me the other day.'

'Right.' Jimmy scoffed and Si could understand why. He hadn't even convinced himself. Perhaps today's kids had just realised earlier than his generation that life no longer offered anybody an easy ride. Nothing could be taken for granted anymore. Perhaps they were just more on the ball than he had ever been and his grumbling was a pathetic attempt to express envy? Si pushed this thought to one side.

'When I was seventeen I wanted to be a professional soccer player. And there I am. Well, I reckon being a soccer player is pretty creative.'

'Could be,' agreed Si.

'I mean, when I went round that Bury defender the other day and lobbed the keeper the write-up in *The Sun* described it as poetry in motion.'

'Yeah, it was pretty good,' said Si supportively, although he'd not seen the goal and *The Sun* had devoted less than fifty words to the match. He wanted to build up Jimmy's confidence. Somehow, although his friend was a talented striker, he'd been overlooked by all the top rank teams. Now at twenty-seven, Jimmy's time was running out.

It had not escaped Si that as Jimmy's career seemed to have plateaued and, barring miracles, was unlikely to progress much further, his own star was rising quickly. Si felt sorry for his friend and slightly embarrassed by the good luck he had experienced recently. If only Jimmy could get the break he deserved. After all, this season he'd averaged a goal a match and was top scorer in the Second Division; but as far as anybody at Millwall Football Club knew, no First Division or Premiership clubs had expressed any interest in signing him. Although *The Sun* described him as a poet of the feet today, in five years time Jimmy would be nowhere. If he was lucky, he'd be looking to open a pub somewhere, cashing in on past glories and resigning himself to maudlin stories of what could have been. The thought was sobering.

'If I score a few more like that, maybe I should publish a video of my greatest goals and call it *Jimmy Sweeney's Poetry Collection*.'

'*Anthology*. Sounds better. More intellectual. *Doctor Jimmy's Poetry Anthology*. Or better still, how about *The Collected Poems of James Sweeney*?'

'Yeah, great,' grinned Jimmy. 'That's great. But it'd have to be Jimmy. Not James. Nobody, not even my mum, calls me James.'

They smiled foolishly at each other, united by a bond of friendship that spanned more than two decades. But in their hearts both knew that nobody but the keenest Millwall fan would buy the video and, rather like Jimmy himself, it would end up on the Woolworth's remaindered shelf, undesired, unsold. Even if Jimmy was the top scorer in the Second Division. These days only the Premiership clubs and their players mattered to the public. And, for the moment, Si seemed to have as much chance of signing for one of them as Jimmy.

Si shuffled the morning papers. Mad cow this and mad cow that. Had the world gone crazy? A few spongy brain cells and the bottom had dropped out of the beef market.

'Government Beefing About Mad Cow Ban' trumpeted one tabloid. The picture beneath it showed the Agriculture Minister wearing a pair of bull's horns. Even the broadsheets had been infected by the hysteria. Si chucked the pile of newspapers under his desk in disgust.

'Write about anything but bloody cows,' Dougy had instructed him last week when panic first swept through the newsprint. It had been like a wave of sewage pushing all before it. Even serious editors had been covered in the effluence.

Thank God he worked on the Diary. Otherwise he too would have been out pestering politicians about whether they would feed their families beef from now on. The level to which journalism could sink was distressing. Pandering to public fears rather than doing the real job.

When Bill came in, half an hour later than usual because of another suicide on the Northern Line, Si tried this argument out on him.

Bill just grunted. 'Serves them all right for eating meat in the first place. Personally I don't give a toss. I'm a vegetarian.'

'Oh.' That took the wind out of Si's outraged sails. He noticed for the first time a definite resemblance between Bill and his cousin Paul. Clearly a generational thing. Luckily, I'm more broadminded, he comforted himself. And, for the time being, his generation ruled over the upwardly thrusting accountant-brains fresh out of college. 'How about a coffee, Bill?'

'Yeah, sure.' And taking his cue, Bill drifted off towards the coffee machine.

Si wondered what he could write about. Something unconnected to bovine diseases. Each day was the same. A pile of faxes from self-publicists, most of which were unusable, a few half-baked stories left over from yesterday and a large empty space to fill—approximately fifteen hundred words worth of white space—in tomorrow's paper.

'Shit, I don't know why I do this,' he groaned. This was

always the hardest part of the day. It was when he felt the full weight of responsibility upon his shoulders and sometimes, if he was honest with himself, it failed to excite him.

He shuffled through yesterday's scraps. Bill had started a story about Madonna in Argentina. Improbably she was cast as Evita in Lloyd Webber's film of his musical. But although this sounded promising material, Bill hadn't found an angle to bring the story to life. Si put it to one side. Perhaps he'd have another look at it himself later on. Then there was a half-hearted attempt to lampoon the Russian Ambassador, who had been blatantly pursuing an opera singer performing at Covent Garden. This had looked a dead cert until Si had phoned the Russian Embassy for a comment.

'His Excellency is not well today and we have nothing to say,' stonewalled a nameless attaché.

Si scented blood. 'Could you say what is wrong with the Ambassador? Is he perhaps love sick?'

'I think your question is impertinent. His Excellency is in hospital since three days. He will be operated.'

'What type of operation?' pushed Si, hoping that it was something ambiguous. A vasectomy was too much to hope for, but perhaps something to do with the heart?

'I can say no more. His Excellency is very unwell. Now if you please I have work to do… Thank you, good-bye.'

Si wondered what to do. If the Ambassador was really ill, perhaps with cancer or even mad cow disease, it would be in bad taste to print the story. Even so, the idea of a great-chested diva mopping the convalescing diplomat's brow would be a winner.

He decided to wait until he could find out what was wrong with the Russian. Better safe than sorry. So far he'd avoided a bollocking from Dougy, but the editor's tantrums were legendary. Si didn't want to be on the receiving end because of some poxy Russian envoy infatuated with an obese, singing tart. The easiest way would be to phone the hospital and pretend to be a relative. Yesterday in the rush to finish the Diary there hadn't been time; but there would be later. Not that the idea of deception filled him with great joy; it was one of the necessary, seedier sides of his job. Si put the story to one side for later. At least that was one piece that would probably make it into tomorrow's paper. Two hundred words down... Only thirteen hundred to go.

Si had one other story which he was determined to use. His first religious piece since Dougy had given him those instructions.

A passing comment of Roberta's had inspired him to take an interest in the Moslem convert Cat Stevens. Roberta claimed that the singer was just one of thousands of people who switched to Islam in the UK each year. Si found this hard to believe, but Roberta cited the authority of her father; Si realised he should not laugh this off too lightly for fear of offending his lover. She was too good to lose so easily. He accepted her assertion but then went off to dig around.

Si found that there were a number of Islamic preachers based in London spreading propaganda via certain Arabic newspapers. They described London and Western society generally as fragmented, soulless and godforsaken; inhabited by sodomites, whores and devils of all kinds. But among these lost peoples the light of Truth was shining, and each day the number of conversions was miraculous. Allah's mercy was manifest regularly.

Si rang up the Grand Mufti and asked him what he thought about these preachers and their claims. The Mufti told him that all the people of The Book were really members of the same faith and that Muslims, Christians and Jews could live harmoniously together. 'All will be revealed in the fullness of time to the true believers,' he intoned softly and declined to expand further.

In a flash of inspiration Si recognised that he should write this story straight. He would begin with a reference to the Shadow Education Spokesman's Commons speech, then use a description of contemporary London lifted from one of the evangelical Muslim journalists, counterbalance that with a quote from the 'Mega Mufti', and finally report that, following the pop singer's example, thousands were converting every day. '*The Diary reports this phenomenon just in case you hadn't yet noticed,*' would be the ironic last line.

Dry, very dry. Si knew Dougy would like it because it could be read in several different ways and was all things to all men. It also meant he would gain extra time to divine the exact nature of Dougy's instructions.

The rest of the leftover material was either too useless for words or too obviously placed at the instigation of some public relations company. They were always ringing up, these PR executives. Jolly, bouncing voices on the phone—'Hi Si... Have I got a story for you...' before delivering some crap idea designed only to market their client's product / film / book / event / whatever... Didn't they realise that he needed a hook to make the story work? Something newsworthy or humorous. PR people were his least favourite breed. Of course there were exceptions: those who catered for his needs as well as their own. But they were very much the exception proving the rule.

Bill came back with the coffee. 'Thanks.'

'Pleasure,' mumbled Bill, clearly not meaning it.

'So what have you lined up today?'

'Gi' us a chance. I've only just got in.'

'Sure, sure,' comforted Si gently. God, Bill could be testy sometimes. But Si tried to remember his management training course: never work against the grain of your staff, move with them. He sipped his coffee. It was boiling hot and almost burnt his tongue.

After a pause Si forgot his management training. 'So?'

'So what?'

'So what have you got that might make a story?'

'Not a lot. Well, there may be something in a comment I overheard at a party last night.' Bill told him about the story he'd eavesdropped. It combined a whiff of financial scandal and infidelity and starred a leading City figure, a property developer and an actress from *Eastenders*; classic Diary material.

'Good man,' congratulated Si when he'd finished. 'That sounds a runner. Maybe even a lead.'

'D'you think so?' Bill perked up. Despite being relatively new to journalism, and notwithstanding the sexual confusion which increasingly tormented him, he was convinced of his destiny: to get on and up. In a year or two he aimed to edit a rival diary or maybe do news... After all, diaries were no place to get stuck for very long. Real journalism was happening elsewhere. Bill was quietly ambitious, but Si was beginning to notice and to use this knowledge to good effect.

'Yeah, you never know. Depends how it develops, eh?'

'Yeah, suppose so. I'd better get on the phone, then.'

'Good idea.'

Bill shuffled off and Si pulled out a blank piece of paper. His plan for the day. He took a pencil, sharpened it and began to map out what would go on the page. Getting going was always the hardest bit. In half an hour's time he'd be fine. He got a kick out of watching the empty space fill up. Beautiful black typescript trickling into all those vacant white gaps. Yeah, he enjoyed his job; well, most of the time. Wouldn't swap it for anything else.

After he'd covered his blank piece of A4 with a complex diagram showing all the options available, he laid down his pencil. With a sigh he realised there was no time like the present. He flicked through the phone book and then dialled a number.

'Hello, can I help you?'

Si affected his best Russian accent by imitating a James Bond villain. Time to expose the naughty diplomat's weakness for Rubenesque sopranos. He thought idly that he might write this up as a sort of spoof *Traviata*, depicting the dying Ambassador sprawled on a *chaise longue* with his fickle lover dancing attendance—not a dry eye in the house. 'Good morning. Is hospital?' Si vaguely remembered chatting up a Russian girl at last year's *Londoner's Diary* Christmas party in the Irish Club: she had explained that in Russian there is no definite article.

'Yes, how can I help you?'

'Good, good. I believe my brother, he is not well and is in your hospital...'

'Could you tell me your brother's name, Sir, then I can try and put you through to the ward.'

'Yes, thank you. My brother... He is Russian Ambassador.'

❁ ❁ ❁

It had been a strangely frustrating day. In one respect things could not have gone better.

Dougy had called him just before lunch to say how much he'd appreciated the Islamic converts story. 'You're on the right track, kid...' Unfortunately, he'd left it at that and Si was still none the wiser whether he'd been on the right track by implying that the Opposition party were in tune with the times and appealed to all religious groups; or, if Dougy had read the story another way, that the Opposition were as ridiculous as the claims that London was infested by evil and that thousands were converting to the teachings of Mohammed.

Dougy had also let out a belly laugh that almost deafened Si, who was holding the ear-piece too close in his anxiety to please his boss. 'I loved the Russian Ambassador piece. Brilliant. Brilliant. Where do you find them, kid?' But without waiting for an answer he'd rung off.

The rest of the day had been dreary and the stories they used were uninspired. Si knew for a fact that he wouldn't be getting a congratulatory call from Dougy the next day.

He left work late and went straight to The Feathers to meet Jimmy. As he came out of the tube he passed a man who made him feel slightly uneasy. Well, not the man so much as a sign the man was carrying.

CHRIST HAS DIED.

CHRIST IS RISEN.

CHRIST WILL COME AGAIN.

It was printed on a sandwich board and enclosed the emaciated body of a forty-something man in a woolly hat and donkey jacket. The man walked ahead of him down the street and seemed impervious to the icy wind which penetrated Si's woollen overcoat.

What had possessed the guy to humiliate himself in public by such an absurd display? Si increased his speed and stepped into the road to overtake, although there was probably space enough to pass on the pavement. You never know, reflected Si, he might be dangerous. But the soft expression which met Si's passing glance was disconcerting.

Si looked away quickly. The man said nothing, but Si could feel his eyes burning into him as he hurried on down the street and turned into the warm yellow embrace of the pub.

With relief, Si sank back into the deep upholstery of the snug bar and waited for Jimmy to bring over the pints.

Roberta arrived as they were merging with the fug over their second drink.

'Jimmy, this is Roberta.'

'Hi,' nodded Jimmy without getting up.

Roberta didn't seem fazed by the cool reception. She'd heard a lot about Jimmy and suspected that their first meeting wouldn't be easy. In her experience close male friendships rarely included women without some initial friction. Many such attachments excluded women completely, such as the ones in her own country.

'Jimmy, it's good to meet you. I've heard so much about you.'

Jimmy immediately reacted. 'Yeah? Like what? I suppose he's told you I'm a failed soccer player.'

'No, quite the opposite. He said you had great prospects.' Roberta smiled.

Jimmy, disarmed, just grunted. 'Some prospects,' he muttered.

Si felt it time to intervene. 'We were just getting another round in. What would you like?'

'An orange, please.'

Jimmy raised an eyebrow. As Si moved off to the bar he made a conscious effort to pull himself together. 'He really said that, did he?'

'Said what?'

'That I had great prospects.'

'Yes, he did.'

'Oh.' Jimmy furrowed his brow. 'Where's the Sudan, anyway?' he asked.

Later, as they left the pub and Jimmy prepared to peel off home, he leaned over to Si and whispered 'She's all right... Not bad at all.'

Si smiled. 'I know. I know.'

⚽ ⚽ ⚽

Jimmy was exhausted. Ninety minutes of running about in the slush playing for a second-rate football team was not his idea of fun. The stadium was on the point of collapse and there was no money to rebuild the crumbling stands with their warping cantilevers and cracking, concrete floors. Vast swathes of orange plastic shone out from the gloom beneath the holed, wooden rooves—empty seats witnessing to the club's dwindling support and dire financial situation. And as for the pitch... The Chairman had clearly resorted to grazing cattle between matches to raise money, such was the state of the churned up turf; more mud than grass.

Jimmy had enjoyed scoring the goal which separated the two teams, but if there weren't any scouts watching, then what was the point? Here he was already twenty-seven, and no prospect of making the top flight. Jimmy knew he was living proof that Nick Hornby had got it wrong when he wrote that there was no such thing as a genius striker failing to get noticed in the lower divisions; the scouting system was *not* foolproof and *everyone* did *not* get watched. But despite this conviction and a growing sense of injustice, Jimmy knew that time was running out for him.

The whistle went. Thank God. He exchanged desultory handshakes with the other team and made his way towards the dressing room. As they walked off the pitch, it was noticeable how much bigger and stronger Jimmy was than his team mates. If the superior girth of his thighs was anything to go by, Jimmy certainly deserved to be in a higher division.

'Well played, laddy... Although you looked a bit bored out there, if you don't mind me saying.'

Jimmy looked at the speaker. He was in his fifties, wearing a heavy duty nylon anorak. His broken capillaries and windburnt face testified to many hours exposed to the elements. 'Thanks. Who are you?'

'Mike McDonald. Pleased to meet you. I think we might be seeing more of each other soon.'

'Oh, yeah? What makes you so sure?'

'Oh, I just know. Trust me.' With that McDonald walked off in the direction of the stairs leading to the Directors' box.

Jimmy sat down and pulled off his boots. Weird guy, he thought.

'I see you met Mike, then?' It was the manager, Steve Burns. They got on all right, but he knew that Jimmy was desperate for a greater challenge than the Second Division.

'You know him? Who is he?'

'A scout.'

'I thought you told me that there wouldn't be any scouts around today.'

'I lied.' Burns grinned. 'I knew you wouldn't play so well if you were nervous about being watched.'

Jimmy's heart was beating ten to the dozen. Clearly, Nick Hornby had been right after all. 'So who's he a scout for? Someone big?'

'Could be. You just keep cool. I'll let you know as soon as there's something to get excited about, okay?'

What a prat. Treating him like a child. But if there was interest in him from a big team like Arsenal or Chelsea... Even if it was only a good First Division team... Then... Who could say, perhaps his career would finally take off?

Despite his irritation with Burns, Jimmy couldn't help feeling on top of the world. Just wait until he told Si. Then again, he reflected, probably best not to say anything until something actually came of it.

⚽ ⚽ ⚽

When the Sleeper first arrived in London he wondered what he'd got himself into. It had all seemed fair enough at home when the English soldiers waved guns in kids' faces and shouted to get out of the road. It wasn't difficult to hate those scared-looking squaddies with their camouflage jackets and ridiculous patrols. They were an invasion force and as such there was a duty to resist them. But in London, at first, it was a bit different. He'd expected to work within a cell, in close contact with other 'soldiers' such as himself. But the leadership had recently decided on a change of tactic, and were now sending young sleepers to integrate themselves into the community, isolated from the organisation except for the most minimal operational contact, until the moment came to act—the awakening.

The Sleeper crossed to Liverpool on the ferry. He knew all about Liverpool, of course, from following the football. And he'd laughed with his family at the reruns of the *Liver Birds* he'd watched on the telly; so it was exciting to sail up the Mersey for the first time, watching the seagulls wheel and squawk over the choppy grey water and taking in the great city's memorable skyline. He'd have liked to stay a few days, but his orders were clear. He grabbed some fish and chips and then took a National Express coach to London. West Hampstead to be exact, where he'd been told to stay until further instructions arrived. Fine, he thought, and went exploring. Carefully, mind, so as not to arouse suspicion, but he wanted to see what was what in London.

The people all seemed okay, not much different from at home. A bit sadder and more serious, but generally the same. He told this to Mrs Donnelley, his landlady.

'Don't be so stupid.' She had a sharp tongue in her head.

The Sleeper liked her to start with, as she reminded him a lot of his ma. But Mrs Donnelley was more passionate and didn't have the tired eyes and sagging body of his ma.

'They're the agents of oppression as much as the soldiers on the Falls Road. These respectable-looking folk are the bastards who pay for freedom fighters and patriots to be locked away and to die from starvation and beatings in English prisons. Don't be taken in by their looks,' and she wagged her finger angrily in his face. 'Don't be taken in...'

He heeded her words and soon saw through the masks of the people around him. The crowds on the tubes and in the buses, they were as much to blame as the English Government. He realised that. The smug bastards... They were the ones who maintained the occupying army in Ireland. It was their sons who'd killed the heroes of Ireland. It was a good feeling to know that soon he'd blast a great big hole in the middle of their complacent lives.

But after a month he'd still not heard anything; and then one evening he and Mrs Donnelley were watching the news as they had tea, and saw that a cease-fire had been declared. 'Oh sweet Mary,' sighed Mrs Donnelley, 'now why have they gone and done that?' A tear ran down her cheek and she left the room.

There was always a lot about Mrs Donnelley's reactions to things that the Sleeper didn't understand; so he thought it best to say nothing. But he was confused, and when he got down the pub later he agreed with Eamon behind the bar who said what a shame it was to have given up the fight and to have fallen into the English trap.

The Sleeper knew that Eamon and all the other so-called 'patriots' in the pub were all mouth. What had any of them ever done in the war? What right had they to be slagging off the leadership?

'But,' the Sleeper said, 'maybe they know what they're doing. A trick, you know, or something, to deceive the bastards...' He noticed that Eamon and the others had gone quiet and were listening carefully. He decided to back off. From then on he only went to the pub occasionally; Saturday nights, normally—and he kept his mouth shut.

But he still heard nothing and began to get angry. Perhaps they really had decided to give up.

'Stay down and don't do anything to attract attention to yourself. Try and live a normal life and blend into the community. We'll be in touch.' That's what they'd said. But that was before the cease-fire, and he wondered if they'd forgotten about him.

Only a couple of months after his arrival, just as he was beginning to think he'd found his feet, Mrs Donnelley turned his little world upside down. 'Sorry, love, but we're going to have to find you somewhere else. My son's coming back from America and he'll need that room.' This was a bolt from the blue. He'd expected to stay in her spare room until he received instructions. Now he'd have to move.

''S all right, Mrs Donnelley, I understand. No problem.' He smiled to show no hard feelings. His ma would have been proud of his self-restraint and politeness. Inside he was boiling.

'Good lad. So you'll be out by the weekend, then?'

'This weekend?'

'That's right. Didn't I say? Oh sorry, love. But my Davie's back on Monday and I'll need time to clean up.'

'Right... Aye, of course, Mrs Donnelley.' The Sleeper made to get up from the tea table. He'd miss Mrs Donnelley's teas more than anything. She made great fry-ups. He supposed he might miss her too. She'd been a bit like a mother to him, and he didn't really have any friends in London. If he was honest with himself, he felt lonely a lot. But then he told himself to belt up 'cos he'd always known there would be hardship. Fighting a war wasn't like real life.

'Oh, and one other thing.'

He stopped in the doorway, leaning on the lintel. He scratched at a grey patch where the white gloss had chipped off revealing the undercoat. 'Yes, Mrs Donnelley?'

'Could you settle the rest of your rent tomorrow as I need to do some shopping for Davie's arrival?'

'Sure, Mrs Donnelley. No problem.' At least he didn't have to worry about money so long as the money held out; despite the cease-fire, he was still able to draw from the bank account. It was the one thing that kept his spirits up and reassured him that this was no surrender; just a tactical move as part of the leadership's long-term strategy. Otherwise, he told himself, someone would surely have been in touch and the bank account would have dried up.

The Sleeper went up to his small bedroom and sat on the bed wondering what to do next. He looked at the peeling, yellow-stripe wallpaper and the cracked mirror. Behind it he knew there was a patch of damp, which no doubt accounted for the musty smell. A garish orange rug with shaggy tassels covered the boards at the end of the single bed, which sagged in the middle; also, one leg was missing and Mrs Donnelley had propped it up with a pile of books rather than pay for a repair. Through the small grimy window he could make out a few rooftops and the backs of small terraced houses. The sound of a baby screaming came from nearby. It reminded the Sleeper of home and he felt his stomach lurch. He wondered how he would find a new place in such a short time?

Jimmy was no dreamer. For him football was a way of life; one which he enjoyed but now that he had become a professional, it was no longer his dream. However, like many people, he did have a secret ambition. Although he told Si most things, knowing that his friend would not take the mickey or break his confidence, Jimmy had never revealed one corner of his life which had been shrouded in darkness since his early teens. And he still didn't want to shine a light into it; not until the time was right. Especially now that he knew Si had once shared the same secret goal. When he was fourteen Jimmy, Si and some other schoolmates took a train to a provincial town one Saturday evening. Not far from London, the town's only claim to fame was the huge stadium recently constructed by local developers. The idea was to draw in the youth from dormitory towns all around London and create a venue for top international rock bands.

Jimmy had never been to a proper rock concert before. He spent the evening mouth-wide-open, mesmerised by the high energy performance. Prince leapt about the stage and effortlessly created electrifying music with his purple guitar. Jimmy couldn't take his eyes off the star.

On the way home some of the others dozed and Si offered round an illicit can of lager. But Jimmy, between swigs, remained silent, lost in a new dream. It was a dream that didn't evaporate in the morning.

Jimmy decided that night that he would be a rock star. He wanted this even more than he wanted to be a famous footballer. The trouble was that until the Prince concert he'd never played an instrument or sung, and he was too shy to start. Only mummy's boys learned musical instruments at school. The kids with the tidy uniforms and short, neatly-parted hair, who spent their lunch hours taking piano lessons and singing in the choir. This was hard to reconcile with his dream. Surely Prince hadn't been such a ponce when he was a kid? Would the delicate Head Chorister metamorphosise into a strutting, groin-thrusting rock 'n' roll icon in later life?

Jimmy couldn't get his head round this puzzle. He was

also afraid that he would be ridiculed by his friends, perhaps even by Si, if he discussed this with them. So he remained silent. He played soccer at lunchtimes and breaks, and jeered at the musical goody-goodies as they minced past, straining under the weight of their cellos.

But the dream wouldn't go away. He lay awake at nights, especially after watching *Top Of The Pops* or *The Tube*, and pictured himself on stage.

His tastes developed, and by the time he was seventeen and playing for Millwall schoolboys, he fantasised about strumming a folk guitar in front of a large band. He dressed like Bob Dylan and Van the Man and put posters of Jim Morrison on his bedroom wall. In his dreams he strode purposefully about a wide stage grasping a microphone and occasionally striking a few rasping chords on the guitar which hung about his neck. The crowd of adoring fans, mostly girls with low cut tops and full lips, blew kisses and screamed whenever he moved. In his sleep Jimmy smiled and, wrapping the duvet cover around him like a spangled cloak, he turned over with a sigh.

And now, ten years later, although Jimmy knew it was ridiculous, he realised he still wanted to be a rock star.

The Sleeper was seriously concerned about leaving Mrs Donnelley's; he needn't have worried.

'My sister's looking for someone to take a spare room in her house. I'll give her a call and see if it's still going.'

Eamon at the pub knew that he was looking for a new place. The Sleeper suspected he'd be able to sort something out. Eamon knew everyone and took pride in helping out fellow countrymen in trouble. He'd been here for a long time. Twenty years by his reckoning; since he was the Sleeper's age.

Eamon returned from the back room where he'd been phoning. 'That's fine. She says go over tomorrow and see her. Here, I'll write down the address for you.'

'Eamon, you're a good man, you know that.'

'Aww, just shut up and take your pint before it goes off.' He handed over the warm glass which he'd been filling. 'That's one thing about the English. They do have good beer. I know I'm not meant to like it really being an Irishman, but I do prefer it to the black stuff.'

When the Sleeper got back to Mrs Donnelley's, he found she'd already gone to bed. That was good because he didn't really want to tell her about the new accommodation until he'd finalised it.

He sat down at the small table in his bedroom and opened the right hand drawer. He ripped a page out of an exercise book and wrote a letter to his ma telling her about the new house he was going to live in and about his friend Eamon. He sent love to his brother and two sisters as usual, and signed off 'Your Loving Son'. She liked that. It'd keep her happy for a couple more months, then he'd write again.

When he'd addressed and sealed the envelope, he looked again in the drawer and took out a small metal box. The tiny key in his pocket opened it. He pulled out a folded scrap of paper. He ripped out another sheet of paper and in block letters carefully transcribed the address Eamon had given him. At school the teacher had always said how well he printed. It didn't look bad, even now after so little practice. He held up the note and admired it. Then he took an envelope and sealed the letter before copying out the address from the scrap of paper. No name, just a PO Box. Finally, he put the paper back in the box and locked it. He closed the drawer and slipped the envelopes into his pocket.

The next day, the Sleeper posted the letters as planned. Later that morning, when the postman emptied his bag, he dropped one of the Sleeper's letters. But before he noticed it lying on the ground, the bitter wind caught it up and carried it into a thorn hedge by the side of the pavement. It lodged there for several days until a small dog saw it and tried to take it in its teeth. But he only managed to dislodge it. Once again a gust seized it, and this time succeeded in blowing it twenty yards away into a shop doorway. A passer-by picked it up and put it in his pocket to post later. It then disappeared for four months.

Si came out of the restaurant and regretted that he had to return to the office. He'd passed a couple of gourmet hours with a pleasant guy from a PR company. The PR company had paid, which made Si feel vaguely self-important. In fact, this was one of the first business lunches that he hadn't had to pay for. He must be getting somewhere if people considered him worth lunching.

The PR executive had predictably pushed his client, but after Si had expressed some interest and promised to keep in touch about progress, they'd moved on to discussing soccer. The businessman clearly felt satisfied that the lunch had been worthwhile, and Si had got away without committing himself to putting anything in the Diary. It had all been a bit of a doddle.

Si wandered along the leafy street for a while, looking in at the shop windows. He stopped when he saw a piece of paper fluttering at his feet. Still feeling rather mellow, he stooped gently and picked it up. It turned out to be a letter for a London address. Someone must have dropped it. Si slipped it into his coat pocket to post later.

The gaunt eyes stared back. Jimmy leaned closer to the window and tried to see through the pane beyond his own dark reflection. The lighting was dim and hardly induced anyone to stop and shop. A few old-fashioned and mutilated mannequins posed drunkenly in the display. But Jimmy's attention was focussed elsewhere. A purple guitar stood propped up in a corner. It wasn't clear whether the guitar was for sale, and certainly whoever had left it there had done so in a careless fashion. It was almost as if someone had leaned it against the wall between sets. But that was impossible because the window fronted a shop in Oxford Street, and nobody played rock concerts in shops.

He pushed his nose up against the cold glass and screwing up his eyes found that he could see the guitar much better. It looked like a Fender but there was no distinguishing mark. A string was missing, otherwise it looked new. How much would it cost? Of course, he'd also need an amplifier. He'd seen buskers on the tube using small battery-operated numbers. They couldn't be too much. Then, when he got better, he could buy a massive mother and let rip with the slick riffs he'd have learnt.

He felt slightly foolish but still grinned childishly. Twenty-seven wasn't too old to become a rock star, was it? Of course, he'd need to form a band. These days record companies normally arranged all that for you, didn't they? So he just had to show that he was a charismatic stage presence and learn to play the guitar. The rest would follow as naturally as day follows night.

Jimmy returned to earth. He stepped back into the icy night and caught sight of a swaying young man smiling idiotically at a window display. Oh shit, he thought. What a dick I am.

He wandered off, depressed by alcohol. The dream was but a delusion. Moreover, if he didn't pull himself together, his football would suffer and that would be the end of his career. Then what? *He'd* finish up as the dustman, not Si.

It dawned on him that Si had a future, regardless of whether he succeeded or failed in his present job. A degree meant you could always get a good job. What did he have, Jimmy Sweeney? What had he got? Bugger all... One O level. In geography. Fat lot of use that would be. Perhaps he should have made more of an effort at school, after all? There again, remembering the anguish of homework, perhaps not.

❀ ❀ ❀

Si was in the the Sudan. The heat stifled him and he had wrapped something about his mouth to keep out the sand. He seemed to be driving from Khartoum airport with Roberta's father. As far as he could work out the car had no air-conditioning.

'You don't know how happy I am that you have embraced the true faith,' said Roberta's dad.

Si felt somewhat removed from the situation. It didn't seem right to disillusion the friendly man in the white robes and turban. Nonplussed, he remained silent but smiled. Like a camel, he reflected. This made him smile even more.

Roberta's father described his background in the Queen's English. 'I used to live in Shepherd's Bush and took the underground train every day to work. I was a presenter on the BBC Arabic Service. I had many jolly times in London... A wonderful time of my life...'

'Perhaps you'll return soon?'

'No, no, I think not.' And the firm look that accompanied these words deterred Si from interrupting further. He resumed his camel expression.

They were back at the house of Roberta's parents. In the courtyard. A marble fountain splashed gently among a spectrum of small tiles. Roberta and he were alone and she was explaining in hushed tones that he was now expected to toe the line.

Si couldn't quite grasp what she was saying, but every time he tried to ask she raised a finger of warning to her lips.

'All will be revealed in the fullness of time to the true believers,' she said.

Si watched the drops of bright water emerge like transparent snakes from the perforated nipple at the centre of the fountain, run over its curves and fall in crystal ropes to the bowl below. He tried to isolate one drop and follow it from its emergence to its absorption in the pool; but no matter how hard he exerted his will, regardless of the tricks he employed such as closing one eye, he failed to distinguish the individual drops. They must be aware of their paths as individual drops, he thought; so why can't I distinguish them? He puzzled at length but couldn't find an answer. Then he realised that Roberta was still speaking to him.

'You must behave like a true believer,' she advised sternly. 'Like Cat Stevens.'

'But I don't even like his music,' protested Si.

'If not, you will be punished.'

Si was dismayed. How had his love life become so serious?

Roberta softened and gave him a winning smile. For the time being, she seemed to have won.

Finally, it all became appallingly clear to him. 'Why?' he cried. But he already knew the answer.

'Because I sent my father the article you wrote about Cat Stevens. He did not understand your meaning because I told him it showed your religious zeal. The passion of a convert. If you now act otherwise, I'll tell my father that you're not a convert. I'll explain your article to my father, and he will not be amused. In fact, I'll tell him that you are an apostate and that will seal your fate.' Roberta drew a curved dagger from the blue wrap which flowed around her limbs like water. 'This will be your fate. This or the religious police who will beat you with sticks until you bleed to death.' Roberta smiled calmly and slipped the knife back inside the folds of her clothing.

She looked around to check that they were not being watched, and then leaned forward, pushing him back towards the edge of the fountain bowl. Her lips brushed against his and Si yielded. He felt the warm water close over his body as they both rolled slowly into the fountain.

When the phone rang it was Roberta to tell him she'd be late and wouldn't arrive at his flat till lunchtime. Saturday mornings—he loved them. Nothing to get up for until Roberta came over. That was on the occasions when she wasn't already there.

His watch on the bedside table showed ten thirty. Another half an hour, then he'd get up and make breakfast. He rolled over on his side and fell into an uneasy reverie. But this time he dreamed of football.

⚽ ⚽ ⚽

Jimmy raised his hand tentatively and bit his bottom lip with the effort of concentration. He struck the strings. God, it sounded awful; and this was meant to be an easy chord. He looked furtively at the closed bedroom door and listened for movement. Nothing. Good. Brenda wasn't about.

Recently his lover had been hanging around too much. He'd have to do something about her before she got the impression their relationship was serious. Heaven forbid. Since she'd lost her job at the PR company she'd been moping about. She was now trying to get her old job back behind the bar at The Feathers. The sooner the better, as that would keep her busy.

He leaned forward and twiddled the volume knob on the small 10 watt amplifier. Lifting cramped fingers off the strings, he consulted the book again. The diagram seemed to suggest that he had to hold down the top string with the third digit, the second bottom string with the index finger and the thick bottom string with the third finger. He carefully twisted his hand into this position and tried to ignore the pain. How long before this became second nature, as the book promised it would with regular practice?

Janggg... The downward blow from his right hand bounced off the strings, and the open G chord clashed alarmingly with a host of foreign notes.

'Shit,' he sighed. This was obviously going to take time. His watch said six thirty. Okay, he resolved, in half an hour I'll go to the pub. But first I'm going to get this bugger right...

⚽ ⚽ ⚽

'Hello, can I speak to Jimmy, please?'

'No, he's not here.' It was Brenda again. Surely Jimmy wasn't making a regular thing of it with her?

'Is that Brenda?'

'What if it is? Who are you?'

'It's Si from The Feathers... You know, Jimmy's friend.'

'Oh, you.'

There didn't seem much more to be gained from this. 'Look, could you tell Jimmy I called? Where is he, anyway?'

'Manchester, he said. He reckoned he'd be back tomorrow.'

'Oh.'

That was strange. Jimmy didn't normally go away during the week unless there was a match. Millwall weren't playing up north, as far as Si knew. But he didn't follow Millwall's fixtures closely, despite Jimmy's involvement. He tried to think of Second Division football clubs near Manchester. Oldham, Burnley, Bolton.... Were Millwall playing Bolton? Then Si wondered if Bolton were really in the Second rather than the First Division. He gave up.

'Well, tell him I called, will you?'

'Yeah.'

'Thanks.' Si leaned back in his chair and watched Bill shuffling papers on his desk while cradling a phone in the crook of his neck. The kid was improving, no doubt about that.

Feeling distinctly uninspired, Si went off in search of the coffee machine. After almost three months at *The Courier*, he was beginning to realise the limitations of the job. Truth was, he'd started to get bored. Well, it was up to him to make his job interesting. After all, everyone had to work, didn't they?

⚽ ⚽ ⚽

'So what were you doing in Manchester?' Si's curiosity got the better of him.

'Manchester?'

'Yeah, I rang the other day and Brenda...' (Si raised an eyebrow as he spoke, but he didn't push it) '... she told me that you'd gone to Manchester.'

'How do you know it was Brenda?'

'I recognised her voice.'

'Oh.' Jimmy looked nonplussed.

'Well, it doesn't matter. I'm not fussed if you want to shag our favourite barmaid.' He smiled reassuringly at Jimmy, who still looked a bit unsure of himself. 'So, what were you doing in Manchester,' Si persisted.

'Oh, not much,' Jimmy said evasively. Until the deal was confirmed he'd decided not to tell anyone, not even Si. It would be tempting fate. And if it fell through he'd look a fool. 'The club sent me up there for a bit of special training.'

'Sounds interesting.'

'No, not really. It's work at the end of the day, like going to an office... No different, really.'

'Ah.'

Jimmy decided to change the subject while Si was still reflecting. 'So, what happened with that girl, then?'

Si shrugged despondently. 'Not a lot.'

'How do you mean?'

'Well, like I said. Not a lot. She rang me last week to say that her dad had told her to come home.'

'Out of the blue, like?'

'Yeah. Well, perhaps he'd got wind of me. I don't know. Anyway, she rings and says she has to go home. She'd already finished her exams anyway, so there wasn't really any reason for her to stay... Apart from me.'

'Oh.'

'Apparently that wasn't enough to keep her here.'

'So, will you see her again? Or is that it?'

'I don't know. She said she'd write as soon as she got home. But I haven't heard anything yet.'

'Perhaps the post takes a while, or maybe her dad's locked her away in a harley...'

'Harem, you mean.'

Jimmy nodded.

'Well, maybe. I don't know. It all seemed to be going so well.'

'She was a great girl. I really liked her.'

'Yeah, me too. I mean, she was all right.' Si tried not to let his face betray him. Roberta had been gone five days, during which time he'd found it difficult to concentrate on his work, to sleep and to do even the basic things necessary to keep body and soul together. It had taken a considerable effort by Jimmy to get him down to The Feathers for a drink.

They sat in silence for a while.

Jimmy's mind had taken a fresh tack by the time he next spoke. 'Did you like school?'

'Huh? School? It was all right. Sometimes. Why? What about you?' Si perked up a bit.

'No, I hated it. Course I did.'

'You seemed to have a good enough time when we were there.'

'Don't be dense. I hated every minute of it.'

'What? Even the football?'

'No, course not. But football was in lunch breaks and after school. Not in lessons.'

'Yes it was. In games.'

'Well, once a week, I suppose so,' Jimmy acknowledged grudgingly. 'Anyway, you were always a teacher's pet. You loved it, didn't you?' Jimmy leered.

'No, you forget that they chucked me out.' Si sounded a bit defensive. 'They wouldn't have done that if I'd been a teacher's pet, would they?'

'I suppose so. But it wasn't as if they expelled you or anything. Just asked you to leave for smoking.'

'I was expelled,' said Si firmly. 'And it wasn't for smoking. It was for anarchistic behaviour.'

'Don't be daft. You were caught behind the back wall with a fag.'

'Yeah, I know. But when old Pig-head told me I'd be out, he said it was for "general anarchistic behaviour". I was an anarchist, you see-'

'Toss. You didn't know the meaning of the word.'

'Bet *you* don't even know what it means now.'

'Bet you I do.'

'Yeah?'

'Yeah.'

'So... What's it mean, then?'

'It means... Like... Not behaving properly, that's what. Like picking your toenails when you're eating.'

'Well, more or less.' They sunk into a maudlin silence over the dregs of their pints.

'Sometimes... Sometimes I feel like that what I learnt at school was quite important.'

'Crap. Never did me any good.'

'Well, maybe. But often I find that the only sense of structure I can find in life are the half-remembered things I learnt at school. Know what I mean?'

Jimmy looked blank.

'Like snatches of poetry or an idea from a book? Even a name of someone I heard about. It can be enough to keep me going when everything seems pointless. Or like when things fall apart...'

'Can't say I've found that myself.'

'Never?'

Jimmy thought for a minute. 'No, never.'

'Oh.' Si sounded disappointed.

'Why? You know I never read books,' Jimmy said gently. And Si thought he detected the faintest note of regret in his friend's voice.

'You told me you were reading *Fever pitch* just the other day.'

'Yeah, I didn't finish it though. Got bored. Anyway, I'm talking about reading books *at school*... When it made a difference to what happened after.'

'Oh, I suppose so. Doesn't matter anyway. School was a long time ago. That was then...'

'And this is now. So stop fannying about and get the beers in.'

'Yeah, why not?' Si smiled for the first time that evening.

'Why not indeed.'

Si drained the suds from his glass and moved towards the bar. He was a good mate, Jimmy. Reliable, there when needed. A good mate. That's what you needed in today's world. Just when everything was beginning to make sense for the first time. A bit of structure and meaning becoming visible. Then the whole thing crashes down in pieces. If it wasn't for Jimmy, Si realised, he'd have been in a right mess.

* * *

Still no answer. He'd give it a few more rings then put the phone down. What was wrong with journalists? Couldn't they even answer the phone?

Jimmy had resolved to tell Si before anyone else. He'd also decided not to tell Brenda and to stop seeing her with immediate effect. It had all got a bit out of control. He'd only meant it as a one night stand, after all.

'Hello?'

'Oh, hi. Is Si... I mean Simon Simpson there please?'

'He's on another line. Can I take a message?'

'Oh, no... Don't worry. Well, could you tell him that Jimmy called. He's got my number.'

'Yeah, sure. Oh, hold on a minute. He's just come off. I'll pass you over.'

'Hi, Jimmy. What's happening?'

'Not a lot. I just thought I'd give you a ring.'

'Really? That's odd. You've never done that before. No,

come on, there's something up. Eh?'

'Yeah. How did you guess? Well, listen, I've just got the most amazingly fantastic news.'

'I'm all ears.'

'I'm going to be a star.'

'Yeah? How's that, then?'

'Well, the boss has just told me Man United want to buy me. Can you believe it? Bloody amazing. He reckons, the boss that is, that it's almost all sorted out. I'm going to Manchester tomorrow to work out the final details. I'll go for a month or so to start with and, assuming it all goes well, they'll give me a three year contract. What about that, then?'

'Grief, Jimmy. I didn't know any of this was in the pipeline.'

'Ah well, I wanted to keep it quiet like until I was certain. But you're the first to know. Honest. And just when I was beginning to think my career would never take off. What do you reckon?'

'Ruddy ace! That's what I think.'

'Yeah, it is, isn't it?'

'We should have a drink when you get back from Manchester. It'll be one of the last decent pints you'll have.'

'What do you mean? The best beer in the world comes from Manchester.'

'Steady, Jimmy. This whole thing's gone to your head. Weren't you telling me the other day that all northerners were prats?'

'They are. But they still make good beer.'

'And they've got the best football teams. Even I know that.'

'Yeah.'

Si could almost see Jimmy grinning at the other end of the line.

'Look, Si, this is it. This is the big one, what I've been waiting for all this time. It's going to be amazing, and this is only the start.'

'Yeah, I'm sure you're right. Well done. You give me a ring when you're back, okay?'

'Don't be stupid. We're going to celebrate tonight.'

'Yeah? Sure, tonight. You're right. This needs celebrating now. Badly. I'm going to buy you a serious drink. Feathers tonight?'

'Sure. I'll be there at eight. Okay?'

'Yeah, see you then... And Jimmy?'

'Yeah?'

'Well done, mate.'

The next call was harder. Jimmy dialled but didn't really have time to compose himself before Brenda picked up the phone.

'Jimmy,' she wailed, 'where've you been? I thought you'd forgotten me.'

'Hi, Brenda. How've you been?'

'What's wrong with you? You sound all cold. That's not my Jimmy. Why don't I come over tonight and warm you up a bit, hmm?'

'That was why I rang, really.'

'Oh. You only ring me when you want something...'

'No, you're wrong. That's just it. I don't want anything. Not any more.'

Jimmy hoped he wasn't going to have to spell it out. He waited for a reaction, but he could already hear Brenda sniffling at the other end of the line. He felt a total snake; but he knew it was the only thing to do.

⚽ ⚽ ⚽

Jimmy moved up to Manchester and stayed in a huge hotel near the city centre. The deal was more or less tied up and only a few odds and ends remained for the lawyers to resolve. Jimmy couldn't believe his new salary, which was three times what he'd been on at Millwall with the prospect of rapid increases, if things went well. He took pleasure in walking the corridors of the hotel, admiring the plush carpets and the gold fittings, drinking champagne in the bar courtesy of Manchester United. He saw glamorous women come and go in the vast lobby, and one evening a famous game show presenter nodded affably to him across the bar. For the first time he felt the heady rush of success and was transported by the prospect of great wealth.

The bartender recommended and served an elaborate champagne cocktail which arrived with a bowl of peanuts and crisps. He then presented Jimmy with the bill.

'Oh no,' countered Jimmy, 'the club will pick that up.' The barman cast him a suspicious look.

'Club? Sir?'

'Yeah, Man United. My new club.'

The barman seemed only partially reassured. 'So if you're a United player, how come I don't recognise you?'

'You will... you will,' smiled Jimmy confidently. As the barman turned away, he sneaked a look at the bill still sitting on the table. Grief, the one drink came to double the cost of a well-lubricated evening in The Feathers. Suddenly feeling rather sober, he reflected that he still had some way to go before he was totally at home with the new surroundings.

Jimmy's old club Millwall, though sorry to see him go since he was their top scorer and with him went any real chance of promotion that season, knew that they couldn't ignore the half a million pounds which United had offered them. That was serious money for a Second Division club. After some half-hearted deliberation the board agreed to let Jimmy go. It had all happened very quickly.

Si didn't expect to hear from Jimmy for some time. He knew his friend would be caught up in the move and was unlikely to have time for the kind of life he'd been living till then. Si hoped that success wouldn't go to Jimmy's head. But even more, he hoped that Jimmy wouldn't blow this chance. It was almost certainly his last opportunity to make it big as a professional footballer.

⚽ ⚽ ⚽

By now Si had established a routine at work and thought he could read Dougy's mind well enough. He had done three religious pieces and Dougy hadn't complained about the generally pro-Government line he'd been taking. He'd decided that this was the message Dougy wanted to get across. So Si relaxed. It was time to really put the boot into the Opposition's education policy.

Si wrote a story about a vicar in Wakefield—an easy hook— who had spouted a lot of guff about daily prayers in comprehensive schools. A few days later, he heard about an Anglican bishop who'd made some injudicious remarks on local radio attacking the Government's education record. Si followed it up and wrote a witty piece pulling the bishop's arguments apart and asking if it was official that the Anglican Church would be taking sides in the election battle.

The day after the piece appeared Dougy called him. 'Loved it, kid. Loved it. You just keep it up, okay?'

Si felt smug. This was child's play. He'd got his job sussed and now he was going to enjoy it.

⚽ ⚽ ⚽

'Jimmy called,' said Bill.

'Oh yes? Did he leave a message?'

'Yeah. Said he'd be back on Wednesday night. He'll ring again.'

Si was excited at the prospect of seeing Jimmy so soon. He'd only been gone a month. It would be great to hear how things were going.

On Wednesday evening they met at the usual time at The Feathers. Jimmy was relaxed because Wednesday was Brenda's night off. He didn't want his former lover to spoil his triumphant return from the north.

'The Boss reckons that if I have another good session in

the Reserves, I might be on the bench for next week's first team match.'

'Shit. That's great. It's really happening for you, isn't it?'

'Sure is.' Jimmy looked well on his success. He wasn't drinking—just orange juice — and the sallow look which had haunted his face for the past year had gone. This was a man reborn and burning with ambition.

When he first came into the pub, a couple of the regulars looked at him a bit oddly—word had spread fast. Not that they approved of his move to Manchester United—they all supported Arsenal and Chelsea. But otherwise nothing had changed in The Feathers. Not even Si, thought Jimmy. Strange, when so much had happened in his own life since he last saw his friend.

'So, how've you been, mate?'

'All right... All right. I got a letter from Roberta the other day.'

'Roberta?'

'The foreign one.'

'Oh yes, Roberta. She was nice, she was. Pity it didn't work out for you.'

'Well, she wants to work things out.'

'Really? How? Is she coming back here, then?'

'No, she wants me to convert and to go visit her in the Sudan.'

'Grief. That's a bit heavy. Convert to what, anyway?'

'To Islam. To become a Muslim.'

'Gawd.'

'That's what I thought. I mean, I'm not really religious but to become a Muslim... That's really asking a lot.'

'And what if you don't? Can't you go and visit her anyway?'

'No. She says her father would never tolerate her going out with a non-believer.'

'You're in a right mess here. Maybe you should convert?'

Si wondered. Why not? It was quite an attractive

philosophy and as religions went it had some good points about it. Si had always had a soft spot for Islamic art and ceramics. 'Maybe. But that's not the half of it. You see, Roberta said that if I went to the Sudan now, without converting, there would be a danger that I'd be killed. By extremists.'

This decided Jimmy. 'Forget it, mate. This is crazy. She's only a chick, after all. Many more where she came from.'

'Yeah, I suppose so.'

'Get yourself a nice English girl. One who doesn't threaten to kill you. Know what I mean?'

'But she was special. Really special in some ways...'

'I don't even want to hear about it. You might end up getting me killed as an accomplice!'

Si managed a smile.

'That's better. Look, there's plenty of girls who'd leap at the chance to go out with a guy like you. Plenty.'

'Yeah?'

'Yeah. Just look at that one over there... No, not there. The one by the bar. With the black jeans on.'

Si began to take heart. It was good to see Jimmy back in London. He brought with him a sense of perspective.

❀ ❀ ❀

Sir Lesley glanced in the mirror and decided that he looked immaculate. Even at his age, he could turn young women's heads. He straightened his bow tie, shrugged inside his dinner jacket and, holding himself erect, returned to the drawing room to await his guests.

Sir Lesley was a self-made millionaire who had long since buried his origins. A shrewd businessman and a friend to what he liked to call 'the political class', he considered himself an influential man. His newspaper was just one way of exerting this influence. Certainly, it was the most public technique he used. As a man of influence and property, Sir Lesley liked to keep a two-bedroom mews cottage in Chelsea. He rarely stayed there, preferring to return to Wiltshire and the young family he had produced with his second wife, Marina. But the mews cottage served for discreet business meetings and occasional dinner parties for select groups of friends.

This evening Sir Lesley was expecting half a dozen guests, including two Cabinet Ministers, the Shadow Spokesman for the Environment, the presenter of a nightly current affairs programme and the head of a merchant bank. The sixth and, in Sir Lesley's eyes, the most important guest was La Contessa di San Benedino, Carla Melli.

Sir Lesley had been introduced to the widow at a Sotheby's reception the week before. He had been struck by her mournful beauty and brooding intelligence. He hadn't met a woman like her before. His interest was heightened by Carla's aloofness and obvious indifference to his presence. But when he had suggested a quiet supper with 'a few interesting friends', she had accepted graciously.

By the time Carla arrived the other guests were already onto their second drink. As she entered the room, the two male politicians leapt to their feet. The Secretary of State for Education, Alison Smith, and the TV journalist Suzanne Radi remained seated. Alison glanced at the newcomer briefly and, once introduced, returned deliberately to her conversation with the Shadow Spokesman, ignoring the frequent glances he cast over her shoulder.

Sir Lesley perched beside Carla, who was the focus of the other guests' attention. 'Carla... May I call you that?'

An elegant nod, betrayed only by a slight play around her mouth, indicated he could.

Sir Lesley smiled as if he'd just been elevated to a peerage, and continued declaiming to his guests. 'Carla lives in London but rarely goes out. We're extremely honoured to have her here tonight.'

Carla offered a demure smile to the collected company.

'Which part of Italy are you from?' fawned the Government Chief Whip. 'Tuscany? I do so love Tuscany.'

'No, not Tuscany.'

The Chief Whip drooped.

'I was brought up in Paris, but my family are from near Lago Maggiore.'

'Oh, how wonderful. I had a holiday near Lugano ten years ago...'

Dinner passed off smoothly, and even Alison seemed to warm to Carla.

After the crème brûlée, Sir Lesley sat at the end of the table surveying the scene and congratulating himself. Talk about power and influence, he thought. I've got it, I really have. Just look at my guests... You should always judge a man by his friends... He waved to the waiter to refill Carla's glass with the excellent Sauternes he'd personally chosen.

'Really my dear Carla, you must have a little bit more wine.'

'Sir Lesley, you are a naughty man.'

'Me? No, I'm never naughty.' Sir Lesley flushed.

'Yes you are naughty... Not just with wine, but also with your newspaper.'

'Oh?' He was slightly taken aback. He hadn't expected her to take a serious tack.

'Yes. Just yesterday I read a story in your paper which made fun of the Rabbi Rebecca Schultz. It said that she was an example of the wet liberalism prevalent among religious leaders in Britain today. And that the future of the country should not be trusted to people like her.'

'Oh...' Sir Lesley vaguely remembered reading the piece in the Diary. It hadn't struck him as particularly offensive at the time. In fact it seemed along the right lines. He was as keen as either of the Cabinet Ministers at the table to pick holes in the Opposition's religious education policy.

'But it was naughty to write that. And to say that she ate pork.' For the first time that evening Carla became really animated. The other guests broke off their conversations to listen in.

'The story said she ate pork? Oh, I doubt it.'

'Are you questioning my word, Sir Lesley?'

'Not at all, my dear... Now, would you like some coffee? We can adjourn to...'

But Carla interrupted him. 'In a moment. But just to finish with this story. The paper said that Rebecca, who is a friend of mine... It said she had advised the journalist not to worry too much about eating pork. And that she had eaten pork herself in the past. Your article made fun of poor Rebecca.'

Carla seemed to realise that she had been on the verge of making a scene and embarrassing her host. She slipped back behind her mask and resumed the flirtation. 'So, you see, Sir Lesley, you *are* a naughty man.'

Sir Lesley tried to smile but was only able to produce a grimace. He was beyond embarrassment. Inside he was boiling. Wait till I get hold of McCormack, he fumed.

'Shall we take some coffee in the drawing room? Alison, why don't you lead the way? Through the door to the right...' Alison threw him a mocking glance and glided out of the dining room. As everyone apart from Carla knew, she didn't need directions. She had spent enough time here in the past to know her way around. Her eyes twinkled as she recalled a certain incident on the dining room table which would certainly have surprised tonight's guests if they'd known. But the real source of her amusement was the way that chit of a girl had torn a strip off Lesley.

As he gave his arm to Carla and felt the limp touch of her hand, Sir Lesley realised with a surge of irrational anger that the dinner party had failed to advance his amorous plans.

⚽ ⚽ ⚽

'What the hell do you think you're doing?'

'What? How do you mean?' Dougy was confused. He had no idea what Sir Lesley was on about.

'Don't muck me around, McCormack. I employed you

to produce a paper, not to offend people. You realise that, don't you?'

'Yes, of course, Sir Lesley. But if you don't mind me asking...'

'I do mind. I mind very much. In fact, I mind immensely. Next time you decide to attack respectable members of the Jewish community, you think again. Okay?'

'Uh...'

'Do you hear me?'

'Yes, Sir Lesley.'

'Good. Good.' Having vented his spleen and frustration, the newspaper magnate calmed down somewhat. 'Okay, well, we'll say no more about it, this time...' He let the threat hang as he pressed the button and cut the line.

Dougy got up and breathed deeply. What the heck had that all been about? He stood in front of the big windows and looked out across Docklands. He loved this view. To him it symbolised the new Britain. Power, glass, money and water, glamorously combined. But even the view couldn't cheer him at this moment. He tried to work out what had upset his boss. Finally, he slapped the glass.

'Damn. It was the bloody Diary.' He walked over and opened the door. 'Martha, get me Simpson up here now. Like pronto. Okay?' Martha returned a scared look as Dougy slammed the door.

'But I thought that was what you wanted.'

'Well, I don't want it any more. Okay? I don't pay you to think. I pay you to get it right. Understand?'

'Yes.' Si looked glum.

'I brought you here because I thought you had potential. Don't blow it, okay? Don't blow it.'

Si just nodded and hoped he would be allowed to leave the room soon. The story had been routine, part of the series on religion and education. He'd done nothing out of the ordinary. Just phoned up Rabbi Schultz and pretended to be a lapsed Jew wanting advice on dietary rules. She'd been sweet and helpful and the piece he'd written had presented her far more sympathetically than had initially been his intention. And now this. Dougy bollocking him for no apparent reason. Si couldn't make it out. But he'd realised at an early stage in the interview that it was prudent to remain silent and not to attempt a defence. Hopefully Dougy would calm down and forget about the whole thing in a day or two.

'And I've been thinking,' said Dougy, as if moving on to an unrelated subject. 'I think we've probably done enough on the religious education stories. For the time being anyway. So drop it now, okay?'

'Sure. Of course.'

'Good. Now, just to be on the safe side, I want you to show me the Diary page from now on before it goes to bed, okay? I don't want any more cock-ups. All right? All right?'

Si groaned inwardly. One of the things he'd enjoyed most about his job was the semi-autonomy he'd had to decide what went into the Diary. It now looked as though Dougy was removing this authority and relegating him to an Assistant Diary Editor role. At least for the time being.

'Yeah. Of course.' Si looked up as Dougy's eyes bored into him like lasers. He looked away and started to move towards the door.

As he went out he passed Martha. She glanced up quickly before looking nervously past him into Dougy's office. Si thought he could see the faint stain of tears on her powdered cheeks. He managed a weak smile and raised his eyebrows. He sympathised—what a nightmare to work so closely with the irascible editor. At least he could now bolt back to his own relatively safe corner of the office. Martha was exposed to Dougy the whole working day. Her gaze flickered back onto Si as he passed. But she didn't return his smile.

⚽ ⚽ ⚽

Si knew he should stop going to parties. He simply didn't enjoy them any more. Even less so since Jimmy had moved away. He'd come to this one with some acquaintances from work and, although he told himself it was history and a waste of emotions, he couldn't help remembering the last such party he'd attended. He missed Roberta.

'God, I'm bored.' A girl standing next to him brushed back a loose strand of blond hair and leaned back against the wall. All around the party continued unabated. 'All these ghastly people. Have you seen our host?'

'No, can't say I have.'

'Well, I wouldn't bother going looking for him. When I came in he was standing right here and I thought it right to say hello, especially since I didn't know him.'

'So how did you get here, then?'

'Oh, I came with some friends, but they've disappeared now. Anyway, I went up and thanked him for his hospitality and do you know what he said?'

'Uh, no.'

'He said, "Hey babe, no big deal. You just go on in there and have fun. There's lots of coke and some serious meat to get your teeth into..." I mean! What way is that to welcome somebody, especially someone you don't know?'

Si sucked on his beer and tried to assess this talkative girl. She was attractive, and dressed conventionally with an Alice band an oversized stripy shirt worn over a short black skirt. Court shoes and navy tights confirmed the look. Normally such women bored him silly, but this one had something about her. A mesmerising vitality and, despite the superficial appearance, a malevolent sparkle in her cornflower eyes that spoke of sharp intelligence.

'So why are you bored? All that coke and... How did you put it? Serious meat? Not very lady-like expressions, are they?'

'Don't patronise me. He said it, not me. I would *never*

use such terms. If you're going to be boring, I'll go and find someone more interesting to talk to.'

'No, don't get like that. I was only trying to make conversation. I'm sorry.' Si changed tack. 'Look, I'm Si, what's you're name?'

'Mary, Mary Cunningham,' and she stuck out her hand expectantly.

Si took it and completed the formal greeting. 'So, what do you do, Mary Cunningham?'

She narrowed her eyes but didn't turn away. 'I work in the City. Emerging markets.'

'Oh.'

'You seem surprised. I'm not as stupid as I look, you know.'

Si blushed. 'I never thought you were. Stupid, I mean.'

'Sure. Anyway, what do *you* do for a living? Fly aeroplanes?'

'No, actually I don't. I'm a journalist.'

'God, how boring. Journalists are all so egotistical.'

'Well, not all of us. But listen, why did you think I flew planes?'

'Oh, because you've clearly got your head in the clouds.' Mary Cunningham burst out laughing. The sound made Si think of a childhood summer holiday in the Highlands. Before he'd become aware of his mother's idiosyncrasies. Partly because of the memory and partly because he found Mary's laugh compulsive, he joined in.

'Shall we find somewhere to sit? I'm knackered. '

'What, not leaving after all?'

'No, not yet.' And leading Mary by the arm, clutching the dregs of his beer in his other hand, he pushed through the crowd towards an empty overstuffed sofa.

❁ ❁ ❁

Roger Gittings, the bumbling Minister for Youth and Sport, seems well-suited to his job. Despite being follicly-challenged, the Minister takes both of his portfolios seriously. At a recent charity event he was introduced to the lovely Mavis Davis, Olympic hopeful and renowned celebrity. Miss Davis' muscular charms were not lost on the Minister, who is said by a friend to be undergoing a rigorous training routine under Miss Davis' strict supervision. No doubt he hopes to recapture his fading youth. Let us hope his wife and the Whips don't take exception to these extracurricular exercises.

Si stopped reading. Not bad, but a bit long. Also a bit too smutty. It wasn't easy to get the balance right between suggestive humour and tawdry lewdness. Bill had taken the Saturday night TV comic approach, but with a bit of polishing it would be all right. A distinct improvement on the series of bizarre pieces Bill had produced in their first few weeks of working together: Si hadn't been able to figure out why his assistant thought that stories about Leonardo di Caprio and Judy Garland were so interesting. Naturally, he'd not published any of them, although he'd realised how upset Bill had been at the time. Si looked up as Bill came into the office and started when he saw that his colleague had shaved off most of his hair and dyed the remnants white. Si looked away quickly and decided to act as if nothing had changed.

'I hate Monday mornings. D'you want a coffee, Si?'

'Yeah, love one. Your story's okay, Bill. I want to tweak it a bit, but we'll put it in today.'

Bill beamed. He recognised that as his hit-rate of pieces published since Si took over as editor had been low, he needed to adopt a more mainstream approach; otherwise, his brief career at *The Courier* would come to a premature end. The chances of landing another job elsewhere were slim as the dust had settled following the turbulence and upheaval of the late autumn.

Si's arrival had been greeted with the same apprehension felt on all the papers as new staff took over key positions; particularly as he'd been hand-picked by the new editor and given an unusual degree of control over the Diary. Bill, unaware of the consequences of Carla Melli's intervention, thought that Si still had considerable autonomy to decide what went into the page.

Despite early misgivings, Bill's confidence was gradually growing both in and out of the office and he now thought that he would be able to work happily for Si after all. Perhaps he did have a future in journalism. Returning to Scotland so soon after arriving in London would have been a terrible humiliation. He could imagine his mates laughing in the pub over their pints of Heavy. Those school friends who'd never tried anything, who were going the same way as their dads, who had zero prospects, and whose brains were shrinking in their skulls with each passing numbing day of monotony... No, Bill wouldn't be going back there. And after years of confusion he was finally beginning to face up to the inevitable; although God alone knew how he'd tell his parents. He couldn't even pluck up the courage to talk frankly to his new mates at *The Courier*. Bill's daydreaming returned to the Diary: if Si liked this story, then he could repeat the approach and, surely, his hit rate would steadily improve. Maybe he would even take over the Diary when Si moved on, although that could be years away. Nevertheless, Bill had patient ambition.

'Hey, Bill? What about that coffee? You're miles away.'

'Oh yeah, sorry, Si. Coming right up.' That served him right for getting carried away in his daydreams.

Bill returned with the coffee.

'Thanks. Did you put sugar in it?'

Bill nodded.

'Great. Right, about this story. I think we need to cut this out and bring this bit up front more. Yeah? And then let's try to put in a quote from Mavis.'

'Mavis refused to comment.'

'Well, let's say that then. Ms Davis declined to comment on her relationship with Mr Gittings. D'you see? Good.'

'We could always try her mum?'

'What?'

'Mavis' mum. She might give us something?'

Ms Davis senior was a renowned self-publicist who had no scruples about using her daughter to achieve column inches. 'Yeah, why not? Good idea. Okay, you get on to Mavis' mum and we'll take it from there.' Si was pleased. Bill was brighter than he'd thought. Perhaps he'd been a bit hard on the kid at the beginning. With a bit of time they could make a good team. 'And Bill...'

'Yeah?'

'Like the hair.'

Bill grinned sheepishly and went off to find a telephone number for Mavis' mum. Si looked at the next story someone had put in his tray. He was soon interrupted by the phone ringing.

'I've never seen it like this before.'

'No, me neither. Spooky, don't you think?' The stillness of central London was broken by the distant wail of a police siren. Si shuddered and hoped Mary hadn't noticed.

'Do you think this'll just carry on? Like before, I mean? It's so depressing to think that everything's back to square one as if nothing happened.'

'I don't know.' Si and Mary walked on in silence. Their steps echoed down Haymarket. A few other pedestrians walked in the same direction.

'Sorry sir, you can't go down there. It's still being searched for evidence.'

'Oh. I wanted to get to Embankment. How can I do it?'

'Well, it won't be easy. It's all shut off round Charing Cross.'

The bomb scare suggested that the cease-fire might be

about to end. The streets were strangely silent, cleared of all traffic to allow the police to approach a phone box in which a bomb was said to be hidden.

A new tension mingled with the smog in the damp air. Or rather an old, unspoken terror which had evaporated in the last few months during the cease-fire. It was almost as if those intervening months had never happened. If the cease-fire collapsed, then the peaceful interregnum would be quickly forgotten.

People hurried past plate glass windows in the West End warily eyeing their reflections lest a sudden explosion should send shards of lacerating glass out on to the street. Everyone remembered previous mainland bombing campaigns.

The cease-fire was so fragile. It took an optimist to believe it could last. The feeling that it couldn't go on indefinitely persisted. On the other hand, the taste of peace was so sweet, it would take a barbaric act to destroy it.

The bomb scare had one positive side. It meant that Si had a legitimate excuse for not rushing back to the office after his lunch with Mary. They had been seeing each other for three weeks now. Just over. That first night at the party had turned into breakfast the next morning at Smithfield market. Arriving in the rain and rushing in for steak and beer as a pallid dawn washed into the capital.

Breakfast had given way to coffee at Mary's—she lived nearby in Clerkenwell in a converted warehouse. They had spent the rest of the weekend together, and it had been Monday night before Si finally got home from the party. After that, they'd continued to see each other, perhaps slightly against the odds. Lunch in Soho had become a favourite Friday rendezvous. Normally, they opted for sushi, as today. Cheap, cheerful and relatively quick. But above all, stylish. And that was what mattered to Mary.

Born and brought up in Hampshire, Mary was an ambitious girl with enough talent and good looks to achieve most of what she set out to do. Last year she'd set her heart on buying a trendy converted warehouse; now Si was part of her ambition. He wasn't complaining.

'I don't know about you, but I feel like a walk. Why don't I take you back to your office?'

'On foot? It's miles.'

'So what? It'll be great exercise. I was only going to sit on the tube. So walking would be much better. Come on.'

Mary looked dubious, but Si was already dragging her off down the street. 'Hey, hold on… Wait for me. You don't need to drag me like a dog.' She skipped to keep up.

When they arrived forty minutes later in the City, Mary stopped and pointed to a tall building. 'That's where I work. Fifteenth floor.' The black glass windows reflected the sickly sunlight—it looked more like a sculpture than a building. This time it was Mary who rushed on, excitedly pulling Si after her by the hand. 'Come on, I want to show you inside. It's an amazing place.'

Si walked after her with an uncertain step. He'd never been one for the City and its financial hi-tech wizardry. Figures dazzled him and he could find no charm in a well-constructed graph. Not that he'd ever really tried. It just wasn't his scene. He allowed his prejudices to dominate when it came to broadening his understanding of such things. Si liked to think of himself as a man of words. A beautifully turned phrase could give him a thrill, and in his scheme of things letters were much more civilised than statistics. The problem was that when he left the newspaper world behind and found himself in the money mile, he was forced to acknowledge that his scheme was flawed. He felt out of his depth and insecure surrounded by a powerful reality he couldn't master.

'Si, hurry up.' Mary waited at the entrance to the building. A rotating steel tube allowed people to enter. A constant stream of sharply tailored suits and expensive shoes rushed in and out of the tube. 'I want to take you up and show you my office. The view's out of this world.'

'Listen, Mary, I've got to get back. Sorry, but I still have to find a lead story for tomorrow's Diary.' He was lying and she probably realised it. After all he hadn't been in any hurry during their long walk east.

Mary hid her disappointment well and assumed a brisk business-like air. 'Hey, no problems. I've got a deal to clinch, so it's probably the best thing anyway.'

Si felt stupid. 'Right. I'm sorry, you know….'

'Don't be sorry. There's nothing to be sorry about. I loved the walk. We should do it again sometime. Okay?' Mary leaned forward and kissed him full on the mouth.

Si managed a smile. 'I'll call,' he muttered, turning away.

'You'd better. I'm a busy woman and I don't like being messed around.' She was only half-teasing. 'Call soon. Bye.' And joining the flow of hi-tech humanity, she disappeared into the silver tube.

❁ ❁ ❁

'Hello, Si Simpson speaking.'

'Hi, Si.' Dougy's distinct drawl made Si sit up in his chair and grope for a pen and paper. He found a yellow sticky in his top left hand desk drawer. 'Now listen, kid, I liked your last piece about the Rabbi. You did good. Much better. Keep it up. You never know, there might be something in it for you, if you pull it off.'

After the initial shock of Sir Lesley's anger over the Diary story on the Rabbi, Dougy had recognised the need to redeem himself. Quickly.

First of all he used his extensive contacts to find out what had caused the outburst and learned of the dinner party and the Italian aristocrat's irritation. Then he decided to talk directly to the Rabbi herself and, after apologising profusely, he had offered in his sugariest tones to run a nice story to make up for any distress *The Courier* had inadvertently caused. After a frosty start, Dougy's charm had paid off. Si was tasked with producing the piece, and the reaction to the published story had been positive.

Dougy didn't dare draw the Rabbi's gratitude to Sir

Lesley's attention, but simply suggested to his new ally that if she was really that pleased, perhaps she could mention it to her friend the Italian Contessa. That was probably the safest way to earn him Brownie points with his boss.

Sure enough, two days later, Sir Lesley had called Dougy to say how pleased he was with the story. 'That's more like it, McCormack. Keep it up. You may have a future yet.'

Such tributes were hard earned. Dougy knew the pressure was off... For the moment at least. And, as he told himself, since he was a generous man, he'd decided to share the glory with Si. Hence the phone call to his subordinate.

Dougy put down the phone. He had said all he wanted to say and wasn't interested in Si's reaction. Keep the kid on his toes, carrot and stick approach. Slap him round the head if he screwed up, and give him praise when he did well. That was Dougy's management policy. He still had faith in Si. After all, it had been his initiative to bring him to *The Courier* during the upheaval. Yes, if Si did well and helped him achieve his objectives, Dougy would make sure he got his due reward. He needed allies in the political game he was playing. And wasn't politics all about helping out when one could?

Dougy leaned back in the comfortable chair and swivelled so he could see out of the huge picture window. He surveyed the metropolis. A warm glow of self-righteousness engulfed him.

⚽ ⚽ ⚽

Elspeth Somerset was making herself a pot of tea. She was in good shape for her age: unbowed and with a slim figure of which women twenty years younger would have been proud. Her straight back led to a taught neck and soft cheeks, slightly tanned from so much gardening; above her smooth forehead, steely grey hair, highlighted naturally by occasional white strands, was pulled back in a pony tail held by an ivory clip.

Elspeth stared out at the barren garden. She hated the winter, so cold, so hostile. Inevitably, her thoughts turned to Bob, whose anniversary fell soon. She made a supreme effort to overcome the emotion welling up within her—even after four years, her grief seemed as fresh as the day she'd found that he'd died soundlessly beside her during the night. They'd never gone in for the convenience of separate beds, although her bossy daughter Beatrice had often suggested it might be—how had she put it? Oh yes—more "appropriate" for a lady of her age to have her own bedroom. Elspeth smiled wryly at the memory.

Beatrice's idea of marriage was clearly so different from her own. How could that be? she wondered idly. How had her daughter grown up as such a prude when she and Bob had done everything to extol the natural and to stress the importance of love? Ah well, children... You could only do so much for them. Then they had to make their own choices; and Beatrice seemed happy enough in her own way, living in chintz heaven, striking airs and graces at coffee mornings with her nauseating friends. And as for Beatrice's poor husband... Well, he'd made his own bed, she reflected, as usual falling back on tried and tested sayings to deal with difficult thoughts.

Ah Bob, Elspeth sighed, staring at the frosted grass on the back lawn. Would the pain never dull? Lord, give me strength to get through this winter. Of course, it won't be long, she told herself, before the snowdrops break through. Then the crocuses, and before she knew it the daffodils would herald the arrival of spring. She loved the white daffodils in particular; so delicate with their bright angelic haloes and strong sunny centres. Like little angels smiling at her, infusing her tired bones with energy and optimism.

For her age, Elspeth was sprightly. She lived alone and, despite the fact that she was now eighty-four, she had no intention of moving to a home. The thought of losing her independence frightened her more than anything; even more than death.

The sugar lived in a tin on the top shelf, to keep it away from the ants in summer. She stood on the stool and plucked it out carefully. She remembered buying this tin—it had been full of biscuits at the time. Must have been before the war, on one of those romantic weekends away. Never very far, of course, in those days one didn't travel much. But she and Bob used to enjoy a trip to the seaside. Normally, they'd stay over in a small hotel on the front. Ah, they had some fun times; very romantic. Bob knew how to melt her heart, and that wasn't all he was good at. Elspeth grinned naughtily. Fancy having thoughts like that at her age. Beatrice certainly wouldn't approve.

Brighton, thought Elspeth in a flash of inspiration; that's where they'd bought the biscuits. Or was it Weston-Super-Mare? Her memory wasn't what it was, she sighed, before clambering back up to replace the tin.

Elspeth put her tea on a small tray and carried it into the sitting room. Then she put on Mahler at volume six, loud enough to block out the traffic at the top of the lane. She was just sitting down to enjoy her elevenses, when the phone rang. 'Hello, Ryburn 4760,' she answered.

'Hi, Gran, how are you?'

'Oh, Mary, how nice of you to ring.'

'Well, I can't chat long, I just wanted to wish you a happy birthday.'

'You are a clever girl to remember. I think your mother's forgotten.'

'Oh, I wouldn't worry, she's probably out shopping in Harvey Nic's for your present as we speak.' They both laughed conspiratorially.

'Will she never learn?' asked Elspeth. 'Doesn't she realise I'd much prefer that new book on Puccini than any of her posh nick-nacks?'

Elspeth had two great pleasures which invigorated and delighted her: her granddaughter and serious classical music, particularly opera. Elspeth was a Radio Three devotee and liked her music to be on the difficult side, not yielding its treasures without a fight. But her daughter loved Classic FM, particularly Simon Bates, whom she considered the epitome of sophistication. Elspeth disparaged this radio station as a mish mash of Mozart ditties and Strauss's greatest hits for middle-brow forty-somethings.

'So, are you feeling okay?' Mary asked.

'Of course I am. Tush, girl, how often do I have to tell you that you're only as old as you feel?'

'Yes, I know, Gran. But eighty-four is a grand old age.'

'It's lucky for you that I can't get my hands on your scrawny neck. I'd give you a jolly good shaking.'

'Oh Gran, you know I'm only joking.'

'Of course I do, my angel. Now when are you going to visit your decrepit grandmother?'

'Well, it's really busy at the moment, what with work and everything. But soon, I promise. Oh, and Gran, I've got a new boyfriend...'

'Oh yes?' Elspeth had been Mary's confidante since her birth. It had really started when as a little girl Mary used to crawl into her bed in the mornings to complain about Beatrice. And Elspeth had always taken Mary's side, indulging and spoiling her.

'I'll tell you all about him when I've got more time. Got to go now.'

'Just tell me what he's called.'

'Simon. Simon Simpson.' It sounded so formal thought Mary, blushing slightly.

'That's a nice name. Well, I look forward to hearing all about him. And don't go getting into trouble or having your heart broken in the meantime.'

'Oh Gran, you know I'm a big girl now.' Yes, but that hadn't stopped her falling for a series of jerks and burning her fingers on several occasions. Poor Elspeth had borne the brunt of those heartbreaks, mopped the tears and offered support.

'Mmm, well, you be careful now. Promise?'

'Okay, I promise. Now, I really must go, Gran. Love you lots.'

'Goodbye darling, and thank you for ringing.'

'Big kiss,' and Mary put the phone down.

Elspeth stood for a moment holding the receiver, lost in thought. Goodness, she wouldn't want to be a young girl in today's world. So tough, without conventions or rules to help you find your way. It was bad enough back in her day, but at least you were reasonably well protected. The world had been a more innocent place, and there had been lots of people around to advise and help you.

Elspeth shivered; even with the heating on high she felt the cold through her parchment skin. She gathered her crocheted shawl around her shoulders and turned back to the sitting room to drink her tea. It was probably chilled by now. But her spirits rose as she heard the symphony building satisfyingly towards a climax. Wonderful stuff. Nothing like it.

❀ ❀ ❀

With education the hot topic at the moment, Arthur Richardson, the notorious writer, has come up with a challenging proposition. When I cornered him at a party last night he was wearing a pink-spotted bow-tie and spun me a line about his latest craze. He suggests that the teachings of nineteenth century Parsee guru Zoroastra should be taught to all British schoolchildren. 'The man was a great educationalist. We shouldn't be afraid of unknown religions,' declares Arthur. I fear Arthur may need to change his neckwear if he wants his theory to be taken seriously.

'Call this a story?' boomed Dougy. 'It's crap, that's what it is. I thought I said no more religious stories?'

'I know, but it's just that we were a bit short of material and....'

'No *buts*. When I say something I mean it.'

'I just thought that since it wasn't very political it would be all right...' Si began to feel unhappy.

Dougy looked at him strangely and Si realised he'd touched a nerve. 'Not political? Not political?' The whisper was more frightening than any of Dougy's ranting. 'Just because you're writing about some past-it celebrity hack and his stupid ideas about an eccentric eastern religion in which no-one's interested anyway doesn't stop it being political. This is more political than you can imagine. I think you'd better realise that before...before...' Dougy tailed off. 'Take this away and chuck it. And pull your socks up, Si, before you blow it.' There was no doubting the sentence's resolution this time.

'Oh...' Si was lost for words. He felt even unhappier. Perhaps this was the end of his meteoric rise in journalism. He would be packing his desk before the end of the day. 'I'm sorry, it won't happen again.'

Dougy looked as if he was going to fly off the handle again, but then he paused and lightened a bit. 'Okay, off you go and get it right next time. Do you hear me? Zoroastra wouldn't be so bad if the electorate included a critical minority of Iranians, but since it doesn't, and since you know what I've said about religious stories, I suggest you go for something a little more...on-beat, shall we say? Get my drift?'

'Yes, yes I do. Thanks.' And feeling like Daniel leaving the lions' den, he walked quickly from the editor's office.

'How did it go?' asked Martha, gentle concern in her eyes as he passed her desk.

'Well, you know how it is...'

Martha nodded. She certainly did.

SPRING

Jimmy's transfer was confirmed just before the deadline. It coincided with a run of form for Manchester United which took them back into contention for the league championship. Ten victories on the trot put them level on points with Newcastle United, who had seemed unstoppable only a few weeks before when they were nine points clear with a game in hand. At that point the Premiership table had looked like this:

	Played	Points
Newcastle	23	54
Manchester United	24	45

As United caught up Newcastle the bookies cut the odds from 15/1 to 4/1 on them finding the Holy Grail of football — that is to say, winning for a second time the mystical Double of Premiership and FA Cup (commonly known as the Double Double).

Jimmy was fortunate to time his arrival with this surge. More fortunate still that injuries to United regulars gave him the chance to contend for a place in the first team, although he had yet to make his debut. Jimmy expected to wake up any day, but while it lasted he was going to enjoy the dream.

Si took his overcoat from the door. A hint of spring hung in the air this week, a potent incense of rich humus and sprouting bulbs. But the mornings were still sharp. As he slipped his hand into the pocket, he realised there was something in the lining. He pulled out a mud-stained envelope bearing an address he didn't recognise. A vague recollection stirred. Shit, he'd picked it up from the pavement meaning to post it as a good Samaritan; but that had been ages ago, just after he'd started his job.

Si bit his lip, a habit he'd retained from childhood. He was slightly horrified that the letter might have contained something important.

For a second he thought of opening it to put his mind at rest. But the feeling of guilt passed quickly. Better to get rid of it as soon as possible.

He remembered to post the letter on his way to work and thought that, despite the delay, he'd done a stranger a good turn.

⚽ ⚽ ⚽

'Mary? Hi, it's Si.'

'Oh, hi. Listen, can I call you back? I'm just in the middle of something.'

'Fine. I'm in the office.'

When Mary called back half an hour later, Si had almost forgotten the original reason for his call.

'Oh yeah, I called. Sorry, I'm a bit up in the clouds at the moment.'

Mary laughed. 'Don't worry, I like that about you. You're quite mad.'

'I know what I wanted to ask you. Would you like to come to a match with me? I've got this friend who plays for Man United—I think I've mentioned him, Jimmy? Yeah? Well, he's playing in London this weekend.' Jimmy was actually playing in a Reserves match against Arsenal, but even so it would be a higher standard of football than most First Division matches.

'Oh Si, I'm sorry, but I've got to work this weekend. So I'm afraid I can't. Why don't I give you a ring when I finish?'

'Yeah, fine. I'd better get back to work...'

'Don't be like that. Come on, we'll go another time. Or we could always do something a bit more civilised.'

'Like what?'

'The theatre, or the opera... I don't know. But soccer's not exactly the most cultivated of leisure activities, is it?'

Si was surprised by his answer. The truth was that his own interest in football had increased dramatically since Jimmy's career had picked up. 'Soccer isn't a leisure activity. It's a way of life.'

Mary laughed. 'Stop being silly and go back to your work. If it means so much to you, of course we'll go to a soccer match sometime. Love you.' And she put the phone down.

Si returned to shuffling idly through the papers on his desk. Eventually he picked up the phone.

An ansaphone responded. Since moving north, Jimmy's lifestyle and accoutrements had changed noticeably. For a start, he was now living in interior designed luxury. Manchester United had loaned him enough cash to rent a three bedroom house in Alderley Edge. 'Of course,' as Jimmy had told Si, 'I intend to buy my own place soon.' His weekly salary was already more than three times what he'd been earning at Millwall, and, if he established himself in the first team, the sky would be the limit. 'What do you reckon to Feraris?' he'd asked Si provocatively. 'Some of the lads have them, and I thought I might buy one ... Just to kick off the collection, mind.' Jimmy had laughed at the time, but Si had been left wondering how flippant the comment had really been. It wouldn't be the first time that overnight riches had gone to a man's head.

When the ansaphone message stopped, Si spoke quickly. 'Jimmy? Hi, it's Si. Listen, about the match this weekend. I'll be there, right, but I only need one ticket after all. Not two, okay? Anyway, talk to you soon.'

Si hung up. He was pleased at his friend's success, although he could see the potential pitfalls. But he couldn't deny that thinking of Jimmy also made him melancholic. Everyone seemed so dynamic and on their way up. But he couldn't even write a story to please his editor, and his girlfriend seemed more interested in her work than him. Keeping himself on track in modern life was as difficult as holding on to a slimy fish; it always seemed to leap out in unexpected ways and elude him. The age of certainties had passed.

⚽ ⚽ ⚽

A fortnight later, Jimmy huddled into his windcheater. After some good performances for the Reserves, including a couple of goals against Arsenal, he'd finally broken into the first team squad. He was surprised that even under the dugout's Perspex protection it was arctic cold. Why didn't the other lads look frozen?

'You nervous, then?' The substitute beside him on the bench nudged him in the ribs.

'No.'

'So why are your teeth chattering, eh?'

'I'm just cold.'

'Sure you are. Well, if you're nervous it's no bad thing. You've got every reason to be. When I first played here I was terrified. The biggest stadium in the country. The noise is deafening when you get out there. And when something goes right, it's like nothing on earth. But if you muck up... Well...' The sharp intake of breath said the rest. 'But I wouldn't worry. The boss won't put you on if it stays like this.'

Jimmy didn't feel reassured. Half of him wanted to get onto the pitch and do what he'd been brought here to do: score goals. The other half of him wanted to run away to the anonymity of The Feathers. A quiet pint with Si.

The northern climes were much colder than he'd imagined. Before starting with United, he'd only visited the north for Millwall's away matches. But now he was living up here, the seductive powers of northern England were beginning to wrap their tentacles about him. He liked the people and he liked the city. Like London, only friendlier and more compact.

A roar from the crowd broke into his reverie. He and all the others in the dugout leapt to their feet punching the air. The noise was deafening. Red and black everywhere, fluttering scarves and flags, shirts and hats... Manchester United had equalised in the fifth round FA Cup derby against Manchester City. After a bad start, the Red Devils had piled on the pressure and were now well in control.

His fellow sub nudged him once they had subsided back onto the bench. 'Well, if we go ahead, then there's a fair chance that one of us will get a game. Good, eh?'

'Yeah, great.' Jimmy wondered if his teeth were audible to those around him.

⚽ ⚽ ⚽

'Oooh,' the roar went up from the crowd in the pub. A pall of cigarette smoke hung over the drinkers. 'Give me another pint!' yelled a voice to the patient girl behind the bar.

'Wait your turn, Mack. I'll be with you in a minute.' The barmaid, a new girl taking Brenda's place for the night, turned to Si, who sat on a stool. 'God, I hate football matches. I don't know what you see in it.'

Si was watching in The Feathers two hundred miles south of Manchester. 'I've got a mate playing in this game,' he confided.

'Oh really?' The girl perked up. 'Which one's he?'

'Jimmy Sweeney. He drinks in here with me normally.'

'Oh yeah? So where is he?'

'Well, he's on the bench, but he might come on soon.'

As if to save Si embarrassment, the commentator promptly announced that Jimmy was warming up on the touchline.

'It's an odd choice being one apiece, but it looks like Alex Ferguson is about to bring on a virtual unknown, a new player at United, Jimmy Sweeney, who's just signed from Millwall for half a million pounds. The question is, who's going to come off?' This was answered a few minutes later when Nicky Butt limped off. Jimmy, bouncing on the touchline, exchanged a brushing handshake with Butt and ran on to the pitch to polite applause.

Nobody knew what to expect, least of all Si. His heart was in his mouth. How would Jimmy cope with this situation? His debut in the Theatre of Dreams.

'That's my mate there,' he boasted to the barmaid. 'D'you recognise him?'

'No, not really, but I've not been working here long. Anyway, he's got nice legs...'

Jimmy's first touch of the ball was inauspicious. He failed to control an easy pass from Ryan Giggs, letting it run into touch. The capacity crowd groaned. Tolerance of unknown quantities was low. With ten minutes remaining and the game one each, United couldn't afford to throw the ball away like that. They wanted to score, and so avoid a replay away from home.

It looked as though a rematch was inevitable when, with two minutes remaining, Eric Cantona picked the ball up on the half-way line and ghosted past a couple of tired City players. From nothing a chance had appeared. It was Cantona with two United players in support and only two City defenders and the goalkeeper to beat. The Stretford End roared the Frenchman on.

Cantona inimitably drew one of the defenders towards him and Giggs made a run down the left hand side. The remaining defender followed him, judging that Cantona would probably try and slide the ball through for Giggs to run on to. But suddenly Cantona stopped, put his foot on the ball, and waited with Gallic arrogance. As the shadowing City man lunged at him with a two-footed tackle, Cantona struck the ball to his right and daintily stepped over the flying studs.

Jimmy saw the ball rolling towards him. Taking his time,

he controlled it and pushed it ahead of him. There was only the goalkeeper between him and the headlines.

On the edge of the penalty box he looked up and, seemingly unaware of the deafening roar of the crowd, the millions of passionate fans willing him to score not only in the stadium but in front of television screens around the world, he looked up and steadied himself. The goalkeeper, faced with no alternative, sprinted towards him, trying to narrow the angle available and to smother Jimmy's shot.

In The Feathers the bar was in turmoil. 'Shoot, you fool, shoot!' shouted a hoary old man, his pint raised towards the TV set.

'Come on, sexy,' purred the barmaid, enraptured by the action.

Si just sat there, gripping his stool with both hands. Come on, Jimmy, come on, mate, he thought. His concentration was such that his eyes ached. Be cool, nice and easy.

'I bet the bugger misses it,' whinged a pot-bellied man beside him.

Si didn't have time to reply.

The goalkeeper was about five yards from Jimmy and moving quickly.

Behind him Jimmy sensed the defenders closing in for the tackle. He had to act quickly or the chance would evaporate in a tangle of legs and boots. He had two choices: either to chip the goalkeeper or to try and take it round him, and then shoot into an empty net. He opted for the latter.

Jimmy dipped his left shoulder, and shimmied towards the centre of the box. As the goalkeeper followed him and dived towards the ball at his feet, he struck the ball with his left foot, dragging it back away from the advancing hands. The ball trickled under the goalkeeper's body and Jimmy was about to tap it on through and towards the net when it disappeared.

One of the City defenders had caught him. A desperately

swung boot cleared the ball into touch. A corner to United. Jimmy hung his head in shame.

The crowd groaned and The Feathers erupted into abuse and laughter. 'Ha, that's the end of it for United.' The regulars, no fans of Manchester United, gloated at this failure.

Si and the barmaid felt Jimmy's pain. 'Never mind, love. He did well to be there, anyway.' Si was heavy-hearted. 'Listen, have another pint. You never know, he might yet score.' But he didn't, and as Si sipped the head from his glass the match ended.

⚽ ⚽ ⚽

The restaurant was virtually empty. Not surprising given the late hour. But Mary had insisted she couldn't get out of work before eleven.

Si had challenged her. 'But you don't plan on working that late every night, do you?' He was worried by Mary's zealous dedication to her job. Sometimes he wondered if she saw him as anything but an amusing distraction to fill up quiet times when she wasn't at the office, to be cast aside as soon as work beckoned.

'No, of course not. Only two or three times a week.'

'Ah, that's fine, then.' The irony fell on deaf ears.

But now Si's patience was running out. He had finished the paper while waiting and now turned back to the sports pages, which he'd read first. Manchester United's draw in the FA Cup at Old Trafford meant a replay away from home at Maine Road. Jimmy's ten minutes received a disproportionate amount of media attention. Uncharitably, and somewhat unfairly it seemed to Si, the journalist reporting for *The Courier* concluded that United's failure to win at home against City was due to the chance missed by Jimmy. Not really fair at all, given that Jimmy had played so little of the match. But, concluded Si, nodding wisely to himself, life wasn't fair, and journalists were as unfair as everyone else. Perhaps not quite as unfair as Dougy McCormack, but then he was no ordinary journalist. Mortal journalists, like the football correspondent—and Si for that matter—needed to be opinionated, polemic and outspoken. That's what sold newspapers.

'Could I have another gin and tonic?' The waiter nodded respectfully and glided away. He reappeared a few minutes later holding a tray on which a sparkling glass sat. In it a pale lime floated symmetrically among the ice cubes. This restaurant was a bit more up-market than Si was used to. Mary's choice, not his. A romantic treat. And some romantic dinner it had turned out to be — just him, the waiter, and several drinks.

The restaurant was now virtually empty and he felt self-consciously alone. Was it so obvious that he'd been stood up? He'd only been there for half an hour.

The waiter floated back towards him—he seemed to be practising for a career on the stage. Probably an unemployed actor waiting to be cast as Frankenfurter or perhaps Lady Bracknell. But the thought failed to keep his spirits up.

'Sir, Miss Mary Cunningham called and left a message for you. She says she's been held up and apologises that she won't be able to join you.'

'Ah… Right.'

'Will you still be wanting to order, sir?' Something in the waiter's manner spoke volumes about what he thought of eager suitors being stood up.

Si determined to disappoint the cocky wanna-be thespian. 'Yes, of course. I'll start with the snails and then have the lamb, please.'

The waiter looked disappointed and, without even bothering to write down the order, nodded and turned away. 'Very well, sir.'

Si caught him as he made to walk off. 'Oh, and to drink a bottle of number sixty three.' If he was going to dine alone he might as well do it in style. The idea of getting a bit tight strongly appealed.

'Of course, sir.' The waiter moved away like the QE II under full steam. Si drained the last of his gin and tonic. He knew his victory over the waiter would prove to be Pyrrhic. He fully expected a miserable day at work tomorrow, hung-over and exhausted. But for the moment he enjoyed some bitter satisfaction.

⚽ ⚽ ⚽

'I saw your column today. It was very good.'

'Really? I didn't think you read *The Courier*. I thought you said it was too downmarket?'

'Well, it is. But someone had a copy in the office and I thought I'd take an interest in your work.'

'How very kind of you.' Once again Si's sarcasm seemed lost on Mary.

'As I said, I thought it was very good. But too political.'

'Why? Wasn't it funny enough?'

'No, not that. It was funny. At least I smiled, I think. No, what I didn't like was the overt party-politicking. It was so cheap.'

Si knew what she was referring to. Since he'd had to show his copy to Dougy on a daily basis, the Editor had started to insist on certain pieces going in which Si would have preferred to chuck out. Not surprisingly many of these were stories with a strong political slant supporting the Government. Disconcertingly, Bill had written most of them. Si wondered if Dougy had started talking directly to his assistant and bypassing him. Only the day before, Dougy had made Si include a story praising a discredited Minister which Bill had put together. Clearly, Dougy didn't find Bill's evolving appearance difficult; even the nose stud hadn't caused problems in the top office. But Si was beginning to wonder what lay behind Bill's evident desire to shock.

Si tried to defend himself against Mary's attack, but apathy prevailed. He just couldn't get passionate about his job any more. 'Sometimes I have no choice. I have to do what I'm told.'

'Yes, I know. You explained. But that's no excuse. If you're going to sell out so easily, why not at least be subtle about it? There's no virtue in propaganda—and that story was nothing more than that.'

Si was taken aback. 'I didn't know you were such a political animal,' he countered.

'I'm not. Money, not politics, interests me. But you obviously are. Or maybe you're not... Simply that you're manipulated by your boss.'

'Is that so very strange? After all, if your boss tells you to invest in a certain market or company, you won't question his wisdom, will you?'

'Of course I will, if I think he's wrong. Sometimes I argue just for the sake of it.'

'Like now?'

'Not like now. This is for real. It's a real problem with you, Si. You shouldn't be so pliant. Be yourself and stand up for what you believe. If you don't want to write something, then don't.'

'I'm not pliant.'

'I think you are. You don't have the guts to publish things that you know your editor won't like. Do you?'

Si looked at her sadly.

'I thought not. You see, Si, I'm not like that. That's why people respect me at work. Because I speak my mind and don't give a damn if I offend people. You've got to be tough if you want to get to the top.'

'At the expense of all else?'

'If necessary, yes. D'you see?'

He nodded. 'I see.'

Mary made to move on to another topic, having ticked off the last of her list of issues to be addressed that day. 'So, what are you doing next weekend?'

'Huh? Next weekend? Oh, I don't know... Haven't really thought about it. Why?'

'Well, I don't have to work and I thought we could go to a football match, perhaps on Saturday, like you wanted to, and then go to have lunch with my parents in Hampshire on Sunday.'

They had been together for almost two months and this was the first time that Mary had suggested going away for the weekend. Their short relationship had been limited to discussing when they would next meet. Normally for dinner and occasionally, when the wind was in the right direction, for sex. So far it had been a fairly clinical affair, no long term planning of any sort.

Si was vaguely aware that Mary had parents, and that they lived in the Home Counties. Her dad was a stockbroker who commuted to London each day. Her mother, about whom he knew nothing, was no doubt a braying, tweedy sort, all weekly manicures and ruthless charity fundraising. The thought of meeting Mary's family raised a host of questions, not least whether he wanted to. But Si felt it would be unfair to voice such concerns. So he consented to the plan.

'Only,' he added, 'there's not much on football-wise this weekend...'

'I thought you had a friend who was some kind of star?'

'Yes, well, no... Actually, he's just on the edge of the big time... Hasn't quite made it yet.'

'Oh well, never mind. We can go down to stay with my parents on Saturday, then. That'll really give you a chance to get to know them.'

'Great,' said Si with a distinct lack of enthusiasm.

⚽ ⚽ ⚽

A loud man with ginger hair barged into the bar. 'Hey, Anne, gi' us a pint, will ya?'

'Ah, you noisy bugger, where've you been all my life then?' the barmaid flirted back.

Si looked up. Since the new barmaid started at The

Feathers, he'd never caught her name. Now he knew.

He recognised the other bloke. Declan, he was called. And despite twenty years of marinated living, he was still a good-looking man, if one ignored the puffy eyes and the web of burst capillaries spreading across his nose and cheeks. Anne apparently did, as she leaned over the bar to plant a playful kiss on his lips.

'Steady, Anne, I'm not half the man I used to be. If you keep that up, it won't just be my nose that's turning red...'

'You dirty old bugger. You just drink your pint and behave. If you're good, I'll talk to you again once I've served this gentleman. And that's more than you'll ever be...' Her smile belied her words.

'Anne, Anne, you're hard on me,' sighed Declan theatrically, and collapsed onto a barstool, brandishing his burnished pint glass like a god on the battlefield.

'Are you listening or not, eh?'

Si turned hurriedly back to Jimmy who sat opposite him, hunched over his beer at the small hopelessly stained wooden table. 'Yeah, course I am... Sorry, go on.'

Jimmy quickly got back into his stride. He'd been repeating the same ideas over and over for the last hour, torturing himself with his failure. Or at least what he thought was his failure. 'I just don't know, Si, I blew it. But they really didn't give me a proper chance. I mean, if they want me to show what I can do, I need more than a couple of minutes.'

'I know, you were unlucky. But you've got to pick yourself up and carry on. You're a great player, Jimmy, and if you stick at it, you'll make it. I'm sure you will. There'll be another chance. Who's to say you won't be on the bench again next weekend?'

'You reckon?' Jimmy looked up hopefully.

'Yeah, I reckon.' He watched enviously as Declan chatted away with Anne at the bar, unaware of the ambitions and cares which hung over the small table in the corner. Why couldn't his life be so carefree? How had he got himself into such a depressing situation? Was it all his own fault?

'Do you fancy another pint?'

'Yeah, I'll get them.' Why not have another? It might help. In any case he might get to overhear some of Declan and Anne's conversation. Some of their good humour might rub off...

'I'll chase mine with a Scotch,' said Jimmy. He didn't have to get back to Manchester for training at The Cliff until the day after tomorrow.

'Fine.' It was going to be a long night.

⚽ ⚽ ⚽

It had rained as they drove down to the country. Mary's windscreen wipers had counterpointed the conversation's more petulant rhythms. She'd been uptight since picking him up, partly because, Si guessed, they were running about two hours later than planned. He also suspected from Mary's behaviour that going home disturbed her natural balance.

Since meeting Mrs Cunningham, or Beatrice as she insisted on being called—such women should not have first names, Si decided—Si had perfectly understood his girlfriend's apprehension. After they'd dumped their bags in their rooms, at different ends of a long corridor separated by Mr and Mrs Cunningham's own room, they'd come downstairs for a drink in the chintzy 'drawing room'.

'You must be exhausted after that drive,' murmured Mr Cunningham sympathetically. 'How's about a drink?'

But just as Si was about to happily concur that he'd love a stiff one, Mrs Cunningham intervened. 'No, no. Not a drink. I know what they'd like... Tea.' And without waiting for an answer she exited briskly to prepare tea.

Mr Cunningham slunk back to his chair by the fire, shook his newspaper loudly and didn't look up. Nor, to Si's disappointment, did he mention the idea of a drink again.

They sat down to a beautifully presented dinner where

the flavour of the food was matched only by the blandness of the conversation—Mary and her mother talked non-stop to, about and over each other, virtually ignoring the two men. It would have been easier if there had been some wine.

After coffee, Mrs Cunningham suggested an early night. 'Bedtime. It's a big day tomorrow and, Mary darling, you need your beauty sleep... No, no protests. That's a good girl. You don't want Simon thinking you're a difficult girl, do you?' Mrs Cunningham threw a well-judged smile vaguely in Si's direction. 'Beware wrinkles, Mary, I can see a few already...'

'Mummy...'

'No excuses. Off you go, good night. See you in the morning.'

'Good night,' said Si as he followed Mary from the room. When they were safely out of earshot he asked, 'Is she always like that?'

'Like what?'

'Well, you know. Bossy.'

Mary paused for a moment before replying tartly. 'I don't know what you mean. My mother's not bossy and I think you've got a real nerve to say such a thing when you're staying in her house...'

'Calm down, calm down. Don't get upset. I didn't mean it nastily. I just... Well, it doesn't matter. Anyway, good night.' And at the top of the stairs he planted a chaste kiss on her rosy cheek and turned down the corridor away from her room.

⚽ ⚽ ⚽

The weather had improved when Si drew back the curtains and took in the view. Manicured fields and hedges stretched verdantly into the distance. The roll of the land invited participation.

At breakfast Si tried to draw Mary's father into

conversation, but he seemed distracted, looking nervously towards the door every few minutes. Mary's arrival didn't help much, although he shot her a thin smile of welcome.

Thankfully, Mary's humour had improved overnight. 'Where's mum?'

'In the garden, I think.'

'Oh.' At that moment Mrs Cunningham walked in. Her husband closed up like a clam and started reading the newspaper with an extraordinary intensity.

'John, I do think the least you could do is help. There I've been, out in the garden picking vegetables for your lunch and do you think to come and help me? Of course not.' Mrs Cunningham sighed theatrically and brushed back her immaculate, ceramic hair. She noticed her daughter and Si for the first time. 'Ah, the lazy bones. You've missed the best of the day, you know.'

'Mum!' protested Mary.

'Well, it's not too late to do something. After lunch we're going for a long walk. That'll blow away all those London cobwebs.'

'I thought we might just take it easy, stay in, go to the pub....'

'Nonsense. You can go to the pub this evening if you insist. But this afternoon, we are going for a walk.' And that was that. Mrs Cunningham moved on briskly. 'Morning, Simon, did you sleep well?'

This seemed more of an accusation than a question and Si answered carefully. 'Yes, very well thanks, Mrs Cunningham.'

'Beatrice, call me Beatrice,' she said coquettishly. Si noticed Mary look away and try to engage her mousy father in conversation.

'Oh sorry... Beatrice. I keep forgetting.'

Mrs Cunningham giggled childishly. 'Well, don't.' She fixed him with a look that made him squirm. 'So, Simon, we understand you're a journalist. But, apart from that, we don't know much about you. Mary has been very secretive. She's been rather unfair keeping you all to herself until now.' Si smiled in what he hoped seemed a friendly manner. 'So do you work for *The Daily Telegraph*?' she suggested with a hopeful look inviting affirmation. Si was not totally unprepared for this as he had noticed a copy of that newspaper sitting crisply folded on the breakfast table.

'No, *The Courier*,' he replied gently.

'*The Courier*?'

'*The Courier* ... It's a national daily...'

'Yes, yes. I know *The Courier*. Not that I read it.' Mrs Cunningham's flirtation had crystallised into hard disdain. 'What led you to work for a newspaper like that?'

'Well, it's a very good paper. I don't really see what's wrong with working for *The Courier*.'

'Of course there's nothing wrong. But it's a little unsound... politically. Isn't it? As far as I can see, it's determined to destroy England and all that we hold dear.'

Si looked to Mary for help with a half-smile.

But if she saw the irony in the contrast between her own opinion of *The Courier* as a downmarket bourgeois rag, and her mother's view of it as a subversive Trotskyite publication, she didn't show it.

Si felt sick. Mrs Cunningham's stony expression seemed to say, 'Go on, then. What have you got to say for yourself, young man?'

'No, I think you're wrong, Beatrice.'

Mrs Cunningham flinched.

Si couldn't think of anything else to say without risking rudeness.

Mrs Cunningham glared at him.

Si tried to assume a bland, nonchalant expression.

Eventually, Mary seemed to notice the developing atmosphere and, breaking off her desultory conversation with her father, intervened. 'Right, I'm taking Si off for a while. I want to show him the garden.'

'Yes, what a good idea,' clipped Mrs Cunningham. 'Lunch will be at one. See you're on time.'

They escaped into the fresh air. But even when they were alone Si couldn't think of much to say. Before he knew it, they were back at the house.

'Don't come any further in your wellies. Put them over there.'

Si meekly obeyed Mrs Cunningham's orders and took off his dirty wellies. He followed Mary indoors and collapsed with her before the fire.

Mrs Cunningham was the kind of woman one instinctively obeyed. Haughty, well-preserved and conscious of her looks, but with as much sex appeal as a Barbie doll, thought Si. As his hostess shooed him into a small room to remove his mud-stuccoed wellingtons, he wondered idly what she had been like thirty years before.

⚽ ⚽ ⚽

'This girlfriend of mine got married last week.'

'Oh yeah. Who?'

'You don't know her. Anyway, she told me about it. Sounded a riot. She left all the arrangements to the last minute and was up till three thirty in the morning writing out place cards and arranging flowers. She started out carefully placing them in vases and ended up chucking them in milk bottles in bundles.'

'Oh.'

'Anyway, the next morning she was at the hairdressers and was stitching her veil...'

'What?'

'Don't be thick. You know, what a veil is. To wear over your hair.'

Si realised he'd been ambushed and affected vagueness. 'Of course. People still do that?'

'Oh yes. At proper weddings.' The way Mary said 'proper' had an ominous ring to it. He resolved not to ask too many questions for fear of showing too much interest.

'So, she's sewing this veil on her lap and all the women

in the hairdressers want to know about her wedding. And several who have already been done insist on staying to see the veil tried on on top of the new hairdo, do you see?'

'Uh huh,' grunted Si in what he hoped was an uninterested tone.

'Then at the hotel they've booked, all the guests get stuck into the drinks before the Registry officials come along to marry them. So half are tipsy in the service, which is in the hotel dining room. And there's the Rolls Royce which circles the hotel twice just for the the hell of it, although all the guests are inside and can't see the bride arriving. Amazing, don't you think?'

'Yeah,' agreed Si although he was having trouble making sense of Mary's rambling. Her face was aglow. He realised that when she was at her most natural, she was not very pretty. Then he felt ashamed for harbouring such a superficial thought. 'Sounds like fun,' he lied guiltily.

'Doesn't it?' Mary paused on a smile.

This was becoming uncomfortable. 'What did you say your friend's name was?'

'Oh, she wasn't really a friend.'

'Huh? I thought...'

'I read about it in a magazine. They had all the pictures too and the costs and contact numbers for the catering companies. Everything you'd need to plan a wedding, really.'

'Oh.'

'I've still got it back at my flat. I'll show you it later if you'd like?'

'Right.' Si felt a burning desire for a pint, some male company and a good game of something sweaty and violent.

⚽ ⚽ ⚽

'Just occasionally, Si, I could do with a bit of romance, you know.'

Si looked blank. He wasn't sure what had brought on this outburst. One minute they'd been discussing how busy their lives were in London—or rather, how high-powered Mary's job was— then Si found himself under attack.

'Uuhh,' he gurgled. He looked around desperately for the waiter. He'd order another bottle of wine. That should distract Mary. But as he beckoned the waiter over, Mary launched her second scud.

'I suppose you think that romance is just the bit before sex... Don't you?'

The waiter obviously caught some of this and decided to stay clear. Ignoring Si's increasingly frantic gestures, he executed an impressive imitation of a turning oil tanker, curving slowly off his original trajectory and setting course for a distant table with a solicitous smile, although there was clearly no need for his services there.

Damn you. Si sucked in between clenched teeth.

'The least you could do is listen when I talk to you.'

Talk? Talk? You call this talking? But instead he said: 'No, you've got me wrong, if you think that. I'm a romantic at heart...'

Mary snorted. 'Romantic. Don't make me laugh. You see, that's the problem with you, Si, you don't have the first idea what you are. You lack self-knowledge. Know what I mean?'

Mary had calmed down and was speaking intensely with her I'm-only-telling-you-this-'cos-I-care look on her face. Si didn't know which of these two Marys irked him more. He let her go on. It clearly made her feel better, believing that she was imparting wisdom to an inferior being.

He stared miserably at his empty wine glass. The worst thing was, she was probably right. If he was honest with himself, he had very little idea who or why he was.

❀ ❀ ❀

'Gran?'

'Hello, my darling. What a nice surprise.'

'Are you all right? Why are you shouting?'

'Oh, sorry. The music's a bit loud. Hold on a minute.'

There was a clunk as Elspeth put the phone down, and Mary could just make out waves of dark orchestral sound crashing around the big rooms in her grandmother's house. She got a sudden urge to jump on a train and take a holiday in the country. If only. These days her time was not her own. It had been different when she was a student. Whenever things got tough at college, she'd take refuge at her grandmother's. In those days her sweet old grandfather had also been there. The recollection filled her with longing.

'That's better. Sorry about that. My hearing's not what it was and I sometimes get a bit carried away. It's such a crime to play Wagner at a low volume on the gramophone, don't you think?'

Mary laughed. Her grandmother sounded so earnest. 'Of course it is, Gran.'

'Oh, I'm so glad you agree. And you know those wonderful speakers your mother gave me really create a very loud noise.'

'Gran, you don't need to make excuses.'

'Oh, I wouldn't want to do that. No, I just don't want you thinking I've gone cuckoo or anything.'

Mary already felt cheered up. Elspeth had to be the best grandmother in the world; probably everyone thought that about their own, she realised. But hers was extra special. 'Gran?'

'Yes, dear? There I am prattling away and you clearly want to talk to me about something.'

'Well, kind of.'

'Go on, dear.'

'You know when you met Grandpa?' Mary could almost hear the pained intake of breath at the other end of the line. She pushed straight on. 'Well, did you know straightaway?'

'Know? Oh, I see what you mean.' The lustre in the old lady's voice had dimmed. 'Yes, I suppose I did. He was so dashing... Why do you ask? Have you met someone?' Elspeth perked up at the prospect.

'No. Well, I don't know. Maybe.'

'Oh, I see.' Elspeth waited diplomatically for her granddaughter to elaborate.

'There is someone but I just don't know where it's leading. Does that make sense?'

'Of course it does. Today, things must be so confusing.'

'I'm not sure it's *today,* Gran. I think it might be me.'

'Nonsense, child. It's not like you to be confused about such things. You're normally so clear-headed and confident.'

'I know. But I don't feel very confident at the moment.'

'Hmm. It's difficult to advise you, Mary, without having met the young man. What's his name?'

'Simon.'

'Oh, so it's the same one as before, then?' She sounded surprised.

'Of course it is. What do you think, Gran? I don't change my boyfriends weekly.'

'Oh well, one never knows. What with the permissive society and so forth. Sounds like quite a lot of fun, if you ask me. If I was your age, goodness knows what I'd get up to.'

'Gran,' Mary exclaimed, outraged.

'Tush, tush. Don't be such a prude. I was a young girl once. I know what goes through your mind when a handsome fellow's about...'

'Gran, you're terrible. There's me phoning to ask for some wise guidance and all I get is encouragement to sleep around.'

'Well, sometimes sex is the best cure for unrequited love.'

'I never said it was unrequited,' Mary bridled.

'Oh, in that case... What's the problem, dear? Just carry

on working your charms and he'll be sure to fall into your net sooner or later. Men are rather stupid at times. You have to be patient, and don't let him see you're particularly bothered about whether or not he responds.'

'I suppose you're right.' Had nothing changed? sighed Mary.

'Of course I am. Don't forget, I've been at this for far longer than you have.' She giggled mischievously, and Mary joined in despite herself.

'Now, much as I love talking to my favourite granddaughter, I must go and turn off the oven. I've got a cake baking. It's to send to your mother,' Elspeth continued, apparently thinking out loud. 'Sometimes I wonder where I went wrong with Beatrice; she can't cook to save her life, and spends all her time at the hairdresser or reading trashy novels. Ah well, no peace for the wicked...' Then she recalled she was on the phone to her granddaughter. 'So, goodbye my dear. I hope you'll ring me again soon.'

'I will. Bye, Gran.'

'And don't go worrying about Simon. I'm sure it'll all work out just fine. Goodbye.' The line went dead.

❀ ❀ ❀

Mary gave Si a video camera for his birthday.

'This is way OTT,' protested Si when he'd finished unwrapping the shiny designer paper: complex asymmetrical patterns just discovered on the tomb walls of an ancient civilisation.

'Don't be silly. It's not every day you're twenty-eight. Now aren't you going to say thank you? I reckon I deserve at least a passionate peck.'

Embarrassed by his churlish reaction, but still astounded by the value of the present, Si leaned across the marble table top and pulled her face gently towards him. He kissed her carefully, self-consciously, with gratitude.

Mary pushed her lips against his greedily, almost as if

she wanted to extract every last bit of passion as recompense for the camera.

A sense of duty more than inspiration moved Si to pick up the camera and christen it with some footage of Mary. He filmed her eating an elaborate ice-cream, smiling attractively through the Dreamboat Surprise which kept threatening to escape through her parted lips and run down onto her chin. The scene was so fifties that Si wondered if it would come out in hand-tinted Technicolor.

'Happy birthday, darling,' she purred, and, leaning towards the camera's silent, dispassionate eye, she puckered her lips into a passable imitation of a film diva. 'Mwwa!'

Si stopped filming and, feeling the familiar physical surge, he laid the camera carefully on the table.

'What do you say? Shall we get the bill and go?'

Mary treated him to one of her rare seductive looks. 'Darling, I thought you'd never ask.'

⚽ ⚽ ⚽

Greta Andrews lived in a big Georgian terrace house in Westbourne Park Road with her husband Michael. She'd first come to London in the early eighties to visit her older brother Eamon. She'd planned to spend the summer, but had ended up marrying a handsome Englishman whom she'd met in Sainsbury's.

'You can't marry him,' Eamon had protested. 'He's a Prod and an Englishman.'

'So what? I thought you were always telling me that the English weren't so bad after all, that they had lots of money and you were happy to take it off them.'

'Oh sweet Jesus. That's different.'

'Is it?'

Eamon furrowed his brow. 'What'll your mother say?'

'I don't care what she says. What's she ever done for me? And since when have you cared what she thinks about anything? Listen, Eamon, I'm marrying Michael and that's that. If you want, you can come to the wedding. But if not, I don't care.'

They got married in the Finchley registry office in October and had the wedding lunch at Eamon's pub. There was a good turnout, although neither set of parents came.

After the couple had left, Eamon and his friends drunkenly agreed that Michael was a good man...for an Englishman.

When the Sleeper turned up on Greta's doorstep she set down the baby and looked him up and down. 'Come in. Eamon told me you'd be coming about now.'

The Sleeper peered past her down the elegant hallway and wondered if Eamon had told the truth when he said the room wouldn't cost much. The house looked posher than any he'd ever been in.

Greta sat him down at a scrubbed pine kitchen table which had a view over the garden. 'Coffee?'

'Aye, thanks. Two sugars, please.'

'They'll rot your teeth.'

'That's what my ma always says.'

'She's right and you should listen to her.'

He thought about what Eamon had told him of Greta's stormy relationship with her mother, but decided not to say anything. Short of anything else to say and not wanting to broach the subject of the room for rent until she did, he asked her how she'd got her name.

Greta laughed and the Sleeper noticed for the first time how attractive she was. She had some of Eamon's better features like the strong jaw and piercing green eyes, but it all fitted together better in her.

'Not very Gaelic, is it?' She raised an eyebrow coquettishly, and he smiled, foolishly tongue-tied. 'Well, Anderson is my husband's name, of course, and he's as English as they come. You'll meet him later, but he's at work now. He works in the City, you know.'

'Oh.' The Sleeper didn't know, and in fact he wasn't sure what people who worked in the City were like. He'd not met any in West Hampstead at Mrs Donnelley's. Presumably, he'd be one of those short-haired, well-scrubbed, tall, public school types in pin-stripes. He wondered how a girl like Greta had fallen for such a man, the antithesis of her working class Irish origins.

'Greta's another story. My mother wanted to call me Mary if I was a girl. After her mother. But my father never got on with my grandmother, too religious, he always said; and so he refused point blank. They almost split up over what to call me. The arguments raged for nine months and they were both hoping that I'd be a boy to solve the problem. I'd have been James then. You see, my father had literary pretensions, and even when I turned out a girl he wanted me to be a writer.'

The Sleeper stared, but she seemed not to notice.

'Anyway, finally, a week before I arrived, my parents went to the cinema to see a film. It must have been a rerun because it was a Greta Garbo film... *Blue Angel,* I think they said. Whatever, they both loved it so much that they agreed on the spot that if I was a girl I'd be called Greta. So there you are.' She threw back her head and laughed again.

He joined in without really knowing why.

That evening he told Mrs Donnelley that he was moving the next day.

'So soon?' she was clearly surprised.

'Aye, I've found a great place. Really posh and you know what, Mrs Donnelley, it's even cheaper than here.'

Mrs Donnelley sniffed and carried on making the tea. 'Well, I've never heard you complain before.'

'No complaints, Mrs Donnelley. It's just I think I've landed on my feet.'

'Pride comes before a fall...'

He laughed. It would be good to exchange fiery old Mrs Donnelley with her laddered tights and greasy teas for the refinement of Greta Anderson's kitchen. If he was going to have to wait around—and as far as he could make out, despite several false alarms in Central London recently, there seemed little likelihood of a break in the cease-fire for the time-being—then he might as well do it in style. Blend into the community, they'd told him. Well that was what he was about to do. To be honest, and he knew it was a terrible thought, he kind of hoped the cease-fire would hold.

⚽ ⚽ ⚽

Si wrapped his overcoat round him as tightly as it would go. It was bitterly cold. Beside him, Mary whinged about the ordeal he was putting her through. 'This is stupid... Si, I'm freezing... How much longer?'

Si suppressed his irritation. After all, it had been his mistake to bring her to the match. 'Another five minutes, my love.'

The capacity Old Trafford crowd roared as Cantona ghosted into space, but he couldn't quite get on the end of a looping Giggs cross.

Mary seemed impervious to the excitement of the sixth round FA Cup tie. 'Then can we go?'

'Well, that'll be half time and then there's the second half...'

'What d'you mean, second half? Are you telling me there's more?'

'Well, of course there is. Soccer matches are divided into two equal halves each lasting forty-five minutes...'

'Si,' she whimpered, 'you're saying that the second half is as long as the first half?'

'Yes, of course it is. That's why it's called a half.'

'Oh, I can't take it much more. I'm so cold. And it's not as if anything has happened. It's so boring.'

Si couldn't disagree with this last point. It had been a dull first half, apart from a disallowed Southampton goal, which had looked perfectly okay to him. Andy Cole had also been pulled down in the five yard box, and United should have had a penalty; but otherwise it had been pretty routine stuff.

But Si didn't mind too much. He wasn't here for United or for Southampton. He was here to cheer on his friend. And he'd been warmed to the cockles by the few touches Jimmy had made. In his first full start for Manchester United he was performing well. Since signing for the biggest club in Britain, Jimmy had gone from strength to strength. Now he was competing for a regular first team place and, although he owed his start tonight to the absence through injury of Lee Sharpe, he seemed to be capitalizing on his chances.

'I'll tell you what... You try and enjoy the match and then I'll treat you to the best dinner we can find in the poshest restaurant in Manchester. How's about that?'

Mary perked up a bit. It had taken some persuading to get her to come up to Manchester for the match; especially mid-week. She wasn't particularly enamoured of the north. Or rather her image of it, as she'd never been to Lancashire before. Si had been forced to resort to bribes such as a night in a smart hotel, and turning the trip into a mini holiday by taking a half day off either side of the game—not easy given that Dougy was breathing down his neck these days. But the decisive factor seemed to have been an article in Cosmopolitan magazine which described Manchester's clubbing nightlife and pronounced the city as the coolest in Europe—this had forced Mary to make a reassessment and agree to the visit.

Mary was nothing if not predictable in her appreciation of what she considered appropriate romantic behaviour by a suitor. Si's dinner proposal had touched the right button. 'Oh all right. You're a real sweet talker, aren't you?' She put her mittened hand in Si's and gave it a squeeze. 'It'd help if I knew which one was Jimmy; then I could cheer him on when he got the ball.'

'Oh, I'm sorry; I assumed you knew. He's the number 22, there, see?'

'In the red?'

'Yes, in the red.'

'If Manchester are in the red, then who's in the yellow?'
'I told you before... Southampton.'
'Ahh.' Mary fell silent for a minute and made a determined effort to follow the game. 'Why is Jimmy number twenty two if there are only eleven players in the team?'
'Because that's his squad number...' Before Mary could ask the obvious, Si explained. 'You see there are more than eleven in the squad and each player has his own number.' He was about to expand that it had not always been so, when an expectant rumble came from the crowd.
Giggs wove past one Southampton player and then knocked it through the legs of another before cutting inside towards the penalty box just beneath where they sat. He looked up and effortlessly lobbed the ball into the box towards Cantona. Three Southampton players crowded the Frenchman off the ball and no other United player was in position to convert the opportunity.
The ball was cleared, but only as far as Jimmy, who was arriving a bit late. He controlled the bouncing ball with his instep, and seemed to search desperately for a United player to pass to. Finding no-one in space, he punted the ball goalwards. It looked more like desperation than judgment, but Jimmy's shot sailed over the goalkeeper, who was five yards off his line. The result looked spectacular.
Si leapt to his feet along with forty thousand others. The noise was deafening.
Looking slightly bewildered, Jimmy eventually emerged from under the heap of ecstatic, red-shirted team-mates, who had buried him as they celebrated the goal. He pulled himself to his feet and, grinning broadly, trotted back to the half-way line. Like everybody else in the stadium, he knew that one goal would probably be enough to put United through to the semi-finals. One step away from Wembley.
Si shouted himself hoarse with delight, and his pleasure was doubled when he noticed Mary beside him, also on her feet, arms raised and cheering for all she was worth.

'That was Jimmy, wasn't it?' she shouted above the din.

'Yeah,' grinned Si, 'that was Jimmy.'

⚽ ⚽ ⚽

The machine clicked on as Si was going out of the door. He paused with his key in the lock.

'Hi, are you there? Darling? No, okay, just to say that I got your message about tonight, but I'm still at work and I'm going to be here for another couple of hours at least. So it's unlikely that I'll manage to join you at the pub. I'll ring later and try to catch you before you go to bed. Big kiss… Mwa!'

The machine emitted a long beep and stopped. Si emerged from his trance. Suddenly resolute, he stepped through the door and slipped the catch behind him.

He soon shrugged off the disappointment, which threatened to overshadow his evening. Jimmy was back on a rare visit from Manchester. Since he'd made the first team squad, he was rarely able to get more than one day off at a time, which ruled out overnight trips to London. Of course they talked on the phone. More than most men, Si imagined. But their friendship had always involved a significant dollop of mutual support and reassurance. They'd grown close over time, and their friendship was more honest and openly affectionate than most male friendships. Partly because of this, he sometimes worried that Mary might misinterpret his relationship with Jimmy—she revelled in intrigue and looked for hidden meaning where the truth was self-evident. As a result, Si had become anxious about introducing the two key people in his life.

Mary's weakness for fantasy was such that she swallowed the conspiracy theories in the Sunday newspapers hook, line and sinker. She still half-believed that Elvis, Marilyn Monroe and Jim Morrison were living on a paradise island somewhere. And she was at her most passionate when she got onto the subject of alien abductions.

Si had been determined to make the evening a success. He'd planned it carefully—a drink at The Feathers, where Jimmy would probably be on good form, relaxed in familiar territory. After that he'd decided to play it by ear, but on the assumption that the evening would be going fine, he'd booked dinner at a little French restaurant round the corner—to show Mary that although Jimmy was a footballer, he knew how to use a knife and fork and could drink wine as well as beer.

He hadn't worried too much about how Jimmy would find Mary. For a start his friend would take longer than one evening to make up his mind, and his initial appraisal would depend on how Mary looked; on that score, at least, Si knew she would impress.

Si strode along the street and fought back the feeling of disgust that threatened to overwhelm him; not with Mary or even with her obsessional, morally suspect job, and certainly not with Jimmy. The disgust, tempered with a splash of shame, was with himself. How had he been so stupid to make such elaborate plans for the evening? And what had he been thinking of when he'd thought of pandering to Mary's snobbism at Jimmy's expense? Why should he worry what she thought of Jimmy?

Jimmy was his mate and had done nothing to deserve such shoddy treatment. What would Jimmy say if he ever found out? He blushed at the thought. Thank God Mary had called off, reflected Si. Just for once, it had been a good thing.

As Si pushed through the crowded bar towards where he knew Jimmy would be sitting, he realised he was still carrying the video camera. He sighed. Ever since his birthday a fortnight before, Mary had insisted that he carry the camera with him whenever he met her. He'd begun to suspect that the gift had an ulterior motive which had more to do with Mary's vanity than with his own pleasure. But he'd refrained from voicing this thought, and accepted Mary's mantra good-naturedly: 'You must film at every opportunity for the next few weeks to make a full and balanced record of your life aged twenty-eight. Your family and grandchildren will thank you for it,' she offered regularly by way of explanation.

Si was not so sure. How would anyone be able to make much sense of his life aged twenty-eight? A fragmented series of events lacking any overall direction or purpose, and only linked by the linear cord of work routines, football and habitual visits to the pub. Perhaps the video footage had some intrinsic worth—it might show how rudderless people could become in a free society. Even so, Si was far from convinced.

But he couldn't be bothered to argue with them, despite his own unhappy experience of family videos: dull evenings during the Christmas holidays trying to set up the ancient machinery, and then embarrassing silences when neither of his parents could remember the name of the person who'd just featured in the last four minutes of flickering over-exposed film. But, he reflected, the irritation of his childhood had faded into a dull ache, and he found the thought of resistance harder than that of inflicting a similar trial on his own offspring. And, God help them, on his offspring's offspring. Would it never stop?

So, when meeting Mary he obliged her by lugging along the camera. It kept her quiet. He'd not gone so far as to take the camera to work, and Mary had not been crass enough to insist on it. If she did... Well, he didn't know what he'd do. But the thought of toting the ugly black Japanese box around at *The Courier* made him wince. Imagine what his colleagues would say. Even Bill might laugh at his expense; and that was something Si could ill-afford, the way things were going. He'd have to pretend he was making a fly-on-the-wall documentary for Channel 4.

Well, he told himself just before reaching the end of the bar, now that I've got it here and Jimmy's not yet arrived, I might as well use it. And flicking the switch, he filmed The Feathers regulars, starting of course with Brenda behind the bar, who grinned sheepishly and then ham-acted the pulling of a pint as if for a TV advert. Zooming in on her face, Si surprised himself with the realisation that she was really not that plain after all. In fact, Brenda was seriously attractive when she smiled. Certainly, much better-looking than Anne, her new colleague.

Jimmy arrived ten minutes later. He ignored Brenda, who'd been chatting to Si. She turned away and began to serve another customer. Si was sensitive enough not to comment.

'Hey, Jimmy mate, I'd almost given up on you.' Si gave Jimmy their usual half-embrace.

'Yeah, sorry. You know how the traffic is. I got caught up round High Street Ken.'

'What were you doing over there? Bit out of the way isn't it?'

'Yeah.' Jimmy looked embarrassed.

'So?'

'Well, I had to meet this journalist for an interview.'

Si raised an eyebrow. 'Great. So you really are becoming famous now, aren't you?'

Jimmy still looked uncomfortable. 'Yeah, I guess. But... I know it sounds silly... But I'd always hoped that if I did make the big time, I'd give my first proper interview to you. Trouble was, I didn't really have much choice.'

'No worries, it's just great to see you.'

'You sure you don't mind? You see, the club told me that this guy wanted to interview me next time I was in London, and like they thought it was a good idea—to mark my arrival you see—and I wasn't really able to do anything about it... Sorry.'

Si was touched and slightly surprised by Jimmy's concern. 'Listen, mate. That's great, but you don't need to worry. I'm not that type of journalist anyway. I don't normally do sports interviews, and I'd be unlikely to be able to persuade my editor to run a feature piece on you yet. Not that you're not becoming famous enough; but the footballing world is a speciality in itself, and I'm not a soccer journalist.' Si realised he was gushing and should have just thanked Jimmy for the thought and left it at that. It was bizarre that they should be so uptight in each other's company after such a short separation.

'Right. Well, that's all right, then.'

'Yeah.' Si tried to lighten the mood. 'Pint? I bet you're gagging after dealing with that hack.'

'Yeah. He really was a wanker. Kept asking me about my childhood, as if that had anything to do with anything. Then he wanted to know what I thought of United and got upset when I wouldn't say anything bad about the Boss or any of the other guys... I mean, what does he expect? I've only just started to establish myself and he wants me to bite the hand that feeds me. He didn't even ask me about that Southampton goal. What a git!'

Si understood why that goal had extra significance for Jimmy. Every national tabloid had run it as the back page headline story with photos of Jimmy in the act of beating the keeper. Even *The Courier* had given the story prominence under the headline SWEENEY'S BIG NIGHT! Jimmy had arrived.

They both laughed and began to relax. Brenda put two pints on the bar.

'Hi, Jimmy. Aren't you going to say hello or have you become too famous for your old friends?'

'Hi, Brenda. How you doing?' Jimmy replied unenthusiastically.

Si thought better of joining in the conversation. The communication between the two seemed to have little to do with the words being spoken. Fortunately, Brenda soon seemed placated.

'So, Si, aren't you going to video Jimmy's triumphant return, since you've already done the rest of us?'

Si looked puzzled for a moment, then realised she was referring to the video camera beneath his stool.

'Oh yeah, right. You don't mind, do you?' he asked

Jimmy, feeling foolish.

'No, sure, go ahead. I love the cameras... You know me! Of course, you'll have to talk to the club before selling it, you know.' Jimmy seemed half-serious, but Si decided it was a joke and laughed.

He shot some stilted footage of his friend drinking a pint and looking embarrassed. Then he filmed Jimmy ostentatiously waving a fifty pound note about as he got another round in and things got better. Si left the camera on during an increasingly raucous conversation. Jimmy relaxed when Si began to imitate a famous soccer TV pundit who always said the same things. Then he did a passable imitation of a *Match of the Day* interviewer. Jimmy played a camped-up version of himself.

When Si got home later that night, half-cut and desperate for sleep, he stuffed the camera in a cupboard. It was a long time before he thought to get it out again.

The seasons in London met seamlessly that year, and it was impossible to pinpoint when spring overcame winter. February had been chilly but bright; March's light breezes promised heat; and April, after a wet start, reawakened somnolent Londoners with balmy caresses. But the spring had definitely arrived by mid-month when it blossomed and progressed triumphantly, adorned with garlands of flowers and perfumed with the musk of a thousand, freshly-mown lawns.

The transition between seasons generated an excitement perfectly in tune with Jimmy's own mood. His first season at Manchester United was approaching a dramatic finale. His bank account had been transformed by United's Midas touch and he now drove a red Ferrari; he never lacked for attractive female company on his nights off in Manchester, and he was about to buy his first house complete with swimming pool, sauna and gym; and importantly for

Jimmy, Si had been suitably impressed by the photos in the estate agent's brochure.

As for his professional ambitions, Jimmy found himself part of a club which was on course to win the Double Double; and if it achieved this Herculean task, it would be the first time in the long history of English football that a club had done the Double twice (United having won both the League and Cup competitions simultaneously for the first time two seasons earlier). Jimmy had to keep pinching himself to make sure he wasn't dreaming. He now had a unique chance to fulfil his dream of making sporting history. United had reached the FA Cup Semi Final and were running neck and neck in the Premiership with their rivals Newcastle. The last few weeks of the season promised to be nail-bitingly tense.

Si was also excited about the imminent arrival of summer. But the upbeat weather didn't reflect his emotional state. A windswept and rainy autumn afternoon would have better suited a growing sense of confusion about the course his life was taking. He recognised the symptoms of dissatisfaction and saw that the cancer threatened to spread to healthy parts of his existence. But it was difficult to envisage, let alone take, the necessary steps to cut it out and make a fresh start.

⚽ ⚽ ⚽

It wasn't only Jimmy's soccer that was going well.

'Smoke on the waaaa-ta... fire in the sky...' Jimmy hit the chords hard as he walked the bar chords up and down the neck of his purple-lacquered instrument. 'Ba, ba, baaaa... Ba, ba, ba ba... Ba, ba, baaaa... Ba, ba....' he shouted as he strummed the riff at the heart of the rock classic.

He'd sneered ten years ago when other boys had claimed they could play this song. But the pleasure he felt as he generated the just-about-recognisable music swept away such memories.

After three months of painful practice, Jimmy was beginning to make progress. He'd told nobody that he'd bought an electric guitar and amplifier, and he was determined to keep it a secret until he became good enough to do his first gig. He would be the new Billy Bragg or Bruce Springsteen. He was going to play a raw, folky but loud and energetic rock. He'd appear on *Top Of The Pops* when his first single went triple platinum in the first week of its release; he'd got it all planned. The football was getting in his way a bit, and he wasn't able to practise as much as he would have liked. But still he was making progress and he reckoned it wouldn't be long now. But first he had to learn some new open chords.

Learning to shape bar chords on E had been an excruciatingly painful process—he'd had cramp in his fingers for hours afterwards; difficult to hide in training at times. But as a result he could now play many more songs than before. Jimmy had read that the real secret was learning to move effortlessly between a series of complex open chords. The mysteries of the suspended and diminished lay before him, and although he had no idea why they had these names, he was totally aware that strummed in a smooth sequence they sounded awesome.

He looked back at his chord book and started to contort his fingers into an unnatural claw. The trick was managing to put enough pressure on the strings once you'd tied your fingers in knots. One last tug on the second finger of his left finger and... Da naaa! An open B7.

'God, that hurt.' Jimmy expelled a satisfied moan, and after exercising his aching fingers, he began again.

⚽ ⚽ ⚽

'You ever heard of Jack Derrida?'

The man with too much blond hair answered confidently. 'Yeah... He was in that movie with Marilyn, wasn't he? Yeah, I remember him.'

Although Si didn't know who Derrida was, he was pretty certain he wasn't a film star. He also knew he had to find out if he was to make any sense of his editor's instructions. His job might even depend on it. How had Dougy put it as he stared out of the huge window in his office? 'Make your Diary like Derrida... You know, Jack Derrida.' Si had nodded, not daring to ask what his boss was on about. Now six hours later he was at a party and desperate to find out who Derrida was. It might be the key to success at *The Courier*.

'No, I don't think so,' replied Si. It was time to leave.

'Yeah, he was. Swear to God...'

Si paused and looked at the surfer. He knew he was a surfer because he'd told him so.

'Hi, my name's Ricky.'

'Oh. Right. I'm Si.'

'Far out, Si. I'm a surfer. What d'you do?'

How could anyone in their right mind describe their profession as being a surfer? Jealousy mixed with incredulity as Si reeled off his standard reply about journalism.

Now after thirty seconds of desultory conversation, Si was tired of his new acquaintance. The whole party seemed to be having a good time. Apart from him. And where was Jimmy?

Perhaps he'd lost the ability to enjoy himself. To let his hair down. Before changing newspapers it had never been a problem. But then he'd taken on a great deal of responsibility with the Diary. Perhaps that was inhibiting him, he wondered, but not really caring whether it was. He just wanted to go. And why did he always end up at such dreadful parties where he hardly knew anyone, and those he did know he didn't like? All these parties seemed the same. Uniformly dreadful, whether they were celeb bashes he had to cover for the Diary or just normal parties held by friends of friends; in this case a friend of a friend of a friend. Si wondered if he was a misanthrope. Then it struck him that perhaps Derrida was a misanthrope and that's what Dougy had been on about? Whatever, it was time to go.

'See you, Ricky.'

'Later…' smiled Ricky, slapping his shoulder. But then the blond boy seemed to have a flash of intuition. 'God, man. What am I saying? You can't split yet.'

'Why not?'

'Hey, we haven't even had a beer. Come on, let's grab a couple and check out the scene. What do you say?'

'It's late, I'm tired…'

'Oh man, are you serious? It's Saturday night. Tomorrow's just sleep time. Don't poop on me, man.'

'I've no intention of pooping. Just going…'

But Si's protests were smothered as Ricky thrust an open bottle of Mexican lager into his hand. Reluctantly, he followed the American away from the door and towards the centre of the party. A tall man sporting a multi-coloured bow tie crossed his path.

'Hey, guys. How's it going? Ricky, are you looking after our friend here?'

'Yeah, we were just going to check out what's doing through there.' He pointed to a darkened room into which Si had not yet ventured.

'Great, great…' He raised an eyebrow. After a small pause during which he looked at Ricky expectantly, the bow tie asked, 'So, Ricky, aren't you going to introduce me to your new friend?'

'Sure. This is Si. Si, this is Richard,' said Ricky with mock formality.

Richard's face lit up. 'Si, it's a pleasure to meet you. Well, we can't stand here gossiping, can we? There's a party to run. See you later, I hope. Behave yourselves.' Richard swung off into the throng.

'Who's he?' Si asked.

'Oh, that's Richard. Your host.' Ricky whispered, raising his eyebrows. 'Come on. There was some good grass in here earlier. Let's see if there's any left.' And he disappeared into the murky den.

⚽ ⚽ ⚽

'Who *is* that guy with the moustache?' The raven-haired girl in the latex dress spoke with a faint South African accent.

'I don't know. Never seen him before. Presumably he's a friend of Richard's. The way he's greeting people, he clearly knows everyone.'

'Not me. You know Richard?'

'No,' admitted Si. 'But I met him earlier.'

'Gay, isn't he? Perhaps the moustache belongs to him?'

Si surveyed the flat's decor and had to agree that the South African girl might be right.

'You gay too?'

'No. I told you, I don't know Richard.' Si realised he might sound over-defensive, but this girl was irritating him. 'Who are you, anyway?'

The latex girl ignored the question. 'There's no need to make excuses for yourself.' She smiled sweetly through blood-red lipstick, which clashed with her hair.

'I wasn't...'

'You should stand up for yourself a bit more. Don't let people trample all over you... He's only greeting everyone to make everyone think he's at the centre of things. I bet he's faking it and doesn't know any more people than I do... Or you, for a matter of fact,' she added disdainfully.

'Hold on, I know some people here.'

'Yeah? Like who?'

'Well, there's my friend Jimmy for starters, he's a famous footballer... Or will be one day.'

'Uh huh, and where's he, then? The famous Jimmy?'

Si looked around, but Jimmy had vanished long ago. Damn you, Jimmy. Pathetically, he was forced to admit that he couldn't see his friend.

'Anyone else?'

'Yes, actually... Ricky.'

'Ricky?'

Si felt foolish. This was a stupid conversation. But he

didn't know how to get out of it. And heaven knows where the American had got to. One minute they'd been chatting and sharing a joint, the next he'd gone. Si realised that meeting Ricky had livened up an otherwise moribund evening.

'Ricky who?' the latex girl insisted.

Si wondered what her reaction would be if he answered Ricky the Surfer. Common sense told him it probably wouldn't help. He wished the earth would swallow him up. His earlier instinct had been correct. Dead on. He should have left when the going was just boring. But the atmosphere had changed and was becoming hostile.

'Listen, it's been a pleasure, you know, brief but entertaining... I must go, bye.' And he turned back towards the front door. The sooner he was out in the fresh air, the better. How he hated parties; especially parties where he knew no-one. And this was rapidly becoming one of the worst—a Party From Hell.

He'd only gone because someone from work had said it would be full of media types and good for contact-making—but he didn't recognise anyone. Even the guy from *The Courier* hadn't bothered to turn up. More importantly, nor had Mary, despite promising that she'd get out of the office at a reasonable hour and meet him here. Jimmy had come along, but had stayed only long enough to meet a vampy blonde. If it hadn't been for his chance meeting with Ricky, Si also would have left hours ago.

'Hey, hey, no need to run off. I was enjoying your company.'

Why was it that strangers seemed to value his company when he'd lost interest in theirs? Clearly, a character defect he should sort out. Probably something to do with his mother... Si decided to be tough. 'Well, perhaps I'm not keen on being enjoyed.'

'Sure you are. You're just been prissy. Belt up. What's your name anyway?'

'Si.'

'Well, hello Si, I'm Lou. Pleased to meet you.' And grabbing his hand she shook it vigorously. Then when Si pulled away she swept back her hair and cackled away at her own joke. 'Come on, Si, see the funny side...' Her accent was becoming stronger.

'Yeah, hilarious. See you.'

'Good idea, Si. I've had enough of this party too. Terrible. Let's go.' Before Si could protest she pushed him out the door and followed. They descended the dark staircase in silence.

On the street, as Si prepared to break off and find his way home, Lou grabbed his arm. 'Where you going, Si? Another party? A rave?'

'No, just home. I'm tired.'

'Come on, Si, you don't look the party-killer type to me. I've got an idea, let's go find a drink.'

'At this time? It's three thirty, nothing's open.' What would Mary say? he wondered. Stuff what Mary would say. If she'd cared so much, she would have turned up.

'Ya, I know a little after hours place not far from here... Taxi!' she screamed waving frantically at a passing cab. Si's protests started to lose conviction and were overruled.

Settled in the back of the cab, Lou pushed back the weight of hair in what Si came to recognise as an habitual gesture. 'Relax, Si. You never know, you might enjoy yourself.' She cackled again loudly, and rolled against him as the black cab swung round in a U-turn and headed off into the London night.

Enjoy himself... If he was honest, that was something he hadn't done properly for a long time.

⚽ ⚽ ⚽

They entered the bar through an anonymous looking doorway off the King's Road. A ferocious-looking bouncer glowered at Si before recognising Lou. 'Hey, babe, how's it going?'

'Great, man, just great,' she answered, pulling Si after her down the stairs. They emerged into a wide area which must once have been a cellar. The whitewashed walls were hung with damask and richly embroidered draperies. Soft jazz smooched over the little round tables and long divans on which lugubrious youths wearing velvet reclined.

A pall of cigarette smoke hung in the air, making Si's eyes water. He needed a drink. It was the only way he could deal with his phobia of smoky rooms. There was nothing worse than a reformed smoker, he knew that and tried never to complain. But sometimes it wasn't easy.

Lou was already weaving her way through the tiny space towards the long wooden bar. Si followed. A few eyes trailed his progress but soon returned to their own immediate surroundings.

A tall boy, sprawled on a threadbare sofa, rolled a joint on a dog-eared copy of *Vogue*. His two companions, one dressed in red and the other in yellow leather trousers, watched as intently as vultures. The tall boy looked up as Si passed, carefully steadying his magazine, concerned that his artwork would be disturbed. 'Careful, man,' he muttered but Si had already reached the bar. The boy returned to his task with renewed intensity.

'What is this place?'

'Oh, just a dive I hang out in. Great, innit?'

Si put on his I'm-a-man-of-the-world look, and nodded slightly. 'Yeah, fine. I've seen worse.'

But Lou wasn't listening. 'Two beers,' she told the barman, who was wearing a rubber tee shirt. 'Cool shirt, Todd.' Si felt distinctly under-dressed in his smart-casuals.

'Yeah, you like it?' Todd seemed pleased. 'I like your outfit too.'

Clearly a club for fetishists, groaned Si inwardly.

Todd stuck two slices of lime in the top of the beer bottles and placed them on the bar in front of Lou.

'D'you have any money?' she demanded.

'Yeah, sure. How much?'

'That's a tenner, mate...'

Si thought better of challenging the exorbitant price and handed over the note. 'Cheers.' Lou sucked her lime and then sipped her beer with an expert air.

Si wondered what he was doing here with this weird stranger. He wasn't even sure he liked her. Distracted, he remembered something that had been lurking in a dark corner of his mind. 'Do you know who Derrida is?'

'No, never heard of him. Is he a rock star?'

'No, I don't think so.'

'Why do you ask?'

'Oh, no reason... Listen, Lou, why did you insist on bringing me here?'

'To loosen you up a bit. You clearly needed it a bit. I bet you never take risks or live dangerously. Come on. Admit it. You don't, do you? You're such a poncey, nineties child, aren't you?'

Her arrogance irritated him. 'This is stupid. What do you want me to say? That I jump off high buildings from a piece of elastic for kicks?'

'No, you prick. That's not what I mean. I might have known that that'd be your kind of definition of danger... Good grief. Bungee jumping. Pathetic.'

'Well, if I'm to be the object of your scorn, I'd rather not be, if you don't mind...'

But Lou completely ignored his attempt to leave. She just laughed at his pomposity and hurt expression. 'Stop being such a jerk. I mean real risk. Not artificial, safety-standardised sport. I mean, have you ever broken the law just for the hell of it?'

'No, I don't think so.'

'What about stealing a chocolate bar from a shop?'

'Yeah, maybe once.' Si was dismayed to find himself playing Lou's game.

'Good, that's better. Maybe I didn't get you wrong after all.'

'What do you mean?'

'So how about something really daring? Have you ever killed someone?'

'Sorry?'

'You heard me. Killed someone. Another human being.'

'You're sick. Of course I haven't.'

Lou took his hand and raised it to her lips theatrically. 'Good. Nor have I. But maybe one day...'

'Listen, Lou, it's been nice, but I really think I should be off...'

'Si, before you go, let me ask you one more question. Okay?' Reluctantly he agreed.

'Have you ever slept with a stranger? Someone you'd only just met, without knowing anything about her? Or, Si, would it be *him*? Only joking, of course it would be her. But seriously, have you slept with someone while only knowing her first name? Have you?'

Si hesitated. Despite himself Lou's intense gaze and soft-voiced provocation was getting to him. 'No. I haven't.'

Lou smiled slyly, and Si noticed a small mole on her cheek for the first time. The deformity was indefinably sexual.

'Would you like to?'

Si stayed silent but couldn't help hoping that this time Lou wasn't teasing him.

'Of course you would. What hot-blooded male wouldn't? But you know that's a real risk these days... Aids and all that. Would you be prepared to take the risk...with me?' Lou prompted. 'No protection?'

Si refused to be drawn. 'Come on, Si, what d'you say? I won't tell you whether I'm clear before, but I promise to after. You can't say fairer than that.'

Si wanted to leave but the excitement dancing in Lou's dark eyes was infectious and he found it impossible to move away. 'Si, you're being shy. Don't be. Go on, just for you I'll make it easy. I'll let you use a condom. Maximum protection, after all. Now, are you prepared to take the risk? Are you?'

'Jesus, Lou, you're not being fair…'
'Fair? Whoever said I should be fair? Grow up, Si baby. Life's not fair. I reckon I'm being about as fair as you'll get. I'm not even asking the difficult questions, like whether you're married or you've got a girlfriend.'
'Why not?'
'Why should I? It's none of my business. Now I'm about to finish my beer and then I reckon I'll head home. If you want, you can take a risk and come too. But if you don't want to, that's your choice. No doubt you're right. After all, I'm sure you've got responsibilities, and you've got to get up bright and early in the morning.'
'Lou, I don't even know you.'
'Of course you don't. That's the point, dumbo. Anyway, I'm not going to push you. Hell, I don't even find you that attractive. But I'm prepared to give you a chance. To prove yourself; to show you're prepared to take *real* risks. Think of it as part of your education.'
Lou downed the suds in the bottle and left the bar. As she passed the three boys rolling up another joint, she leaned over the magazine. 'Hey, d'you mind if I have a puff?'
The boy rolling looked up, a stupid expression on his face. 'Sure. Just wait till we finish getting spliffed up.'
But Lou interrupted him. 'I don't need to wait.' And taking a deep breath she blew the flakes of broken cigarette tobacco and resin into the yellow leather lap of the nearest boy.
'Shit, what d'you do that for?'
'Mother…'
'Oh noooo…' protested the triumvirate.
'I told you all I wanted was a puff.' Her laugh sounded like breaking glass, and still smiling at her own joke she strode out of the club.
'Stupid bitch. That was the end of my stash,' moaned the roller as he scrabbled around on the floor trying to retrieve the little brown lumps.
'Oh nooooo,' wailed red trousers, mourning the

premature end to his evening. 'Oh noooooo.'

At the door Lou turned and gazed back into the dark cavern to see if Si had decided to follow her.

⚽ ⚽ ⚽

'Shit, Si, what do you mean nothing happened?' Jimmy was annoyed by Si's reluctance to reveal where he'd got to at the end of the party.

'I don't see what the big deal is. After all, have you told me where you were when I came looking for you? Hey, have you?'

'No, but that's not the point. Anyway, if you want to know, I was outside snogging that girl, you know, the pretty young blonde one in the blue dress.'

'Jimmy, you dick... She must have been jail bait.'

'Calm down, calm down... Nothing happened. It was just a bit of fun.'

'That's what they all say. Your Honour, nothing happened. Just a bit of slap and tickle... They'd put you away, Jimmy. *The Sun* would love it. SOCCER STAR IN UNDER AGE SEX SCANDAL... I can see it now, complete with fuzzy photographs and no-details-spared captions explaining what each photo represented.'

'Listen, I'm telling you I didn't bone her. Right?'

'Just looking out for your interests, that's all.'

'Well, if I need that I'll ask you, okay? Anyway, you're trying to change the subject, you slimy bugger. What happened, then? Who was she?'

'How do you know it was a *she*?'

'Well, I'd assumed you were straight at least... Or have you got a big confession to make?'

'No, you prat, what I meant was, how do you know I went off with someone at all? I might just have gone home. To sleep. Not so unusual at two in the morning, is it?'

For the umpteenth time that morning Si experienced the strange mixture of relief and inexplicable guilt. He'd woken up feeling like death, the noise of the party still crashing around his skull. The cushions he'd formed up into a makeshift mattress had failed to soften the floor's impact on his body—he ached all over. Si pulled on his scattered clothes. One sock simply refused to be found, so he abandoned it. Before leaving the flat, he glanced into the bedroom. Gazing at Lou's naked back, he was overwhelmed by gratitude to the handful of sober brain cells which had helped his better self conquer the strong animal urge to sleep with the stranger. His guardian angel must have been watching over him, he decided. The unaccustomed thought made him smile.

He let himself out of the flat. It took a moment to find his bearings—this was a part of London Si hardly knew. He hailed a cab. It was seven fifteen, and the streets were still reasonably quiet.

Back at the flat, he immediately checked the ansaphone. Thank God; no message from Mary. What he feared most was that she'd find out he'd not been home. If he was lucky he might just get away with it. He noted with some surprise the extent of the loyalty he felt to his girlfriend. He must be growing up, he told himself wryly.

Despite having refused Lou's mortal challenge and exchanging nothing more life-endangering than one false kiss which had immediately filled him with disgust, he felt physically dirty, so he took a bath.

The hangover was getting worse, and Si decided to go round the corner to the greasy spoon for a full breakfast: a cracked mug of sugared tea accompanied by a plate of sausages, three rashers of bacon, mushrooms, two eggs sliding over golden triangles of fried bread and, to cap the feast, baked beans on the side. That cheered him for a while. But all day at work he kept breaking off from what he was doing as he recalled the events of the previous night.

'Don't bugger around with me, Si. I know you didn't just go home. I know you...' Jimmy's laddish banter ended Si's daydream abruptly.

Do you, do you know me, wondered Si? How could Jimmy know him? As The Who had put it: *How can you say you know me / When I don't even know myself...* Perhaps Jimmy knew him better than most. But he was judging Si by his own low moral standards, and Si recognised the acute gulf that lay between them. Growing up together could create strong bonds and loyalty. But friendship didn't mean understanding. They were two very different people doing very different things. So how could Jimmy claim to know him?

'Ah, come on, Si, if you're not going to tell me, who are you going to tell? Eh?'

'Yeah, all right, I'll tell you everything. Not that there's much to tell. But go get me a pint first, okay?'

Jimmy grinned victoriously and scampered off to the bar. Another midweek night in the pub, thought Si. Nineties life... Great, wasn't it?

⚽ ⚽ ⚽

Si was bored at work; he tried to ring Mary. No reply. So he rang Jimmy.

A female voice answered. She declined to give her name, but told him Jimmy was out. 'Playing soccer,' she said, 'training.'

Who was this girl? He supposed it might be the blonde Jimmy had got off with the other night. But surely she hadn't moved up to Manchester after a one night stand. No, Jimmy was obviously playing the field.

Then Bill came back with the coffee and a bright idea for a story. 'I've got a pal who works in an art gallery and she says she saw Will Carling and the Princess of Wales at an opening last week. Apparently they were getting on really well.' He raised an eyebrow and waited for his editor's reaction.

Si sipped his coffee slowly before reacting. 'Bill, that's old news. It was all over *The Sun* months ago. Nice try, but we're meant to come up with scoops. And anyway royal stuff is too hot for the Diary... You know that. Dougy would take it straight to the news boys, or to that toad Andrew Smaltings-Rogerson.'

Si was no fan of *The Courier*'s balding royal correspondent. The hack had made it perfectly clear that he had no intention of fraternising with an upstart nobody such as Si.

'I know that,' said Bill patiently.

'Really? So what's the story, then?' Si felt despondent. Bill's thinking had never struck him as particularly original.

'Well, my friend told me that Will Carling was interested in buying a picture...' He paused for effect.

'Yeah?'

'A portrait of Diana's mother... Now what about that?'

'Still too hot for us. Tell the news boys. They may be interested but I doubt it. This is probably one of those stories we should just sit on. At least for the time being.'

Bill looked crestfallen.

'Nice effort, though. Keep it up, eh, Bill?'

Bill cheered up a bit.

'By the way, did he buy the picture?'

'So, how's work this morning?' drawled Ricky.

'Well, it's not really morning any more, is it?'

One thirty in fact, and Si was hard at it putting the final touches to his lead story for the day. A celebrity adultery-and-shopping book launch had produced a gobbet of gossip the previous evening. The usual tripe really, but it made good copy. Some bimbette snogging someone else's husband. In fact the authoress' husband—hence the story.

'Yeah, I guess you're right. Hey man, I mean I only just woke up, that's why I thought it was the morning like.'

'Right.' Since their first meeting at Richard's party, Ricky had attached himself to Si. He rang him at least once a day about nothing mostly and they met a couple of times a week after Si finished work. Ricky had grown on Si and since Jimmy had gone north, Si welcomed the American as a substitute. But he was slightly bemused by Ricky, who seemed to do nothing in London and have no plans. Questions produced the same non-committal 'I'm a surfer looking for a wave...' line, which didn't help much. Clearly Ricky wasn't short of money. Si couldn't help feeling envious of his ability to exist for each new day.

On the whole, Si looked forward to his lazy conversations with Ricky, but appreciated the fact that he would not be disturbed in the mornings when he had to get the day's work sorted out and assign stories to Bill and the other Diary staff. The mornings were quiet because Ricky never got up before midday.

'So what's your scoop today?'

'What?'

'Your scoop? You know, your job, man?'

'Oh, right. Well there's this writer who's just about to lose her husband...'

'Doesn't sound that interesting to me.'

'No, but listen, will you. She wrote this book about glamorous people bonking each other's wives and husbands and they launched it last night.'

'Were you there?'

'Yeah, for a while.'

'So?'

'So the blurb on the cover describes Jane Furness, the author that is, as a happily married mother of two children. And, *quelle surprise*, Mr Furness was making out with some girl at the party. They thought they were out of sight but...'

'But you saw them?'

'No, not exactly. But someone I know did.' Si felt dirty. This kind of story often made him feel like that. But Dougy considered such gossip to be bread and butter for the Diary. If he couldn't pin down what Dougy wanted on Jack Derrida, or whatever he was called, then Si had to keep his boss happy with this kind of fodder.

After the last marriage-break up trumpeted by the Diary, Dougy phoned especially to say well done. 'More of the same please. That's what we want, Si. Some sex to add spice. Counterpoint, really. Know what I mean?'

Si had grunted affirmatively, although again he wasn't really certain of Dougy's meaning. But, if Dougy liked marriage break-up stories, Si knew he should produce them; even if he felt uncomfortable doing it.

'Great story, Si,' Ricky's voice oozed sarcasm. 'Catch this, man, I'm off to get some brunch and then I'll meet you tonight. Seven thirty at Larry's Bar.'

'Well, tonight's a bit tricky...'

'Why, what's up? You got plans? A chick?'

'No, no chick.' It felt foolish using Ricky's Californian sun-soaked expressions. It was raining outside, for God's sake.

'What, then? A better offer?' Ricky sounded a bit uptight all of a sudden. Strange, unlike his cool hipster image. 'Hey, no problem, man, like we can hang out later, okay.'

'No, listen, Ricky. My mate Jimmy's playing soccer tonight and I want to watch him. It's on the box...'

'The box?'

'TV. So why don't you drop by and we can watch it together? You might learn something about English culture.'

'Hell, I know all about English culture. Emma Thompson and Kenneth Branagh and all that stuff. I got enough culture Stateside.'

'No, you plonker. Real English culture. State of the art stuff. What drives this country. Not your stereotypes, but football—that's far more real. It's the religion of the masses.'

'Oh.' Ricky seemed non-plussed. A rare event. 'Like opium, you mean? In that case, okay, I'll give it a go. What time, then? And where?'

'Come by my place at seven thirty and we'll go down The Feathers in time for kick off at eight. Okay?

'Sure. I'll catch you then.'

'Later,' mimicked Si.

'Later, man,' replied Ricky without the slightest hint of irony.

⚽ ⚽ ⚽

'Could've been killed... Blown to pieces.'

Si was telling Ricky about his afternoon and the latest bomb scare in Central London.

'You sure were lucky. What I don't get is, why do these guys keep planting bombs anyway? I thought there was a cease-fire.'

'There is. Only they keep sounding false alarms to keep everyone on their toes.'

'So there wasn't an explosion in the end?'

'No, not even a bomb. Just a scare. But it disrupted the whole of London all the same.'

'Right. But what do they want? That's the bit I don't get. I mean, there's already an Ireland, isn't there? That's an independent country?'

'I think they want the bit in the north too. You know, Northern Ireland. That's still part of the UK.'

'So what's the problem, man? It makes perfect sense to me. Why not let them have it? Then the bombing will stop permanently.'

'I'm not sure it's that simple.'

'I figured it wouldn't be. Things never are in Europe.' Ricky grinned and sucked down the rest of his beer. Well, he called it beer but, as far as Si was concerned, it was lager.

'Surely Ireland should be all one country, united, you know. Keeping a bit separate is like so colonial. You Brits should give it back.'

'But it's the Northern Irish, who don't want to go back.'

'Why not? Don't they want to govern themselves?'

'Well, they do already. They have MPs in Parliament, and they consider themselves British as much as the rest of us on the mainland. And I suppose they are.'

'I find this so confusing, man. So who are the IRA trying to persuade by bombing London?'

'I don't think it's a matter of persuasion. More like coercion or intimidation. They want to persuade the government to pull British troops out of Northern Ireland.'

'Sounds fair enough to me.'

'Yeah, but the thing is a lot of people in Northern Ireland don't want the army to go. And the government thinks that if they pull out the army then the paramilitary organisations will fight back against the IRA and there'll be a bloodbath.'

'Oh. That wouldn't be good.'

'No,' agreed Si. 'It wouldn't.'

'Complicated, really.'

'Yeah, too much history.'

'Too much history,' nodded Ricky. 'That's you British all over. Too much history. Stops you even taking a shit without getting lost up your own arses. You've too much history.'

Si changed the subject. They were in The Feathers and the match was about to start. 'God, I'm ready for another drink.'

'Yeah, sounds cool. I'll get it this time.'

'Be quick, they're about to kick off.'

'Like the wind, man. I don't want to miss a minute of this great cultural-religious experience.'

'You scoff.'

'Moi?' Ricky raised his eyebrows and flashed a Venice Beach smile.

'Yeah, you,' called Si after his new friend. Ricky was already halfway to the bar and may not have heard him.

❀ ❀ ❀

All the Sleeper's preconceptions of Michael Anderson were wrong. For a start he was younger than his wife, often wore jeans to work, stood five foot eight in his stockinged feet and rarely carried a briefcase. He laughed a lot, mostly at his wife's comments, and drank a good deal more than he laughed. Englishmen weren't meant to be like this.

The Andersons welcomed their lodger as if he was a younger brother. The rent was a nominal one hundred pounds a month.

'We prefer not to let the room, than to have someone we don't like. The money's not important,' Michael told him.

The Sleeper couldn't understand how they could like him without knowing him. When he asked, Michael laughed. 'Greta told me I'd like you, and I trust her judgement implicitly. She tells me the Irish have a gift for character insight.'

'Oh?'

'Yes, apparently it dates from the time of the druids.'

The Sleeper smiled uncertainly. Was this a joke at his expense? English humour was something he'd yet to get to grips with.

After that, he didn't see that much of Michael, who was away during the day. Since the Sleeper didn't have a job, he kept Greta company or minded the two children when she went out. In the evenings he went to Eamon's pub or to the cinema in Notting Hill Gate and tried to give the Andersons some space. They seemed a happy couple, but occasionally when he came home late at night, he heard them arguing in the front room. When that happened he just went straight upstairs to bed.

The Sleeper listened to the news and read the newspapers—normally *The Irish Times*. But even that was disappointing, as it was totally biased in favour of the Irish government. Bruton's election victory filled him with deep depression, not because he cared for either party, but because he could see that the Irish political system was in the pocket of the English, no matter who was Taoiseach.

Time passed but the freezing, miserable weather continued. He stayed in more often in the evenings and waited for a sign of change. But neither on the news or in any other way could he detect a weakening of the ceasefire. Even the bomb scares seemed to send the wrong message— many commentators thought they were carried out by a small fringe group without the means to pull off a significant terrorist attack. For all the Sleeper knew they were right. But the worst thing about being stuck in limbo out of contact was that he no longer knew if he wanted to be involved in the action or not.

Since moving to Westbourne Park, he was less lonely. He spent the day chatting with Greta, and she inspired new sensations—not always comfortable ones.

He also got to know a few English people. Jo who ran the newspaper shop was from Yorkshire and spoke with an accent hard to decipher. But he was a good man.

So was Lenny, the tramp who sat on the bench just along from the Andersons' house. Often the Sleeper would spend a couple of hours in the afternoon talking to Lenny about his travels. The tramp even reckoned he'd been to the Sleeper's home town. But the way he described it didn't seem right at all. He was probably lying half the time, but the Sleeper enjoyed his company anyway.

Lenny's favourite topic of conversation was the English Government and how it did nothing for the homeless. 'Not that it'll change if the other bloody lot get in. They're just as bad. Bloody toffee-nosed lot they are...' And he was off. Sometimes for up to an hour without drawing breath. But listening to Lenny was stimulating: it helped fuel his hatred of the English political class.

Michael Anderson also helped strengthen this conviction. Not that the Sleeper had anything against him personally; just that he was always so cheerful and successful; and when he was around, Greta talked less to the Sleeper and more to her husband. The Sleeper took to leaving the room soon after Michael entered in the evenings. Of course, he was polite and subtle about it, but his landlord's presence was irritating. To be sure, he realised that as a guest in the house he shouldn't do anything to upset Michael. The time for revenge on Michael and his kind would come later.

⚽ ⚽ ⚽

The church clock struck three. 'Sun's nearly over the yard-arm...'

'Say what?'

'I said,' enunciated the tramp carefully, 'that it's time for a drink.'

'Ah, you eejit. I thought that's what you meant.' The Sleeper cracked up laughing. Lenny was a laugh a minute, he really was. He'd already had a skinful long before the sun got anywhere near the yard-arm. 'I thought the yard-arm was like when the sun sets?'

Lenny pondered this. 'Sometimes it is,' he conceded. 'But on other occasions, it isn't.' He nodded sagely to himself, and his matted silver hair swung back and forth in front of his ruddy cheeks.

The Sleeper watched the old man fascinated. He particularly marvelled at the network of minuscule blood vessels spreading just below the transparent skin covering the nose.

'Will you get away,' he exclaimed at Lenny's sophistry. 'I never knew that. And when would it not be?'

'Not be what?'

'Over the yard-arm?'

'Are you still prattling on about that? The young today...'

The Sleeper bit his bottom lip to control the giggles threatening to overtake him.

'And you needn't laugh, you cheeky blighter.'

'Lenny, I wasn't laughing, I promise you.'

The tramp harrumphed and shifted in his overcoat. He wrapped it tightly around him, and then leaned over and peered into the Victoria Wine carrier bag at his feet. After snuffling about for a while, he straightened up brandishing triumphantly a can of extra strong lager. 'I knew I had one somewhere in there.' Lenny pulled back the ring and took a swig. 'So, young lad, you can stop staring at me and tell me why you're not at school.'

'Lenny, I've told you a thousand times. I don't go to school. I'm twenty years old.'

'When I was twenty I went to school.'

'Get away! Nobody goes to school that old.'

'Well, I did. But things were better then. It was a different country.'

The Sleeper cut him off before he could get started on one of his nostalgic reveries, which inevitably involved a good deal of racist diatribe against the 'immigrants that took all our jobs and homes away.' Not that they'd taken Lenny's away, mind. As the Sleeper had found out after a bit of probing, Lenny had been married for fifteen years. The couple was childless and began to blame each other. Eventually, the marriage broke down in acrimony, and Lenny walked out—'I just woke up one morning and said to myself I've had enough. So I packed my rucksack, left the wife snoring and muttering her crazy dreams, and hit the road.' He'd not only abandoned his wife and home, but also his job as a warehouse foreman. When the Sleeper had asked him if he regretted the loss of family, comfort and a secure future, Lenny challenged him. 'I don't know who you are, young lad, to be asking me that. I can't exactly see you in a good job, now, can I?'

'Yeah, yeah. I've told you... I'm looking for the right job to come up.' The Sleeper deployed his usual cover story. A job in the advertising industry. It had almost gone wrong with Michael, who'd offered to use his contacts in the business world to sort out an interview. The Sleeper had quickly had to insist that he was grateful but was determined to do it by himself. Since then neither Greta nor Michael had pursued the question of employment; just an occasional throwaway line about how was the job-hunting going. After all, they figured, he was a nice kid and what business was it of theirs? And it was useful to have him round the house to help out with the children when Greta was really busy.

Lenny drew heavily on his can. The sucking noises gradually came to an end and he scrunched it up. 'That was good,' he sighed contentedly. He stood up stiffly and walked, as he always did, to the corner along from his bench, where he carefully dropped the ruined can into the bin. 'Doing my bit for the environment, you see.'

The Sleeper smiled. 'Good on you, Lenny.'

'Not that I'm one of those Greens, mind you, cause I'm not. Bunch of namby pamby lefty farts they are. As much use as a pork pie at a Jewish wedding...'

The Sleeper waited for him to calm down. Eventually, the time seemed opportune to sound out Lenny about what had been bothering him. 'Lenny?'

'Yes.'

'Can I ask you a question?'

'Of course you can. What else have I lived all these years for? But to be a font of wisdom, a Tiresean oracle for today's blind youth, a rudder for their foundering bark...'

'Yeah, that's great Lenny. I'm really grateful and all that,' the Sleeper hurried on. Sweet Mary, when Lenny got going, there was no stopping the man. Talk about blarney. 'You see, I've got this problem bugging me...'

'Go on, I'm all ears.'

The Sleeper couldn't help glancing idly at the two mauled protrusions on his friend's head. They looked like they'd been through the wars. One even had a chunk missing; he was a real alley-cat, was our man Lenny.

'Right. Well, do you think it's right to fall in love with a married woman?'

'I'm not a priest,' growled Lenny. 'If you want confession

then just go up the road there. I'm sure the father would be glad to hear your story.'

'No, just hold on, right? I've not done anything. I'm just asking you a question, what if? You see what I mean?'

'Mmmm. Well, get on with it then.'

'So I'm asking you. Do you think it's all right?'

'To fall in love with a married woman? Is that what you're saying?'

'Yeah.'

'I guess it depends what you mean by love.'

'What?'

'Well, love can mean many things. Do you mean, is it all right to admire and worship a married woman? If so, then no problem. There's no law against unrequited love, in fact, society used to be based on it, and it inspired some of the most exquisite literature.'

'Did it really?' The Sleeper sat up with hope sparkling in his eyes.

'Yes. About six hundred years ago.'

'Oh.' He sank back dejected.

Lenny pursued his theme. 'But I suspect what you mean is—is it acceptable to covet her? Or do you really mean,' Lenny stared sternly at the Sleeper, 'is it okay to screw her?'

The younger man blushed. 'I don't know, Lenny. I mean, it'd be nice... But I'm just worried that I might be falling in love with this wonderful lady who's married. And I don't know what to do about it.'

'Well, in all honesty, I can't really advise you. I can tell you it's morally wrong to commit adultery; and I can say that in some countries you would be risking your life to muck about with a married woman. But since the laws of this land offer no guidance, and even the Church doesn't seem to know its own mind these days, I can't really tell you whether it's *right* or not. I guess what I'm really saying is, don't do anything in a hurry.'

The Sleeper stared at the piece of dirty pavement between his feet. This wasn't getting him anywhere. He might as well head back to the house and leave Lenny to his drinking. 'Thanks, Lenny, you've been great.'

'Any time, young man. Come by soon and we'll have another little chat. Nothing I enjoy more than setting the world to rights. And if I can help out my fellow man in the process, then all the better.'

'Yeah, thanks. I'll be seeing you around, then.'

'Goodbye.' Lenny seemed to swell with innate dignity. He stretched his arms and puffed out his chest like a robin; then he hunched over his plastic bag again in search of sustenance. The Sleeper turned disconsolately on his heel and walked off down All Saints Road towards home.

⚽ ⚽ ⚽

Brenda was serving behind the bar, as usual. She didn't mind really. As jobs went it was okay, and the crowd at The Feathers were a good bunch on the whole.

She realised she'd been lucky to have got her job back so easily after that poxy PR agency kicked her out. Just because she wouldn't sleep with her account director.

Everyone had laughed when she'd threatened to sue for sexual harassment. 'You've been watching too many films, love... You'd have no chance of proving anything.' And they'd been right. So, yes, she was quite lucky that The Feathers had taken her back.

Lunchtime had been quite busy. Apart from Patrick, who always came in for a half of stout just before his lunch, most of the lunchtime drinkers worked in the area. They didn't really overlap with the evening crowd.

Brenda preferred the latter, and had got to know them much better than the besuited lunchtimers. One or two she had got to know too well, like Jimmy. The memory brought back a painful ache in her lower stomach, like the beginning of the curse. It had probably been for the best that Jimmy had moved away when he did, and the last few times he'd been in with his friend Si, she'd got on much better with him. Water under the bridge...

Brenda liked Si more now. She'd been a bit hard on him in the past. He was always polite to her and took an interest in what she thought about things. He never seemed to mind listening to her blabbing away, which was good because she recognised that some people found her constant chatter irritating. Not Si. In this and so many other things he was very different from Jimmy.

It was hard to see why they were such good friends. They were very different, after all, and didn't seem to have that much in common. She thought they'd been at school together, but was that enough to sustain a friendship ten years later? With blokes it probably was. They had very different friendships from most girls, who tended to hang around in small posses with ever-shifting permutations of best friends within the group; you never knew who was slagging you off behind your back. But guys were different.

Si and Jimmy seemed more openly affectionate than most male pairs she watched in the pub. There seemed to be none of that hearty back-slapping and false bravado. But just as much beer swilling, no doubt about that. When she'd first got to know them, she'd wondered if they were gay. Since her fling with Jimmy, she'd decided that he at least was very straight. But there was something attractive and supportive in their relationship. It raised her spirits to see them together.

As she wiped glasses and replaced them carefully upside down on the shelf, Brenda wondered whether Si had a girlfriend. Funny that, she'd never thought to ask. Si occasionally met girls at The Feathers, but none of them had appeared more than a few times. He seemed the romantic type, though. A bit shy and serious perhaps, but charming and what her mum would have described as One of Life's Gentlemen. Brenda smiled at the thought. No doubt her mother would like her to end up with someone like Si. Some hope. She sighed and rubbed a puddle of spilt beer with a small Guinness towel.

She'd have to ask Si about his love life next time he was in. As a joke, mind, without letting on that she might be personally interested. He would certainly be a good catch for any girl. He had a good job; some sort of journalist, she thought. And no doubt he earned a good salary. If he had his own flat around here, then he must have quite a bit of cash. Yeah, she decided, she'd have to find out a bit more about Si's situation. But more in the spirit of adventure than out of any real expectation of success.

⚽ ⚽ ⚽

Michael was often away on business; the Sleeper didn't know where, but he knew his landlord sometimes went abroad. When Michael was away the Sleeper used to stay in to keep Greta company. She couldn't really come to the pub because of the kids, who called him 'Baa' because they couldn't pronounce his name properly. But once the kids were in bed, Greta and he would go downstairs and watch TV. It was mostly crap, but he loved sitting there with her, just the two of them.

The Sleeper never really thought that anything would happen. After all, Greta was married, ten years older and the sister of his best friend in London. He never expected anything and certainly the first move didn't come from him. His ma, like Lenny, had taught him that it was wrong to get off with a married woman. Also, he wasn't the most experienced man in the world when it came to women. So he missed the warning signs. He would have been quite happy just to make the most of the shared evenings, and enjoy Greta's company all to himself.

But she had more in mind than that. About the third time that Michael went away for a couple of nights, the Sleeper came home with some shopping for Greta. He'd been up the shop with Jo buying a *Standard* and having a chat. Jo was a Leeds United supporter and the Sleeper had been giving him a ribbing about how crap they were doing and how Man United were starting to storm back up the league. Even at that stage with Newcastle way out in front he'd been convinced United would win the Premiership. At least the Premiership, maybe even the Double. The Sleeper had always supported Man United, mainly because his family had always done so. But also, back home nobody really thought of them as an English football club. They had always had so many Irish playing for them; even now, with Irwin and Keane and so on.

So, when he got back from the shop, he had a great big grin on his face and was about to tell Greta about what Jo had said when he realised that something was wrong. She was in the kitchen, cooking with her back to him. Nothing unusual about that, but when she turned round and wiped her hands on the apron he could tell she'd been crying.

'What's up?'

'Nothing.'

'Nothing? So why are you crying?'

'I'm not crying. All I need is a hug.' Greta held out her arms, and although he'd never held her before, it seemed innocent enough to wrap her in his arms. He'd never realised quite how small she was. She buried her face in his jumper and he was surprised that he could see over the top of her head. The kitchen clock showed six forty five.

'That's better... Thanks.' She gave him a squeeze and turned back to the cooker.

'What are we eating?'

'Steak and potatoes and carrots.'

'Wow. What's the occasion?' Although Greta could cook, she normally limited herself to pasta because of lack of time.

'No occasion. Could you lay the table, like a good boy?'

'Sure.'

'Do you ever miss home?'

'Yeah, of course. I miss my family a bit. But I think I'll probably go back to see them in August. I wrote my ma as much the other day.'

'That's good. Good that you get on with your ma. Mine doesn't speak to me since I married Michael.'

'That's terrible. Why?'

''Cos he's English and, worse, he's not a Catholic.'

'Oh.' Although the Sleeper had been brought up on the same precepts as Greta, and had never questioned them before, it suddenly struck him as a bit odd that people should hate other people just because they believed different things and lived in other countries.

He carried on setting two places for dinner, trying to remember if the spoons went clockwise round the table. He never could remember that, and at home he'd always got a clip round his ear when he got it wrong. That happened almost every time it was his turn to lay the table on Sunday. He bit his lip and tried to remember. Clockwise, surely it was. He laid clockwise.

Dinner was quiet. Greta didn't say a thing and only answered his talk with smiles and nods. She asked how the steak was and he told her it was 'brilliant'. That was about it. He felt pretty uncomfortable by the time they cleared up and went to the sitting room to watch TV.

'Are you sure nothing's wrong?'

'No, why?'

'Well I was just wondering. Maybe I've done something wrong. What is it?'

Greta laughed. 'You've done nothing wrong. Quite the opposite.' She looked at him with her piercing eyes and without quite knowing why, he blushed. He tried to turn the TV on, but the remote control wouldn't work. 'Stop playing with the TV,' Greta ordered.

'Sorry?'

'I said stop.'

The Sleeper put down the control obediently.

'You know that nice hug you gave me before? Why don't you come and give me another one... To cheer me up.'

'Oh... Okay.' He moved next to Greta on the sofa and turned awkwardly towards her. He felt her head come to rest on his shoulder. Then his heart began to beat uncontrollably as he felt Greta's moist kisses on the back of his neck. He was terrified that she would stop when she heard his heart beating. And then it was dreadful because he could feel movement beginning to poke the inside of his fly. He thought he'd die if she noticed. Thank goodness they weren't embracing standing up, like before. She would have been sure to feel it pushing against her.

Greta raised her head from his neck and brushed her hair out of her eyes. 'Hey, Baa,' she said, using the kids' nickname for the first time. It seemed to mark a change.

'Yeah?' he answered, trying to sound normal, but failing dismally. She must have noticed because she giggled.

'Stop looking so serious.'

'Yes.... Right.' He tried to look happier, but all he could think about was his erection and whether she'd notice and think he was trying to molest her.

'Baa? What do you think I'm doing?'

'Uh... I don't know.'

'You don't know?' A small smile played at the corners of her mouth and he noticed she was wearing some sort of faint lipstick. He couldn't take his eyes off her glossy lips. They were slightly parted and seemed very close.

'Well, I suppose, having a cuddle... Yeah?'

'I suppose so.'

Her lips seemed to be increasing in size and he wondered what it would be like to lean across the few inches separating their faces and kiss her slowly, like in the films. Immediately, he regretted the thought because he felt a nudge from below and realised that Greta would have to be blind not to notice.

'What else?'

'What else?'

'Uh huh... What else am I doing?'

'Uh... I don't know.' He felt his face burning up. It was like being stuck in a nightmare, except it was really pleasant at the same time.

'Well, silly. I'm trying to seduce you. Didn't you know?'

'Oh…' But he didn't say any more because he found out what it was like to kiss those lips, and it was a thousand times better than he'd imagined it would be. And then he stopped worrying about his erection because it became obvious that Greta had noticed, and there was nothing he could do about that.

❀ ❀ ❀

Si had put the page to bed early and was reasonably satisfied with his labours. A story about a rising film star borrowing a dinner jacket to attend the premier of his new film; another about an eccentric raising money for charity by cycling around the borders of Kuwait.

Then there had been the scoop of the day. A long piece speculating about an ex-Cabinet Minister's motivation for joining forces with a new arts foundation promoting a little known sculptor. Si had been able to reveal that the sculptor happened to be the Prime Minister's godson, who had failed to graduate from art school the summer before. Because of the political sensitivity, Si had checked that one with Dougy even before he started writing it up.

To Si's relief, Dougy had been delighted. In recent weeks it had become obvious that much of the Establishment was preparing for an Opposition victory in next year's elections. Sir Lesley, ever the political optimist, had instructed his editor to ensure *The Courier* ingratiated itself with the future government. Si's story was pitched just right.

'Good stuff, Si, but play down the PM angle. If it's got more than a grain of truth in it, then let's stitch up that brown-nosing bugger.' He was referring to the ex-Cabinet Minister. 'No doubt he's after his peerage. Let's hope we can blow the whistle on it, eh?'

So that's how Si had written it up, suggesting that the PM was an innocent party and that his godson was not to blame for accepting the foundation's support; but that either the ex-Minister and the foundation were bad art critics—in which case they shouldn't be responsible for such large endowments to artists—or that something more devious lay behind the grant...

Si waved goodnight to the remaining Diary staff. Bill was still around. He seemed to be getting keener recently and there was no longer any doubt about his ability. The lad was improving by the week. Although logic told Si he was being slightly paranoid, he couldn't help feeling less than pleased to see Bill still beavering away on the phone. Bill raised a hand in farewell as Si went off towards the lifts.

He soon forgot his work. Sitting in the back of the taxi on his way to Mary's flat, he was as excited about the Manchester United match he planned to watch on TV as about spending an evening with his girlfriend. Better be careful not to show it, he told himself; she wouldn't be impressed.

Things hadn't been too good with Mary recently. He partly ascribed this to some lingering guilt he felt about his encounter with Lou—he shivered when he thought what might so easily have happened. It was stupid to feel guilty, he told himself; he hadn't really done anything wrong. But he couldn't totally exorcise the darker feelings that he'd faced that night.

The deficiencies in Si and Mary's relationship went beyond anything the Lou incident had uncovered. Si noticed that the gaps between his meetings with Mary were lengthening and they spent much of their time bickering. It was increasingly apparent that something needed to change; only Si didn't feel like a crisis at the moment. He resolved to wait until there was no alternative to taking a decision, one way or the other.

However, Mary was not as contemplative and indecisive as Si. He'd hardly got through the door when she set into him.

'Where have you been? I thought we said seven?'

'Yeah, I know. I'm sorry. I got caught up and I thought

that you wouldn't be here till later. Sorry.' Si shrugged pathetically.

Mary scrutinised him as if he were a small, hairy, many-legged animal. 'Well, don't think I'm going to sit around here and watch the football with you tonight. I've been patient enough already. Let's go out and eat, okay?'

'Can't we watch Jimmy for a while? It's already half time and it's a big match. Only his third first team start.'

Mary's fierce glare cut him short.

'I guess it would be over by nine fifteen...' Si tailed off.

'You stay here if you want. I'm off.'

'Where?'

'What do you care?'

Good question, thought Si. He said nothing. He knew from experience this was the best tactic.

'Well?'

'Well, what?'

'What are you going to do? Are you going to watch the soccer or come with me?'

'Uh, I don't know. Let me think about it a sec...'

'Oh!' Mary stamped her foot with rage and reached for her keys. 'You're impossible. Anyone would think you were more in love with your friend Jimmy than me. Well, I'm not going to put up with it. You're just like my mother said you would be. I'm going to take one of the rich good-looking guys at work up on their offer and have a really good night out. There's enough of them after me, you know. I can't think why I haven't done something about it before.'

Si wondered whether she hadn't in fact. Where else had this sudden attack come from? He suppressed the suspicion as, with irritation, he recognised the symptoms of jealousy. After all, he wasn't so virtuous himself. 'What do you mean, I'm like your mother said?'

'What?'

'You said I was like your mother said I would be.'

'Oh, I don't know. She just said you'd probably turn out like my father. Wet, and a failure of a man.' Mary looked sad.

The storm seemed to be passing. But Si was struck by her words. Did one have to be successful and aggressive to be a real man these days? Whatever happened to all that talk of men becoming more sensitive and understanding and women preferring it that way? Obviously not, at least in Mary's case. She shared her mother's views. The thought made him shudder. But Mary looked vulnerable now, standing confused in the doorway. Neither in nor out; like the rest of our generation, thought Si. What a mess. But he could feel his heart melt and he stretched out his arms. Reluctantly, Mary allowed herself to be drawn into them and leaned her head on his shoulder.

'I'm sorry,' she snuffled. 'It's just that I missed you.'

'Yeah, I'm sorry too,' muttered Si. 'You were right, I guess... Let's go to the pub, eh?'

That was how Si came to miss Jimmy's first hat-trick for Manchester United, which won a vital match and set him firmly on the path to soccer stardom and United to winning the Championship.

⚽ ⚽ ⚽

As usual, Mary woke with the birdsong. It had been a habit from childhood which she'd carried to London. At home, of course, there had been a whole orchestra to transport her from dreams to daylight, but now a solitary starling soothed her waking. She rolled over onto her back and opened her eyes.

Another day at the office. She enjoyed her job most of the time, and she knew she was good at it. The money was excellent too. But what was it all for, she wondered? In the clarity of dawn—the LCD on her radio alarm blinked 06:15—she paused to reflect on her life. A rare moment in the hurly burly of work.

Si groaned on her left. He was still fast asleep. How sweet he looked with his George Clooney hair cut and a tightly clenched fist poking over the edge of the duvet. It was strange how their relationship had developed. She'd had to make most of the running, she realised, because he was so introverted and laid back. She now knew that this was just a veneer, an act for society. After the best part of four months together—the long dark months when London works too hard and forgets how to enjoy itself—Mary thought that Si worried too much. He worried about his work, and he looked for meaning unnecessarily. Life was quite simple really, it didn't need angst-ridden self-examination to work out that we were all really insignificant in the great scheme of things. You just had to get on and make the best of it. For her that meant being successful in her job. For Si, she wasn't so sure. He certainly didn't seem happy in his job, but he didn't seem to know what else he wanted to do. Sometimes, she wasn't even sure he wanted to be with her, and thought that, but for force of habit, they might have split up long ago.

But Mary was increasingly clear in her own mind what she wanted. Si drove her up the wall at times, but he was the best boyfriend she'd had. She could see a future for them, once Si got his head together. Of course, she would be wise to keep that thought to herself—she knew how terrified men were of the M word. She was young enough to wait... Time would bring its own answer.

The birdsong became more intermittent. 06:24. Did that bloody clock never stop flashing? How on earth did it keep going for so many separate little bursts of energy? Quite remarkable. But then again, she supposed it was no different from her heart, which she could feel gently pulsating, pushing the blood around her loose limbs.

Mary pulled herself together. Time to stop daydreaming and to get up. Otherwise she'd be late for work. It was all right for journalists like Si who could roll in after ten, she had to be at her desk by seven thirty. The joys of the financial world. They claimed that the pay compensated for the long hours, but if one worked out the hourly rate, it was more or less the same as less demanding and supposedly badly paid jobs. A mug's life? No, she loved it really. Perhaps it would be different if everyone didn't think she was a high-flyer? Yes, almost certainly. But, she always had the option to stop and do something else; even have a family. Get up, and stop being so predictable, ordered a little voice in her head.

Mary slid out the side of the bed and realised that she was naked. The memory of the previous night made her spine tingle, and she smirked as she fumbled for her towelling bath robe. It was cold and she shivered. She stole a glance at her sleeping lover before heading for the bathroom.

The bedroom door shut and Si rolled over to a more comfortable position. He found the warm spot which still smelt of Mary and snuggled down into the dent in the mattress, pulling the duvet around his shoulders.

'Wake up, dozy, I'm off.'

'Wha... What's going on?' Si poked his head out. 'It's early, why are you waking me up?'

'I thought you might like a cup of tea?'

Si groaned.

'I'll put it here, okay. Just on the floor. Don't leave it too long, or it'll go cold.'

Si mumbled insincere gratitude.

'See you tonight, okay? Give me a ring later.' Mary leaned over the bed, feeling stiff in her high-buttoned white blouse and tight suit. She kissed Si on the cheek, which was the only bit of his body exposed. 'Bye. Love you,' she whispered.

'Yeah... Bye,' he slurred.

Mary picked up her Hermès bag and closed the door softly behind her. Si rolled over, tucked his head under his arm and fell back into a dreamless sleep.

⚽ ⚽ ⚽

It was just after four and the kids were about to return from school. Greta had gone to fetch them. The Sleeper sat in the armchair in his room and looked out the window. He loved the view of tall Victorian buildings shaded by Arcadian streets. So peaceful, in stark contrast to his inner turmoil. A warm breeze shivered the tops of the poplar trees and he remembered how his ma used to sigh when things were really bad back home. Then, as usual, his thoughts turned to Greta.

The first time they'd made love was like nothing he'd ever known. It was like going to heaven. Blinding light, a feeling of weightlessness and an incredible warmth. They didn't make it upstairs; just did it on the couch where they were. He didn't really have much to do in the event. Greta did most of the work. He was impressed that she seemed to know what she was doing. He'd been concerned because it was his first time and he didn't want to tell her. He'd had a protected upbringing, and his ma wouldn't let him go out with girls like some of his friends did. So he'd never had the chance. Anyway, he thought, he was glad he hadn't. It made doing it with Greta all the more special.

'Thank you, Baa,' she said afterwards.

'Thank you? Why are you thanking me? I should be thanking you.'

'No, you're the one who's being lovely. Did anyone ever tell you what a lovely kid you are?'

'I'm not really a kid. After all, I'm twenty now.'

'No, you're not a kid...Did anyone?'

'Anyone what?'

'Tell you how lovely you are?' Greta rolled off his chest and propped herself up on her elbow. He tried not to stare at the swing of her breasts.

'No. I don't think they did.'

'Well, they should have.' She leaned forward to kiss him on the forehead. 'You are quite lovely.'

He looked into her emerald eyes and realised with a shock that he was in love. Foolishly and head over heels in love. This was another novel experience. It was slightly confusing. He realised that he had to be a bit careful.

During the training before he left Ireland, they'd told him, 'Don't get tangled up in personal relationships. You're there to do a job, never forget it.' The job. This was clearly what they'd been thinking of when they said that. He hadn't paid much attention then, but now the meaning of those words became clear. To be honest he felt pretty confused. His life before Greta seemed almost to belong to a different person.

'Why so down? Didn't you enjoy it?'

'Yeah, like nothing before.'

'Good.' Greta looked relieved. 'If you're a good boy I might let you do it again later...'

The reflection in his bedroom window grinned impishly back. He supposed he must have been a good boy.

⚽ ⚽ ⚽

Despite his winning goal against Southampton in the sixth round of the FA Cup, Jimmy hardly dared hope start the match against Chelsea. It was the semi-final and victory would guarantee United a place at Wembley. But injuries still troubled several of the team's regular strikers, and Jimmy thought he had a good chance of being picked to sit on the bench; that could lead to another chance to show his talents, if the manager decided to make a substitution.

Then, at the end of midweek training, Alex Ferguson called him over and told him that he would be in the team from the start of the match. Jimmy was ecstatic.

'Great... That's really great... Thanks,' was all he could say.

Ferguson just looked at him steadily and nodded, the hint of a smile playing at the edge of his dour mouth. 'Don't thank me... Thank th'self,' he said. 'You're doon well, Jimmy. Just do well on Sunday too, okay?' He patted Jimmy on the shoulder and walked away.

When he got back to his hotel room, Jimmy began to realise what his selection really meant. This was it, the big chance. The whole footballing world would be watching the FA Cup semi-final. If he did well, he'd be catapulted to stardom. If he failed he might not get another chance to play in the first team for a long time.

The intense fear which overcame him drove away sleep, and desperate to off-load some of the excitement and terror, he picked up the phone. There was no-one in Manchester to whom he could talk. So he rang Si.

'Hello,' groaned a voice after half a dozen rings.

'Hi, Si? It's Jimmy… How are you?'

'Jimmy you git, it's three o'clock in the morning. What the hell are you doing ringing me, eh?'

'Yeah, sorry about the time…' In the background Jimmy could here a woman's voice complaining.

'Yeah, I hope you are. I've got to go to work tomorrow.'

'Oh, right. Yeah, sorry. I just thought I'd give you a ring.'

'Listen,' muttered Si sleepily, 'If you've just rung for a chat, could we do this in the morning? And then I'll kick your butt when I next see you.'

'No, nothing special. Sorry mate, we'll talk tomorrow. By the way, who've you got with you?'

'None of your business.'

'It's not Mary, then?'

'Course it's bloody Mary… Ow! No, I didn't mean it like that, I was just saying to Jimmy… Oh never mind.' Si's voice boomed louder as he stopped talking to Mary and spoke into the receiver again. 'Now look what you've done. You've woken her up and got me into trouble into the bargain.'

Jimmy laughed. 'You see, you are glad I rang you.'

'No, I'm not. Honest, Jimmy. Not a bit glad. Hey, are you drunk? Bet you are. As a skunk, no doubt. I thought professional footballers were meant to be sober during the season.'

'Course I'm bloody sober. No, what I was phoning about… It's important, Si.'

Si's curiosity began to conquer sleep. 'Go on, I'm listening.'

'Right, well the Boss, he's picked me for Sunday. The Chelsea match.'

'What? On the bench?'

'No, you prat. Playing from the start. Centre forward. What do you think about that, eh?'

Si sat up in bed and turned on the bedside lamp. Sleep fell from him like a shroud and he was oblivious to groans from the slumbering form beside him. Strands of Mary's hair splayed out over the crisp white pillow like the Medusa's serpentine locks. ' Wow... Now that *is* news. Well done... Bloody well done...'

'That's more like it. You'll be there, I hope? And bring Mary. It's about time you introduced me.'

'Yeah, sure. If you get us tickets. Of course we'll be there. Jimmy, that's great, really great.'

'Yeah, I know. Those were my very words when the Boss told me.'

'Poetry man, sweet poetry.' And at that moment this seemed the most apposite form of words available to celebrate the event. 'Great. Really great.'

⚽ ⚽ ⚽

The following week, Si and Ricky were walking through Soho discussing Jimmy's inspired performance in United's victory over Chelsea. Mary's work obligations had prevented Si from taking her to the match, but he'd gone on his own. Ricky had watched it on TV. As they strolled, they glanced in shop windows looking for clothes. Ricky wanted a pair of crocodile skin winklepickers.

'What d'you want them for?' Si asked incredulously.

'Well, I've always wanted a pair, and now that I'm going to play in this band I need to sharpen up my image. Know what I mean?' Ricky had announced that he would be joining an R and B group. Singing, he claimed. It was the first Si had heard of Ricky doing something about his musical ambitions.

'Yeah, ever since I was a kid. I used to play the guitar but really my talent lies in singing, fronting the band.'

'Right.'

'And Ricky R—that's going to be my stage name—well, he'll need a cool pair of shoes.'

'I suppose he will. What's the R stand for?'

'Dunno. Doesn't need to stand for anything. Just sounds cool.'

Apparently the band had already been going for a year, but apart from a few gigs they hadn't got anywhere. But then they hadn't been fronted by Ricky before.

'So when's the first gig?'

'Not sure, man. But there are rehearsals this week and next and then I guess we'll be ready to go on the road.'

'Really? Where you going? On the road like?'

'Probably Kilburn.'

Si raised an eyebrow but managed not to laugh.

'Okay, it's not far, but best to start in London and then work out to the provinces. On the road's an expression, that's all. It's all about rock 'n' roll living, man. Get hip... Get cool...' Ricky swung a high five in his direction.

Si pretended not to notice. He didn't like to admit it, but he was slightly envious of his friend's new-found sense of purpose.

'Okay... So what's the band called?'

'At the moment they're called The Moguls, but I think that's dumb. When I asked why, none of the guys could tell me. Sounds like a mixture of Hollywood and the Swiss Alps...'

Si laughed involuntarily. 'Suppose so.'

'And I've got a plan to turn this band around. Really make it something. Could be hot shit if we do some practice. The drummer's good and the bassist's not bad. But the keyboard player makes Ray Manzarek look disabled, and the lead guitar must be Eric Clapton's younger brother. With me at the front geeing the whole act up... Man, we'll be unstoppable.'

Listening to him, Si almost believed it.

'Shit, there they are.'

'Who?' Si looked around, half-expecting to see Ricky's band.

'Not who, what. My shoes. Check those mothers out.'

Si had to admit they looked beautiful; if you liked that kind of thing.

Miracle of miracles, they fitted. Ten minutes later they were back outside the shop and Ricky was strutting carefully down Wardour Street, avoiding muddy patches and piles of rubbish; more like a Regency fop than a budding rock star.

'You know what I'm going to call my band?'

'*Your* band?' quipped Si.

But Ricky didn't react. 'The Crocodiles. What do you think? Cool, huh?'

'Mmmm… Could be. Yeah, it's not bad. Why not?'

'Yeah,' grinned Ricky, 'why the hell not. Rock 'n' roll baby, rock 'n' roll,' and he leapt into the air, neatly clicking the steel-shod heels of his new shoes together. The sun caught them and bounced off the metal and undulating leather. The flash of light seemed a good omen.

❀ ❀ ❀

The first night grew into an affair. Soon the Sleeper and Greta were sneaking kisses not only when Michael was abroad, but also during the day when the kids were out of the room. The Sleeper stuck to his routine for the evenings, but noticed that Michael came home later these days, normally after the Sleeper had gone out to the pub. Also, the evenings when he opened the front door to the sound of fighting seemed to become more frequent. He didn't want to ask Greta about Michael or the arguments. He was afraid she might decide to end the affair if he asked such personal questions. Despite himself, he found the situation becoming more intense.

The Sleeper wondered how Michael failed to notice the guilt written large across his face. He used to resent Michael, but now that he was doing something which would really hurt his landlord if he found out, he felt bad about it. He despised his own weakness.

Sometimes, when he was talking to Michael, he'd become convinced that Greta had left a lipstick stain on his cheek; he would rub discreetly at it.

'What's wrong with your face?' Michael would ask.

'Oh nothing. Caught myself shaving, that's all.' He felt the heat rising in his cheeks.

But Michael seemed not to notice and turned away. The Sleeper knew he was making a mistake getting involved; but he couldn't help it. So long as no-one found out then it wasn't a problem, he told himself. He refused to confront the bigger questions which lurked in the shadows at the edge of his mind.

Just after Easter he received a letter. It wasn't the first one he'd got since moving into Westbourne Park Road because his ma wrote a couple of times with family news and to ask when he'd be coming home. He hadn't been home since coming to London, but thought maybe he'd go during the summer, if he'd still not heard anything by then. Greta handed him the letter with a smile at breakfast. She'd been up for a couple of hours with the kids and getting Michael off to work.

'Hey, dozy, you've got a letter.'

It had a London postage mark, but he didn't need to open it to know who it was from. It had been so long since he'd last heard anything that it came as a shock. He thought they'd forgotten about him. He'd got so caught up with Greta that he'd almost forgotten why he'd come to London in the first place.

The Sleeper toyed with the letter over his toast and tried to convince himself that he hadn't hoped that they'd forgotten about him; but he knew he was lying to himself.

'You going to open it or what?' demanded Greta nosily.

'Oh, no. I'll read it later. After breakfast.'

She gave him a strange look. Then one of the kids started screaming and she turned away to comfort the child.

The Sleeper tucked the letter in his pocket. Later, when he was alone in his bedroom, he ripped it open. The message was brief and gave little away. Just some instructions to be at a pub in Hammersmith on 30 April. Nothing more. He mentally cancelled his trip home. The letter could only mean one thing— he remembered what they'd told him. His heart was beating terrifyingly fast, and he felt sick.

The flames engulfed the letter and black flakes floated into the sink. When there was no white paper left, he wafted at the smoke—surely Greta would smell the acrid stench of burning? He scrunched up the ashes and turned on the tap. They left a black stain on the porcelain as they spiralled down the plughole.

⚽ ⚽ ⚽

The first gig was in the upstairs room of a Kilburn pub. Si turned up early to give a hand in setting up. But Ricky and his new friends had already played a couple of warm-up numbers. Of course, there was no-one there yet. It was ten past nine. The landlord, a grumpy old bugger with holes in his cardigan, kept popping up to check on them.

'What's he worried about?' muttered Ricky.

'Dunno. But I don't like 'im.' This from Art the drummer.

As far as Si could see, Art was the most articulate of them all—apart from Ricky, of course. The other band members stood in their own little worlds, tunelessly playing to themselves. What a bunch, thought Si. What the hell is Ricky doing with this lot?

But Ricky stood proud centre stage. He'd back-combed his blond mane and was wearing the crocodile winkle-pickers; he looked pretty slick dressed all in black with that shock of hair and those extraordinary shoes.

Somehow Ricky had got his way with the name too.

The Moguls were history and tonight's gig was billed as the launch of The Crocodiles. That's what it said downstairs on a blackboard outside the pub.

TONIGHT! THE LAUNCH OF THE CROCODILES. THE HOTTEST NEW BAND TO HIT LONDON SINCE SPANDAU BALLET. 10 PM PAY ON THE DOOR.

Si suspected Ricky had written the quirky notice. He was right.

'Why Spandau?' asked Art.

'It'll attract attention.'

'It looks stupid.'

'Yeah,' chimed in the others.

'Makes us sound like a bunch of ponces,' complained Art eloquently.

'Come on, guys. Wise up. It makes us look like we're in the same league as Spandau.'

'But we're not. We're a rock and roll band. Not mincing New Romantic tossers.'

'Ah, come on, guys,' sighed Ricky; and using the same technique as he'd employed to change the band's name, and to ease himself into the role of lead singer and unofficial manager, he painted a picture of The Crocodiles' future. 'Can't you see it? Wembley Arena, playing to fifty thousand... The Hollywood Bowl .. Screaming chicks... Rock 'n' roll, man... Yeah? Well, trust me. I'll get you there, okay.'

'Yeah,' grinned Art and the entranced band members nodded.

'Effing cool,' one managed.

'Yeah...,' agreed Ricky. After a pause he clinched the deal. 'So Spandau stays?'

The expressions hardened slightly, but nobody protested. Ricky's sweet talk had won the day.

⚽ ⚽ ⚽

'You all having a good time?' screamed Ricky into the microphone, sweeping his hair back as he did so.

Si admired Ricky for his guts. It wasn't easy to stand on a low stage in a small room facing fifteen bored looking punters and give out that you're Mick Jagger.

'Cool... Well, this is a pussy-whipping song we're gonna start with. It's called *Brown Sugar.*'

The guitarist, Dog, as he liked to be known, struck the first notes and Art clattered his sticks. They were off.

Si hadn't quite known what to expect; but this wasn't it. Ricky had warned him that most of the set would be covers. But this was a cover with a difference.

Ricky gathered the mike-stand to him, jutted his pelvis towards a striking girl at the front—she was already beginning to look more interested—and strutted. He flicked his amazing shoes into the spotlight and marched up and down; not easy in a space two metres square. But nobody seemed to notice the cramped conditions.

'Brown Sug-ar...' howled Ricky and strutted.

He was good, thought Si. Really good. Next time he'd have to bring Mary. The poor girl was still working, he imagined. He hadn't pushed her to accompany him in case The Crocodiles turned out to be embarrassingly bad. But not only could Ricky sing, he also transformed on stage into a rock star. Si could already imagine his friend playing stadiums. It seemed just round the corner. And the band had only played one number.

What's more, Si could see why Ricky had been so keen to join the bunch of troglodyte musicians formerly known as The Moguls. These guys might find the word 'chord' hard to spell, but they could certainly play. They were tight, and Dog's licks cut like a hot knife through butter.

At the end of the first song Ricky leapt into the air, legs splayed. Joe Strummer would have been proud. 'Yow!' he screamed as he hit the ground and the song finished.

Really together; amazing for three weeks' rehearsal, thought Si.

The rest of the set was the same. Slick and compelling. The Crocodiles looked like they'd been playing together for years. It didn't last long—they only had eight songs so far; but none of the audience was complaining. In fact, they came back for an encore of *Brown Sugar* before unplugging.

The small crowd, which had been swollen by some drinkers from the pub downstairs, was generous in its applause.

'We'll be back next week,' called Ricky as he stepped from the stage. Si had no doubt that the turnout would be higher.

'Great stuff.' He slapped Ricky on the back.

'Thanks, man. It was okay.'

'Okay? You're going to the top, man... Yeah!' Si grinned.

'Yeah, I know.' And Ricky threw him a high five and a hug.

⚽ ⚽ ⚽

Jimmy was going from strength to strength. 'Si... I'm in the starting line-up again. Tomorrow against Coventry. The boss told me today.'

'That's great.'

'And what's more, the boss reckons I've a good chance of playing at Wembley if Roy Keane's suspended.'

'Fantastic.'

'Yeah, isn't it? Not for Keano of course, but for me,' Jimmy added. For an instant he felt a twinge of guilt about profiting from his colleague's misfortune, but the feeling passed and he carried on happily. 'Just think, only a few months ago I was nowhere... Nobody... Playing for a second-rate, Second Division team. Now look at me. Sometimes it's all a bit like a dream, eh?'

Si could understand Jimmy's point. Twenty-seven's late

for a soccer player to break into the big time; but that's what his friend seemed to have done. He was fast becoming one of the most talked about players in England. His arrival at United had coincided with their rise through the league. Jimmy hadn't played much of a part in the Championship race—as opposed to the Cup where his contribution was clear—but he had shared the glory as United recovered a twelve point deficit from Newcastle. The Tynesiders, under the charismatic Kevin Keegan, had dominated the Championship all season. But now, with four matches to play, their run of bad luck had allowed United to overtake them and top the table. Heady stuff; and Jimmy was part of it.

'So you'll watch the match, then?'

'Yeah, course I will.'

'Good.' Jimmy seemed pleased. 'And you're sure you can't get there?'

'It's good of you to get us tickets, but I just won't be able to get out of work in time. You know how it is. Anyway, I'll be down The Feathers with my pint watching.'

'That's great. I'll put one in the net for you, okay?'

'You do that.'

'Yeah.'

In fact, Si didn't get to The Feathers until after the kick off. But he was in time to see Jimmy come close to scoring. He was in the right place to meet a Ryan Giggs cross with his head and direct it firmly goalwards. The Coventry keeper was off his line and watched helplessly as the ball sailed over him.

The red hordes in the stand behind the goal leapt to their feet with an expectant roar. But this subsided into a deep 'Aaaah' as the ball smacked against the crossbar, and a Coventry defender cleared the rebound.

A ripple of applause, like the Centre Court at Wimbledon except stronger and with added testosterone, greeted Jimmy's effort. He turned and trotted back towards the United half. The camera zoomed in and a white box appeared beneath the picture of the young man with his head held high: *Jimmy Sweeney, No.22, centre forward for Manchester United.*

'Only a handful of appearances for United,' the commentator was saying, 'but already showing great promise.'

'That's my boy, Jimmy,' said Si softly. Jimmy looked calm, enjoying himself. Si had noticed how when the attack broke down, Jimmy had looked across to Giggs and applauded his world-famous team-mate's precision cross. Clearly, he was already part of the United machine, at home among the stars.

Si felt a warm glow surge within him. He was surprised to find tears prick behind his eyes. But no, that was wet. Men only loved women. Mates were... Yes, mates were mates. You didn't *love* them. But no doubt about it, he was proud of Jimmy.

The other feeling Si experienced was even harder to define. It was a sentiment shared with millions the world over. Like all humanity, Si was subject to the religious urge—the desire to express his spiritual self, his higher being—which takes many forms, and is often channelled into ritual or a set of conventions. However, Si was finding in the rites of football a channel for this urge. A blind alley symptomatic of the age, but one which brought to the surface the nobler side of Si Simpson; the searching soul seeking to return to its origin. So as Si felt himself moved almost to tears by Jimmy's participation in a slick sporting performance, he was half-conscious that it wasn't just affection for his friend that was inspiring him; something profound and important, long-buried, was moving within him.

Ricky arrived ten minutes before full time. 'Sorry I'm late. Christ, the traffic, man—unbelievable. Another bomb scare. I think it was a hoax again in the end.' He settled into his chair. 'Have I missed anything cultural?' he asked with gentle irony.

Si grinned. Ricky had become a soccer addict. The first match Ricky had watched had been a knock-out success: Manchester United had thumped Southampton, and Ricky had been spellbound. He was now threatening to send off to join the MUFC Supporters Club. Si thought this might be simply a Californian over-reaction, but wasn't going to say anything.

'No, it's nil nil.'

'How's our guy Jimmy doing?'

'Okay, okay. Hit the woodwork once, and he's had a busy game.'

But no goals and United really needed to win this match. All three points would give them an almost unassailable lead at the top of the Premiership. There would then be a strong possibility of them winning the mystical Double Double.

Most eleven-year-old boys and all professional players dream of winning the Double. A team achieves this on average about once every fifteen years (although it has happened more frequently in recent seasons than in the distant past). So, by a rough calculation, about one in half a million British males realise the dream, assuming there are no foreigners in the side—a rarity nowadays, so the odds against are likely to be even longer. But Jimmy might just become one of the few, realised Si. All credit to him. Then he would achieve his ambition of entering the soccer history books.

This thought made Si slightly melancholy. How would *he* achieve *his* ambition? What *was* his ambition? With a lost feeling, Si realised he had no clear idea. He'd drifted from college to journalism without a vocation. Chance seemed the only explanation for where he now found himself. It struck him that it didn't need to be like this; he could take control of his life. But how? By chucking in his job? Wouldn't the euphoria of freedom be short-lived, giving way to a realisation that he'd made a great mistake? He might become bored. And wouldn't he miss the money, the status that being a journalist on a national daily afforded? It would be difficult to come back after such a decisive break.

A terrifying abyss started to open beneath Si's feet. Was he just a coward, as Mary had once intimated? Someone who would just drift through life, weak, and with no direction. Or did he have the courage to try and impose some order on his fragmented life? Did he dare leap into the unknown, putting material and social concerns behind him? How did he know that when he landed on the other side life would hold any more meaning? The questions flashed like shooting stars across Si's dark consciousness. Long after the doubts faded in intensity, he continued to mull over the question of meaning. After all, he realised, that was the crux of the matter.

Ricky was settling down to watch the closing minutes of the match. 'Hit it, you mother!' he screamed as a United player wasted an opportunity to shoot. It looked as if the game would end as a draw.

The commentator noted that a few people could be seen leaving their seats.

Unbelievable, thought Si. If I was there, no way would I be leaving. United matches were always so unpredictable—you never knew when they might score. And then it happened. Sharpe controlled the ball on the half-way line and chipped it forward to Jimmy. His red shirt was hanging out and Si noticed how bandy his legs appeared in the long white shorts. Strange, given that Jimmy's thighs were so massive—but compared to those of other Premiership players, they were nothing special. Jimmy took the ball cleverly on the outside of his boot and looked up. There were three Coventry defenders in sky-blue shirts between him and the goalkeeper. To his right was Giggs, usefully placed to put in a cross. The safe option would have been to pass to Giggs; but Jimmy seemed to have a flash of intuition. He drew in one of the defenders, and just before he reached him, he slipped the ball into a gap on the left hand side of the penalty box. There seemed to be no-one else there. But Jimmy's peripheral vision had spotted Cantona gliding ghost-like towards the box. Clearly, the Coventry players were not aware of the threat.

'Oh Jimmy,' Si moaned as he watched his friend hit the ball into the empty space. But the words were hardly out of his mouth when Ricky shouted, 'Great pass, beautiful!' Cantona appeared in yards of space, with an open path to goal. He gathered the ball and, cool as a *concombre,* slotted it into the net.

'Gooooalll!!!' yelled Ricky, and he, Si and two thirds of the crowded pub leapt to their feet. The pub went wild for a few minutes. Many of those watching, the remaining third, obviously loathed United. Their glum faces told the story. But Si and Ricky were over the moon. A great goal, made by Jimmy.

'Your guy, he's really great,' said Ricky after the match was over and United had established themselves firmly at the top of the Premiership. 'I'd like to meet him sometime. You must introduce me when he's next down here. Or better, why don't we go to watch the next match, if he can get us tickets?'

'Yeah, why not?' Si thought about it. He hadn't considered introducing Ricky to Jimmy before. They seemed like separate parts of his life, and he generally preferred to keep his life clearly compartmentalised. It was safer, and less complicated that way. But why not?

⚽ ⚽ ⚽

'What's wrong?'

'What d'you mean, what's wrong?' Jimmy slumped over his pint. 'We lost. That's what's wrong.'

'Oh that. Yeah, sorry. A bit of a disaster.'

'Well, not a disaster,' said Jimmy defensively. 'But certainly a setback. We're still two points clear at the top of the league.' He showed Si the back page of the newspaper in front of him.

	Played	Points
Manchester United	35	73
Newcastle	35	71

'Yeah, I suppose you are.'

Jimmy was in London for the day. The afternoon before he had played in United's 3-1 defeat by Southampton. A shock result. Some of the newspapers blamed the new additions to the team, such as Jimmy, for weakening the side and disrupting the rhythm.

'I doubt I'll get picked for Wednesday.'

'Yeah, course you will. You're a striker after all—it was the defence that screwed up.'

'That's not what *The Sun* says. And we didn't exactly score a bundle did we?'

'Mmmm...' Si hoped Jimmy would cheer up. After all, fortune had hardly neglected him recently; a footballing rags to riches story or what? But how quickly people take changed circumstances for granted.

'I think the worst thing is that Newcastle won.'

'Yeah, I see.' Newcastle, chasing United for the title, had closed the gap with a 1-0 victory over Aston Villa that afternoon. With three matches left it could now go either way, although United were still the bookies' favourites. Certainly, the title seemed destined to be decided on the last day of the season.

'Bugger.' Jimmy slammed the table.

'Cool it, man,' soothed Si.

'Cool it? You sound like some American twat.'

'Yeah, well, I've got this Californian mate. He says it a lot. I guess it might have rubbed off.'

Jimmy looked at Si suspiciously.

Si went on regardless. 'Actually, I thought we might get him out for a drink next time you're down. He's a good bloke. You'll like him.'

'Yeah?'

'Yeah.'

'Is he an intellectual bugger like you? I don't think I could handle another.'

'No, don't worry. He's a surfer.' Si refused to let Jimmy's obnoxiousness get to him. He'd seen his friend in these moods before. They were generally a pose designed to tell the world that he didn't give a damn.

Jimmy realised Si wasn't going to rise and grinned sheepishly. 'Oh my God. A surfer. In London? Right... Well, why don't you bring him to the next match then, eh? And tell him to bring his board.' They both cracked up.

'Yeah, right. Great.'

'So what's his name then? The surfer.' And Jimmy laughed again at the thought of a surfer in London.

'Ricky.'

'Ricky?' mimicked Jimmy. 'Grief. This is worse than I thought.'

'Well, if you don't want to meet him...'

'No, I was only joking. I'm sure he's great. Real cool, eh?' He looked straight into Si's eyes. After an awkward silence, they shared a smile.

'So are you heading back up north tonight?'

'No, I'm here until Tuesday morning. No training tomorrow.'

'Right. Another drink tomorrow night, then?'

'Yeah, it would be rude not to. After all, one or two won't hurt, will they?'

⚽ ⚽ ⚽

'I'm just off down the shops. Do you want anything?'

Greta thought for a moment. 'Pick me up some milk, will you? There's a sweet lad.'

'Sure, no problem. I'll see you later.'

'You'll be back for lunch, will you?'

'Oh aye. I will. Best bit of the day.' They shared a smile. 'Bye.'

Greta listened to the door click to, and then continued loading the kids' clothes into the washing machine. If only her mother had told her how much washing children generated, she'd surely have thought twice before breeding. But, she thought with uncharacteristic bitterness, her mother hadn't even turned up to her wedding. So expecting her to provide helpful maternal advice was asking a lot.

Greta sighed and stuffed the last bundle of soiled garments into the voracious machine's mouth. After slamming the door shut and turning it on, she straightened up and stretched backwards. The pain in her lower back wasn't getting any better. Old age, she lamented. She flicked on the kettle. Time for a coffee. These days she seemed to measure out her days in cups of instant coffee. Hardly an idyll; but, she chided herself, there were many worse off, and she really shouldn't be complaining.

The sky was overcast and the chill made the Sleeper snuggle deeper in his jacket. At the top of All Saints Road he looked about for Lenny. The bench was empty; a few straggling pedestrians made their way down the hill. A couple of drug dealers loitered in doorways—trade started early these days.

The Sleeper disapproved of drugs. He'd tried dope back home as a kid, but his mother had drilled into him the dangers of hard drugs—'See what happened to your cousin Brendan,' she used to say sadly; and although he'd never known what had really happened to Brendan, whom he'd hardly known, the impression stuck. He thought Michael was probably into charlie. Once coming in from the pub, he'd heard Greta screaming something about coke being all to blame for their problems. But it wasn't any of his business, so he didn't pry.

Abandoning the idea of a quick chat with Lenny, he walked briskly to the newsagent. As usual, Jo stood behind the counter scowling at his customers. When he saw the

Sleeper he nodded a welcome. 'Now then, young 'un. How goes this morning?'

'Great, Jo. Just fine and dandy.'

Jo looked surprised. 'That's odd, 'cause what with your team getting thrashed at weekend, I thought thee'd be a bit down in mouth.' Thinly concealed pleasure broke through as he smiled mockingly.

'Aye, I might have known you'd harp on about that. Well, even champions can't win all the time. And we had a weakened team you know. Lots of reserves and new players.'

'Eeeh, lad, you can't have it both ways, you know. Only last week you were telling me how fantastic that new striker... What's his name?'

'Jimmy Sweeney,' prompted the Sleeper patiently.

'Aye, that's the one. Well, he was playing, wasn't he? So, don't be making excuses for 'em.'

The Sleeper relished his banter with Jo. It was rare that he was on the receiving end as Manchester United had been doing so well recently. Of course, Jo, as a Yorkshireman, hated United. 'So, how did Leeds do?' The Sleeper knew the result of course: they'd lost one nil at home. But he wasn't going to miss the opportunity to retaliate.

Jo's face clouded over. 'Bloody awful. Can't even win at Elland Road these days. Hopeless. I reckon they should sack manager. Then buy a new team. It ain't like the old days... I tell you, when I used to go and watch them in the days of Billy Bremner, now, that was a champion team. They'd have walked all over your poncy Man U, no trouble.'

'Dream on, Jo. Hey, I knew I came in here for something.'

'Oh aye, can't be wasting the day, I suppose. *Courier* and *Irish Times*, as usual is it?'

'Yeah, thanks, Jo.' The Sleeper counted out his change and gathered the newspapers—one for the Andersons and the other for himself. 'See you, Jo.'

'Not if I see you first, lad. Oh, and send my regards to that pretty landlady of yours.' Jo winked.

The Sleeper blushed to the roots of his hair. 'Yeah, course I will.' He waved a hand and left the shop as quickly as possible. Behind him he could hear Jo laughing at his embarrassment; a raucous, timbrous laugh brewed deep within that vast beer-invested belly.

He headed back towards home intending to pick up Greta's milk at the Seven Eleven.

Crossing the road by the church, he spotted Lenny. The tramp was lying on the low wall next to the graveyard, apparently asleep. The Sleeper wandered over. 'You awake, then, Lenny?'

The whimper of a wounded animal emanated from the prostrate figure. 'I'm dying.'

The Sleeper bent over his friend. 'What's wrong?' Suddenly a thought struck him. 'You been hit by a car, is that it?' Lenny was always vulnerable to being run over, swaying drunkenly on the kerb. 'Don't you worry. I'll get an ambulance.'

A gnarled hand on his sleeve prevented him leaving in search of a phone. 'No, don't do that. I've not been hit by a car.'

'So what's wrong with you, then?' The Sleeper's concern was turning to irritation.

'I knew it was a mistake. I've always kept to the lager before. Tried and trusted. I was a fool to drink it.'

'Drink what? What did you drink? Meths, is that it? Ah, you stupid eejit.'

'No, I didn't drink meths. Do you take me for an idiot? I've no desire to commit suicide. And you mind who you're talking to, young man.'

'Yeah, sorry, Lenny. I'm just a bit concerned for you, that's all.'

Lenny belched and slowly sat up. He beckoned the Sleeper to sit beside him on the wall and patted his knee. 'Yes, you're a good friend to me. I'm feeling better already.'

'So what did you drink, then, that poisoned you so bad?'

'Brandy. I found a half bottle in the bin down there, and

seeing I'd run out of cans, I couldn't really stop myself. Fool that I was.'

The Sleeper laughed. 'Are you telling me you can't handle a drink stronger than lager?'

Lenny looked shamefaced. 'I've never had that problem before. But I must be getting old. And for so long now I've just stuck to lager. The occasional bit of beer, but mostly lager. I guess the grape is stronger than me.'

'What?'

'No matter. Onwards and upwards. That's what they used to say at school. I've never asked you. Are you a public school man? I imagine you are, being such a nice young man.'

The Sleeper looked at the grimy ravaged face sunk into the desiccated body about which hung the rancid smell of human excrement. 'You were one of those posh public school boys?' He was incredulous.

Lenny straightened himself and stuck out his chin. 'What makes you think that I might not have been?' He looked slightly offended that anyone should question his education. 'My present state should not conceal from you that I am a gentleman by birth and breeding.'

'Get away. You're a laugh, you are.' The Sleeper fell about.

Lenny watched him with a pained look. 'I'm glad that I amuse you. But if you don't mind, I am feeling unwell and would prefer to be left alone.'

'Oh Lenny, man, don't take it to heart. I'm sorry if I've upset you. I didn't mean to be rude. Can I stay a bit longer?'

'Well, if you must. But I expect a bit more respect in future. After all, I'm at least twice your age.'

'Thanks.' They sat in silence for a while. A small dog strolled past. It seemed to know where it was going. The sun came out briefly; then it clouded over again. It even looked as if it might rain.

Lenny broke the spell. 'I intend to be buried here,' he pronounced.

'What, here in this churchyard?'

'Yes. So that my friends can visit me easily.'

'Well, not too soon, I hope.'

'One never knows. Maybe even tomorrow? The way I was feeling an hour ago...'

The Sleeper smiled. 'Just stay off the brandy; then you'll live to a grand old age.'

'The only problem is that the priest is putting obstacles in the way.'

'Obstacles?'

'He insists that I become a Catholic. Totally unreasonable, I think.'

'So this is a Catholic church?'

'Yes, and I'm an Anglican. I mean, I explained to Father Theodore—don't you think that's a silly name? I do. Anyway, I told him we believed in the same God and that as a good Christian I had every right to be buried in my local parish church.'

'What did he say?'

'He said that I should go to the Church of England place over the way.'

'So why don't you?'

'Well, it's not so pretty. And I never sit outside that horrid new church to socialise with my friends. Only here.'

'Aye, I see the problem.' The Sleeper thought for a moment. His face lit up. 'I've got the answer.'

'You have?'

'Aye, it's simple. You convert.'

Lenny's disappointment was visible. 'You think I haven't considered that? Of course I have. But I don't think I can bring myself to do it.'

'Why not?'

'When I suggested it to Father thingamajig, he said it was not something to be done lightly. There were all sorts of considerations.'

'Like what? I thought the church was always trying to recruit new people.'

'Questions of faith. Sacraments.' Lenny delivered these

words like a judgement.

'Well, I'm a Catholic and I've never had to worry about them.'

'Ah, that's because you're one of the lucky ones. Born into certainty. The life of the righteous. Hereditary membership.'

The Sleeper looked mystified.

'The problem arises when you try to join your Church. The entrance exam is really rather rigorous. Now I'm perfectly happy to have regular little chats with the priest and to discuss theology. In fact, there's nothing I like more than a little bit of theology...' Lenny tailed off, lost in thought.

'And?'

'Oh yes, excuse me. Quite lost myself for a moment. As I was saying, a bit of Socratic dialogue never hurt anyone and I'd be delighted to debate the finer points of the Gospels. But this Father Theodore,' he pronounced the syllables with distaste, 'he says that I must be prepared to listen and then accept the teaching he would offer. Dictatorship, that's what it sounds like to me. No doubt he'd want me to worship graven idols, eat human flesh and believe in angels. Well, I just won't do that. I've got principles, after all.'

The Sleeper looked puzzled. 'But Catholics don't do that, do they?' He thought of his devout mother and just couldn't recall her doing other than going to church most days, crying a lot, particularly after his dad left, and wearing black more as she got older.

'Oh, I see. You're not really a practising Catholic, are you?'

For no explicable reason, the Sleeper felt guilty. He hadn't thought of his religion for months until now. It had never been something other than a backdrop in his life; like being a boy, or being Irish. No, in fact, being Irish was something stronger, more real. 'What I mean is, Catholics don't eat flesh.' He racked his brains. 'It's the communion, that's all. Don't you do that in your church?'

'Yes, but it's different. Anglicans don't believe in transubstantiation. At least I don't.'

'What's trans-sub-stan...' He gave up. 'What's that when it's at home?'

'It means the sacrament when the bread and wine turn into the body and blood of Christ. Anglicans believe it figuratively and your lot take it literally.'

'No, they don't. You're being daft. When I was a lad I used to take communion all the time. But it never turned into flesh and blood in my mouth. I promise you, Lenny. You've got it wrong.'

'Hmmm.' Lenny was thoughtful. 'Perhaps. But the priest seemed pretty clear... And what about worshipping Mary as the Mother of God? Isn't that what you do? That's proscribed in the Ten Commandments.'

'I'm not really the man to talk to, Lenny, but I remember we used to pray to Mary for various things. I can't quite remember what. But I don't think we worshipped her.'

'And angels? What a load of hocus pocus.' Lenny rallied accusingly.

'Oh, I don't know about that. It'd be nice, though, wouldn't it? I guess it's just stories, really.'

Lenny clearly wasn't fully satisfied. 'Well, I'll have to think about it. I suppose I should have another chat with that priest to clear a few of these points up.'

'Aye, you do that. Sounds a good idea to me.'

They sat quietly for a few more moments and watched the first prostitutes come out for work. A panda car sped by, siren blaring. Just another day in Notting Hill Gate.

'Well, I'll be off then, Lenny. Got to get back for lunch.'

'Right. Goodbye. And thanks. We had an interesting chat, didn't we?'

'We certainly did, Lenny. It's always a pleasure.' The Sleeper walked quickly home, leaving the tramp on the church wall staring into space.

'I'm home,' he called.

'Good timing. We'll eat in five minutes.'

The Sleeper dropped the papers onto the table, made a face at Greta's youngest, who watched him from the high chair, and took off his jacket.

'Did you get the milk?'

'Ah, sweet Mary. I knew there was something.'

Greta looked disappointed.

'Now look. I'm sorry. See, I'll get it after lunch. Okay? And I promise you, I'll make it up to you somehow. Okay?'

Greta cheered up. 'You will? How'll that be, then?'

'Oh, never you mind. I'll find a way…' And they both laughed with nervous anticipation.

❀ ❀ ❀

'When we were small… my ma used to feed us nothing but grits somedays…'

'What are grits?' slurred Si.

They were back at his gaff, slouched on the floor drinking whisky. Si was already beginning to look towards his bed. As predicted, the second gig had been an even bigger success than the first and celebrations had led to many drinks. Too many. He had a mounting, bilious feeling rising within him. Soon he'd stop drinking. After this whisky. But it would be a waste not to finish off the glass.

Ricky, still flying on adrenaline, seemed more awake than ever.

'Grits are like cereals, you know. You eat them for breakfast.'

'Right.' Si felt his eyelids begin to fall. Not far away he could hear a train cut though the embankment. The post train or the milk train, he supposed. Perhaps they were one and the same? Carrying milk and post together to save money. It certainly made sense. He pondered this as he listened with half an ear to Ricky.

'Sometimes I was so hungry I couldn't stop my stomach rumbling in class. The teacher used to look at me kind of pitiful like, but she couldn't do anything.'

'Where was your dad?'

'My pa went off when I was about ten. Son of a bitch...' There seemed little to add. 'But my ma did her best for us kids. We were four. I was second youngest. That's when I decided to be a rock star...'

'Mmm...' nodded Si as he fell asleep.

⚽ ⚽ ⚽

Si woke first.

The sunlight streamed in through the big window and surrounded Ricky with a halo. His burnished hair shot out in all directions. He sat in the same position he'd been in the night before and must have fallen asleep mid-story.

Si vaguely remembered something about a childhood of grinding poverty followed by Ricky making a serious amount of money quickly, just before coming to London. How he'd done this, he hadn't explained... Or at least Si couldn't remember.

Si slumped gracelessly on the floor. 'Oh...' he moaned. He knew the whisky had been a mistake. Why, why hadn't he listened to the voice of his own experience? 'Oh shit.' Si raised himself to all fours and crawled into the bedroom, pausing only to gulp down a couple of glasses of water. Kicking off his shoes, he burrowed deep into the duvet. With a bit of luck he'd feel better next time he woke up.

⚽ ⚽ ⚽

'The famous Jimmy... It's great to meet you, man.'

'Yeah and you.' Jimmy looked far from convinced. 'Si says you're a wild man.'

'I don't know about that. But I just love your soccer. I've watched all your games recently. Ask Si, if you don't believe me.'

Si shuffled awkwardly from foot to foot and smiled

tensely as they both turned to look at him. Si and Ricky had come to the players' entrance, which was under the stand away from the main turnstiles, to pick up their complimentary tickets. But Si hadn't planned on introducing Ricky to Jimmy until after the match. However, by chance Jimmy had been standing in the reception area chatting to another player when they'd walked in. Si nodded to affirm Ricky's claim. He felt foolish. 'Yeah, he's become a real fanatic.'

'Great, great.' Jimmy was having difficulty not being rude.

'It was real good of you to get us tickets for the match. It's the first time I've seen a game live.'

Jimmy looked over his shoulder towards the glass security door beyond which only club officials and players could go. He wasn't making much effort to conceal his impatience. 'Well, I hope you enjoy it. It's another cruncher. Listen, I must be getting back. I need to change and ...'

'Yeah, sure, no problem. Well, it's been real cool to meet you.'

Si threw a warning glance at Jimmy. But he need not have worried. Jimmy retained his impassive expression.

'And, Jimmy, next time you're in London ...'

Jimmy left him mid-sentence as he greeted a passing team-mate. 'Hi Gary. How did it go last night?' The two players had a brief, hearty exchange before Jimmy turned back to his guests. 'Hey guys, I'm sorry, that was really rude of me. It's just that Gary...' he paused to gather his thoughts and then clearly thought better of explaining. 'Oh, never mind.' He made to go.

Si was fuming. But Ricky was undeterred. 'Jimmy, as I was saying, next time you're in London come and see my band play. I'd love to return the favour, although it's hardly in the same league.'

'Band?'

'Yeah, didn't Si tell you about The Crocodiles?'

'Uh no...'

'Oh, I'm sure I did,' blurted Si, now even more uncomfortable.

'So, what kind of a band is it?'

'R and B, mostly covers, but we're already working on a few of our own numbers. We're gonna be big. Catch us while you can.' Ricky shimmied and did a few of his Mick Jagger steps to emphasise the point. He grinned.

Jimmy grinned back. 'Wow, that's great.' Jimmy suddenly came to life. Bemused, Si watched his friend open like a flower to the sun.

'Yeah, real cool.'

'I'd love to come and see the band next time I'm down in London.'

'Anytime, man, just say the word.'

'You know, I'm a bit of a musician myself,' said Jimmy shyly.

'You are?' asked Ricky, interested.

'You are?' Si echoed. This was the first he'd heard of it.

'Yeah, well, a guitarist really.'

'What, classical?'

'No. Rock 'n' roll.'

'No way...'

'You're kidding,' said Si, totally amazed. Jimmy was the most unmusical person he knew.

Jimmy ignored Si.

'What's your axe, man?'

'Fender copy,' blushed Jimmy. 'It's got a great action.'

'Yeah, real cool.' Ricky reflected a moment. 'Listen, you should come and jam with us. That'd be awesome.'

'Yeah, I'd love that. Next time I'm down, okay?'

'Okay,' exclaimed Ricky and punched Jimmy on the arm.

'Didn't you say you had to be going or something....' Si prompted.

'Yeah, I should really.' Jimmy left reluctantly after executing some extraordinary American basketball handshake which Ricky taught him in less than twenty seconds.

'Great guy, really cool.'

'Yeah, he is. We should go too. There's just time for a quick drink before the match.'

They walked back outside into the crowds of milling supporters. Si wondered what Jimmy had been on about. Surely he wasn't telling the truth? And if so, why had he never mentioned it before? The meeting, about which he'd had serious reservations, had gone well. But Si was left deeply puzzled.

⚽ ⚽ ⚽

The Sleeper had been in the pub about an hour and was on his third pint when a ginger bloke sat down beside him. They both stared up at the big TV screen and watched the soccer. The pub groaned as Man U failed to score. But it didn't matter as they were winning 1-0 already. The Sleeper had always supported United; since he was a wee kid. So he didn't mind waiting. In fact, he was almost hoping no-one would come.

'Your team is winning?' carrot head asked after a while.

'Wha'?' The Sleeper jumped at the expected words. 'Oh, yeah, a walkover,' he blurted, completing the sequence.

The man raised his fiery eyebrows and leaned over. 'Call me Ginger.'

The Sleeper wanted to crack a joke about the name, he was so nervous. But he managed to restrain himself. 'Right you are. Pleased to meet you. I'm...'

'I know who you are. You're Baa.' His laugh was unpleasant.

'What do you mean? How do you know that name?'

'Ah, we know a lot about you. Don't forget it.'

'Now wait a mo...' But the protest was feeble and Ginger brushed it aside.

'What are you drinking? Eh? D'you want a drink or not?'

'Bitter,' the Sleeper muttered.

'Bitter? English bitter? You'll not have a Caffery's with me?'

This didn't sound like a question, so the Sleeper nodded.

'Good lad.' Ginger patted him on the shoulder and pushed through the crowd to the bar.

As he waited, he watched that new signing, Jimmy Sweeney, score a great goal from the edge of the penalty box. He was a steal at the price, thought the Sleeper, and Millwall must be kicking themselves for not asking more. You could say one thing for Ferguson: despite his many critics, he bought his players well. Everyone had said Sweeney was past it. Even a keen football fan like the Sleeper had never heard of him till two months before. But since Sweeney signed for United he'd done really well.

This pleasant distraction ended as carrot head returned.

'You know, we only got your letter the other day. Thought we'd lost you, not hearing anything from you for months.'

'I posted it when I moved. I don't know what could have happened to it.'

'Is that so, now? Sure, the date on the letter suggests you're telling the truth. But the postmark was for March so it must have been sitting somewhere for ages. Anyway, we'll give you the benefit of the doubt. Lucky for you it got to us in the end.'

'Why lucky for me?'

Ginger looked around before replying, and then spoke in a conspiratorial whisper. 'Because, eejit, otherwise you might have missed out on your chance to change the course of history and fight for Ireland.' He explained briefly that the cease-fire was fragile and that soon it would be broken. 'Who knows when or where. But when it does... You'll be ready.'

The Sleeper nodded. Why did he feel so uncomfortable? Wasn't this what he'd come to London for all those months ago? Wasn't this the chance he'd been waiting for? Had he changed so much? Or perhaps, just grown up a bit? For Christ's sake, he was only just twenty. But then he realised he was being stupid, and tried to shut out such weak thoughts. He steeled himself. 'Right. Go on.'

⚽ ⚽ ⚽

It was the night before the last match of the league Championship. Manchester United were playing away at Middlesborough. Newcastle United would be playing Tottenham Hotspur at home the same day. After Newcastle's victory against Leeds, it had looked like the two teams chasing the Premiership title would be on equal points for the last match of the season. But because they had conceded a late equaliser against Nottingham Forest, Newcastle now found themselves two points behind United.

To win the Championship, Newcastle needed to win and hope that United lost. United, on the other hand, only needed a draw to be sure of the Championship on superior goal difference.

	Played	Points	Goal Difference
Manchester United	37	79	+35
Newcastle	37	77	+29

Jimmy knew he should be feeling relaxed. But although his team were now firm favourites, he was nervous as hell. It might be United's third title in four years, but it would be his first. And what if he made a mistake which led to United losing? It didn't bear thinking about.

'I could murder a beer…' he groaned.

His team-mates, sitting with him in the hotel watching Saturday night TV, laughed. 'Some chance.' Alcohol was banned until after the FA Cup Final the following week. It was going to be a tough seven days as United attempted to repeat the Double. It still seemed like a dream to Jimmy. Only a few months before he'd been a nobody, stuck at Millwall. Now he was participating in football history. Sometimes he didn't want to blink, fearing he'd wake up.

'I think I'll crash out,' he said.

'Yeah, not a bad idea,' said one of the more experienced players.

'Night.'

'Night.' Jimmy sloped from the room. He was terrified at the thought of tomorrow's match. Terrified, but exhilarated. It would be broadcast around the world to countries of which he'd never even heard. Amazing. To be so small yet so universal... He thought about his family and friends. I bet Si'll be watching, he reassured himself. He tried ringing him from his room. But there was no answer. Probably at The Feathers, thought Jimmy enviously.

Downstairs the other players were finishing up their orange juices and mineral waters. 'Nice guy, Jimmy.'

'Yeah, but I hope he doesn't go soft on us tomorrow.'

'What d'you mean?'

'Well, he's only just made the big time. Pressure could get to him, know what I mean?'

'Oh right. Like you're not going to feel the pressure at all tomorrow, eh?'

'Well...'

'Well what?'

'Yeah, I suppose you're right. It's going to be a big one.'

'Mmmm...' An apprehensive silence descended. 'But you may have a point. After all, he's only played ten full matches. Hope he stays cool.'

'Yeah, we could do with a goal from him too.'

'It'd be nice.'

'Yeah. Wouldn't it.' And with that, feeling slightly less nervous about their own prospects, the other players also went upstairs to bed.

⚽ ⚽ ⚽

Jimmy needn't have worried. David May headed an early goal to put Manchester United in front, and then as Andy Cole acrobatically flicked the second into the Middlesborough net, Tottenham scored against Newcastle. Jimmy had a quiet day, although he supplied the pass which allowed Ryan Giggs to score the third. Three nil to United. Champions yet again.

	Played	Points	Goal Difference
Manchester United	38	82	+38
Newcastle	38	78	+29

Si watched his friend running round the pitch draped in a United scarf, red, black and white clashing wildly with United's blue away strip. The camera caught Jimmy looking like a startled rabbit as he held up the huge trophy. He kept it at arm's length as if the silver object might bite. The look of disbelief and amazed pleasure was mirrored on Si's face in The Feathers.

'Our lad did well,' said someone.

'He did, he did,' agreed Si coughing away, a husky edge to his voice. He wiped a rogue tear surreptitiously, hoping no-one would notice.

Mary sat next to him. She'd agreed to come and watch in honour of the occasion and because their relationship was on an up-turn after a difficult period. They'd both agreed to try harder to compromise and share their time. 'Why are you crying?' she demanded.

'No, I'm not crying... It's the smoke, that's all.'

'Ridiculous. It's only a football match.'

Si thought better of replying. He didn't want an argument to spoil the moment.

'When are you going to introduce me to your famous friend then? It's about time.'

'Who, Jimmy? Well, I've tried, you know. But either you didn't turn up or it didn't work out for some reason.'

Mary sniffed derisively. 'You haven't tried very hard.'

'Fine, fine. I'd love you two to meet. I'll work something out soon. Next time Jimmy's in London, okay? But it'll probably be after the Cup Final. I imagine he'll be totally caught up before then.'

'When's that?'

'Next Saturday.'

'Does that mean we have to watch it?'

Si looked at her sadly. 'You don't need to if you don't want to. I wouldn't have any difficulty in getting rid of the ticket.' Si knew that Ricky for one would leap at it.

'Oh, so we're going to the match?'

'Yeah, if you feel like it.'

'That's different. I just didn't fancy sitting in this grotty pub again cricking my neck to see the screen.' Mary brightened. 'I've never been to Wembley.'

'No, I don't suppose you have.'

'How exciting.'

Si looked at his girlfriend suspiciously. But there was no trace of irony in her expression.

Si reflected on Jimmy's achievement as United celebrated the first leg of the Double. League Champions, and Jimmy was one of them. That alone was more than most people achieved in a lifetime. And of course, there could be more to come. Manchester United had to win the FA Cup Final against the mighty Liverpool if they were going to achieve the Double for the second time... The Double Double. Jimmy had a real chance of achieving a certain immortality: to become one of the elite whose names would be recited reverentially by schoolboys for decades to come ('Jimmy Sweeney... He won the Double with United in 1996, didn't he?' 'Yeah.' 'Wow, I'd love to meet him someday'). But to do that he'd need to get a game at Wembley and United would have to win—a team like Liverpool wouldn't be a walkover. It was far from certain that Jimmy would be picked. There were plenty of experienced players, household names, trying to edge him out and regain their places.

But for the moment the sun was shining on Jimmy. Next week's Cup Final would come soon enough, thought Si.

⚽ ⚽ ⚽

'I watched this programme last night.'

'Yeah?' Bill stirred his coffee, listening to his immediate boss more out of duty than interest. The morning had been slow so far.

'Yeah, they were debating whether to put the national sports stadium in Manchester or London.'

'And?'

'Well, they couldn't decide.'

'They've got one already. Wembley.'

'I know, but they want to build a new one.'

'Oh.'

'So they asked if it'd be necessary to knock down Wembley.'

'Weird.'

'Yeah, perhaps. And if it was going to be at Wembley, they'd knock down the old one.'

'So?'

'So, someone said something really interesting.'

'What?'

'They asked would we need to deny British fans three years of international sport while they rebuilt the stadium.'

Bill looked mystified. He wasn't used to Si being so garrulous.

'D'you see? It's a bit like Britain's problems on a bigger scale. Like if we're going to sort out the UK, perhaps we need to start from scratch and reinvent ourselves to fit into the modern world. That might take at least three years of denial, but the end result would justify it. D'you see?' Si was becoming whimsical.

'It's a bit early,' mumbled Bill.

Si looked hard at him. Then caught himself. 'Yeah, I guess you're right. Let's leave the thinking until after lunch. Let's just get on with some journalism, eh?'

'Yeah, sounds good to me,' nodded Bill, obviously relieved.

'So, who d'you think'll win the Cup Final, then?'

⚽ ⚽ ⚽

Jimmy didn't sleep a wink the night before Manchester United played Liverpool in the FA Cup Final. He'd been floating on air since collecting his Championship medal the week before, but at about midnight the magnitude of what was still to come hit him like a revelation.

Alex Ferguson had not announced the team publicly, but Jimmy knew he was in the side. There had been a team meeting on Thursday behind closed doors when the team had been read out. To his amazement, Jimmy found himself in the starting line-up. Famous players with much more experience, such as Lee Sharpe and even the club captain Steve Bruce, were left out.

A huge weight of responsibility rested on his shoulders. And he couldn't even phone Si or anyone else to tell them that he'd be playing because there was an embargo on the team announcement until just before the match. Jimmy also realised that telling Si would be to put his friend in the difficult position of sitting on a story, powerless to act. Could even Si's strong loyalty withstand the professional pressure to pass the news to a colleague on the sports pages?

Breakfast was a quiet affair apart from a few of the lads trying to crack jokes to dispel the tension hanging over the cornflakes. Jimmy mooched about the chintzy hotel waiting for the bus to take them to Wembley. He was still in awe of many of his team-mates and suspected that some resented his arrival and place in the first team.

Occasionally, he came across huddles of two or three of his fellow players slumped in deep armchairs, chatting with forced humour. He smiled and nodded but didn't join any of them, not wanting to intrude on the friendships forged during several long Premiership campaigns. He was acutely conscious of the short time that he'd been at the club.

Jimmy wished Si was there. They could have had a laugh together. He only had that kind of friendship with Si.

After what seemed an eternity they all assembled in the lobby. Decked out in the navy blue suits which they'd been measured for a fortnight before, they trooped out to the coach. There was something uncanny about so many young stars in sharp tailoring rather than football kit. Of course, it could have been worse; at least the cut was classical and done in Savile Row. Heaven knows who made the extraodinary three piece fashion suits which Cup Final teams in the seventies used to wear. But despite this sartorial compensation, Jimmy was not alone among his team-mates in feeling uncomfortable in a suit and tie; he'd have preferred jeans and a tee shirt.

It was a short drive to the stadium. Jimmy sat next to Ryan Giggs, who seemed as calm as ever. They chatted sporadically about last year's final in which United had been beaten by another Merseyside team, Everton. It had been a terrible experience, coming as it did straight after failing in the last match to win the Championship; the antithesis of this year.

'But today'll be different,' Giggs prophesied, as deadpan as ever.

Jimmy prayed that he was right. Last year he remembered watching the Final with Si in The Feathers. As he recalled, both of them had been quite pleased to see Everton, the underdogs, beat United. That now seemed a lifetime away.

'You nervous?'

'Yeah. Terrified.'

'Don't be. Believe me, once you get out there it'll be fine... Like any other match.'

'I suppose so. Only there's a lot hanging on this, isn't there? More than your average match.'

'You mean the Double Double?'

'Uh huh.'

'Yeah, I guess so. But let's just get on with the job and enjoy it, eh?'

Jimmy nodded gratefully, encouraged by his team-mate's unfazed attitude. Impressive, especially since he was still several years younger than Jimmy. 'Yeah, right,' he grinned.

Then they were driving through the singing, smiling crowd and soon afterwards inside the stadium. Some of the players went out to inspect the pitch. Jimmy felt so nervous that he didn't want to move from the refuge of the dressing room. He sat on the blue bench quietly by himself watching the others come and go, talking loudly to cover raw nerves. The white walls stared back at him and he felt oppressed.

Only Eric Cantona seemed completely detached from the pressure of the occasion. He sat still in the corner, meditating. Jimmy noticed that he glanced occasionally at a crumpled paperback by someone called Jacques Derrida which he was holding between the thumb and forefinger of his right hand. Jimmy hoped he was plotting a masterstroke to unbalance Liverpool and push the advantage United's way. But it did seem a bit late in the day to be reading football strategy books, even if they were in French. Well, who was he to raise such doubts, thought Jimmy humbly. Since arriving at Old Trafford, he'd had been so awe-struck in the great player's presence that he'd only exchanged a few pleasantries. The Frenchman seemed aloof, above it all somehow.

Jimmy took off his jacket and hung it on one of the hooks above the bench. Then he checked that Albert and Alec the kit managers had laid out his strip and that his boots were ready. As ever, the backroom boys had performed their duties impeccably. Jimmy contrasted the United set up with his experience at Millwall. The two clubs were worlds apart. For instance, at United there were always at least four shirts available for each player, two long sleeved and two short sleeved. But at Millwall there had been times when he'd even had to take his kit home for washing and to clean his own boots.

Jimmy looked up when an official poked his head round the door. Seeing an unreceptive dressing room, he quickly withdrew it. Then Jimmy realised Cantona was watching him.

'You are nervous?' Cantona closed his book carefully.

'Yeah, I think so,' blushed Jimmy.

Cantona nodded unsmiling. 'You must not be. It will be good today. You will see.' A mischievous twinkle played in the corner of the older man's eyes.

Jimmy forgot his nerves and believed his captain.

⚽ ⚽ ⚽

Si and Mary were sitting among the players' guests, high in the stand. The sun had descended in the sky and long shadows fell across the emerald pitch. His teeth and those of some United spectators around him were chattering. He could see the tension etched deep into the brow of a teenage girl draped in United's colours sitting on his left—one of the players' girlfriends.

Jimmy's generosity in inviting them as his guests had made an impression. Si had been really touched by the gesture.

'Hey mate, that's really kind…'

'Don't be thick. Stop being grateful. You're my best mate, what else d'you expect?' Jimmy had tried to make light of it. Si unable to say anything else, had given Jimmy a hug.

'Cut it out. What'll people think, eh?' Jimmy pushed him gently away. But the moment had been a good one, an instant of emotional honesty which would outlive at least one of them.

Si pulled himself together for fear that Mary would

notice and not understand. Why were women allowed to parade emotions, but men had to preserve a gruff mask? Si watched Mary carefully ploughing through the official programme, studying it as if it were company accounts.

'They've got nice legs,' she said, pausing on a picture of the United team. 'Thighs to die for,' and she giggled naughtily. Despite his butterflies, Si felt uplifted and a deep wave of affection for Mary surged in his chest.

United were trying desperately to break through Liverpool's defences. After over an hour of play there were still no goals and both sides were playing badly. At times it seemed more like a comedy of errors than an historic match between the two most famous football teams in Britain. The only consolation, thought Si, was that United were playing less badly than Liverpool. But both sides were suffering from acute nerves.

Jimmy had been virtually non-existent so far, apart from one shot way over the bar. Even Giggs, for all his pre-match confidence, was having an off-day.

'This is terrible,' complained the teenage girl on his left, biting her nails.

'Yeah,' agreed Si, noticing that she'd now run out of fingers and was onto her thumb. If it carried on like this without a goal they'd all die of stress. He reckoned the tension had already knocked ten years off his life.

'They're bound to score soon,' said Mary. She was transfixed, totally absorbed in the spectacle, having learned from the glossy programme what all the fuss was about.

'Yeah,' said Si without confidence. It was going to be settled by a single goal either way. The danger was that an error by United would allow Liverpool to go ahead, and that would be that. No, please God, no. Let United win and let Jimmy score the goal, he prayed silently.

⚽ ⚽ ⚽

Jimmy was having a nightmare. He'd known it would be bad, but this was ten times, even a hundred times, worse than anything he'd imagined. Every time the ball came near him he couldn't move his legs fast enough to catch it. He felt as if lead weights were in his boots holding him back.

Five minutes to go and it looked as if extra time and even a replay was inevitable. What a terrible match. He wondered if he'd blown his chances at United as he watched Gary Pallister stop a half-hearted Liverpool attack.

Jimmy was only amazed that he hadn't been substituted yet. The Boss had pulled off Andy Cole, but Jimmy was still on the pitch. He knew that, like Cole, he was principally there to score goals. And so far he had not. As the seconds ticked away, he began to feel his United career drawing to a close. He'd had his opportunity to score after twenty minutes, but he'd snatched at the shot and ballooned it over the crossbar. The Liverpool fans had jeered him and, although he knew he shouldn't allow it to get to him, he'd been rattled by the volume and animosity of their taunts.

Pallister still had the ball and tapped it to Roy Keane. The voluble Irishman had been magnificent in holding United's midfield together—a rare point of stability in a jittery performance by the League Champions. Keane, looking assured, ran forward with the ball to the half-way line before taking a one-two from Cantona. Now inside the Liverpool half, he looked right and, seeing Jimmy in space, pushed it forward to him. 'Jimmy, yours,' he shouted; more a command than anything else.

Jimmy thought for a moment that he wouldn't be able to control the ball, it was coming too fast. But he caught it on the outside of his boot and it spun off in front of him along the manicured turf.

The sun came out as Jimmy pursued the ball, deaf to the rising crescendo of expectation from the United supporters.

He moved towards the penalty area and looked up to see if the shot was on. As he did so, a Liverpool defender hurtled into him and slid the ball away from him.

Damn, thought Jimmy, as he tumbled face down onto the ground. He'd squandered a good opportunity.

Pulling himself to his feet, he realised that the ball had gone behind for a corner and United still had the advantage. He jumped up and went to stand on the near edge of the five yard box.

David Beckham positioned the ball and ran up to take the corner. 'Becks... Here,' cried Jimmy. He broke forward in an attempt to lose his marker, keeping his eye on the ball as it curved towards him. It was high and spinning outwards, away from the goal.

Summoning his remaining strength, Jimmy leapt as high as he could into the air. He just connected to flick the ball with his head towards the goalmouth. The Liverpool keeper launched himself and punched clear Jimmy's attempt. As Jimmy fell to the ground, he found the Liverpool keeper tumbling over him.

What happened next made footballing history. As Jimmy rolled around trying to disentangle himself from the Liverpool keeper, the ball flew out to the edge of the penalty area. It looked as if Liverpool had survived the attack and a goalless draw was unavoidable.

Then from nowhere Eric Cantona swooped like an angel of destiny, a one man legion of honour. He appeared at the edge of the penalty box and bent himself at almost ninety degrees to the vertical; somehow he managed to hook his right foot around the rebounding ball. Cantona took it on the volley and the ball miraculously sped back towards goal. Amid the chaos, over Jimmy's body and the prone goalkeeper, between three defenders frozen and impotent, unable to block the shot, the ball rocketed; only that it all seemed to happen in slow motion, and the ball almost appeared to weave its way between the players.

Then the white sphere hit the back of the net and the

world turned red, the red of United.

Cantona had kept his promise. It was a good day; a great, historic day; the best day of Jimmy's life. He and United had won the Double Double.

As Jimmy ran to congratulate his captain, he passed James, the Liverpool keeper, despondently pulling the ball out of the net. He patted him on the shoulder. The keeper had done all he could to defend his goal, but it hadn't been enough. The two opposing players exchanged a look. Even if Jimmy had wanted to say something he couldn't have—the noise of the delirious United celebrations filled the stadium, obliterating all other sound.

Jimmy ran past the disconsolate goalkeeper and, giving vent to a massive but inaudible victory yell, ran on to embrace the goalscorer.

SUMMER

With the first intimations of summer, the city rose to the challenge. Rosy-cheeked children rushed to the parks and sucked ices. Dapper businesswomen swung Chanel jackets across bony shoulders and strode purposefully from the underground to their air-conditioned offices.

The newspapers trumpeted that the summer promised to be one of the hottest on record. Despite the heat, the city speeded up and glistening, racing green MGs, driven by Ray Ban posers in Polo shirts and chinos, raced bicycle messengers in tight satin shorts down dozy Belgravia streets. Roller-bladers clad in improbable armour skated dangerously along the pavements of Battersea and Fulham, trying to avoid wrinkles in the bubbling tarmac and the drooling dogs, which skulked in the shade and dreamed of brisk winter walks.

⚽ ⚽ ⚽

'Darling, that's great,' raved Si's mother. 'We'll see you at about eight thirty, then.'

Si listened to her blow the customary kiss down the phone before closing his mobile—a recent imposition intended to allow Dougy to talk to him at all times. Si resented it as deeply as a dog its leash. He looked thoughtful as he walked back through the park to *The Courier* building. A trip home to the county of Easfolk needed psychological preparation.

Si had realised in his late teens that nobody was responsible for the family into which he is born. This was fortunate, and since then relations with his own family, in particular his parents, had changed for the better. Previously his father's idiosyncrasies—pipe-smoking, dahlia-growing kind of idiosyncrasies—had been a source of deep embarrassment. He had felt this to such an extent that taking friends home was always a trial; and even now he had never taken a girlfriend to meet his parents.

Si's mother was less an embarrassment than a mystery. One week, she devoured books about eastern religions; the next, she attended evangelical revival churches. She was passionate in what she termed her search for the Truth.

Once she had tried to draw a parallel between Si's journalistic ambitions and her own spiritual path. 'Darling, don't you see, we're both striving for the same thing. It's like George Trevelyan says, we are reborn anew and each soul is on a higher plane, reaching out desperately to get to the Truth at the centre of the universe.'

Si hadn't protested, although he knew that his mother's understanding of modern journalism was clearly limited. The search for truth only acted as an excuse for the real business of selling newspapers. When business success and revelations of truth for the greater good coincided, fine... But that was the exception rather than the rule.

Once Si realised that, despite an accident of birth, he was not expected to take responsibility and could not be judged because of his parents, then he began to appreciate their better qualities.

He noticed how his father controlled his temper even in the face of extreme provocation; for example, when Si accidentally 'weeded' some expensive prize flowers when trying to help in the garden. His father just pointed out the error, leant on his spade and, contemplating the mangled remains of his cherished plants, stoked his pipe and smiled benignly at his errant son. No words, just a few puffs before the pipe automatically extinguished itself again. Si appreciated that.

He also realised that his mother could be a valuable asset. Although he found her mystical ramblings incomprehensible and bizarre, friends he brought home, including Jimmy, were fascinated by her.

'She's great,' enthused Jimmy. 'I wish my mother was like that.'

And Si felt a sort of pride watching his mother, blonde hair pulled back with a silk scarf, talking non-stop for half an hour without interruption from Jimmy. Even more bizarre was the fact that Jimmy had never shown any religious or intellectual leanings before or since. But he hung on every syllable as she explained the Tao.

Si passed through the security check and flashed his pass at the guard, who wore a black uniform and looked like Officer Dibble from *Top Cat*. Would he really be capable of deterring any would-be terrorist from storming the building? It seemed unlikely. But who would want to attack *The Courier*'s offices anyway? Even in the cease-fire, perhaps the IRA? The newspaper had been consistently critical of Sinn Fein's duplicity in the bomb-shattered times before this peaceful interlude. Not that anyone would have much to gain from such a crass action. But then terrorists seemed not to understand that they stood to gain nothing from blowing up civilians. Odd, really, that they bothered at all, reflected Si. Anyway, there hadn't been any bombings in London for the best part of a year now, and the cease-fire seemed to be holding.

He stepped into the lift and, pressing the sixth floor button on the panel, wondered what it would be like to be blown to smithereens. Would he be able to appreciate the sensation or would he be already nothing, non-existent, by the time the blast ripped his body apart?

The thought was intriguing and he pondered it for the rest of the day. As he put on the kettle he imagined he was triggering a bomb... As he pressed 0 on his phone and when he opened a door, he held his breath to see if the action would lead to an explosion.

Si was still wondering about it when he knocked off that evening. Somehow he'd managed to scrape together enough material to fill the page. Insipid stuff, he knew it. But any passion for his job had more or less gone, and increasingly he wondered if he retained enough ambition to get him through the day. The shadows were lengthening and Si was aware that his position was becoming untenable. He couldn't hide from himself forever; life was too short.

Bill, true to recent form, had produced two good pieces which had carried that day's Diary past the Editor's censure. Dougy had wanted to know how Si had found out about the past of the Head Chef at Zeno's (a new ultra-fashionable Notting Hill restaurant). Apparently the cook had started out as a factotum for a notorious Lebanese arms dealer. Preparing food had just been one of several duties; the others were less savoury. Anyway, Dougy decided after a few seconds of indecision, that he liked it.

Si couldn't be bothered to lie, and admitted that the story had all been Bill's efforts. He didn't feel self-destructive enough to admit that he hadn't even proof-read the piece carefully before putting it to the Editor.

'Mm,' intoned Dougy, 'he's doing well, Bill, isn't he?'

Si tried to mirror Dougy's thoughtful look and nodded slowly. After that he left the eagle's nest office as quickly as possible. Stopping only to chuck the approved page onto Bill's desk, asking him to deliver it downstairs, he grabbed his bag and made for the lift.

Si went straight from work to the station, where he picked up Mary in front of the main ticket office. He was on time, but she'd been waiting quarter of an hour already and made sure he knew this.

Si had been dismayed by Mary's enthusiasm to meet his parents. A weekend *à quatre* loomed and it was unclear how it would pan out.

It was the first time he'd been fond enough of any girl to want to take her home; or, more accurately, to agree to her demand that he introduce her to his parents. As they stood on the platform waiting for the six forty which would take them to the little Easfolk village where he'd grown up, he wondered again if he was doing the right thing. Perhaps Mary would get the wrong idea and assume the next step would be a proposal. He felt nowhere near ready for marriage yet. Wasn't this just giving her false expectations? The arrival of the train distracted him.

'It's here Si, stop day-dreaming. The least you can do after being so late is to talk to me.'

Despite the unfair criticism, Si followed Mary obediently through the automatic doors which beeped repeatedly and then swooshed shut behind him. Like entering the command deck of the Starship Enterprise... Or a gas chamber.

⚽ ⚽ ⚽

Si was at his desk. How long this could go on he didn't know. He knew what he should do, but doing it required more courage than he could muster. And he wasn't even managing to do the job well any more. He felt caught in no-man's-land between two safe and correct courses of action.

Now, instead of rewriting a piece he'd researched earlier, he was reading a book of poetry. Mary had given it to him last weekend in Easfolk. His parents and Mary had got on extremely well and after cautiously observing them for the first evening, Si had decided to join in and enjoy the weekend as well. It had been a great success and as a result his relationship with Mary seemed to have moved onto another, highly satisfactory plane.

Mary said the collection was one of her favourite books. So far he had not discovered the same truths within the pages, but he was persevering in the hope of understanding Mary better. Only one poem had really struck a chord with him.

> I go to Ely to sustain my soul
> And the Island wind restores me whole.
> Within steep vaults of lofty stone
> The beast within groans and is gone.
> On knees of bone I gaze ahead
> Beyond the choir, to when I'm dead.

And in the gloom a glow surrounds
My quietening heart and present sounds.
The grandparents stand at the mortal watch;
The parents, ageing, now hear the clock;
And I, with no more than twice this more,
Find comfort in these mortal laws.
I go to Ely to sustain my soul
And the Island wind restores me whole.

Si hadn't heard of the poet before, but this song of death seemed strangely joyful and he could identify with the mortal mood. It was rare to find a modern writer with so clear a perception of death; recognising within that great unknown cause for calm and pleasant expectation rather than nihilism or terror.

The phone rang and Si put down the slim volume.

'How's the page going?'

'Fine, fine,' lied Si.

'Yeah? Well. I hope so. Bring it up to me as soon as you've got all the bits in place, okay?'

The requirement for Dougy to approve the Diary every day before it went to press held him like a ball and chain; there was still no sign that Dougy would lift the injunction.

'Only temporary, mind. Understand? Just until we get it back on track, up to your previous standard. Okay?' That's how Dougy had explained retaining control when Si had asked recently if they couldn't now return to the previous arrangement.

Despite this half-reassurance, Si wondered how long it would be before Dougy permanently removed his remaining authority. In his heart he knew he didn't really care any more. The glittering prizes of journalism no longer held the same fascination. It could only be a matter of time now.

The Sleeper collected the first part of the kit the week after the meeting in Hammersmith. 'Just a small amount of explosive,' Ginger had said. But within a fortnight the Sleeper held a small arsenal. He suspected that his operation was not the only one Ginger was masterminding. As he had been instructed, he hid the material in a lock-up garage in Kilburn.

Ginger obviously had a sense of humour because the ordnance was always packed in identical Manchester United sports bags, which locked with a small key. The Sleeper wondered if Ginger knew that he'd once had a very similar bag; he used to take his sports kit to school in it. Or perhaps Ginger had been inspired by United winning the Double Double with Cantona's cracking goal? Even Greta had appreciated that one. Anyway, the Sleeper reflected, he found it strangely comforting to associate the operation with his football heroes.

After the last delivery, he saw Ginger once more. Again in Hammersmith, but this time a different pub.

'Now sit tight and wait to hear from us. Okay? And if you must shag your landlady, do it discreetly? We don't want you getting murdered by a jealous husband now, do we?' Ginger grinned. 'Not when you're about to be a hero.'

The Sleeper nodded. He was in so deep there was no point in trying to resist or even contemplate a change of course.

'Good man.' Ginger turned and, without shaking hands, walked straight out of the pub. The Sleeper didn't see him again. Not in the flesh anyway.

According to CNN, the new government in Madrid was making heavy weather of the economic inheritance bequeathed to it by the outgoing administration.

Si had been to Madrid once. He'd spent two days a few summers ago researching a feature as a cub reporter desperate to make an impact. The piece had eventually appeared under the title *Madrid After Dark*. Si had been disappointed because the detail of his sleepless visit had been erased by some dumb sub-editor who failed to understand that the repetitious references to drinking beer were essential to the article. As far as Si could work out, the Madrileños measured out their lives in small glasses of beer, *cañas,* as they called them.

Little happened before seven in the evening, but even mid-week the city bustled until three or four in the morning. The bars overflowed with people of all ages drinking *cañas*. Everyone seemed to be having a great time, without a care in the world. During the working hours a heavy inertia descended across the dusty streets. The heat oppressed and little work seemed to be done.

Si was not surprised by CNN's report. But he thought it would take a lot to make Spain adopt the work ethic. Long may it remain unchanged, he smiled to himself. Si had loved his blurred, sleepless forty-eight hours in Madrid. A great city which could teach London a lot about night life, certainly during the summer months.

Si flicked off CNN as the soapy news presenters—the man imbecilic and the woman disconcertingly cross-eyed—began to repeat the stories he'd listened to just fifteen minutes before. He found satellite news useful from a professional point of view; he could catch up with the main news any time of the day or night. But since its advent, the quality of news reporting had suffered and Si suspected that even tabloid newspapers offered a better analysis than CNN or Sky's so-called 'informed comment'. Ten minutes a day of this stuff was about all he could stomach. But it was marginally better than working.

Si forced himself to concentrate on the job in hand. 'Hey Bill, how's your story coming?'

Bill grunted.

It was one of those days. It always got tricky in midsummer, but this year the stories seemed to have dried up early. It was only June. What would they have to write up in August, if they were already printing pieces of such low quality?

He'd sent Bill off earlier on a wild goose chase to draw a connection between recent gossip about a government reshuffle and the BSE crisis. He suspected that there was nothing in the story told to him by a notoriously untrustworthy backbencher. No doubt the MP was trying to score points off the Agriculture Minister or the pro-European faction in the party. Si wouldn't have minded if the story was credible. But it seemed far-fetched to suggest that the Prime Minister had timed the release of new information about BSE as part of a strategy to sacrifice the Europhile Agriculture Minister, thereby allowing him to sack the poor fellow and increase support for more Eurosceptic policies. This was so circumstantial and tenuous that Si would not normally have bothered following it up.

But these were not normal times. There was a dearth of stories and Si knew that Dougy would come down on him like a ton of bricks at the first opportunity. If he was going to leave *The Courier*, he wanted to jump—not be sacked for incompetence.

Si wondered what other jobs he could do? He was just another over-educated generalist, trained by a decadent society to appreciate literature and abstract art, but incapable of explaining how a kettle worked, let alone how to build a house or mend a car. Those were really useful things to be able to do. It wasn't as if he was really contributing anything to the greater knowledge of mankind. Bottom line, he was a crappy journalist doing a shitty job, being paid to poke his nose into other people's affairs, interfering where he wasn't wanted.

'Do you fancy a drink?'

Bill looked up with a blank look on his pug features. The sun had brought out his Scottishness, spraying a rash of ginger freckles across his face.

'A pint? I don't know about you, but I really feel I'm not getting anywhere here.' Not that he'd even started to tackle the story Dougy had pushed his way that morning. Si hated Dougy's so-called 'leads'. He just couldn't seem to get them right, to get into his boss's mindset.

'What about the story? It's already three thirty.'

True, if they went out for a drink they'd be hard-pressed to get the page together on time. Well, one drink would probably be just about all right.

'We'll only go for a quick one. How about it... That place just over the park? I'll buy.'

They sat on the wooden benches contemplating the river. The Thames flowed past thickly, as exhausted by the heat as everyone else. Washed out, dripping office workers in suits, bred for English weather not continental heat, wandered despondently by.

In the park—as the thin strip of yellow grass and three trees sandwiched between the road and the river was optimistically called—some pink individuals lay prostrate before the sun god. Why was it that whenever the sun came out, the normally reserved and prudish English abandoned their inhibitions and stripped almost naked? If only they had the bodies to get away with it. But these red blobs were typical: grey bras, flabby chests and summer skirts tucked into oversized knickers, which had been designed for undercover protection on cold winter nights.

Si watched a fat girl with compassion. The poor thing was so obviously suffering but seemed determined not to miss even one photon of potential tan. Elephantine thighs, puckered with cellulite, rolled over the dry, ochre grass like lard on toast. The girl mopped her perspiring brow furiously but seemed to have abandoned the rolls of sweating torso which flopped over the waistband of her skirt.

Si looked away in horror. This was terrible; no way to live. He was tempted to wander over and offer the girl a drink, to tell her to stop being silly and to cover up. But knowing the reaction this would provoke, he just sighed and abandoned the fat girl to her self-inflicted humiliation.

Bill sat on the bench beside him sipping a pint. 'Did you watch the Cup Final?' Si asked. He'd asked the same question a few weeks before but couldn't remember Bill's answer.

'What Cup Final?'

Si wondered how to take this. He looked at Bill, taking in the shiny nose ring and the surrounding, inflamed skin which seemed to be going septic; at least his colleague's hair had grown a bit, although Si was unconvinced by the red tint Bill had recently applied. But perhaps most disconcerting about Bill's appearance today was the studded metal collar around his neck. This accessory was making its debut appearance. Si had managed during the morning to resist the temptation to nickname Bill 'Fido' or to make doggy jokes. He feared that this would only be met by a serious sense of humour failure.

It wasn't easy making conversation with Bill. On paper his subordinate was quite bright. And there was no doubt about his growing ambition. Bill clearly intended to take over the Diary at some stage. But despite this, Bill had few social skills and often appeared to be thick as two short planks. Si suspected that much of this was deliberate and that Bill got a perverse pleasure from testing those who conversed with him. He probably regarded conversation as a sort of duel in which the winner was the one who managed to psyche his opponent into social niceties. No doubt Bill scorned Si's interest in his views, considering it a sign of weakness.

Si groaned inwardly. It was definitely one of those days. Bill was probably right to adopt the stonewall approach. He would make a good journalist one day, if he had the breaks. Compassion and understanding rarely sold newspapers.

'Yeah, I watched it... Weeks ago, though,' admitted Bill eventually. Perhaps he had been psyched out himself by Si's protracted silence? 'Crap, wasn't it?'

‘True, it wasn’t great. But I suppose that the best team won in the end, didn’t they?’

‘I hate Man United. They were crap. Even the goal was a fluke deflection.’

‘Oh, I don’t know. It looked pretty inspired to me, the way Cantona cracked it through the defence. Fairy tale stuff, eh?’

Bill looked at Si as if he’d just confessed that he was an active paedophile. ‘It was crap,’ he repeated sullenly.

Si studied the bottom of his pint glass. Against his better judgement, he pursued the subject. ‘What did you think of the new United lad?’

‘Which one?’

‘You know... Jimmy Sweeney’s his name, I think?’ Si hoped that this disingenuous approach might allow Bill to break with form and compliment his friend. He’d not mentioned his friendship with Jimmy to anyone at work before. But somehow it seemed important that a sceptic like Bill should appreciate Jimmy’s success.

‘No idea. Can’t say I noticed him. Even if I had, I doubt he was very good. United were crap. I really hate them. More than anything, I think.’ Bill pondered this for a moment, an unusually alert expression illuminating his blunt features. He nodded sagely. ‘Yeah, definitely. More than anything.’

Si felt unutterably depressed. He suppressed a desire to grab Bill’s dog collar and twist it until his colleague lay choking on the ground. Instead, he thought grimly that Bill clearly revelled in mediocrity, knocking talent and cynically undermining true excitement; blinded by petty jealousy. He clearly had the right skills to work on the Diary. Si realised it was going to be a long summer.

‘Let’s get back shall we? We’ve got a page to finish.’

Bill grunted. They raised themselves from the bench and shuffled in silence along the dusty street towards the hulking *Courier* building.

⚽ ⚽ ⚽

Mary pressed the button and turned off the telly. They were in Si's flat ensconsed for an evening of take-away curry, an episode of *This Life* and if they had the stamina, for a video recording of last Friday night's *Friends* and *Frasier*. In Si's book this was the perfect way to unwind. But Mary was now introducing a dissonant note.

'So where does it end, Si? Do we just go on like this until we die?'

Si recognised the thought. The easiest thing in modern life was to keep going in a straight line: work, friends, films, sport, dinners out and so on. No need to do anything radical. Why rock the boat? He suspected that was why so few of his friends had married yet or had kids or done any of the great life-affirming acts which had traditionally measured out the span of human existence; the events between birth and death which endow direction and meaning and give the lie to Beckett's supreme, nihilistic image of women giving birth astride a yawning grave. Si wasn't sure how his contemporaries measured out their lives. They didn't really. They just assumed their present existence would continue forever. Perhaps that's why they were so serious, so purposeless, so unattuned to the spiritual? Because endless life was such a depressing prospect.

'So? What have you got to say, then?' Mary demanded.

Although Si recognised the question, he had not expected his girlfriend to put it to him; and he certainly didn't have a clear answer.

'The thing is, Si... I love being with you. We go well together. But we're not getting any younger and I need to know how serious you are.'

'About what?' It began to dawn on Si that Mary was coming at the question from a slightly different angle.

Exasperated, she shook her head violently. 'About me, you idiot. Oh, I don't know why I bother.'

'Right, I see. Sorry, I just didn't quite understand.' Si

played for time. 'Well, yeah, I agree. We're great together. But I guess I thought we could carry on like this for the moment. After all, we haven't known each other that long, have we?'

'Six months, Si. How long do you need? In another year I'll be thirty. Do you realise that?'

Si hadn't really thought about it. But now he did he saw what Mary was driving at. It wasn't that he didn't think he could marry Mary; he just hadn't thought they were anywhere near that stage yet. Obviously Mary had other ideas. 'Listen, my love. I see what you're saying. But give me a bit of time, okay? I'm still trying to get my life under control, you know, at *The Courier*, and I'm not quite there yet. But trust me. I'm not messing you around. Right?'

Mary seemed reasonably satisfied with the answer. She calmed down. 'Okay. I'm not pressurising you or anything. I just sometimes wonder if you feel the same as I do. I'm sorry if I was unreasonable.' She leaned over and kissed him.

Si gathered her in his arms. For the moment the storm had passed. After what he judged to be a respectful interval, Si pressed the remote control and *This Life* flickered back on.

⚽ ⚽ ⚽

Resigning was far easier than Si had thought it would be. It was so evidently the right thing to do.

'Bill, how you doing?'

Bill looked up with a curious look on his face. A mixture of embarrassment and pity. 'Morning, Si.' Despite the clock showing eleven thirty, Bill's voice contained no note of irony. 'Look, Dougy's been on the phone. I think you'd better ring him.'

'Did he say what it was about?'

'Something to do with last night's page. He thought it wasn't that good.'

No, I bet he didn't, thought Si. It had been a pretty pathetic effort, even he knew that. Not only were there no stories about at the moment, but in the July heat it was hard to motivate himself to get out and dig them up. Bill had come up trumps with a story about the editor of a literary magazine, but one story was not enough. He'd had to resurrect a couple of old cast-offs and stretch the boundaries of journalistic license on another to make it even half-interesting. Even then the Diary had only filled two thirds of the space allotted to it. Dougy would surely not have accepted it without further work. But he'd been away and Si had left it with the Deputy Editor who hadn't commented.

'Thanks, Bill.'

'Do you want a coffee?' Bill was increasingly eager, helpful and professional. He knew his star was rising and it didn't cost him anything to be kind.

Perhaps he's taking pity on me, thought Si. But he couldn't feel any rancour towards Bill. Good luck to him. 'Yeah, I'd love one. Thanks.'

After shuffling through a few faxes and routine mail, Si picked up the phone. 'Is Dougy there?'

'I'll just put you through.'

Dougy didn't hang around. 'Listen kid, I don't care what time you choose to pitch up in the morning. But I do care about this newspaper. What you served up last night was crap. If I'd been around I would have refused it. Unfortunately, I wasn't. What's the excuse, eh?'

'No excuses. I know it wasn't good but...'

'Not good? It was diabolical.'

'Yeah. It's just there's not a lot about at the moment... You know, it's a lean time for Diary stories.'

'Don't bullshit me, Si. I know about newspapers. I've been doing this since you were in nappies. Of course there aren't any stories... That's why you're paid to find them. Do you get where I'm coming from?'

Si knew Dougy was right. He was just making excuses

to himself. There were always stories in a city like London. Just sometimes one had to try harder to find them. That took determination and drive—two qualities Si had been lacking recently.

'Now listen up, kid. I'm not about to sack you. This time, anyhow. I still think you've got what it takes. But don't let me down again, okay?'

'Okay. I mean I won't. Today's page will be much better, I promise.'

'It'd better be.' And Dougy was gone.

But it wasn't. Bill found a fun angle on the Edinburgh Festival: a bright, varsity comic duo with the talent to follow in the footsteps of a panoply of stars from previous generations. But while Bill tapped away happily on his word processor, Si's leads all ended in frustration.

He skipped lunch and tried phoning contacts who had produced successful stories in the past. He drew a blank.

Then Bill got a call from one of his many sources with a bit of gossip about the opening of a new restaurant. He finished off the Edinburgh Festival and cracked on with the new piece.

Meanwhile, Si made himself a second coffee and leaned back in his chair, deep in thought.

It became apparent to Si that he had to be courageous. For the first time in his life he had to take a really difficult and crucial decision. He'd always done what was expected of him; it occurred to him that he was aptly named: *si* meaning 'yes' in several languages. This provoked a wry smile but no real happiness. It was inescapably clear that at the age of twenty-eight he needed to say 'no' for once and take control of his life.

He had proved that he could be a journalist, maybe even quite a good one. But in his heart of hearts he knew he didn't really want to be an editor one day; and more importantly, he didn't want to be a journalist now. In fact, he probably didn't want a career at all. Not that he was lazy—no, it was just that he needed to believe in what he was doing.

Si wasn't sure what he would do, but right now he wanted the time and space to change direction. Of course, he would need money to live. But for the moment he had enough savings to live on for at least six months. Until the fog cleared and he found out what he should do. He had no doubt that he would find the right course if he took the time to look around carefully.

Si took the decision and after that it was easy. He left Bill absorbed in writing about the restaurant, and wandered up to Dougy's office.

The editor was on the phone when Si reached the outer office. It was no longer the relaxed waiting area it had been in Martha's time. The new girl looked tired, but she was sharp and professional. Not a spare smile in sight. Si waited until the red light on the PA's switchboard went out and then went in.

'Dougy, have you got a moment?'

Dougy was standing behind the huge black desk. Beyond him the vast picture windows showed the Docklands spreading out on either side of the gunmetal grey river. Dougy nodded and looked at Si expectantly.

'I've been thinking and I don't feel that I should carry on editing the Diary...'

'Oh come on, Si, you don't really think I can give you your own column yet, do you?' Dougy was incredulous. 'Not with the shit you've been pumping out recently.'

'No, that's not what I meant. I know it's not been going well. You see, I think I need a bit of time out, d'you see? Of course, I wouldn't leave until everything was sorted out and so forth...'

Dougy cut him short. 'You mean to say you want to resign?'

'Yes, that's it. As I say, I'm perfectly happy to stay as long as you need me. Until you find someone to take over and...'

'Why, Si? I know you've had a tough time recently, but I still believe in you, kid. You can go far if you want to.'

Dougy was finding it hard to understand.

'But that's the point. You see I don't want to any more.'

Dougy wasn't listening. His brow suddenly furrowed. 'I see, someone's offered you a better job. Who is it? *The Mail*? The gits, I might have known.'

'No, it's got nothing to do with *The Mail*...'

'Who, then? If it's *The Daily Telegraph*, I'll ruddy kill them. Listen, kid, whatever they've told you, don't believe it. We can work this out between us, okay? I can't promise you a big raise now, but assuming things go well over the next month, I'll make sure you get a good bonus in October. How's that? Can't say better than that, can I?' Dougy paused.

Si tried again. 'Look, Dougy, I'm sorry, but nobody else is involved and it's not a question of money. It's about me... You see, I need to get a grip on my life. To control it rather than allowing it to control me. Do you see?'

Dougy obviously didn't. He clearly thought Si had taken leave of his senses. Leaving for a better job, *that* he could understand. Even accepting less money for improved career prospects, okay. But just leaving? No, he didn't believe it. People simply didn't do that these days. Career and success were everything; what was left if you rejected them? Si had to be hiding something from him. Dougy hated losing staff to another newspaper, no matter how badly they might be performing for him.

Along the river, somewhere towards Gravesend, the horn of a barge echoed with a mournful finality. Like the ultimate, quavering note of *The Last Post*.

Si left the office having done his best. He told Bill what he had done, and said he would recommend his assistant to succeed him as Diary Editor.

Bill tried hard to conceal his delight, and said how much he'd miss Si and so forth. But Si wasn't fooled. He knew this was Bill's dream come true, and hoped for Bill's sake it would work out. There was always a risk in trying to run before you could walk. *The harder they come*, Si quoted silently. Yet Bill seemed up for it: driven, and fiercely ambitious, he had certainly become more competent in the last few months.

Then they scraped together the page. When they had finished, Bill took it up for Dougy to approve. Ignoring the lift, he skipped up the stairs two at a time. He realised that he was truly happy for the first time since coming down from Scotland. It had been a confusing period. Half the time he'd felt desperately insecure. And his sexual confusion hadn't helped. He hoped that now he'd conquered his first goal and won the job he wanted, he might have the confidence and clarity to tackle a much more difficult challenge. It was clear what he had to do; but how would he deal with his family? And what would Dougy say? Bill felt his happiness quaver and his stomach contract into a hard little ball. Oh God, he wasn't there yet. One step at a time, that was all he could manage.

While Bill was away, Si wrote a short formal letter of resignation explaining that he would work out his month's notice if required and recommending Bill as his successor. Before leaving for the night he dropped it off with Dougy's PA and sent a copy to the personnel department. Then, having completed his own piece of midsummer madness, he walked out into the balmy London evening.

As Si left *The Courier* building, he felt a great weight lift from him. He knew he was doing the right thing. Not just intellectually, but emotionally and even morally the decision seemed correct. The only thing he couldn't understand was why it had taken him so long to reach this point.

The sunshine washed over his pallid face and, as if for the first time, he looked and marvelled at the beauty of London. The cars glinted as they flowed like water down the dusty street. A flower-seller smiled at him as he passed her brightly adorned booth. Si smiled back and surprised himself by not feeling foolish. A huge warm wave surged up within him and he felt more open and alive than he could remember.

How long would this feeling continue? How long before

he became used to his new condition of freedom and slipped into imprisoning routine again? Surely there was some way of preserving this inspiring vision of life? But even this sober thought couldn't diminish the joy he felt.

Everything seemed possible now. Social convention and inhibition appeared absurd. He saw a bag lady standing on the edge of the pavement waiting for the unforgiving traffic to let her cross, and he instinctively took her arm and helped her shuffle to the other side.

When he had landed her safely on the far pavement, he saw her glance fearfully towards an old cane shopping basket on wheels sitting in a doorway. Understanding the plaintive look in the woman's eyes, he fetched the basket for her. Even the all-pervading smell of stale urine failed to affect him. The woman mumbled something and looked at him with evident surprise. Then she grasped the handle of her trolley firmly in gnarled hands, and tugged it slowly along the street after her.

Si stood for a few minutes watching the hunched figure shuffle away. Then he recrossed the street and carried on walking away from *The Courier*. Avoiding the cracks in the pavement, he thought that perhaps he could detect some meaning in all the apparent chaos of his life. Maybe all the pieces did add up. He wondered if it was simply that the answer was there for anyone to see, but until now he'd failed to look. Once he had seen an illuminated expression gracing the face of a man in a sandwich board; Si recognised in that emaciated, religious eccentric something of his present self.

The emotion within him surged again and welled up behind his eyes. He dismissed the tears with a blink and a smile. This would never do. He needed to compose himself for Mary. Otherwise, she'd think he'd taken leave of his senses. He wasn't quite sure what he would say to her. But he knew it would be important.

❀ ❀ ❀

The message arrived. No sooner than expected, but sooner than the Sleeper had hoped. Scribbled on the back of a postcard of Central London featuring a big red bus, and signed by Ginger: 'Shopping on 15 September.' That was all. It was the green light to put into effect the plan which had been explained in Hammersmith. The Sleeper had severe doubts, but there was no turning back now. He managed to suppress his qualms by thinking about the cause: all the martyrs murdered by the English, the soldiers waving guns at small kids on the streets in Belfast, all the weight of history pushing at his back to continue the struggle...

But the burden was heavy, even if he knew he was doing the right thing. He shut out thoughts of Jo, Lenny the tramp and all the other friends made in London. God help him, he thought, it had been almost a year since he first moved into Mrs Donnelley's. What had happened to her and her son Davie back from America? He hadn't really thought of Mrs Donnelley since moving out.... Since Greta. And that was the worst of it. He knew that after going into action, his life could never be the same.

The plan was to wait a while in London, carry on as normal, and then go to France for a bit. Ginger had arranged a job in an Irish pub in Paris. Then he'd receive further instructions. Ginger had promised that he'd be able to visit his family soon—before Christmas, he'd said. But the Sleeper knew that his time with Greta was coming to an end. That hurt. It hurt a lot. At times, it hurt so much he wished he could turn his back on the cause and run off with Greta. Somewhere romantic like Hawaii. It always looked amazing in the films. But he knew this wasn't really an option. Ginger, or someone like him, would find him sooner or later, sure they would. And everyone knew what happened to deserters.

❀ ❀ ❀

When Dougy realised there was nothing he could do to keep Si, he agreed a transitional period of two weeks and made Bill the Diary Editor. Si came in late and left early, offering advice and helping out where he could. But he realised it was better to leave Bill to his own devices. After all, the new Editor was already familiar with the job's requirements and execution. The fortnight passed quickly.

Si had been concerned that Mary would take his resignation as further proof that he lacked mettle. She had surprised him.

'Darling, that's the best news I've heard for a long time. Brilliant. Mummy will be delighted. She never did approve of you working at *The Courier*.'

'Mm, I guessed as much.'

'So what'll you do instead?'

'I haven't made my mind up yet. I thought I'd take a bit of time to work things out.'

'Darling, that's fine. So long as you're happy. I've got enough money for both of us. You could even sell your flat and move in with me.'

'That's really sweet. But I think my savings will get me by for at least the next six months.'

'Six months? Goodness, how long are you planning to stay unemployed?'

'Well, I don't really see it as unemployed. More a case of changing direction. And if you've been ploughing ahead on the same bearing for a decade, you build up a certain momentum. It can take some time to alter course smoothly.'

Mary seemed slightly reassured. 'Right, I think I see. Anyway, it's brilliant news. It'll mean we have more time to spend together.'

'I suppose so. But that implies your taking more time out from your job too. After all, you work far longer hours than I do.'

'You're right. I'm also going to turn over a new leaf. I'll

make an effort to get out earlier in future.'

Mary's reaction was far more encouraging than he could have imagined; although how long her tolerance would last was not clear. But Si determined to make hay in the meantime.

'You do that, my love. Turn over a new leaf, that is. I guess I've not just turned over a new leaf, not even started a new chapter. I've chucked the whole sodding book away.' They laughed together. The idea was both exhilarating and deeply daunting.

❀ ❀ ❀

The train drew into Ryburn with a hiss. Mary chucked the Louis de Bernières novel into her bulky, new Kenzo bag and left the carriage. She was the only one to get off at the tiny station. She looked around at the short platform, the delicate Edwardian wrought iron and the big clock. It was amazing this branch line to Oxford had survived the Beeching Plan. She decided that Ryburn's chocolate box qualities made it the kind of village where politicians had weekend retreats; hence the reprieve when the axe had dropped on thousands of similar village stations. Such a cynical thought, she noted happily, was out of character for her and owed much to the considerable influence of Si.

Mary watched the train slide away into the long horizon, as in a western movie; only no smoke. Opposite the platform, fields of poppies and corn stretched away up the hill towards a small farmhouse. Even the pylons at the top of the slope managed to look picturesque.

Mary felt her insides dance a quick jig, as they always did when she arrived to visit her grandmother. She loved Ryburn; it reminded her of her childhood and the long summer holidays; the time when she believed she would live forever, and every experience was a new one. She'd never imagined—even as a fourteen-year-old snogging that boy from Ryburn post office—that a time would come when there was nothing new; just new ways of doing the same things.

The taxi followed the familiar route. Out of the village and onto the causeway. Down the lane lined by high bushy hedges and dry ditches; 'rinnies', that was what they called them down here. Mr Johnson the taxi driver knew Elspeth. 'Mrs Somerset's a wonder of the world,' he marvelled. 'You wouldn't know she was a day over sixty. Backbone of the village, she is. Just the other day she rang my wife and offered to bake some cakes for the fair.' The Ryburn fair was the big social event of the year round here. People came from up to twenty miles round. Mary remembered waiting with barely contained excitement for the day to arrive.

'When is it?'

'Oh, next Saturday. You'll be staying for the fair, then?'

'I wish,' sighed Mary. Today was Sunday, and she'd be leaving later today to get back in time for work tomorrow. She'd originally planned to come down yesterday, but a last minute crisis had meant an unscheduled half day in the office. It was high time she took control of her life.

'Oh, you can't miss the fair. Nothing like it in these parts. But then again, I suppose it'd be nothing special for you London types.'

Mary didn't react to the implied rebuke. Mr Johnson was quite right. London certainly destroyed all sense of proportion. 'So what else has been happening?' she asked breezily. Mr Johnson rose to the challenge admirably, and during the five minute drive he brought her up to speed with the latest village gossip. It had been too long since she last came down, thought Mary. She barely recognised some of the names featuring in the monologue.

The car swung past some large wooden gates and into a gravel drive; Mr Johnson dropped her under the big yew tree in front of the white-washed house. Everything looked so green for this time of year. Must have been all the rain of which Mr Johnson had complained. The taxi driver waved across the lawn and Mary noticed her grandmother crouched over the flower bed. Elspeth waved back without standing up.

'Hello, Mr Johnson. How's Sarah?'

'Oh, she's fine, thank you, Mrs Somerset.'

'Good, good. Tell her I'll ring her about the fair. I've done a couple of sponges, but I want to let her have a chocolate cake too.'

'Right, I will. Sounds delicious.'

'Not for you, mind. For the cake stall.'

'Ah well... It was worth a try,' he grinned. Mary noticed that his tummy bounced up and down as he spoke; he resembled a telly-tubby, she thought. 'Must be getting on. Bye then, Mrs Somerset.'

'Goodbye, Mr Johnson.'

He waved a cheery hand in Mary's direction and slowly drove away.

'Hello, Gran.' Mary bent to give the old lady a kiss. 'No, don't get up.'

'Yes, I must. I've been weeding away for the last hour. My old back can't take much more. Mary noticed how neat the freshly tended bed looked. She gave her grandmother a hand up. 'Well, let's have a look at you... You're obviously not getting enough sunshine and fresh air,' Elspeth scolded. 'You shouldn't work so hard. I keep telling you.'

'I know, you're right. But it's tricky, Gran. Wow, it's good to be here.' They walked arm in arm back towards the house.

'It's good to have you here. You know, it was autumn last time you came to see me.'

Mary felt a pang of guilt. 'I'm sorry, it's just been so busy.'

'But not just work, eh?' Elspeth had a wicked twinkle in her eye. 'Clearly this Simon Simpson is quite something.'

'Oh Gran. It's not that serious, really.' Mary frowned. Who was she trying to fool? After all, Si had been the main reason she'd decided to come and see her grandmother.

She needed to talk to someone who could give her good advice.

Elspeth pursed her lips and snorted quietly.

'What's that for?' demanded Mary.

'What's what for?'

'You know perfectly well. I know what that snort means.'

'So why are you asking then?'

Mary giggled. 'Okay, you're right. It is a bit serious. I'm not quite sure what's going on... So, I need your advice.'

Elspeth sighed. But inside she was delighted to find herself still needed. 'Well, darling, all in good time. Let's have a nice cup of tea and you can tell me all about it.'

Mary clung more tightly to her grandmother's bony arm and gave her a kiss on the cheek. 'I knew you'd understand. You are wonderful, Gran.'

'Nonsense. Just doing what grandmothers are meant to...' she smiled. The two women went in through the back door and, in the cool of the spruce nineteen fifties kitchen, they busied themselves making tea.

⚽ ⚽ ⚽

Si was enjoying his new found freedom. Endless August days stretched before him with no deadlines or pages to fill. He no longer had to worry what Dougy or anyone else thought; he could do as he wished, when he wanted. The initial euphoria still hadn't worn off and it was almost a month now. The work ethic had shrivelled within him almost without a whimper. It had been much easier than he'd expected.

Part of the thrill had been the rediscovery of London. It might be a difficult city to work in, but it was fantastic for those with time to enjoy it.

Si stopped before a window. Something childish stirred within him.

Boots Galore, he read on the glass. Beyond the pane,

racks of individually stitched cowboy and biker boots marched towards him. He noticed that only one of each pair was displayed. It gave the scene a faintly medical air, as if the shop sold artificial attachments for the one-legged. But suspending his disbelief, and reminding himself that where there was one boot a second would be close by, he pushed open the door.

It wasn't boots he was in search of. He already had a pair of plain black leather boots, soft to the touch and hand-made in Mexico. He'd bought them when he went for a two week holiday with an old girlfriend.

Sun, sea and sex, the brochure had advertised. They certainly got the first two; but even the holiday company couldn't rescue their disintegrating relationship and there was little romance. By the time they returned on the charter, they'd decided to 'stay friends'. Even that didn't happen. Si hadn't seen her for a couple of years and, with Mary absorbing his attention, he had no desire to now.

But he had brought back the boots, of which he was rightly proud. Not that he'd had much chance to wear them until recently. Thrusting young journalists on *The Courier* wore brogues or practical DMs.

What had drawn Si into the shop was the sight of a bootstrap. Ever since his Lou Reed-dowsed teens, he'd loved the idea of bootstraps—studded pieces of leather and chain gratuitously fastened around a boot; and he knew that what his Mexican boots really needed were bootstraps. Just like the ones in *Boots Galore*.

'Are you a dancer?' asked the shop manager; platinum blonde—dyed probably—late thirties, flirtatious, but hard-edged: Si couldn't work out if she was taking the mickey. He hardly had the taut body of a professional athlete. She'd probably seen straight through his assured, street-wise questions about bootstrap use and expense, and took him for a City executive, closet queer, or a fetishist. Or even all three. Si imagined many of her customers fell into these categories.

Her lingering gaze made him blanch.

Was it just his imagination that an ironic smile played around the corner of her painted lips?

'Sorry?'

'Do you want them for a stage performance?'

'Oh, I see what you mean.'

The woman raised a practised, finely-pencilled eyebrow.

'What makes you think I'm a dancer?' Si felt flattered for some inexplicable reason.

'I don't. I've no idea who you are. You could be the Archbishop of Canterbury for all I care.'

'What? And wear them under my cassock?'

'Yeah, why not? I'm sure priests wear stranger things than that...'

Why not indeed, thought Si. He bought the straps, some with large silver studs to go across the front of the boot. He left the shop with a spring in his step.

Glancing at his watch he saw he had just enough time to get to his meeting with Ricky. A late afternoon drink and then maybe a film in the evening. By the time he got out Mary would be leaving work and might be on for some dinner. Why hadn't he cut loose earlier? This new life was great.

For the first time in years he was able to relax completely. He slept better, read the books he wanted to, and as a result had started to get things into proportion. It was hard to recreate even temporarily the state of mind which had been his every day reality until so recently. How had he allowed himself to be convinced by the gods of ambition and public success? It was clear that true meaning lay elsewhere.

It hadn't taken him long to realise that Ricky had known this all along. Far from being a wastrel, the Californian used his time wisely. He pursued his vocation—to be a rock singer—and avoided distractions.

Of course, the biggest distraction was a routine job which ate up the best part of the day and sucked out all energy so that the remaining hours were needed for recuperation.

Even through his convert's zeal, Si recognised that for some people the two went hand in hand; the working day was the pursuit of the true goal. But for him it hadn't been the case. He knew that from the way his spirit grew daily now that the shackles had been removed. New and exciting dimensions appeared before his open eyes; whereas before he would have perceived them but myopically, now he could take time to study their forms and recognise the vast possibilities.

Ricky had initially been a help as he embarked on his new life; not only had he been available to talk things over during the day, but he had also pointed Si towards stimulating reading matter; just what the situation required. Although Si had soon tired of Ricky's trite American self-fulfilment guides, they had steered him in a new direction and had stimulated his interest in the spiritual and religious inner life. Si found himself reading a couple of hours every morning before starting the rest of his day.

Even his mother's initial dismay about her son 'dropping out', as she put it, evaporated when he explained what he was reading. She enthusiastically recommended several titles to him and offered to send him copies of other books. The irony was not lost on Si. He hoped his father wouldn't be too upset. But it took a lot to disgruntle the old man. His son's lifestyle change would probably do no more than inspire a thoughtful pipe in the garden.

Si was still no closer to discovering what he should do when his money ran out; but, as he said to Mary, he was seriously engaged in research.

'Clover, Clover, come back... Clover...' Si and Mary watched a young mother chase after her wailing toddler. They exchanged a look, the same thought in both their minds. No, they were nowhere near even contemplating kids, although marriage, or at least co-habitation, seemed increasingly feasible, even to Si. But no hurry. He certainly wasn't planning to broach the subject. How could one hurry anything on a day like this? God, it was good to be in London when the sun was shining.

They lay on a grassy bank in Battersea Park watching the roller-bladers whooshing past.

'Crap, not bad, crap...' Three teenage boys moved along the hot tarmac in ungainly fashion, unaware of Si's appraisal.

'Now that's what I call skating,' said Mary admiringly. Si followed her gaze and watched a muscular guy in baggy shorts and little else apart from a personal stereo twirl and sashay among the pedestrians. His motion seemed effortless, motor-driven. Mary's eyes opened even wider when wonder-boy shimmied past executing a perfect pirouette in front of them.

'Okay, okay... You'll overheat if you're not careful.'

Mary laughed sexily. 'Come on then, lover, you cool me down.' She rolled over on her side and placed her elegant pale hand on Si's chest. It looked so small compared to his bulk. Si reached up and gently pulled her head towards him. Their kiss, now so familiar, was slow and tender. Mary closed her eyes and pushed herself across the ground so she could feel his body against hers. 'That's better, I feel like I've had a cold shower,' she lied when they finally came up for air.

Si lay back and watched the sky. He loved feeling small and insignificant like this. Mortality gave him a much greater buzz than any chemical-induced experiences.

'Penny for your thoughts?'

'I was just thinking...'

'Thinking what?'

'Oh nothing.' Mary hit him softly on the chest. The great bone-lined cavern seemed to echo within him. 'Well, about life, how short it is and yet how long.'

'Profound.'

'No, it's not. Everyone knows it. I just wonder how many people enjoy knowing it?'

'Well I can tell you that I for one do not. The thought of growing old puts the willies up me...' Mary giggled. 'An unfortunate expression. I don't actually mind having the willies put up me, in fact I quite like it.' She started to slide her hand down Si's chest and onto his belly. Laughing, he rolled over to face her. 'Old age can't be a lot of fun, can it?'

'Depends on your health, I suppose. I rather fancy the idea of looking back on a full life knowing you've done what you wanted to achieve, and that soon you'll be forgotten and on a higher plane.'

'How morbid. What do you mean by that? Are you getting spiritual on me? You sound like your mother when you say things like that.'

'God, don't say that. Anyway, I can't possibly sound like my mother, she only speaks in Tongues at the moment... I can't possibly compete. I don't even know what Tongues is.'

'Nor does she from what she told us last time we went to Easfolk. But your mother's great. You shouldn't knock her. She's honest about herself, and what I really love is that she just doesn't care what anyone else thinks of her. I wish I could be like that.' Mary looked wistful.

Si was surprised. He'd never heard Mary express any regret about her character in the past. Her self-confidence was one of her great qualities. 'I don't want you to be like my mother. No way.' He opened his eyes in mock horror as the thought sunk in. 'I couldn't possibly go out with someone like my mother. I like you *just* the way you *are,*' he sang teasingly.

'Oh, you big softie. You're quite romantic when you want to be. I think this stopping work thing was a good idea.'

Si thought for a moment. 'Yeah, so do I. I feel so much more alive. I think more, I enjoy doing simple things more. I even sleep better. I wonder how long before I start getting bored, though?'

'Make the most of it, you lucky fool. I'm jealous, you know. Deeply jealous. There's me slogging off to work and you chilling out at home doing nothing.'

Si looked offended. 'Not nothing. I'm working out what to do next. That's quite different from idleness.'

'Of course it is darling, of course it is.' Mary's raised eyebrow and twinkling eyes belied her sincere tones.

'No really, I'm not just wasting my time. I need to do this. To get my life in order. I thought you understood that?'

'I do. I was only joking. I love the fact that you're always there when I want you, and you're so much happier. It's great, for me too, you know?' She pushed him onto his back. Si watched a small bird—a sparrow perhaps?—fly overhead. The balmy warmth of the day washed over him. A dark object suddenly blocked out the sky, a lock of hair tickled his forehead and soft lips pressed against his. What a life, he thought gratefully.

⚽ ⚽ ⚽

'Okay, I'm down in London a week on Wednesday and Thursday. So let's do this long-promised lunch with your mystery missus on Thursday.' Jimmy had just got back from training.

The new season had started and he was carrying on from where he'd left off. He'd done well during Manchester United's summer tours.

'Thursday's fine. I'll just have to check with Mary, but I'm sure she'll be on for it. And what are you doing on Wednesday?'

'I'm meeting your mate Ricky for a jam. The Crocodiles are rehearsing and he's asked me to come along.'

'He did?'

'Yeah. Great, isn't it? God, Si, you don't know how excited I am about finally getting to play with a rock band.'

'I was meaning to ask you about that. I mean, I had no idea....'

'Well, I kept it kind of secret. But I've been practising and I've got quite good.'

'Excellent. So where are you meeting Ricky?'

'He said he'd ring me nearer the time to let me know.'

'So you've talked to him quite a bit then?'

'No, not really. Just a couple of times since you introduced us. We fixed this jam session before I went off to the Far East with United. I'm looking forward to meeting up with him.'

'Right. So, is it just music or shall I come along too on Wednesday?'

'No, don't worry. I think we'll just do the music. You and I can meet up Thursday.'

'Oh, all right. So, let's talk nearer to the time then, shall we?'

'Yeah, I'll give you a call on Thursday morning first thing. Okay?'

'Fine.'

'Good. See you then, mate.' Jimmy rang off and wandered off to the spacious kitchen of his new luxury home in search of refreshment. He planned the rest of his day: an afternoon playing with his new video game, practising his electric guitar and then perhaps an early evening round of golf with one of his team-mates; dinner out as usual, but an early night as there was training tomorrow and a big match later in the week; he expected to keep his place in the first team. Jimmy was finding fame and success a comfortable burden.

⚽ ⚽ ⚽

It was all over the news on Monday 12 September. Three days later the Sleeper was still dazed. The English security forces had somehow found out that Ginger was organising arms runs into London. They'd busted the house in Hammersmith and shot him through the front door. Ginger was dead. Apparently, his real name was Martin

Coughlan—the Sleeper hadn't known that, but he recognised the picture straight away. The other two men in the house—neither of whom the Sleeper had met—had been arrested.

The news claimed that the police had found an extensive arsenal—enough to mount a huge bombing campaign. Commentators concluded that the cease-fire seemed likely to end soon.

How many others like me are there, the Sleeper wondered? Sleeping in London until called to go into action. By the sound of it, Ginger and his mates had been running quite a few lads.

He felt no sorrow for Ginger's death. A bit of admiration and respect, yes. He'd died a martyr, fighting for the cause. But he'd not liked him personally. And he'd hated that Ginger had known all about the affair with Greta.

The Sleeper hadn't wanted Greta to be involved. He still didn't. After long thought in his bedroom, he devised a way of ensuring she could avoid being implicated. Although he recognised it was rash, he decided to record a last testament on tape, so that if something went badly wrong for him in the next few days, she could use it to prove her innocence.

'If you're listening Mr Policeman… Whoever you are…' he spoke into the small dictaphone he'd bought for the purpose, 'pay attention… Greta Anderson has no idea who or what I am… What I'm doing or anything. Okay? Got that? Good.'

Of course, hearing about Ginger put the shits up him. If they knew about the arms smuggling, surely they know about his operation too? Also, the two blokes arrested in Hammersmith might have known about him. What if they'd been tortured and had given him away? But so far nothing had happened. He didn't seem to have been followed, and nobody had been round asking questions, as far as he knew.

The Sleeper had even been up to Eamon's pub to take the temperature; it was tepid, the same as always. The regulars greeted him the same as ever. Nothing to worry about. Of course, everyone was talking about it, saying what a disgrace that the police had opened fire without giving proper warning and that the only proper response from true Irishmen now would be to fight back. Not that any of them had any intention of doing so.

The Sleeper started to despise them all. He couldn't help it. Sitting there with their Guinness in front of them, listening to the fiddle music from back home, with their fat beer bellies wobbling and spouting about a united Ireland, when none of them had ever done anything to help make it a reality. Well, I'm different, he thought; I believe actions count more than words, like my ma taught me.

In his bedroom, The Sleeper picked up the dictaphone. 'Greta, if you're listening to this it will be because... Something has happened. I don't expect you to understand, but I hope that this will help you to remember me as I was when others are telling lies about me. I imagine many others who never knew me will try and persuade you that when I was with you I wasn't what I seemed. Believe me, I was. Perhaps you alone know me as I really am.

'I'm not recording my story for history's sake. No, it's an insurance policy really. For you. If you're listening to this, you'll know why you need it. Just give it to the police if they arrest you, okay?

'Remember me as I was... Your Baa; and don't forget I love you. Okay? Right... Well, I'll take a break, then I'll tell it as it was.'

⚽ ⚽ ⚽

The jamming session was a great success. Jimmy's hours of practice had paid off and he had become a competent twelve bar blues man. Nothing fancy, mind, just a few imitative licks here and there. But enough with the right effects pedals to add a new angle to The Crocodiles' slick sound.

'Jimmy, that was real cool.'

'What, that riff at the end? Yeah, I was working on that last week. Seems to come off now.'

'Good, real good,' grinned Art.

'Wild,' said Dog.

Jimmy smiled as happy as a sandboy. This was childhood dreamtime.

'You sure you're not gonna be down for longer sometime? Then we could really do some stuff. Maybe even gig together.'

Jimmy was ecstatic. 'You mean like on stage with you guys? I'd love that.' Then his expression clouded. 'But I'm not going to be able to manage more than a day or two at a time during the season. And next Summer's so far away, who knows what'll be happening?' He didn't dare to even express the thought clearly to himself, but Jimmy had seen an article suggesting that he might yet play for his country in the World Cup qualifying matches. The idea was beginning to take root. Who could rule it out? If he had a good season with United, it wasn't totally out of the question. But his disappointment at being unable to perform with The Crocodiles, in the near future, was more immediate.

'Yeah, sure. I understand. You're a big time soccer star. And this is just small time rock 'n' roll; but you're always welcome to jam. Just let me know when you're around, okay?'

'Sure, that'd be great.'

'Enough yakking. Let's do one more, then catch last orders. '

'Okay, Ricky. What'll it be then?' The rest of the band looked instinctively to their lead singer for an answer. So far he'd delivered and they now had as many gigs as they wished to play. Still pubs and clubs, but their reputation was growing steadily in the independent music press.

'Let's hit *Gemini Jane*, okay?' This was one of their own compositions: to be accurate, Ricky's composition, into which he'd built the band parts bit by bit. It was a hard hitting R 'n' B number with enough original touches to give it commercial potential. What they really needed was a good producer to turn them into a recording band; but not even Ricky had planned that far ahead yet. The first step was to build a reputation and then find a record company.

'Jimmy, you'll pick it up. It's basically a twelve bar on E, okay?'

'No problem,' grinned Jimmy as he adjusted the strap of his guitar in anticipation. 'No problem.' This was even more fun than playing football for Manchester United. Life was smiling upon him, he decided. But that was how it should be.

'One two, one two three four...' shouted Ricky, and began to strut as the chunky bass riff kicked in.

⚽ ⚽ ⚽

The office was like a steam room; sod's law that, as London baked in an Indian Summer, the air-conditioning should break down. Mary hunched over her desk and pressed on her voice mail. 'You have two messages. Press five for new messages.'

'Get on with it, you stupid cow.' Sometimes Mary loathed this woman, even if she was nothing more than a disembodied electronic voice.

'Temper, temper,' teased Rory, who sat at the adjacent desk.

'Get lost, Rory,' she snapped.

'Oh, PMT? Or is it that you're just not getting enough?' Rory raised a camp transatlantic eyebrow. 'There's no need to take it out on your poor phone, you know. It can't help being a pre-historic bundle of IT.'

'Piss off, Rory. Just mind your own business.'

Rory sighed dramatically. 'Girls today... I don't know. Just no... etiquette.'

Mary deliberately swivelled her chair so that her back was towards him. How she hated open-plan offices. No privacy. Whoever had come up with the idea had clearly never worked in close proximity with one hundred fellow creatures sweating in the airless confines of a fifteenth floor with phones ringing off the hook all day and computer screens cynically destroying all hope of retaining twenty-twenty vision beyond one's youth.

'First message,' intoned the electronic voice.

'Hi… Three o'clock, Calvin calling. You know the number and the deal.' She glanced at her watch. Ten minutes since her main client in New York had rung. She'd ring him back in just a mo'.

'Mary? It's Si. I'll try later.' Mary immediately pressed the automatic dial for Si's flat.

'Hello?'

'Hi, darling. How are you? You rang.'

'Oh yeah. That was quick, I only left the message two minutes ago.'

Mary wondered if she was being too keen. She never knew with men. Either they complained that you were too aloof and distant; or, they ran away when you tried to be obliging and enthusiastic. She decided to play it cool. 'Oh, I didn't realise. I must have been on the line to someone else. I'm in a bit of a hurry, so can you make it quick?'

Si sounded hurt. 'Oh, sorry to waste your precious time…'

Damn, she'd got it wrong. As usual, thought Mary glumly. She gave up the act. 'No, don't be like that. Of course I've got time for you. As much as you want, my love.'

Si softened. 'Good. Sorry, if I was uptight. You know how it is… Tough day in the flat doing nothing,' he quipped. Mary waited for him to go on. 'I just wanted to check you were having an all right day.'

'That's sweet. Yes, it's okay. Not brilliant, mind, but okay. Bloody hot.'

'Yeah, isn't it great? I'm about to go off to the park and try out those roller-blades.' With typical generosity, Mary had bought them both blades last week when she'd been in the States on business.

She surprised herself by feeling happy that Si was having a good day; even if she was cooped up and feeling like a boiled cod. Normally, she would have been deeply irritated and jealous of a friend having fun while she suffered. God, it must be love, she thought, her pink skin flushing to red. 'That's great. I wish I could be with you.'

'Yeah, me too,' Si replied nonchalantly.

I wonder if he means it. Si sounded so breezy and insouciant. Changing direction really had been a good move for him. Not just resigning from *The Courier*, but also starting to read more and really explore what he wanted to do with his life. Even all the spiritual stuff his mother had got him into seemed to have helped; although Mary sometimes worried that he might go all evangelical on her. 'Listen, darling, I must go. Have a good skate, and don't break a leg, okay?'

'Yeah. I'll be thinking of you. Stay cool.'

If you only knew how uncool I am, thought Mary. 'See you tonight, then.'

'I'll be waiting. Dinner at eight?'

Mary giggled. Definitely one of the best things about Si's new freedom was his willingness to cook for her. And, after a dodgy start, he was getting better. 'Can't wait. What are we having?'

Si put on an appalling French accent and unwittingly demonstrated how the banality of uxoriousness increases to fill the time available. 'Well, I thought Madame might enjoy some poached salmon with a warm rocket salad and croutons followed by summer pudding and clotted cream, accompanied by a sophisticated little wine I found today...a superb white burgundy dribbling butter and with a powerful nose of freshly cut lemongrass...'

Mary could stand no more. 'Stop, stop,' she wheezed, 'it sounds fabulous. Promise me something.'

'Anything, *ma chérie*.'

'Promise me, that whatever you decide to do, you won't become an actor.'

Si sounded offended. '*Pourquoi?*'

'Just don't, okay?'

'Okay. See you.'

'Love you... Bye.' Mary wiped her eyes and looked around. Fortunately, no-one seemed to have noticed her having a good time. If they had, intrusive questioning would have been bound to follow. Another joy of open-plan working.

She spun her chair back towards the computer screen. Her screen-saver told her in no uncertain terms that *TOP TOTTY KICKS TUTS*—not her phrase, but suggested as a motto for her by one of the vice-presidents. She'd taken it as a compliment six months ago. Now she wasn't so sure. Is that really what her colleagues thought of her? If so, shouldn't she be concerned?

God, it was hot. If she was going to get home by eight, she'd need to pull her finger out. Right, Calvin; down to earth with a bump. She grimaced as she forced herself into serious business mode and pressed another automatic dial button on her phone.

⚽ ⚽ ⚽

Jimmy looked out of the window at the blue cloudless sky and brown fields. It was only ten, but the dew had long since evaporated from the tired grass. Better late than never, he thought. It had been such a bloody awful summer.

Exhausted Friesians moped in the shade of tall, solitary trees. Probably contemplating a BSE future, mused Jimmy. Personally, he couldn't see what all the fuss was about. After all, hardly anyone had died of this new disease as far as he could work out. He still ate beef, loved it; in fact, he made a point of telling everyone that he did.

Another hour and they'd be at Euston. Amazing, the train was on time for once.

He was looking forward to London, as ever. Not just returning to the metropolis where he'd lived a decade, but also to seeing Si. Even though he got on with the lads at United and the city was good for a night out, it wasn't really the same.

Thinking of Si reminded him; tomorrow they were having lunch with Si's new girlfriend. Well, not so new, it seemed. Just that Si had been keeping her to himself. But it was obviously starting to get quite serious. The plan was to meet at The Feathers for a swift one, before going off to a restaurant or something. She sounded a bit fancy, this girl; in banking or something equally brainy. Jimmy wasn't sure if he'd like her. Well, it was only a lunch. Then he'd spend the rest of the day with Si on his own. But before all that, he looked forward to meeting up with Ricky and his band for a jam.

The train entered a tunnel and, without a view to stare at, Jimmy picked up *The Mirror*, his favourite paper at the moment. Of course, as he'd protested to the lads at United who'd ribbed him about it, this had nothing to do with the fact that *Mirror* readers had voted him player of the month—the new season was only a few matches old, but he was already having a ball.

The front-page headlines were all about Government sleaze and the Opposition being twenty points ahead in the opinion polls. Boring. The election was still eight months away, but there was little else in the news. Politics really turned him off. He turned to the back page in search of football news. If he was lucky, there might even be a mention for United's new star striker, Jimmy Sweeney.

⚽ ⚽ ⚽

It had taken over an hour, and the Sleeper had used three little tapes telling his story. He realised that if ever anyone played them, only one person would listen sympathetically; to everyone else he'd be simply a terrorist.

The Sleeper had almost finished, and suddenly noticed that the effort of concentration and recollection had drained him completely. Exhausted, he clicked on the machine and spoke softly towards it. 'This is more or less it. I'll have to go soon. Still no sign that they're on to me. Sometimes, to be honest, I half-wish they were. I woke up this morning realising that this was the crunch... I'm about to do something so important that the rest of my life and many other people's lives will never be the same again. I guess some people may be killed. And for that I'm sorry, especially if they're just innocent passers-by. But... How did my ma put it? Oh yes... You can't make an omelette without breaking some eggs.

'I was really shitting myself first thing this morning, though. I had some breakfast, cornflakes as usual, with Greta. Michael had gone off much earlier. She was a bit distant, but that might be my fault for not paying her enough attention in the last few days. What with Ginger and all, I've been a bit distracted. We didn't say much over breakfast until Greta said something really odd.

'"Baa, I've never asked you... But are you religious?"

'"No, not really. I mean my ma brought me up to be a good Catholic of course... You know, I went to mass until I left home, more or less every Sunday. But not since then."

'"Oh"

'"Why?"

'"Well, I was thinking I might go to mass this morning. D'you want to come?"

'I was surprised, but the more I thought about it, the more I realised I wanted to go to mass with Greta. It seemed right somehow. Not just to go with her. But also because of what I'm about to do.

'So we went round the corner to the Catholic church, which had a ten thirty mass. There were a surprising number of people. A lot of old 'uns but also some younger types. I wondered why they weren't at work. The priest was also quite young. The reading was a passage I knew backwards from when I was small. But until now I'd never understood it. It was about walking through the valley of death. Then we sang a hymn, *Amazing Grace*, and I remembered the story about the lighthouse keeper's daughter, and I kind of imagined Greta as Grace Darling rescuing me from the storm. It was such a beautiful piece that I felt tears coming and I had to stop singing in case Greta noticed.

'The rest of the mass was more or less normal. I thought my ma would have been pleased to know I was in church.

'When it was time to take communion I waited until right at the end. I wasn't sure if I should. I remembered that you weren't meant to if you'd eaten less than an hour before. I glanced at my watch but couldn't remember if we'd finished breakfast before or after ten o'clock. Then I thought I hadn't been to confession for over two years. Wasn't it a mortal sin to take communion without having confessed? And if I did confess I'd have to lie to the priest anyway... I couldn't possibly tell him I'd been sleeping with a married woman.

'By this time, everyone had gone up and the priest was about to turn back to the altar with the salver and chalice. But suddenly I had a burning urge to receive the bread and wine and rushed out of the pew.

'Greta had already been up and back and was praying. I don't think she really noticed my haste.

'I walked quickly up to the priest, who waited for me to reach him, a curious look on his face. Almost inviting me to confess. My heart was thumping and I bit my lip as I put out my hands... I couldn't remember if it was left over right or right over left. So at the last minute I put my hands behind my back and stuck out my neck and tongue. The priest placed the small white disc on my tongue and I swallowed it whole. Then I sipped from the cold metallic-tasting cup. The wine felt warm like blood and the sensation made my stomach churn.

'I walked back to my seat and joined Greta on my knees. I felt something immense surge up within me, out of focus, impossible to grasp... More than emotion... More like pure power. I clamped my eyes shut and tried to pray. But my mind just flickered like a TV after the video's finished.

'When I opened my eyes everyone was leaving the church. Greta and I stood up, smoothed down our clothes and, without a word, we walked home.

'I feel stronger now. More prepared. In a few hours I'll have done what I have to do. Everything's more or less ready. I've just got to pick it up from the garage, assemble it and take it there.... Carefully, mind... They warned us in training these things were sometimes a bit unstable... But it should be okay. After that it should be easy. No problems. Just leave it where I've been told to and then... Well, then the end of the cease-fire I suppose, and one day they'll recognise me as a hero.

'With a bit of luck I'll be watching it all on the news tonight with Greta curled up beside me. Michael's away for a few days abroad, so once the kids are in bed we can make love. Tomorrow, again... And maybe I'll take her somewhere special to eat? There's an expensive Thai restaurant round the corner she often talks about. We've never been. I'll use some of the money they've given me for France to spoil her. I've got to make the most of the time that we have left together. She's the only woman I've ever loved... Like a lover that is...

'Right. I guess that's it. Time to go.' The Sleeper clicked off the dictaphone.

⚽ ⚽ ⚽

The big summer which Si had yearned for had finally arrived. The heavens were indigo and so high and clear. Si thought that if only his eyesight was strong enough he would be able to see beyond the atmosphere, the stratosphere and all the other limiting spheres and find a bit of meaning. But, he lamented, his eyesight was still deeply mortal and not up to it.

The books on mysticism and Buddhism, which his mother had sent him, had stimulated him and increased his knowledge and awareness of his own insignificance and ignorance. What they hadn't done was to provide any sort of answer. Despite this, he revelled in the heat of sunny London. Life seemed extraordinarily good.

He walked up the Haymarket with Jimmy. It was busy, and shoppers heading to or from Piccadilly crowded the pavement. Tourists sweated heavily as they trailed after bullying guides. A young Japanese girl waved a raised umbrella threateningly above her head as she berated her bovine charges.

Si wondered if the tourists were enjoying themselves. The poor things had paid a fortune, quite possibly several years' savings—after all, most Japanese tourists were ordinary working people. And what did they get? A week of following an umbrella and being herded around by snappily dressed young guides determined to wring out every last yen in commission and tips. Some holiday.

Si could picture Mary's parents being herded around on some stultifying, middle-class tour of Greece or Egypt, all perspiring complaints about the hotel plumbing and the prices of fake artefacts. Compassion overwhelmed him.

But he couldn't see Mary herself putting up with such abuse; not his little Mary. Pity the poor guide who took her on. With a smile, he thought they'd probably end up paying commission to her. But, he reflected, feeling slightly guilty, her independent-mindedness was one of her most attractive characteristics, and it wasn't that she was avaricious, just careful with money.

They passed a theatre showing a much-praised revival of *The Importance of being Earnest*. Si had wanted to take Mary, but she'd opted for *Evita* at the cinema instead. This had provoked some serious questions, such as how could he really consider spending the rest of his life with a girl whose tastes and values were so out of kilter with his own? As usual, he'd reached no conclusions. Time would tell, he'd decided. In the event the musical was superb entertainment, and he'd agreed with Mary that Madonna was brilliant.

Si's musing, partly induced by the unexpected warmth of the day, ended abruptly as a young man called out to them. He'd recognised Jimmy.

'Hey, Jimmy, how you doing?'

Si watched Jimmy's reaction closely, but his friend just grinned.

'Good luck at the weekend, mate,' and with a wave the bloke passed on down the street.

Manchester United had made a strong start to the new season, and after his contribution to winning the Double Double, Jimmy was now a regular in the first team. He'd scored four goals in the first five games, which made him United's top scorer so far. The team were playing Aston Villa on Saturday, and Jimmy was odds-on favourite with the bookies to score first.

'Does that happen often?'

'No, just every now and again. It started after the Cup Final.'

'So you really *are* a star now.'

Si hadn't meant to mock and hoped Jimmy wouldn't take it the wrong way; but he didn't seem to mind.

'Give over,' he laughed and punched Si on the arm. 'Famous my arse. Just 'cos someone recognises me means nothing.'

But despite this modesty, Jimmy looked pleased at the idea that he was becoming a star. And why shouldn't he? Si realised he was feeling a bit edgy. Putting any negative thoughts firmly behind him, he put his arm round Jimmy's shoulder in a matey fashion and gave him a squeeze.

'Come on then, superstar, I want you to meet Mary; and if we don't hurry up she'll have left. Star or no star, my girlfriend don't wait for no man.'

After nine months of effort—admittedly, sometimes half-hearted—Si was going to introduce Mary to Jimmy. The plan was to have lunch at Andante, a trendy restaurant in Soho where Si used to take some of his contacts at *The Courier*'s expense. It was his first time back since leaving the Diary, and he wondered if it would feel very different to eat there as a man of leisure.

Fortunately, given Andante's prices, Mary had offered to pay. She did that more and more these days, since he'd ceased to have a regular income. Initially, Si had found it a bit difficult, but now any chivalrous misgivings had evaporated. It made sense: Mary earned a big salary; she wanted to eat out, not him; she wanted to pay; he earned hardly anything now; so let her pay. After all, it was an egalitarian society, wasn't it? This just showed how modern their relationship was.

'I'm looking forward to meeting her,' said Jimmy. 'It's about time you introduced me. Especially if it's getting serious. I've never been out with a girl for more than a month.'

Si pretended not to know what Jimmy meant; he didn't want to discuss the future of the romance until Jimmy had met Mary. After all, there was a good chance that they wouldn't get on. Then what? Could he carry on as before, reconciling himself to the fact that his best friend and his girlfriend had to be kept apart? Si realised he was characteristically creating problems which didn't exist and might never arise.

'How did it go with Ricky last night?'

'Fantastic. I reckon when I get too old for this football lark, I'll become a rock star.'

'What, like Julio Iglesias?'

'I might have known you'd take the piss... Anyway, I suggested to Ricky he come along and join us.'

'What, today?' Si was slightly horrified. Jimmy plus Mary was a complicated enough sum without adding Ricky.

'Yeah. Only he's busy for lunch, he said, at a place not far from here in fact. Apparently he's fixing up a gig for the band in a pub just off Oxford Street.'

'Oh well, another time...' Si breathed a sigh of relief.

'Yeah, but he might meet us for a coffee later. He's got my mobile number in case.'

Si focused on his inner self—as one of his mother's books had taught him to do in times of stress—and immediately felt calm, despite the lingering prospect of having to deal with the three separate pieces of his life simultaneously. He'd made great strides in the past two months, and his life was much less fragmented; but there was still some way to go before he felt mature enough to deal with a fully integrated, coherent existence. He glanced at his watch. Five to one. Mary had been waiting ten minutes. Better hurry up.

They reached Piccadilly and, crossing to the left of Eros, washed along by a flood of German tourists, turned into Regent Street. The sun glinted off the elegant crescent and, not for the first time, Si wondered at London's glory. Simple understated lines borrowed from Rome, but breathtakingly modern on a sunny English day.

⚽ ⚽ ⚽

The Sleeper finished writing the letter to Greta. Among other things, he told her where to find the dictaphone so she could play the tapes. He folded the sheet of paper carefully and put it with the three small tapes into a plain manilla envelope. He sealed this carefully and left the room.

In the kitchen Greta Anderson was giving her youngest an early lunch. The child had thrown most of it on the floor. The rest was spread liberally around his mouth and clothing. Greta sighed.

'Hi.'

'Hi, you,' she looked up and watched him standing in the doorway scratching the chipped paint. 'You all right, Baa?'

'Yeah.' He waited in the doorway watching, fiddling

nervously with his watch strap. 'Greta, I've got something to ask you.'

'Uh huh?'

'Baa, Baa, Baa...' chanted the child, demanding his attention. But he ignored this and the spoon being waved threateningly in his direction by the infant.

'This envelope... Do you mind keeping it safe for me?'

'Course not.' Then her face clouded. 'Why? Are you going away or something?'

'No. Well, maybe. Don't know yet. But it's just that if I do, I need to keep this safe, you see?'

'Are you going to tell me why?'

'No.'

Greta looked at him sadly for a moment; she seemed to realise she was looking at a stranger; she nodded. 'Okay.'

The child began to howl. 'Oh, be quiet,' sighed Greta from the heart. 'Please be quiet.'

'And see, if...if something happens...'

'What?'

'Something... You'll know what I mean if it does...'

Greta raised her eyebrows ironically. No doubt, thought the Sleeper, she thought he was being silly or over-dramatic; but there was no scope for further explanation.

'If something happens, you can open the envelope. Okay?'

Perhaps something in the way he said this persuaded Greta not to make light of the request. She looked at him for a few moments. Her piercing green eyes drilled into him, but failed to extract any further information. Then she sighed and put the envelope to one side. 'Yeah, okay,' she said and returned to feeding her demanding son. Immediately, he stopped crying.

'Bye bye Baa, bye bye Baa...' The child waved a little hand.

'Hey, I'm not going anywhere, you tyke.'

But the child thought otherwise. 'Bye bye Baa...' he intoned, enjoying the sound of his own voice.

The Sleeper waited in the doorway for a few seconds, fixing the scene in his memory. Then he went up to his room. Not long now. Wasn't this what he'd been waiting for? Of course it was. He lay on his bed and stared at the ceiling for a while.

At twelve fifteen he went out.

'So where are you going, young man?'

The familiar voice made the Sleeper stop in his tracks. Damn, this was the last thing he needed. He turned about and composed a smile of greeting. There was no point in raising suspicions, even those of a drunk old man. 'Hi, Lenny. How's it going?'

'Fine, fine.' Lenny caught up with him and fell into step. 'In fact, quite wonderful.' Something had clearly happened. The weathered face cracked into a broad grin. 'You'll never believe it...'

'Go on, try me.'

'Well...' Lenny looked round dramatically before continuing. 'I've got it all sorted out.'

'What?' Despite himself, the Sleeper was intrigued.

'You know. What we were talking about the other day.'

The Sleeper racked his brains. They'd talked about so much, most of it trivia and instantly forgettable. What could Lenny be on about? He sighed. 'I give up.'

'The big issue. That's what. I've been talking to that Father Theodore...'

'I thought you didn't like him?'

'Oh, whatever gave you that idea? The Father's a fine man, a holy man, he is.'

The Sleeper waited for his friend to go on.

'So I checked out with the father if Catholics are cannibals and he said just what you did. They're not.' Lenny stopped and examined the Sleeper's face for a reaction. Evidently satisfied by what he saw, he went on. 'When you eat the bread, Catholics don't believe it really turns into human flesh. But it doesn't just remain as bread either. No, what the father said was that it's a sacrament between man and

God; so something mystical happens to it, something beyond the comprehension of human understanding.'

This all sounded far more complicated than anything the Sleeper had been taught as a child.

'I can't tell you what a weight off my mind that is,' said Lenny.

'Great. It's a bit odd, though, don't you think, that the answer is something you can't understand?'

'I know, I know,' Lenny replied patiently. 'But that's where *faith* comes in.'

That was a word the Sleeper remembered his mother using a lot. 'Ah, faith. Is that what it means, then?'

'Yes. Amazing, don't you think? So, anyway, when the penny dropped I realised that there's really no reason at all why I shouldn't become a Catholic.'

'No?'

'No. And there's a very good reason to do so...'

'So that you can be buried in the churchyard?' The Sleeper looked over his shoulder to where he could just make out the spire and the weathervane.

'Exactly. Not that I've got any complaints about the Anglican Church—it's served me well. But one has to be practical in such trying circumstances.'

'Aye, I suppose so. What does Father Theodore think?'

Lenny looked thoughtful. 'Well, I'm still working on him. But I think he sees I'm ripe for conversion, and a few more of our little chats should do it. We're doing intercession next.'

The Sleeper restrained himself from asking what that was; it sounded quite sexy. He really had to get on if he was to keep to the plan. But he needn't have worried; Lenny was obviously keen to get off.

'I'll tell you all about it next time I see you, okay? Must rush... I'm trying to work out whether I'd prefer a plot near the church wall, or round the back outside the east transept.' Without further ado, Lenny turned on his heel and strode vigorously back the way they'd come, his gaze fixed firmly on the church spire. 'Goodbye,' he called with a cheery wave, without looking back.

The Sleeper watched him go, envious of Lenny's certainty.

The bus took him to Kilburn, where he unlocked the garage. As he swung back the door, light streamed in; the space looked dank and empty. The Sleeper stepped into the gloom and flicked a switch behind the door. A strip light spluttered into action and the Sleeper closed the door behind him, locking it with a bolt.

The unforgiving illumination showed a small pile of cardboard boxes in one corner, an old card table and rickety wooden chair in the centre of the concrete floor. The Sleeper had salvaged the furniture from a skip. He set to work.

First, he unpacked his boxes. He placed the three main ingredients separately on the table. He sat down. Before starting the assembly, he sat quietly recalling instructions and training in his mind. It was a long time since he'd actually made an improvised explosive device, or IED as the Brits called it—and this was the first time for real—but he was more or less confident that he could remember how to do it corr-ectly. All the same, he wished there was someone he could call just to check a couple of small details. 'Stop being daft,' he told himself. 'It's easy, just get on with it.'

The Sleeper picked up a metal cylinder, the size of a cigarette. He attached the electrical detonator carefully to the circuit board. He placed the small clockwork egg-timer into position beside a nail hammered hoizontally into the side of the wooden casing. As the dial rotated, it would shoulder up against the side of the nail and close the circuit. He inserted a light switch into the circuit as a safety precaution, up for safe, down for armed. Then, he turned to the amorphous lump of white matter—it looked and felt like putty. The Sleeper had never, even during training, handled thirty pounds of Semtex before. He bit his lower lip in concentration as he slowly pushed the detonator into the yielding mass. Just like playing with plasticine as a kid, he thought. He recalled how some of the explosive used in training had smelt of almonds—but this stuff had no odour. Okay, almost done. He took a deep breath. Was he going to flick the safety switch now or at the target? he asked himself. As far as he could remember it depended on the situation. After a moment's thought he decided that as the plan involved planting the bomb in public and there would be little opportunity to fiddle with the mechanism at the last moment, he should set it now. After all, he was going to set the timer before leaving the garage, so it made sense to do the switch too. He turned the dial on the timer—the bomb would go off at two o'clock allowing him ample time to get up to the West End, leave it in the rubbish bin outside the Café Royal and make his escape. Finally, hesitatingly, he flicked the small metal rod down into the armed position. The Sleeper rocked back in his chair and surveyed his handiwork with satisfaction. It had been quite easy after all; child's play, really.

After a couple of minutes, he emerged from the garage, locked up and left carrying a red sports bag with black and white trimmings.

He knew where he was going. He'd already walked the route twice. But this wasn't a recce any more. This was for real. Previously, the bag had contained a bundle of rubbish, old newspapers and the like. This time it was much heavier, and his arms ached. He handled it carefully, avoiding lamp-posts and other objects which might disturb the contents. He thought about the size of the bomb and bit his lip. It was huge. God knows what would happen when this mother went off. Certainly, he didn't want to be around when it blew.

⚽ ⚽ ⚽

Mary was running late for lunch. She'd not been able to get out of work on time because a client had rung her. She'd never admit it to Si, but sometimes she felt like a slave to her clients. If they wanted something, she had to jump. Her own life had to take second place. These days slaves were an expensive commodity—hence her hefty salary.

Such dark thoughts made her question how much longer she'd be able to sustain the patience and hypocrisy. She'd taken the call and politely answered a string of stupid questions, reassuring the client through clenched teeth that she was delighted to help.

There must be more to life than making money. It struck her that this was probably the first time she'd admitted the fact. Occasionally, she surprised herself by envying Si his freedom. Perhaps she should take a leaf out of her grandmother's book and move to the country and have a garden. That would be nice. But not yet. In a few years time. She found herself thinking how fulfilling it would be to have a family.

Snap out of it, she told herself. You've got a great job, with amazing prospects. How could you contemplate another existence? Well, marriage would be nice, okay. But watch it... A baby. God, that'd be death for your career...

Mary took a cab to the top of Regent Street, but seeing the traffic crawling along she decided it would be quicker to walk. She was almost a quarter of an hour late. Apprehensive though she was, she was looking forward to meeting the famous Jimmy at long last. If he was so important to Si, then she really should make an effort. But what would she find to talk about with a footballer? Si, she supposed.

In front of Liberty's window she stopped to study her reflection. She smoothed her navy Chanel skirt, plumped her hair and practised a smile. Not bad. It would have to do. If she was any later, it would be beyond fashionable. At least she didn't have to worry that Si would leave the restaurant. He had nothing else to do apart from wait for her; and even if he had other commitments, she knew from past experience that he would wait devotedly until she arrived. She smiled at the thought. He really was very sweet, and she was a lucky girl.

⚽ ⚽ ⚽

'I love London when it's like this.'

'Yeah, me too. Pity it's dull and grey most of the time.'

'No, it isn't. Just this summer. Normally, the weather's quite good.'

'Maybe,' Jimmy sounded dubious. 'Well, whatever, it's better than Manchester. Up there it just rains, non-stop. Terrible.'

They paused to cross the road. As they waited, a man crossed in front of them. He was carrying a Man United bag.

'Watch out, Jimmy. Your fans are everywhere.'

'What do you mean?'

'That guy there. He's a Man U supporter. If he recognises you he'll be wanting your autograph.'

'Ah, piss off.'

But Jimmy need not have worried. The Sleeper walked straight past them, frowning with concentration.

Jimmy and Si reached the opposite pavement and walked into the restaurant.

'Can I help, sir?'

'Yes, thanks. I've got a table for three booked under the name of Simpson.'

The Maitre d' looked at the page of the large bound book in front of him. 'Yes of course, sir. We've reserved one of our best tables in the window for you.'

Si looked knowingly at Jimmy, who just raised a sarcastic eyebrow.

'If you'll just follow me...'

❀ ❀ ❀

Ricky stopped and polished the toe of his boot on the back of his left leg. That was better. The black leather shone in the bright light. Then he entered the pub.

The darkness of the interior forced him to strain his dilating eyes after the pupil contraction of shimmering Oxford Street.

Once accustomed to the gloomy interior, he strode confidently towards the bar. This was a big opportunity. If The Crocodiles played here, the A and R men would come. It was a regular talent-spotting venue. Bands queued up to play on a Saturday night and often did it for nothing; the chance of being signed up by a record company was a big enough incentive.

Ricky had no doubt that The Crocodiles' time was about to come. The only thing was persuading the pub manager of this fact.

He slid a cassette out of his inside jacket pocket and leaned across the bar towards a man cleaning glasses.

The man eyed him warily.

Ricky cleared his throat and gave his best smile. Then he started the patter.

❀ ❀ ❀

Unusually, the lunchtime crowd in The Feathers was fairly thin. Many of the regulars had chosen to have their lunch outside in the bright September sunshine.

Brenda's feet hurt and she wished she'd not wasted all that hard-earned cash on fashion shoes. The Edwardian clock behind the bar said two minutes past one. Another two hours till she got her break. Then she could put her feet up and have a cup of tea at home. It was only ten minutes walk to her mother's flat, in the opposite direction to the smart terraces where Si lived; but she winced at the thought of walking along the hot pavement in those stupid shoes.

She'd be back later, of course. And the evening crowd was much more fun. Moreover, there was always the possibility that Si would pop in for a pint. Or two. They'd been getting on particularly well recently. Not that she'd made any progress in fulfilling her romantic fantasy, although Brenda's crush on Si was as real as ever. But since he'd packed in his job, he'd become much more relaxed and talkative; prepared to share his thoughts with her. He didn't seem to mind that she sometimes couldn't understand what he was talking about. He seemed particularly keen on religion recently. She'd never really had much time for such hocus pocus, but Si's chatter was amusing. The odd thing was, he was always asking questions, not of her, but of himself. And he never answered them before putting another question. But never about Jimmy and her; she half-hoped he would—it might mean Si was interested in her. However, she enjoyed his company and her heart beat faster whenever he pushed through the doorway and greeted her with an airy wave.

A man in a grey pinstripe waited to be served. Probably a solicitor or an estate agent. There were a lot of those working near The Feathers. She forced a smile in his direction. 'What can I get you?'

'A tomato juice, please.'

A solicitor, she decided.

It was the hottest day of the year, but otherwise there seemed nothing unusual about the dog whining in the park. The mongrel started to emit a thin moan and kept it up for a few minutes. Bristling with miserable anticipation it strained at the makeshift lead.

'Shut up, Tex,' barked a middle-aged man sitting on the bench beside the dog. Then he returned to his newspaper.

Big Ben struck one o'clock, but no-one seemed to notice. The park was full of people on their lunchbreak. Tourist couples strolled around the lake and took photos of Buckingham Palace through the trees. Day-dreaming civil servants in suits munched sandwiches and perspired on benches. A group of small children down by the lakeside fed scraps of stale bread to the swans. The magnificent ivory birds craned their necks gracefully to retrieve the food as if they were doing the children a favour. Hundreds of ducks bobbed serenely on the glassy surface.

The noise caused people to stop walking. Some looked up into the sky, perhaps expecting a supersonic aircraft to cut a thin white scar through the blue. Cameras were lowered briefly. Sandwiches hung in the air mid-bite. The children feeding swans stepped back in fear as the birds reared out of the water screaming and spreading their immense, powerful wings. The ducks took to flight, wheeling in a terrifying flapping arc, beating their way to the end of the lake and back in a dense flock.

After the bang a dangerous silence, thick with uncertainty, descended on the park. Then, gradually, people forgot, started talking again, resumed their strolls and lunches, and the birds glided back to the lake. The dark swarm of pigeons which had taken to flight at the noise, curved around the trees and landed abruptly on the grass as if driven by a common thought.

Only the mongrel Tex did not relax. He kept barking as he had done since the boom shook the park. Barking fit to burst. Nothing his owner could do would calm him.

Then the sirens started and a pall of dirty smoke rose in an apocalyptic pillar, like a crude brushstroke on a virgin, azure-washed canvas.

❀ ❀ ❀

Greta stopped reading the newspaper. She must have read the article half a dozen times already. She sat quietly, lost in thought for some time. How long, she didn't know. Occasionally, her unfocussed eyes rested unseeing on the letter beneath her hand.

Her thumb ached from holding down the play button on the dictaphone she'd found in Baa's room. She'd listened to the three tapes all the way through. Baa's recordings lasted well over an hour. And the voice was so serious; she had difficulty associating it with her boyish lover.

Then the phone rang. It rang half a dozen times before she heard it. From upstairs came the sound of children fighting. She brushed a tress of auburn hair from her face and pushed back her chair from the kitchen table.

Greta was slightly surprised not to wake up. It might so easily have been a nightmare. But if so she was still caught up in her dream.

She noticed the early autumn sunshine streaming through the windows as she stood up. The phone was still ringing and, rubbing her aching eyes, she walked over to answer it. No doubt, the police would be back again soon. They'd said as much earlier, when they came to tell her that Baa was dead. Perhaps this was them? She knew it was only a matter of time. She knew all this, and although she now knew why her lover was dead, she simply couldn't begin to understand.

EPILOGUE

Si opened his eyes. He felt so relaxed. A fly spun around the lamp above him. Feeling slightly chilly, he tried to pull up the bedclothes. The pain was excruciating and immediately he remembered everything. Through scrunched up eyes, he fought back the tears which always followed.

'Ah, so you've decided to wake up at last. We're honoured to have you back, to be sure we are.'

Si realised that, for once, he had managed to control his tears. Progress. Pity his body still looked like a teabag and felt like a pin cushion.

'So, do you want some breakfast? I mean it's only twelve o'clock, but you've been asleep for fifteen hours. I wish I could have the luxury... Some hope.'

'You need to get blown up to get that honour,' Si joked feebly.

'Yes, on second thoughts, I'll settle for my six hours a night.' Penny was wonderful. In the fortnight he'd been at Saint Mary's Hospital, she'd nursed him constantly. Dedicated beyond the call of duty, always cheerful, the young nurse had pulled him back from the edge.

'Now seriously, fifteen hours is a great improvement. You're over the worst, the doctor says. Sleeping like that, you'll be back on your feet in no time.'

Si knew she was lying, but he didn't care. The important thing was to forget that first week of sleepless agony, when his injuries had been so severe that even breathing seemed brave, and the only rest he'd got was drug-induced.

Now things seemed to be looking up.

'Any news on Mary?'

Penny shook her head. Mary had been injured more severely than any of them, having been the closest of them all to the epicentre of the blast. She was still in intensive care, although stable now. It had seemed at one point that she might not make it. Si had only been told this several days after the immediate danger had passed—at the time he would not have understood.

'And Jimmy?'

'No change. The bandages come off next week. We won't know until after that. And maybe not even then.'

Si and Jimmy had been inside the restaurant, a hundred yards from the bomb; when Andante's vast plate glass window had been blown in, they had been caught in a storm of glass shards. Si had his back to the window and had been peppered like a pheasant. Jimmy had taken the blast face on. The surgeons feared he might have lost his sight for good.

Si sank back into the bed. It still hurt. He ached everywhere. Not for the first time he wondered, *why*? Why them, just when things were going so well for them all?

'You rest now,' Penny advised. 'I'll be back soon.'

Si watched her departing form as she softly closed the door. Then he closed his eyes.

⚽ ⚽ ⚽

'You've got a visitor.' Penny looked unsure whether to let the intruder in. But as she dithered, the door flew open. A huge bunch of tropical flowers entered. Ricky followed noisily.

'Surprise!'

Si managed a weak smile. Apart from his parents, he'd not had any visitors. The doctors advised at least another week of total rest before he had regular visiting hours.

Penny left the room discreetly.

'Hey man, how's it going? We thought you might poop on us at one point. But now they say you're gonna be fine. Isn't that great?'

'Hi, Ricky. Thanks for coming.' Si didn't feel strong enough for conversation.

'No problem. Sorry I didn't make it sooner. But they wouldn't let me. God, they're strict round here. That nurse'—he cast a surreptitious glance over his shoulder—'she's a tough one. Treated me like I was the one who put you in here.' He laughed loudly but cut himself short. 'Sorry, I guess that wasn't very funny.' Ricky looked a bit lost for what to say next.

'Yeah, it was funny enough. Only, I can't laugh. It hurts too much.'

Ricky grinned, clearly relieved. 'You know they found out who did it?'

Si nodded. Barry O'Reilly, a twenty-year-old member of the Provisional IRA had been killed in the blast. The police said the bomb had probably gone off prematurely, although they were still trying to fathom why O'Reilly had flicked the safety switch off before reaching his target. The explosion might have been triggered by movement of the bag in which it was being carried; or O'Reilly might have bumped into something. It was unclear what the target was, although it seemed that the intention was to end the cease-fire with maximum impact. An explosion in the West End of London certainly fitted the bill. To that extent the operation seemed to have been a success, O'Reilly's death apart. The bomb had carved a huge swathe of destruction down one of the busiest shopping streets in London; five people had died, ten others were still in hospital and many others had suffered minor injuries from flying glass. Barry O' Reilly had left his mark in many places.

'What could have made a kid like that so full of hate? Defeats me. I suppose it was justice that he was killed by his own bomb.'

Si's eyes filled up with tears. He felt very sorry for himself suddenly. Ricky must have noticed. 'Oh, listen, man, I didn't mean to upset you. I'm really sorry. Hey, why don't I tell you about the band? We got this gig at The Goat In Boots, you know, the pub on Oxford Street where all the famous bands play on their way to the top? In fact it was the same day as the bomb. I went and talked to the manager and played him a few tracks, and he signed us up. We're playing next month. You see, they've got so much demand, they book at least a month in advance. And hey, man, it was a close run thing you know.'

'What?'

'Getting the gig, man. It almost didn't happen.'

'Why?'

'Well, talk about luck... Well, not exactly luck, that's the wrong word in the circumstances...' Ricky looked disconcerted again, his usual ebullience gone.

'Go on.'

'Yeah, well... Just as we shook hands on the deal and had finished sorting out the details, the bomb went off. Boom, just like that. Know what I mean?'

Si nodded.

'Yeah, course you do. Sorry, I forgot for a moment.'

'And, although we were round the corner from Regent Street, we must have been five hundred yards away from the bomb; but all the windows blew in and everything shook, like an earthquake, man. At first we thought the explosion was outside, but then we realised that it was some way away.' Ricky paused. 'Now, what was I saying? Oh yeah, it could have been a disaster... Well, it was, I know, but I mean for the band. You know what I mean?'

Si smiled reassuringly.

'If the bomb had gone off any earlier, there'd have been too much chaos to clinch a deal. As it was, I just rang up the next day to check that The Goat In Boots would be repaired in time and that the deal stood. It did.' Ricky looked at Si. 'Sorry, that was all a bit confused, but you know what I'm trying to say, don't you?'

Si managed a nod. 'Every cloud?'

Ricky looked blank. Then recognition dawned. 'Exactly man. Exactly. I guess I'm just real pleased to see you... Alive, that is.'

Silence fell between them. The silence of hospitals and big institutions, textured with distant muffled voices and midday birdsong.

'Well, I'll leave you these.' He placed the blooms in an empty vase, wrapping paper and all. 'I shouldn't tire you out any longer. That dragon of a nurse told me I had only ten minutes. See you, then.'

'Ricky, thanks for coming by.'

'No problem, man. I'll be back soon, okay?' And, with a broad grin and a lazy, surfer's wave of the hand, Ricky swung out of the room. How, Si mused, did Ricky manage to preserve a suntan when autumnal mists had descended on London? Impressive. But there again, perhaps it wasn't real.

⚽ ⚽ ⚽

Si started to feel strong enough to have visitors every day—mostly his parents and Ricky. Bill from *The Courier* had come once, looking very self-conscious. Si had imagined it was because of the hospital and the unease which grips most people when faced with the seriously ill. But it had turned out to be far more interesting.

'I brought you these.' Bill shyly presented some wilted pink and white carnations wrapped in soggy paper.

'Hey, you didn't need to.... But thanks anyway. So have a seat.' Si gestured to the functional chair beside the bed. He noticed that Bill had lost the nose stud and had shaved his hair almost down to the scalp. The fuzz which survived had returned to its natural brown hue. He wore a tight white vest under a black leather biker's jacket. Strangely, Si felt that the flowers seemed to complement the outfit.

'No, I can't stay. Got to get back to finish off the page.' Bill shifted uncomfortably from foot to foot.

Si realised he hadn't thought about *The Courier* once since the accident. His time there seemed like ancient history. 'Yeah, of course. How's it going? Dougy treating you well?'

'It's going great,' Bill brightened. 'I love the job... You know I really appreciated the way you sorted it at the time so I could take over. I didn't really make it clear then, but thanks, you know.'

'Oh come on, don't make me blush. I'm weepy enough as it is at the moment.' They exchanged a smile. Bill seemed more relaxed now. Si thought with a slight twinge of regret that perhaps he'd been a bit hard on the lad when he'd been his boss.

'Oh, and by the way, Dougy's no longer at *The Courier*.'

'What? Did he resign?'

'No, sacked. Sir Lesley decided he'd had enough of him, for some reason. Nobody really knows why. But some people say it's all tied up with Sir Lesley's new mistress. Some high-class Italian bird. Apparently, she took a dislike to Dougy and insisted Sir Lesley put a woman in charge.'

'So who's the new editor?'

'Not so new… But I suppose you probably haven't been able to follow the news recently.' Bill stopped, suddenly unsure of himself. Noticing Si's impatience for the name, he went on. 'Well, do you remember that woman before, you know, before Dougy? Mini Bournemouth? Well, Sir Lesley brought her back.'

'Wow. I thought she'd retired. Spending more time with her family and all that.'

'She did. But perhaps she spent too much time with them because…' Bill paused for effect and raised an eyebrow, 'she got divorced and started editing *Jezebel*, a new magazine for high-brow, professional women. And that's how she met the boss's aristocratic Italian floozy. I imagine it can't have been easy for Sir Lesley to swallow his pride. But as far as he's concerned, what Carla says goes these days.' They both laughed at the thought of *The Courier's* unloved owner having to grovel to Mini Bournemouth. 'Apparently, she demanded serious money to come back. But he paid up. He had to.'

'Extraordinary. The world keeps turning, eh?'

'Sorry?'

'Oh nothing, just thinking out loud. So, what's she like to work for, this Mini? She left just before I arrived.'

'She's a tough cookie and I've heard some of the old

hands say her sense of humour has suffered since losing her husband to a nineteen-year-old bimbo. But she's much better than Dougy. We seem to have hit it off okay. And she was really sweet when I broke my news...'

'What news?' Si interrupted Bill's breathless flow.

Bill looked surprised. 'Oh, didn't you know?'

'What?'

'Well, I suppose you've been out of touch for a while and all....'

'What?' Si wanted to know.

'Well, I came out in August. It just suddenly became obvious that it was the right thing to do. And God, what a relief. I can't tell you how much better I feel now.'

This hit Si like a bolt from the blue. He'd never for a moment considered Bill might be gay. Extrovert, trying to make a point, a fashion victim... All these yes. But gay, no. God, how dense he was. Talk about wrapped up in his own world and impervious to others...

This situation was a new one to Si; he wondered what he should say? 'Congratulations'? 'Yeah, great'? 'I never imagined...'? Now it was his turn to be stuck for words. 'But isn't that fantastic?'

Bill nodded, clearly pleased by Si's reaction.

'Have you told your parents?'

'Yeah, they were really cool about it. Amazing to think I was so terrified. I guess until you test them, you never really know how they're going to react. I went up to Scotland especially to tell them, and all my family are being excellent.'

'Great.' Si wondered what to say next. 'So do you have a steady boyfriend?'

Bill laughed loudly. 'Steady? God, no. The steadiest thing I've got is a hangover. I also have a nipple ring.' He laughed again.

Si knew his eyes were wide as plates. But he found he couldn't do anything to look less surprised.

If he noticed Bill didn't show it. 'I'm just having fun. I

don't want to tie myself down yet. No commitment, that's my motto. And I'm having a ball.' A wicked grin spread from ear to ear.

'Great. I'm really glad things are going well for you.'

'Listen, I must go. I've stayed far too long as it is. Oh, and before I forget, everyone sent love and said to get well soon. They want to do a feature on you, I think. But I'll try and hold them off for as long as possible.'

'Thanks. Please do. I can't think of anything worse than being interviewed. And Bill...'

'Yes?'

'I appreciate you coming.' Bill raised a camp eyebrow and Si reddened. 'You know what I mean,' he said. They both laughed again and Bill left.

⚽ ⚽ ⚽

A week later, Penny pushed a wheelchair into the room. 'What's that for?'

'You, of course. The doctor says you're now strong enough to join the walking wounded.'

'Walking?' Si cast her a sarcastic look. 'You reckon?'

Penny was unmoved. 'If not actually *walking*, then let's say the *rolling* wounded. Okay?'

Si groaned. He didn't feel ready for such a big challenge. 'Do I have to?'

'Of course. You can't lie in bed forever you know. You've got to get up and about. Come on, brighten up. You'll enjoy it. Just think, you can visit Mary.'

'Really?' Although Si knew Mary was in the same hospital and had spoken to her on the phone, he hadn't imagined she was so close. 'How far away is she?'

'Not far... Up one floor and a couple of wards across, in North Wing.' This meant little to Si as since his arrival he'd spent all his time in his room. But, for Mary, he was prepared to make the effort and explore.

⚽ ⚽ ⚽

Si scooted along the shiny corridor, his rubber wheels squeaking when he turned corners. He negotiated the lift without mishap—why, he wondered, had it seemed such an obstacle during the two days in which he'd mentally planned this trip? He'd even made Penny sketch him a floor plan of the hospital. But now, after short recces into the ward and offices surrounding his room, he was on his way.

North Wing was a recent extension to the old Edwardian hospital. As he came out of the lift, Si immediately felt the difference. Everything was brighter, slicker and more modern. It felt more like an art gallery than a hospital. Si imagined that even the scalpels were sharper round here. He followed the directions Penny had given him and wondered if he'd been right to refuse her assistance. She'd wanted to push his wheelchair, but they both knew the offer had little to do with Si's physical strength. He'd already proved he could manoeuvre his vehicle. Penny's concern stemmed from the conversations they'd had about Mary, particularly Si's fears that she might blame him in some way for her injuries.

'Don't be ridiculous. You didn't set the bomb off .'

'No, I know. But I did set up the lunch. Any other day and it would have been fine, but…' Si's self-confidence seemed to have been as damaged as his flesh.

'Twaddle. Now look. She'll be dying to see you. Didn't she say so on the phone?'

'Yes, but…'

'No *buts*. Okay?' Penny's tough look, a look Si had come to recognise meant no nonsense, calmed him.

Yet now that he was about to reach Mary's ward, his resolve was faltering. 'I'd like to see Mary Cunningham, please.'

The nurse behind the desk looked at him. 'Are you her boyfriend?'

'Yes, I am.'

'Well, she's been expecting you. Come on, I'll take you down.' The nurse took a firm hold of his wheelchair and manoeuvred him expertly down the corridor. Si sank back and suddenly realised he was exhausted. The effort of getting to the ward had been the most exercise he'd done since the fifteenth of September.

The nurse stopped outside a swing door with a porthole above Si's head. She peeked through and then entered. 'I won't be a moment. Don't run away now.' She threw a parting grin at him and winked.

Si waited for what seemed like an hour. He wanted to stand up and look through the window to see what was going on. But his legs weren't up to that yet. They were still covered in starry red scars, and the deep wound on his groin, where a piece of glass the size of a sideplate had sliced him, was still extremely delicate.

'Okay, let's be seeing you then,' the nurse said cheerily. She made to push the wheelchair forward.

'No, it's okay. I'll do it.'

Something in Si's look must have struck her because she backed off without a word. Smiling encouragement, she held the door open.

The first thing that Si noticed was that Mary was not alone. An old lady stood between him and the bed. She had a short silver ponytail and wore a tweed skirt and cream blouse. Her ruddy complexion betrayed a country life. She watched him intently as he paused in the doorway.

Beyond the stranger, Si could make out Mary's head on the pillow, the rest of her body concealed beneath white sheets arranged in a strange shape—presumably they concealed various contraptions to take the weight of the bedclothes. He'd been warned that she had been 'very unwell' and that she was still a long way from recovery. But he hadn't expected to find her such an invalid.

'You must be Simon.' Elspeth stepped forward. 'Come on in, my dear, we've been expecting you.'

Si trundled forward. Mary's grandmother was more or

less as he'd expected; only more so. Her presence seemed to exude calm. But Si couldn't make the jump from this lady to Mary's prissy mother. Perhaps Beatrice Cunningham had been adopted?

'I'm afraid she's dozed off, but I imagine she'll wake any minute.' Elspeth looked at him gently. 'She's been so looking forward to seeing you.'

'It's nice to meet you. I mean, having heard so much about you.'

'Yes, and you, dear.' Elspeth gave him a knowing look. 'I'd expected Mary to bring you down to see me at some stage, but one never knows what the future holds...'

Si nodded. 'How is she?'

'Better. Better than she was, that is. She can now sleep by herself, which is a blessing. Before she would have woken up every hour but for the sedation.' Silence descended on the room.

Si plucked up courage. 'Will she walk...again? You know what I mean?'

Elspeth pursed her lips. 'Oh, of course she will. The doctors think it will take time, naturally; but yes, she *will* walk.'

Si wasn't entirely convinced. Elspeth seemed to be reassuring herself rather than him. But now wasn't the time to challenge her. 'If you don't mind me asking, has she said anything about me?'

'Oh goodness, yes; of course she has. Lots, in fact.'

Si persevered. 'I mean, I've been really worried that she'll blame me for what happened.'

Elspeth looked at him maternally and thought for a moment before answering. 'I can't answer that, my dear. You'll need to ask her.'

A voice from behind her made a barely audible sound. Elspeth turned to face the bed and Si edged forwards, his hands on the wheelrims.

'Sorry, darling, what's that you said?'

This time the voice was stronger. 'I want to see him...'

Si could hear the pain riding on each syllable. In response

to Elspeth's gesture he rolled up to the bedside so that his head was level with Mary's chest. Her eyes were open and staring at the ceiling. He tried to read her expression, but the neutral cast was inscrutable. Taking a deep breath, his heart beating madly, he spoke in a hoarse whisper. 'Mary… It's Si.'

Mary's lips twitched. With what was obviously a great effort, she twisted her neck about thirty degrees towards him. Si leaned forward to rest his elbows on the bed.

'Thank you for coming to see me.'

He choked back the emotion which threatened to betray him. He had decided to be strong and his resolve was being tested to the full. 'I've missed you.'

The response came clear and quick. 'Me too.' At last, Mary managed to move her head far enough to see him. The effect was instantaneous. Her smile shone through and the passive veil evaporated. 'Oh Si… What a pair we are.'

In the many scenarios Si had imagined for their first reunion, this had not featured. He was unsure what to say. 'How do you mean?'

'Well, you know… We're not exactly the most mobile of couples are we?'

If it hadn't hurt so much, Si would have laughed with relief. 'I suppose not. Never a dull moment with us.'

'No. Never.' They looked at each other in silence. It seemed to Si that he was seeing Mary for the first time.

Elspeth discreetly backed out of the door. Passing the nurse in the corridor, she smiled. 'Pure *Tristan und Isolde*. I think she'll be okay now.'

The nurse nodded sagely. This eccentric old woman had certainly added colour to the ward in the past few weeks, although it was often difficult to understand what she was on about.

'Oh, and nurse?'

'Yes?'

Elspeth put a bony finger to her cracked lips. 'Shhh… I wouldn't bother disturbing them for a while. They've got quite a lot to catch up on.'

With a slight spring in her step and feeling lighter of heart than she had since hearing of her granddaughter's injuries, Elspeth walked towards the hospital gardens. It was high time she got some fresh air. She'd been cooped up in that room for far too long without a break. Yes, some fresh air and a few laps of the little garden, that should do the trick.

❀ ❀ ❀

The ambulance dropped Si off at his flat. A golden light blurred the edges of the Georgian buildings, but only a few parchment leaves remained on the trees lining the street. Last time he'd been here, it had been a scorching summer's day and the fully laden trees had cast a deep, dappling shade over the pavement.

'You sure you don't want a hand, now?' offered Mike, the ambulance man.

'No, it's only up one flight of stairs. You guys have already done more than enough. Thanks for everything.' Si shook Mike's hand and, placing his crutches gingerly on the pavement, hobbled slowly towards the front door.

The key was in his pocket. He took it out of the jeans his mother had brought him while he was in hospital—his own clothes had been shredded and blood-sodden in the blast. Balancing precariously on one crutch, he turned to wave goodbye to Mike. The ambulance pulled gently out from the kerb and swung off towards the river.

The plane trees at the end of the street refracted the thin, November sunshine, and the church clock struck the half hour. Si watched the splintering light, mesmerised by the breaking colours.

Someone, his mother he presumed, had cleared his mail from the shelf in the communal hallway; a couple of envelopes from that morning's post awaited him.

It took him a while to get up the stairs. But eventually he was home.

Si had insisted that no-one should bring him home from the hospital; he'd decided he needed to complete the painful journey of the last weeks alone; to mark an ending—that was how he'd explained it to his mother. She'd seemed to understand; but he still half-expected to find her waiting for him. However, the flat was empty. It looked tidier than he'd ever seen it—except for when he'd first viewed it with an estate agent three years before. The late morning light streamed through the French windows and, although there was no heat in it, the illumination raised Si's spirits briefly. The glass table sparkled with recent polishing; and a few magazines, which he'd bought almost two months ago, just before the bomb blew his life apart, sat in a neat pile to one side. He deliberately untidied them.

For a moment, Si wondered what to do next. He unloaded a few possessions from the small canvas bag: some neatly folded clothes, a personal stereo, two classical music CDs and a book. Then in the absence of inspiration, he did what he had repeatedly imagined he would do.

He'd pictured this moment of homecoming so vividly over the past weeks; his imagination had helped him during the long hours on his back, sandwiched between starched hospital sheets, trying not to breathe too deeply to minimise the pain across his chest. From the fragments of memory and the hours of solitary meditation forced upon him, he had put together the pieces, creating a picture which had previously eluded him. And one thought—his intended first action on returning home—had helped him smile when even his sapling faith bent in the howling gale of the horror, and he thought he had an inkling of what was meant by walking through the valley of death. And even after the pain had dulled and he became mobile, whizzing around the hospital corridors in between his visits to Mary's bedside, the homecoming vision continued to burn brightly.

The video camera was where he'd left it, in the cupboard next to the boiler. He brushed off half a year's dust and weighed the cyclopean box in his hands. Surprisingly light for such a valuable load. He recalled how he'd grown to dislike the machine when Mary insisted he use it. Now her nagging seemed inspired.

Si rested silently for several moments, lost in thought; like an old man in a retirement home.

Snapping to, he rummaged at the back of the cupboard for the wire he knew would be there. Then he plugged one end into the camera and the other into the back of the video machine. After a few minutes he succeeded in getting a picture and rewound the tape to the beginning.

Si felt focused, controlled and ethereally calm. Again he paused for a moment in thought, but this time quickly recovered himself and pressed the green play button.

He moved back and sat on the floor leaning against the sofa, his legs stretched out in front of him. He still found it impossible to bend them more than about forty-five degrees. As the screen came alive, he forgot his aching body.

The fragments of footage shot in Mary's flat, restaurants, the street, and even in a taxi transfixed Si. There was one ridiculous scene where Mary dripped ice cream all over herself. And he laughed out loud at some of his repartee with Jimmy in The Feathers, as seen through the unforgiving lens. That had been when Mary stood them up and they'd ended up getting hammered together. That had been a good night. The pieces began to slide gently back together, to make sense in a way they'd never done before. Si noticed that, almost magically, the ragged edges of the recent violence seemed to be smoothing out the familiar chaos, like a spatula stroking rough clay.

When the video clock said that twenty-seven minutes had elapsed, the tape ended. Si didn't move for a long time. He thought mainly about Jimmy, whose damaged eyes meant he could not have the solace of watching images from the past; tragically, it was now clear he would never again play top flight football. What would become of his friend? Si wondered. Soon after the bomb, Jimmy had been moved to a specialist eye clinic outside London; as a result, they had not met since the fifteenth of September. The few phone conversations they had attempted had spluttered to a halt after a short time as each of them stumbled into unmapped emotional marshes—for the time being, their friendship seemed inadequate, unable to offer a safe path through the suffering.

Someone went past in the street outside ringing a bicycle bell. A beam of sunshine moved slightly and lit up Si's immobile face. As the light scorched his petrified cheek, he allowed the tears to overspill his tired eyes.

The phone began to ring. The sunbeam moved further into the room and spread across Si's whole body, surrounding him with a warm halo of soft light. The phone rang again and again before Si registered the noise. Returning from within, he raised his head like the Phoenix, and slowly the world came back into focus. He pushed back his shoulders, shook his head as if waking from a deep sleep, and the anguish on his face subsided; it was replaced by a weary, but gentle and peaceful expression.

The phone was still ringing and now Si leaned forward to pick it up. He knew who it would be. The faintest trace of a smile showed at the corner of his shining eyes.